D1131200

THE WHITE ROSE

THE
WHITE ROSE

BY

Jan Westcott

G. P. Putnam's Sons
New York

Copyright © 1969 by Jan Westcott

*All rights reserved. This book, or parts thereof, must not be repro-
duced in any form without permission. Published simultaneously in
the Dominion of Canada by Longmans Canada Limited, Toronto.*

PRINTED IN THE UNITED STATES OF AMERICA

F
W524w

BC#30928

For my husband

6-28-96   Stk Sales $1.25

QUEEN
ELIZABETH: My lords, before it pleased his Majesty
To raise my state to title of a queen,
Do me but right, and you must all confess
That I was not ignoble of descent;
And meaner than myself have had like fortune.
But as this title honours me and mine,
So your dislike, to whom I would be pleasing,
Doth cloud my joys with danger and with sorrow.

KING EDWARD: My love, forbear to fawn upon their frowns:
What danger or what sorrow can befall thee,
So long as Edward is thy constant friend,
And their true sovereign, whom they must obey?
Nay, whom they shall obey, and love thee too,
Unless they seek for hatred at my hands;
Which if they do, yet will I keep thee safe,
And they shall feel the vengeance of my wrath.
WILLIAM SHAKESPEARE, *King Henry VI,*
Third Part, Act IV, Scene 1

RICHARD, DUKE
OF GLOUCESTER: Why, then, I do but dream on sovereignty;
Like one that stands upon a promontory,
And spies a far-off shore where he would tread.
King Henry VI, Third Part, Act III, Scene 2

PART ONE
The Crown

Chapter 1

IT WAS January first, 1461. The big hall at Grafton where she sat that night was decorated for Christmas. Mistletoe hung from the balcony, ivy twined about the heavy stair rail, the ancient suit of armor was crowned with holly and the antlers on the wall, symbols of her father's and brothers' prowess at the hunt, were festooned with ribbon. Logs burned in the fireplace and gay pennons with her father's and mother's badges fluttered along the paneled walls.

The packages of gifts had been opened; her two-year-old son and her baby boy had been put to bed, along with her four youngest sisters. Her mother was in London, tonight an embattled city with its gates barred and its shops closed; her father and her brother Richard and her husband were near York with the army of the Queen, England's beautiful French Queen. In the hall at Grafton now, besides herself, Elizabeth Woodville Grey, were her brothers Lionel and young Edward, solemnly playing chess, and four teenage sisters. John, who was fifteen and fretting because his father had not permitted him to join the deadly struggle of Lancaster and York, was playing cards with his sister. She was inattentive.

He said, "At least we know where everyone is, Bess. At least there is no fighting tonight."

A Christmas truce had been declared, so Elizabeth Woodville nodded.

Her hazel eyes regarded her brother fondly but worriedly. "We don't know where Anthony is," she reminded him. Anthony was twenty, she about eleven months older; the two oldest of the Woodville tribe, they had been very close.

John started to play a card; his hand stopped midway, holding

high the big colored knave. He tossed it to the table and jumped
to his feet.

"Horses!" he shouted.

Was it their mother? Was it their father? Pell-mell, exuberant
with John first, they rushed to the huge doors, throwing them
open wide, not feeling the bitter-cold January air; light poured
out from behind them into the courtyard as the horse beats
slowed and became sedate; as the men ahead running from the
lodge gates carried torches high they could see who it was, and
all gathered together at the edge of the court they raised their
voices.

"Happy New Year. Anthony!"

Astride his big horse Anthony held his hand up, his face under
the red cap handsome and smiling. "Happy New Year!" he
shouted back, and the men with him took up the greeting till the
court was filled with laughter and noise the way it usually was
when the Woodvilles were at home.

They rushed down into the court now, crowding around him
while he hugged Elizabeth and shook hands with John and Lionel
and Edward, clapping them on the back, kissing his three sisters,
and finally picking up the youngest, Kate, and carrying her back
into the house at a run.

"By God, it's cold," he said, setting Kate on her feet.

Light came on in the kitchens. The manor servants came in to
greet the oldest son, to shake hands and wish him well. "Hot
spiced ale," they promised him.

Anthony had a kiss for his former nurse; food was being produced—cold beef, chickens and wedges of cheese, and apples
from the storerooms—and the hall at Grafton was so filled with
sudden happiness and laughter and talk that Anthony didn't realize that it was his coming that had released it, for it seemed just
the same as always to him.

"Your gifts, Anthony, Anthony!" Lionel, trying to make himself
heard, was carrying Anthony's New Year's gifts on a pewter
platter.

Anthony opened them one by one, in turn giving a bright coin
from his purse. "I had no way of buying presents," he explained,
which they knew.

And even though he was carrying very important news he said
not a word of it until he had thanked each one of his brothers

and sisters and hung the gold chain Elizabeth had given him around his neck. Suddenly there was silence. Eight pairs of eyes regarded him.

"I guess you missed Mother and Father," he said suddenly. "And Richard and John Grey."

At the mention of her husband's name Elizabeth looked at him sharply. "Anthony," she said, and stopped. She was sitting next to him on the bench before the fire; the younger Woodvilles had dragged cushions to the hearth and were sitting in a circle on the floor around their oldest brother and sister.

She knows, he thought; she senses. They were startlingly similar for all his height and breadth and her slender figure and astonishing beauty. Her hazel eyes, flecked with gold, studied him. Her gilt hair was drawn severely back from her oval face. "Anthony," she prodded.

"Yes, I have news," he said. "But first, Father and Richard and John Grey are safe."

There was a sigh; Elizabeth bit her lip. "But there was a truce."

He nodded. "The Queen broke it. There has been a terrible battle in front of Sandal Castle where the Duke of York was keeping Christmas. The Duke was so angry with the Queen's breaking the solemn truce that he rushed out with his men and his son Edmund, and they were all killed just like fish in a net. They were slaughtered like deer in a buck stall, Bess. The Duke of York is dead."

The younger Woodvilles' eyes were fastened on Anthony. Good Lancastrians that they were they weren't sure whether their brother approved of this.

"I don't approve of the Queen breaking the truce, Lionel," Anthony said. "But the Duke of York and the Earl of Warwick are our principal enemies. And now the Duke is dead."

"Maybe Warwick will run away," John offered. "He did once before."

"Perhaps," Anthony said. He glanced at Elizabeth. "You see, John, Warwick is already gathering men to come north to fight our Queen. At least so the rumor goes, and I am going too, north to join Father and Richard."

"There will be another battle," Elizabeth whispered.

He shook his head at her. "If we can confront Warwick with enough troops, he may retreat and flee. That is what I hope, Bess.

Tomorrow morning I am going to the village to see if there are some who want to ride north with me."

John leaned forward but before he could speak Anthony said, "You can't come. Father forbade it three months ago. Mother would never forgive me if I took you. Wait till next year when you're sixteen."

Elizabeth thought suddenly, Next year. Next year and the year after that.

John Woodville raised a blond eyebrow. "I wasn't going to ask to come. Personally, Anthony, I am beginning to think that all this rushing about with swords in defense of a French Queen is silly."

Lionel cleared his throat; his voice squeaked with earnestness. "You see, Anthony," he said, "we learned in school that a ruler must be forceful. Our King cannot be forceful because he is sick. A man who doesn't speak for six months is hardly a fit ruler."

"The old King himself appointed the Duke of York his successor and the protector of the throne," John said.

Lionel cleared his throat again. "Well, obviously, John, the Duke was no match for the Queen since she has vanquished him and he lies dead."

Anthony said, "Will you stop arguing for a minute? I know I should be used to it, but for better or worse we have a saintly, sick King." Henry's face rose before Anthony, ascetic, withdrawn, the eyes sad in a thin face. "But he has a son and a Queen and his son does not deserve to be disinherited. That is what the Queen is fighting for, her son. And that is why we fight. And we love our King. We are sorry for him. We want to protect him."

"It is a crusade," John said, "and crusades are out-of-date, Anthony."

Anthony was curious. "Why did you ask Father before then? He said you wanted to go with him."

"I wanted to be with him in order to protect him and I'd still like to do that."

"I see. Well, I'll protect him, Richard and I."

John shrugged. "You may be sorry you don't have my good right hand at your side. I hope to God you're not. But if you're going in the morning you should get to bed. I'll help you, Anthony. I'll go get some hot water too."

He raised Anthony's saddlebag to his shoulder. Elizabeth

thought, A servant could have been called but John wants to do it; we should be thankful that we love one another. John wants to go to help, not because he wants to fight for the Queen. Would it be best? Should she persuade Anthony to let him go? If there were more of them would they be safer?

"Anthony," she said.

"No, Bess. He's too young."

That was his last word. And when she went to bed later, troubled, worried, she thought of her father and Richard and her husband. And now Anthony. What were the odds that all of them would return? All night long she tossed in a nightmarish sleep.

Edward, Earl of March, oldest son of the Duke of York, slept peacefully, sprawled in his big curtained bed.

He had spent Christmas at Shrewsbury and he was there on January second when the news of his father's and brother's death was brought to him. With him were a few young men, Walter Devereaux, Richard and William Herbert, Humphrey Stafford and William Hastings. Hastings could not keep the whole story from pouring out, although he tried. The betrayal of the truce, the father's anger and the injudicious rush from the castle, the death of the Duke and the death of Edward's younger brother as he knelt before Lord Clifford. Then the Queen had set the severed head of the Duke of York up on the Micklebar Gate in York and crowned it with a paper crown and bits of straw.

Hastings watched Edward's face. Edward was standing. He towered over most men, six feet, four inches of young man, for he would not be nineteen until April. Thoughts were whirling around in Hastings' head. His lord Edward Plantagenet then was heir to the throne. Henry VI, the ill King, had named Edward's father his heir. Now the Duke was dead. Hastings, emotional, went down on one knee.

"Your Grace," he said. "My liege lord."

Edward looked down at his bent head and he touched him on the shoulder, pulling at his jacket. Edward wanted nothing but to be alone and in the chapel. Edward turned and left the room; he was sick and sore and burning with rage and hatred. But he was the kind of man whom adversity made twice his size, and his quick mind was already seizing on the problems facing him; he was going to pray not only for the souls of his father and brother

but that Almighty God would help him, Edward, judge aright
and wise. Hastings stood at the back of the small chapel and
watched him cross himself before the host and go down on his
knees.

Edward had parted from his father in December. With the
Queen on the march, seeking forcible custody of her sick husband, Edward's services had been called on and he had been sent
to Wales to raise men for the Yorkist cause. So as he knelt the
first fact that presented itself was that he had an army. He was
young, he was strong, he was surrounded with young, strong men.
Slowly Edward got to his feet. Yet caution inserted itself. Already
the lesson of hasty action had been learned. As he came out of
the chapel he studied openly the faces of his cohorts; his dark
eyes thoughtful, without a trace of the usual merry wit, the dart-
ing humor. A different task was now thrust upon him, very different, and a different task upon them.

He set his companions about a table. At the head of it he
lounged in his chair, and his outward indolence was deceiving;
it would deceive many men during the years ahead. In the first
place, there was never enough room for his frame in any chair;
his big booted feet stuck out and lay crossed at an angle. He was
rarely armed and as elegantly dressed as his slender purse would
allow. He looked like a Renaissance Prince, brown-haired and
brown-eyed, and indeed there was no man he admired more than
Francesco Sforza, the Duke of Milan. Around the table they
talked earnestly; there was no smiling. They advised the sending
out of messengers and dispatches, for they must know what was
happening in London and in the rest of the realm. They must set
spies on the Queen and outriders to smell out any movement of
Lancaster forces. And finally they would ride and fight with him
to death if need be!

"Scarcely," said Edward. "We'll have as little dying as possible."

They didn't notice that he himself had actually said little.
Whatever plans he had made he had kept within his big chest.
The only plans that were vouchsafed to them was that the army
was to be made ready to march.

Without haste Edward moved his men so as to keep himself
between London and the Queen's forces. He knew better than to
attempt a fight with a weary fellowship of men; more than that,
he wanted time for these men to realize he was their commander.

He spent hours with the common archer; he supervised a number of contests after they bivouacked for the night. Sometimes at night around a big fire, they—someone—would notice his tall figure standing just outside the light of the flames; he was listening to their talk or their songs. Meanwhile messengers rode daily into the camp.

The Queen was hesitating. The King was still in London under the care of the great Earl of Warwick, who was going to set forth with him and challenge the Queen once and for all. Edward read the letter from Warwick and burned it. But the rumor spread among his men. "The Earl is on the march. Shouldn't we join him?"

Even his young inner group posed that question. And Edward procrastinated. He looked thoughtful and yawned.

"We'll wait and see, we'll have an archery contest. I always like them." His smile flashed out. All afternoon he watched the contest, and at the end distributed prizes, clapping each winner on the shoulder, consoling the loser. Hastings watched him among the men; he was friendly, truly friendly; he thought nothing of flinging an arm about another man casually.

The next day the dispatches arrived for which he had been waiting, and he ordered his men to swing around and to march toward Herefordshire. The dispatches had disclosed with certainty that the Earls of Wiltshire and Pembroke had landed on the coast with an army of Bretons and Irish. Now there was need for haste, now the time had come; now he must intercept the Earls before they made contact with the Queen's forces. When Edward's orders were given William Herbert nodded.

"I see," he said. "You were right."

He had wanted not only to intercept the Lancaster forces and to prevent them from reaching the Queen; he wanted to come upon them with fresh, eager, rested troops. Carefully he laid out the route on the maps, moving his men just as he moved his pawns on a chessboard. Carefully each day's march was calculated; carefully scourers were sent ahead; Edward was now doing what he already had a genius for—being a soldier. He disliked fighting, but once embarked on a campaign he thought sometimes that another personality had engulfed him; almost as though the light chain mail exchanged for his usual elegant dress had exchanged him for another man. But he was used to it. As he would say later, he had been in the saddle since he was thirteen, in the saddle with a sword in hand.

Edward caught up to the Lancastrian forces as he neared Wigmore, at a place called Mortimer's Cross. They reached there in adequate time the night before for a good night's sleep. It was February first and cold; January had just died. From a slight eminence Edward surveyed his camp, the cheerful fires, the restless horses, and he worried about the cold keeping his men awake. He himself felt no need for sleep; he'd been careful to provide himself with plenty in the past two weeks. Now he felt calm and confident and he moved among the fires, content to let the other men take over, the soldier who had no problems but the winning of tomorrow's battle; they were little enough compared to the other cares life thrust upon one. He moved among the men, sometimes joining their talk. He told them, "Spare the common man. It is his leader that is bringing him to fight against you."

He had already listed in his mind the Lancaster leaders who must either be destroyed or won over. In all of England there were no noble names fighting with Edward Plantagenet save the Nevilles and their chief, the Earl of Warwick; all the other nobility were ranged against him but not the common man. "Spare the commons," Edward repeated. "Spare the commons."

The next day dawned. Edward had slept lightly for a few hours preceding the dawn. It was still cold; he washed and ate some bread and ale. The Lancastrian forces were very near and the enemy was not too anxious for battle, his outriders and spies had reported. They were trying to avoid him but that was impossible now; by noon he should be facing them at Mortimer's Cross.

He had the time well calculated; an easy morning march should accomplish his task, and he would be face-to-face with the Earls of Pembroke and Wiltshire. So he set his men to breaking camp and feeding the horses and he figured at ten o'clock it would be time to march.

So exactly at ten, with the reins of his horse in one hand, at the head of his men, preparing to mount, he looked up at the sky.

The peculiar light had made Edward look up. Every man did the same. There were three suns shining. In the cold February morning a murmur and mutter ran through the massed men and Edward felt a shiver of horror and wonder as he stared, and the light hurt his eyes. Then he glanced at Hastings near him and at

William Herbert. What he saw forced him into an involuntary movement of which he was seldom guilty, and his big hands clenched as he thought he saw victory slipping from them because his men were afraid, afraid of a curious phenomenon of light—up in the sky were shining three suns.

Edward commanded his trumpeter to sound the horns. They rang forth and Edward gained the saddle of his horse; he swung around to face his men.

His voice rang out. "Be of good comfort and dread not!"

From his mounted vantage point he surveyed them, holding one hand high. A sigh rippled from the throats of his listeners; as they fixed their eyes on him, the light shone like gold around his head. "Do not fear, for this is a good sign! For three suns in the firmament, shining full clear, betoken the Father, the Son and the Holy Ghost." He let his voice stop and he smiled. "Therefore, let us have good heart and in the name of the Almighty God go against our enemies!"

Edward saw Hastings' face; he looked as though he were about to shout and cheer, and Edward heard the beginnings of swelling sound from the lips of his men, and he held his hands high to stop them. They quieted. Carefully he divested himself of his helmet and handed it to the nearest man. Then he dismounted.

"We shall pray."

He knelt on the ground, his dark head bent. His men followed suit. After a long two minutes Edward rose and spoke to the kneeling men.

"I have thanked God," he said, "for this omen for our cause."

His voice was somber. The plumed helmet was placed on his head and he mounted; the trumpets and horns blew bravely, their clarion call to arms sounding through the morning, mingling with the wild cheering. Edward thought, Was it an omen for good? Anyway the Lord had helped him, and for that he offered his devout thanks. He spurred his horse; he was going forward to his first venture, alone. In the skies there was just one sun now, as lonely as he was.

Edward intercepted the Lancastrian forces just where he knew he would. He set the mounted men in two wings; he himself commanded the center as he always did and would. Edward fought on foot like his men, and this was a simple strategy, the battle at Mortimer's Cross, a determined assault.

The Lancastrians broke and fled quickly. Edward pursued the fleeing army as far as Hereford, leaving a field of three thousand dead, his officers reckoned. Wiltshire escaped, but the Earl of Pembroke was captured and quickly beheaded in the market-place at Hereford. Edward commandeered one of the houses in the town for his quarters; it overlooked the square. An old woman came with a basin and washed the blood from the face of the Earl of Pembroke and combed the matted hair; she set candles burning about the pole. A soldier came to ask what to do, and Will Herbert told him to leave the old woman alone and let her care for the dead. Then he shut the door on the scene. He was thinking of Edward, leading his men into the thick of the fighting; he was thinking he would never desert him, never; he was wondering whether they would join the great Earl of Warwick now. But it didn't matter to him; he would do exactly as the young Earl of March commanded him.

The Earl of Warwick, Richard Neville, wealthiest and greatest noble of the kingdom, was Edward's cousin; Edward was related to all the Nevilles through his mother Cecily Neville. Edward's messengers were quick and reliable, and they brought him the news that his cousin would reach the main Lancastrian forces under the Queen in a matter of days. Edward knew the great Earl well, very well. He had shared his exile in Calais and had fought with him in the field; soon Warwick would be meeting a competently commanded force and Edward knew that he might very well lose. Would it avail if he, by forced marches toward York, came up in the rear?

For a day he pondered this. There is no one more alone, Edward thought, than the heir to the throne, and he would have to make his decisions alone. But there was an obvious and wise course open for him and it was the one he chose. By the time he reached his objective, his men would be unweary; they would have fought no more battles, their morale would be high and the prize in Edward's big hands. The following morning, February sixth, his orders came.

"Where?" asked Hastings.

Edward was leaning back indolently among the pillows in his

bed. He spoke only one word. He said, "London." Then he repeated it. "London."

Edward started for London by easy stages, keeping himself and his men between London and the Lancastrians to protect the city. On the eighteenth of February the news of Warwick's defeat reached him; the Earl had fled the field, abandoning the poor King, leaving him sitting under a tree, singing and talking to himself. Warwick's forces had been utterly routed; the Queen and her Northerners but twenty miles from a terrified London. The rumor was that Warwick had fled to Calais.

News from London arrived the following day. The city had barred its gates, Edward's mother had sent his two younger brothers to Burgundy in fear of their lives, the Chancellor and Archbishop Bourchier had fled to Canterbury. There was but one question Hastings asked.

"But where, my lord, is the special messenger to Earl Warwick?"

"He hasn't returned," Edward said. He paused. "My guess is that he is escorting the Earl to me."

There was gloom about the council table. Will Herbert thought Edward seemed unconcerned. He was his usual calm self. Edward glanced about at their faces. Occasionally he let them in obliquely to what he was thinking. Negligently regarding the ring on his finger, he said, "I fully expect to meet my lord of Warwick in a few days. He will find safety with us." There was accent on the word "us." Edward looked at their faces to see if they understood the import of it—that is, it was meet and fitting that even a great Earl should find safety and succor at the hands of the Earl of March: If there were to be a new reign there would be but one master of it.

"And second, gentlemen, after we see to the welfare of our capital, then there will be time enough to take care of any dissident elements in the realm."

But now events followed swiftly. As Edward had predicted, Warwick met Edward's troops at Chipping Norton. Edward embraced his cousin in front of his men; the horns blew and the Earl was welcomed with all ceremony into camp. Edward's eyes glinted with hidden amusement as Warwick realized suddenly that he had been rescued by his young cousin. Warwick blurted out, "I could wish it were otherwise." He was gruff and blunt, this man.

Edward said, "We are happy to be of service to you, my lord."

They reached London by the twenty-seventh of February. In the meantime Margaret, the Queen, but twenty miles from London, learned that the young Earl of March was on his way and, in a moment of indecision, returned to York to avoid another battle. Edward's troops would be fresh and it seemed unwise to challenge him now. So on the twenty-seventh of February London learned that Margaret had retreated and, even better, a deliverer was at hand. On that morning Edward's van arrived at the gates, gates hastily unbarred and thrown wide as the citizens of London welcomed Edward with relief.

They had seen him before, of course. But not like this. For days there had been fear and unrest. There had been rioting and fighting, theft and pillage. Sober citizens trembled in their households at night; men secreted their jewels; many had sent a coffer of worldly wealth out of the city for safety. Noble Lancastrian and Yorkist women and children were in terror of their lives; even the King's physician, William Hatclyf, had fled. It had been a terrible year, too, with great ice storms and drought and comets of ill omen, and there seemed to be more men in sanctuary than there were in the palaces and noble homes. Edward rode through the city, made his offering at St. Paul's and then, good son that he was, rode straight to Baynard's Castle to comfort his mother.

In Westminster the second lady in the kingdom, good Lancastrian that she was, watched from her windows. She was Jacqueta, born a Princess of Luxembourg, Duchess of Bedford, the title which was still accorded her even though after the great Duke's death she had wed secret with a plain English knight, a Richard Woodville. Jacqueta was thinking of Edward's mother, Cecily Neville, of York. She was thinking with what joy and with what tears Cecily would greet him and hug him. Jacqueta thought, Why, he is younger than Elizabeth or Anthony; he is just about the same age as Richard.

The February afternoon darkened; the candles were lit. Outside in the city bonfires burned and doorways were decorated. Jacqueta did not know what the morrow would bring; she sat dwelling on the past, in the window seat, wrapped in her cloak, for it was cold. What would the great Earl of Warwick do now? Before, with Henry in his hands, he had been able to head a government in Henry's name; now the Queen had Henry back with her. Jacqueta thought she understood Margaret, the Queen, better than anyone else in the realm. In the first place they were both French. Both had been brought to England—Margaret to marry the King and Jacqueta to marry the King's uncle. But there the similarities ended. For Margaret had mated with the shy, simple Henry and years had passed before she had a son. Jacqueta remembered well what poor Henry had said when he had been shown his son. The first time he had turned his head away and not spoken, for he had fallen into one of his fits of madness that lasted six months and he did not speak. But when finally he emerged from that dim world and Margaret had shown him the infant prince, he had said wonderingly, "He must be the son of the Holy Ghost."

No wonder, Jacqueta thought, that half the kingdom believed the child somebody else's. And how much of a reproach I must have been to her, I, always carrying another child. And delivering them successfully. Now, she thought, she must decide for them and live for them successfully, for the fortunes of her family were paramount to the Duchess of Bedford. Once more she reviewed the fact that her husband and two sons were with the Queen; God keep them. Disaster had already struck the family in the battle between Warwick and the Queen, for Elizabeth Woodville had feared aright, her husband had been killed; Jacqueta had lost a son-in-law of whom she was both proud and fond and her two grandsons had lost their father.

Jacqueta kept thinking of Edward. Not for nothing was she born a Princess; the shifting sands of political destinies had been her toddling ground. But it was late. In all of her forty-two years Jacqueta had never wasted a penny, a moment of time or thought. She should go to bed and she did.

When the sun rose the following morning the refugees who had fled the city were returning. First to come was the Bishop of Exeter, George Neville, brother to Warwick. He went straight to Warwick and Edward and was immediately given the task of preparing a speech to be delivered the following day, March first. Edward was moving fast.

That day Edward rode through the streets and out the city

gates to his troops; when he returned Jacqueta saw him. Around
her the people cheered; they thought he looked like a young
god, so tall and so handsome. Jacqueta didn't; she thought he
looked like a true Prince.

Edward had interrupted a day-long conference with Warwick
to ride out of the city. He said negligently he needed fresh air.
Impatient at this sign of youthful inattention to important business Warwick spent the time while Edward was gone to confer
with his brother George on the doings of the morrow. Edward
came back into the room at Baynard's Castle, but before settling
down he said he was hungry and, it being four o'clock, he wished
dinner to be served and asked especially for some of the Gascon
wine his mother had said was down in the cellar. Warwick
grumbled.

"A civilized man pays attention to fine food," Edward said
mildly. It crossed his mind to explain to Warwick that he had
gone to review his men because it was a military duty since he
was going to use them soon. But the wine had been brought him,
and when he tasted it he didn't bother to explain to Warwick but
sipped it appreciatively. Then his boots were removed and he
eased his feet into slippers. Warwick stamped about the room,
for he didn't want to talk before servants, but Edward sipped his
wine. He was remembering that a year ago his father had
marched into Parliament and laid his hand on the throne before
realizing that he did not have the consent of the lords, and he
had had to retreat awkwardly. His father and Warwick had quarreled later. Edward remembered himself coming between them,
saying, "Speak ill of no man, and it will be well."

But now there was no Parliament sitting, and moreover Warwick did not have Henry as a puppet King. Instead he had the
Earl of March.

After dinner was served Edward dismissed the servants. Warwick then had his brother the Bishop read to Edward parts of
the speech prepared for the morrow. As he ate, Edward digested
not only his food but the speech, and the time. He reckoned he
should leave London in less than two weeks and there was a
great deal to be done.

His logical mind was attacking the problems. Since the nobility
were hostile to him, since they preferred, and why should they
not, a weak King, a saintly, mad King, because they could then

do as they pleased, arm their retainers, make mockery of the laws, send their own hirelings to sit in Parliament, why should they want Edward, Earl of March? Why indeed should Warwick want him? Warwick was listening impatiently to his brother's speech. Edward found no flaws in it. The Bishop was explaining carefully Edward's right to the throne, doubly descended from the great Edward III. Edward's mind wandered since he knew his genealogy as well as the Bishop. He was wondering whether Warwick realized whose idea it was that the case be presented, not to Parliament, which wasn't sitting anyway, thank God, but to the people. Edward's sense of humor asserted itself, and he began to think it comical that the Earl had forgot whose suggestion this was; Warwick was cutting his meat with his dagger; Edward had chosen the game birds and he kept absently calling for a servant with water and towel, and then because there were no servants in the room, he kept rising and going over to the ewer on the sideboard. The candles had been lighted and in the paneled room Edward's clothes were a blaze of color, the short cloak faced with red velvet, setting off his brown hair and eyes. The Bishop paused suddenly in his long recitation of why Edward was heir to the throne and looked across at Edward's face, and the Bishop suddenly thought, Why, what I've been saying is true —this young man *is* a Prince.

Warwick coughed. "Then tomorrow," he said, "at St. John's Field this speech will be read to the commons gathered there."

Edward said, "I have asked some comrades to bring some of my soldiers, too." He paused; would Warwick take the hint?

He did. "I'll have all men who wear the ragged staff there too."

"Good," said Edward. He rose. "Now if you will excuse me?" Absently he started for the door. Neither man questioned where he was going, yet Edward stood for a moment at the door; then he came back into the room and went over to the Bishop and put his hand on his shoulder. "Thank you, sir," he said, "thank you very much." His honest smile flashed out; it carried a warmth that shone steadily in his eyes, and the Bishop smiled too at this open show of gratitude.

"You're welcome, my son," and his voice had a little catch in it, for he was moved.

"Until tomorrow then," Edward said gaily, and was out the door in a sweep of cloak and hose.

He let himself quietly out of the house, this house which was the Duke of York's town house. It was going to be his habit to go out alone among his people. He was unafraid and unarmed. And although Edward had a highborn mistress, who was bearing his child, it was London which was his first love, the jewel of the realm. Edward, now Earl of March, went first to church. He would have preferred on this night to make his offering at the shrine of Becket, but a pilgrimage to Canterbury would have to come later. Tonight, alone, before the altar he prayed once more for guidance and wisdom and love, and he thanked God for the miracle of the three suns and for the faith that the Lord had shown by the phenomenon in the skies. Edward had almost no money, but he left what he had and went out into the streets and made his way slowly, enjoying his walk through the streets to the dwelling of the Seigneur de la Barde. The Seigneur was the representative of the Dauphin of France. On the throne of France was Charles VIII. The Dauphin, his son, was at bitter odds with his father and now residing in the court of Philip of Burgundy, and because Charles was supporting the Lancastrian cause, naturally his son, Louis the Dauphin, had sent an old friend and soldier to give his support to the Yorkists. It was this man whom Edward wanted to see tonight; it was imperative that immediately it be made clear to the realm that he, Edward, had the support of other nations. For this purpose Edward was going to ask that the Seigneur give him armed aid—it could be and would have to be a token force, but it should be present when he marched from London, as indeed he must. Edward, who disliked fighting, nevertheless was certain that the first thing he would have to do would be to defeat Margaret the Queen and her hostile nobles and defeat her as completely as possible.

Edward had been born in Rouen. He spoke fair French, which stood him in good stead that evening. He came away with the Seigneur's firm commitment that he and his banners would accompany Edward into the field.

When Edward came back to Baynard's Castle he said good night to his mother and sought his own apartments. Will Herbert was already in bed but Hastings was awake and tending the fire. Upon Edward's request he set out paper and pens and made sure of the candles. Then in his slippers and heavy furred cloak Edward worked on far into the night. He wrote the first draft of the speech he would make, and he wrote a number of long memoranda. At three he put away the papers carefully in a small chest, threw off his cloak and slid into bed, giving Will Herbert a push with his big hands so there would be enough room. Soon he slept.

The next day was the first of March. The Bishop made his speech, the opening shot of the clumsy bombard in the political arena. The massed soldiers and commons cheered. The Bishop asked them, "Is Henry fit to rule?"

"Nay! Nay!" came the shout.

The Milanese ambassador was there. He wrote, "And all the city was glad and said, 'Let us walk in a new wine yard, and let us make a gay garden in the month of March with this fair white rose, the Earl of March.'"

Edward spent most of the day at his table, working. He went out for another walk with Hastings. In the late afternoon a group of captains and citizens came to Baynard's Castle and Edward received them. They told him the people wanted him and had chosen him to be their King. Edward was so charming they forgot this had been planned. Outside, the crowds gathered and Edward came to the big doors. He didn't speak to the people; but they watched him eagerly, with pride in his handsome youth, and they cheered wildly when he shook hands with each of the captains as they filed out of the house.

"What did he say? What did he say?" they asked as the men came down among them.

"He said—he thanked us! He said—we did him a great honor!"

"What else did he say?" they cried, not having heard enough.

A tall man answered, his voice ringing out in the sudden hush. "He thanked God."

There was silence. Then way had to be made through the crowd for some members of the Yorkist nobility. That day all the Yorkists who were in the city came to Baynard's Castle, and on the third of March the commons were summoned at nine in the morning to St. Paul's.

Did they want Edward for their King? the Chancellor asked.

"Yea! Yea!" The answer poured from hundreds of throats.

Events were happening so fast that Edward's mother could scarcely keep up, with the providing of food, too, so the Earl of Warwick sent over some servants and cooks and more food. She

was harassed by all the comings and goings, and her pretty face
was tense.

"I want to speak with you alone, Mother," Edward said at her
elbow and she jumped.

He laughed. He set her down in the window seat and waited
till the door was closed. "You are so calm, Edward," she said.

"You reprove me for my calm? Mother, I want you to invite
some Lancastrian ladies to attend you tomorrow when we go in
procession. I have ordered your litter draped with blue velvet
and sprinkled with white roses and suns, which shall be my badge
—the white rose and the three suns, that miracle which was
vouchsafed to me. Tomorrow I want you to ride with the Duchess
of Bedford. She will come, I think. She is close to the former
Queen but she will come."

"Invite that woman?" Cecily said, horrified.

Edward hardly heard her. "The Duchess of Bedford receives a
pension from the crown. You will say nothing of that. But the
Duchess is undoubtedly thinking of it."

"Edward, that is bribery."

"Be sure you charm her. I'll do the bribing later. You may have
forgotten, but the Duchess of Bedford is the sister of le Comte de
St. Pol and Prince Jacques of Luxembourg."

Edward glanced down at his mother's face. It had only been
two months since she had been so cruelly widowed and deprived
by an act of wanton murder of her seventeen-year-old son. She
had borne this with such stoicism—perhaps the excitement of
these last few days had helped her forget even though it must
also serve as a reminder that her husband was dead. But through
the very act of being born her son Edward had much to be grateful to her for, for she was the great granddaughter of Edward
III, thus presenting her son with a stronger claim to the throne
than had his own father. He was thinking of her gallantry and
of her deprivation. They had always been very close as a family.

"As soon as I make the realm safe I'll send for Clarence and
Richard. I've written them both and I promise you I'll find a
prince for Margaret."

"What did you write them?"

"To behave themselves," Edward said. "To remember that they,
no matter how young, are representing England in a foreign

court." His mother looked reproving, so he added, "I also sent them five pounds I borrowed from the Bishop."

"Oh, Edward," Cecily said. It was difficult for Cecily to realize that this son of hers, who would not be nineteen until April twenty-sixth was now the head of their family; it was easier for her and her fierce pride to accept the fact that he was going to be the King.

Tomorrow he would go to the abbey. In the shadowy room Cecily could feel the proud presence of her ancestors, her grandfather John of Gaunt, her beautiful grandmother Catherine Swynford; the love that any woman feels for her firstborn son radiated from Cecily.

"It is fitting you shall be Edward IV!"

Edward's sense of humor deserted him. She was sitting straight and proud. No matter what fierce winds blew about her, he thought, she is as sturdy as the great castle in Westmoreland, where she had been born, and holds her head as high as its ancient battlements. Edward knelt.

"My beloved son," she said. "May the blessings of God be upon thee."

Edward dressed carefully the following morning. It was the fourth of March. Black velvet with gold facings, a shirt of finest white cambric. When he appeared the crowds of people were already thick about Baynard's Castle. Edward on horseback was a sight that medieval London would never forget. He looked like a young god, a magnificent Prince, a deliverer, a man, a King.

The procession began. At the Cross the Chancellor repeated his first speech, which Edward had listened to three days before. Then they went through the city to Westminster, all of London streaming after. At the great hall of William Rufus Edward dismounted. He towered above all the rest of the crowd. On foot he went up to the chancery and before the Archbishop of Canterbury, the Chancellor and the lords spiritual and temporal of the realm—those that were in London—he took the oath. His firm voice sounded out, plain to be heard.

"To keep the realm truly and justly, and to maintain the laws."

The Archbishop placed the royal robes on his shoulders and

the cap of state upon his dark head. Then he went and sat in the seat, as King.

There, in simple language, he made the speech he had written four nights before, explaining his right to occupy the throne, speaking to the lords, the bishops, the monks and the people. Hushed silence greeted him as he finished and rose. He walked through the palace to the abbey now, and the abbot and the monks were waiting for him with the scepter of Edward the Confessor. They led him, among them, to the high altar and tomb of the Confessor for him to make his offerings.

When his tall figure returned to the choir, he took his seat upon the throne, and the people knelt and the choir was filled with the sound of the "Te Deum." Edward, Earl of March, was become Edward IV of England.

Edward returned to the city by boat; he dined and lodged at the episcopal palace. The next day, March fifth, the "Te Deum" was sung again at the abbey and the new King proclaimed, but Edward was already busy with the affairs of state.

He dated his reign from the fourth of March. On the fifth letters missive, prepared the day before, were hurried to all parts of the realm. In the morning he received the Mayor Lee and the alderman, with citizens. With anxious faces they asked that he be "good and gracious to the city and confirm the ancient liberties and franchises, as his progenitors had done."

Edward said, "I promise it faithfully." He paused. "But I command you to see that our city is well guided and that it remains faithful to me after I set out, as I mean to do and as I must."

They thanked him. The following day Edward's first proclamation was read.

"Margaret, calling herself Queen, has brought our old enemies into the land, the French and the Scots. They are pillaging the country, the towns, the abbeys. Therefore let it be known that we are setting forth, and also let it be known that no man, under pain of death, shall rob or despoil our women or our churches."

A proclamation went out to the fleet too, which was to follow him north. And grace and pardon were extended—of life and goods—to any adherent of the former King who would tender submission to the new King in ten days.

The Duke of Norfolk set out north immediately. Warwick followed him. Meanwhile there were not enough hours in the day for Edward. He appointed his court, his Chancellor, his Treasurer, the Keeper of the Privy Seal. Warwick was created Chamberlain and Constable of Dover and the Cinque Ports.

He named his council and for his personal household, Hastings as chamberlain, John Fogge as treasurer.

On March eleventh Lord Fauconberg, another Neville, left London in command of the foot. Three great guns trundled alongside. Edward himself was trying to raise money.

The treasury was bare, indeed it was worse than bare. Henry's misrule had carried the realm deeper and deeper into debt each year. Edward borrowed four thousand pounds from the mayor and the alderman, of which one hundred fifty was allotted to the royal household; a citizen named Hugh Wych loaned a hundred pounds. The Bishop of Exeter, George Neville, the new Chancellor of the realm, raised money on his jewels. Streams of people waited to see Edward in the anteroom. Finally, it being impossible to grant personal interviews, he startled the company by strolling out among them. A wealthy woman who made her living in silk offered him ten pounds. He asked his treasurer to put down the loan, and he gave her a kiss and thanked her. The Duchess of Bedford was in the room. Edward went over to her. She brought a fine jewel.

Edward thanked her; he knew that her husband and her two oldest sons were with the so-called Queen.

"We shall write you regarding your pension," he said.

And he found the time to dictate a letter to her before he left, saying that the crown would continue her pension.

Nonetheless the hours, the days, were speeding on. On March thirteenth, early in the morning, Edward left London. The night before he reviewed all that had been done. All positions of importance were filled by men who were loyal at the present time. Enough money had been borrowed to pay his soldiers and to pay for the next month's household. Around him were still his group of young men; he would reward them greatly in the days to come. In the North both Norfolk and Warwick had raised troops. London would stay loyal; the mayor and the aldermen had no hope of getting their money back if they didn't. As far as Europe was concerned the King of France was supporting the mad Henry, but Philip of Burgundy had sent some men, and they were led by the Seigneur de la Barde, who bore the proud banners of Louis, the Dauphin of France. The rest of Europe would wait and see.

The sun shone bright that morning. Edward knew he was leaving London an uncrowned King and that it might be months before he were crowned, if ever. All he had was the consent of the people. Would it be enough? He was confident that it would, and his new banners, with the flaming suns of York, floated bravely over his head as the gates of London closed upon the last of his men.

Once in the saddle, riding out to confront his enemies, Edward left all disquiet behind him. Fifteen miles a day was enough to push his foot; by March sixteenth he was forty-five miles from London and the following day he reached Cambridge. Here he was joined by Sir John Howard, who bore a hundred pounds from the abbot of Bury St. Edmonds. Now began Edward's maneuvering to push the Queen's forces into battle. During that week Warwick joined him with fresh troops, and Lord Fauconberg and the largest part of the foot met at rendezvous on time. Edward gave them two days' rest, then he pushed on to Pontefract and Ferrybridge. When he arrived there he knew his scouts were right. Margaret and Henry must be near, eight miles beyond the river, his spies had said, for the bridge across the river was gone.

Edward set his men to rebuilding it. The weather was poor, cold and windy. It was Friday. Wrapped in his cloak, he paced the riverbank and watched the work; he reckoned it would take all day tomorrow to rebuild; meanwhile, across the river, spies must be watching him.

Saturday night the big bonfires burned in the camp all night long and on the bank, where shifts of men labored.

"As soon as it is finished and the last plank laid, they will attack," Edward said.

Warwick looked surprised.

"Not with their main body," Edward said. "But I'll lay you heavy odds they make a raid."

He left the tent. There was the sharp smell of rain or snow in the air; there were no stars. Hastings and Will Herbert were with him. Again Edward went down to the bank of the river. The body of archers protecting the laboring carpenters were at their posts, peering through the black, cold night. Edward's mind was visualizing the Lancastrian forces.

They were drawn up beyond the valley of Tintingdale on a plateau nearly a mile in breadth, which dropped suddenly on the west to a narrow, deep stream called Cock Bech—on the east it extended to the road to Tadcaster and York. Edward wondered if they had been foolish enough to destroy the bridge over Cock Bech; his scourers were divided on that point.

Hastings shivered in the wind; its icy fingers ran down his back even through the woolen scarf he had wound around his neck. It must be two in the morning, he thought; the black water of the river made him even colder.

There was a fire burning on the bank, and Hastings stepped closer to it, when he felt Edward's hand on his arm, drawing him away.

"If you want to get near it you'll have to squat like those." Edward gestured to the knot of men about the fire.

Ahead of Hastings was the new-laid bridge. Far out on it torches flared, and one could hear the sound of hammering and occasionally a bit of sound of a man's voice, snatched out of his mouth and flung on Hastings' ears. Between the torches, in the blackness of the bridge, were a small body of archers; it was some of these, temporarily relieved, who crouched about the fire, warming their hands.

"The danger will come when they reach the other side," Edward said, peering through the blackness.

"What have they gained by this, sir?" Hastings asked.

"Time," said Edward. He shrugged. "It may redound to their advantage. Maybe they're expecting more Scots, maybe Trollope (he was the Queen's cleverest captain) entertained the thought of attacking in the rear. But he doesn't have time enough to move that unwieldy body."

When Edward had found the bridge destroyed he had sent Norfolk on a wide rearward flank to protect against sudden attack from behind. He was thinking that on the morrow he would allow Norfolk some rest and leave his men in the rearguard. Hastings was thinking suddenly of Edward's safety; his tall figure so unmistakable; suppose, Hastings thought with sudden horror, a longbow was being raised at this very moment? A flare of light suddenly came from the fire and threw Edward's dark face in relief, then Hastings could even see the brilliance of his dark eyes, the mobile, wide mouth. It was the cold, cold hour of the night when thoughts as black as the night descend; even the trees looked menacing, the black water swirled. Across the water the camp which they couldn't see: All the nobility of England were gathered there, Hastings thought, except for the Nevilles, Warwick and his brother Fauconberg, and the Duke of Norfolk —all the rest waited like angry tigers at the thought of this new, young King. Defeat tomorrow would mean death, Hastings knew; death on a village green or in a market square, death in front of Margaret's eyes and the eyes of the young Prince, her son, who would watch in his brave new suit of velvet and beaten gold. It had been different at Mortimer's Cross, Hastings thought. That had seemed like a fine adventure. He glanced at Edward's face; was he too thinking that tonight might be their last night to live, to make love, to savor wine, a good horse, the horns of the hunt? Suddenly even the cold became precious to Hastings, the black night, the nasty, whining wind and those horrible writhing trees. At least he was alive; he drew a deep breath of the bitter air and it set him coughing.

Edward slapped him smartly between the shoulder blades. Hastings looked up into Edward's face; in the darkness he saw only the outline of his face. The helmet Edward wore made him look slightly Italianate.

"Suppose an arrow?" Hastings gasped.

Edward smiled at Hastings. He knew very well that without him there would be no chance of victory tomorrow and that his own life and his own wits were the only things that stood between all these men, the few nobles, the commons, and a miserable bloody death. It had been his choice, he knew. There was many an imponderable in war and he had a weak link: Warwick. Secretly Edward was amused at Warwick's feel for battle and he wasn't sure of his physical courage. He had just come from Warwick's fancy tent; there were so many banners flying furiously on it that Edward had thought with a smile they might pull the whole thing from its stakes. He had said mildly—it had not been an order, for Edward did not want to order the older man about; he had been too good a friend—that they would fight on foot; there would be no body of nobles on horseback ready to flee. The men would fight harder if they were right beside them, Edward said. He watched Warwick's face carefully to see the effect of his words.

Warwick had nodded. Edward had then said good night and left the tent. Well, Edward thought, tomorrow will see. He knew very well that standing there, in his black cloak, with the heavy, simple helmet made for battle and not for show, he was an uncrowned King, fighting the loyal forces; he was the usurper, the intruder; his sense of politics had already told him that for years he would be regarded by some of England and most of Europe as the outlaw King. But he was satisfied. He was content with his claim; ever since his birth he had been prepared for this; he came naturally into kingship; it suited him; he was ready and so was England. That night, under the starless black sky, in the pureness of youth, he swore that he would bring justice and peace. And although the way ahead was black and bitter as this March night, and only March can be such a mean bitch, Edward thought, I shall be the King of England as long as I live, and I shall keep the realm, as I swore, before the shrine of Edward the Confessor; I swore that to God Almighty.

The night was lightening. Edward's dark eyes narrowed, and he took a step forward and slipped in the mud. He grabbed for Hastings and righted himself, swearing under his breath.

There was a sudden commotion at the other end of the bridge; they were finished, a shout went up and then Hastings saw men coming back, running, their tools in hand. Gray streaks lighted the Sunday morning; Hastings suddenly realized it was Palm Sunday; he stood there, stiff as steel, waiting to see what would happen, but it was just the excitement of finishing the bridge and Hastings saw that Edward was regarding him with amusement.

"Would you rather be in early mass?" he gibed.

"By God, I would," said Hastings.

Edward flung an arm around his shoulders. "There's something I've promised myself for this day," he said, and explained no further. For he was watching the dawning day, and through the gray mist on the river he thought he saw movement on the opposite bank. He handed his cloak to Hastings and now stood armed and dressed in mail; he unsheathed the heavy sword and started running forward just as Hastings heard the horns on the opposite bank and also heard Edward say, "Tell Warwick we are under attack!"

On the other side of the bridge it was Lord Clifford who led the attack. It was Lord Clifford who had killed Edward's brother as he had knelt before him. Hastings had disappeared and Will Herbert ran alongside of Edward; Will was amazed, because Edward was calling, ordering his men toward him and off the bridge to safety instead of attacking. Will was so surprised he actually didn't take it in and ran forward on the rough-hewn planks until he heard Edward's sharp command to him to return. Then Edward himself took to his heels and ran up the slight slope away from the bridge, everyone else coming pell-mell after him. Hastings had reached Warwick, and Warwick had been told what to do. By the time Will Herbert reached the top of the rise, a body of archers were fitting the arrows; the line of longbows raised. Will glanced at Edward, standing to one side, his face now cold and set, and then Herbert suddenly perceived the strategy.

"What a fine target," Edward said. The opposing force under Lord Clifford had reached the bank and was spilling out onto it in haste, just like a line of dominoes.

Edward was wondering whether they would perceive they'd won the bridge too quickly and easily, but he wanted to time it right and get as many men on his side of the river as possible. He waited. The archers waited. Will Herbert thought his heart would burst with excitement, for Edward always seemed to turn a battle into a heady fray. There was a banner in Edward's hand, with the flaming suns of York on it. He raised it high and brought it down. The three big bombards fired and Will jumped. At the sound of the guns, which were aimed across the river and fell on the opposite bank, the archers then loosed the murderous arrows; a hail of them enveloped the bridge and the banks. In ten minutes, when Will Herbert reached the bridge at Edward's side, they were slippery with blood.

The fighting on the bridge was sharp and quick. Lord Clifford was killed and his body fell into the river; Edward reached the other side, mighty sword in hand, and again raised the banner and waved it. The mounted horsemen ready for pursuit came over slowly to test the new bridge; Edward watched them gallop off and spread out in the hunt for fleeing men before he turned and made his way back to the other side. There was only one casualty. Warwick was wounded slightly, his leg grazed by an arrow.

Edward was worried about the weather. There was occasional thin, icy rain, spatters of it, and he wished to postpone the confronting of his enemies no longer. Quickly the camp was broken and the men set forth across the new bridge, and Edward reckoned it would be afternoon before they reached the entrenched Lancastrian army.

Edward rode first, Warwick following; the drama of the bridge and the letting of his own blood seemed to rouse the Earl to a fever pitch of excitement, as though he were truly the legend which he had created, the great Earl, the greatest flower of English nobility, the wealthiest, the most generous, the most admired and loved. Riding his great charger, with the warm blood trickling a bit down his leg, his fine plumes adding more height to his helmet, he was the legend living indeed, and the admiration of his followers surrounded him in a warm aura; he was as proud as the peacocks that strutted in the Tower garden.

Edward was pleased to have him in such fine fettle; nonetheless he cast increasing glances at the sky, the dark, blowing clouds, the smell of ice and snow in the air. As they rode that wind blew in their faces and they would have to ascend the hill to the plateau on which the Lancastrians rested with that wind full in their faces. But it must be today, Edward was sure. Tactically there might be trouble; but psychologically it was right; his men were ready to fight; they had just had the good, sharp taste of victory and they were hungry for more.

Edward never pushed his men unless it was a matter of retreat. Thus it was afternoon before the whole Yorkist force arrived at Tintingdale, and with dispatch Edward drew up his force in battle formation, himself commanding the center.

On horseback, he addressed his men. "Spare the commons." It was his battle cry, far different than they had ever heard before, but Edward wanted a country to rule, not a graveyard. And then, "We shall fight on foot among you."

He dismounted. Alongside of him Warwick dismounted too. Edward's personal groom took the reins of both horses, but Warwick suddenly cried, "Halt!"

He drew his sword, and before Edward's eyes he drove it into the beast's neck. Edward turned aside.

"I shall fight to the death, on foot!" Warwick roared as the horse fell into a pool of blood at his feet.

His men cheered mightily; Warwick stood astride the dying horse as though he had slain a dragon.

Flamboyant fool, Edward thought, we can't afford to kill horses, and at the same moment a sharp rain beat in his face; then it died, the wind stilled and it was suddenly colder. Edward cursed the weather, stepped around the dead horse and cast one glance upward at the slope where the Lancastrians waited for him. His horns sounded. Edward was armed with his great sword, a battle-ax stuck in his belt, the visor of his helmet open. At the bottom of the hill the Yorkist army began to move slowly up the hill. At that precise moment the wind began to blow again sharply, and with it the promised rain. Edward felt the rain, then he realized he was seeing it, that it was blowing from behind him and that it was not rain but sleet; a curtain of sleet was between him and the waiting Lancastrians, and what was more, it was blowing in the enemy's faces and moving like a God-given protection in front of him.

Edward gave a mighty shout, signaled the horns and then he charged ahead as fast as he could to save enough breath when he reached the opposing forces.

His men followed, and followed fast; the arrows of the Lancastrians were going over their heads, the aim was bad, the archers could not see and Edward attained the plateau; then there began a hand-to-hand struggle with swords and daggers, spears and battle-axes; with the precious sleet blowing in the faces of his enemies, he moved forward with it at his back.

The battle of Palm Sunday Field lasted until ten at night in the foulest weather England could produce. Back, back were driven the Lancastrians. They had destroyed the bridge across the Wharf; it flowed deep and swift and many drowned in it.

Edward pursued his fleeing enemies. Edward's mind was behaving as it always did in the midst of battle; it was calm as though it were standing off from him, directing him, making every sense in his body doubly sharp, all-knowing, all-directing. Alongside of him Hastings felt no fear at all. The slashing, determined attack of Edward, forward and forward—Hastings followed suit, using his battle-ax; ahead of him on one side he saw Blount, hewing his way.

But there were more and more of them. Trollope himself now, and Hastings saw him fall, mortally wounded. The sleet continued, then it was driving snow; it lay on the ground, bloodied, and the hours wore on; the afternoon light was dying. The men were wearying and Hastings began to feel afraid when suddenly it was all over. Edward's carefully kept fresh troops under the Duke of Norfolk poured onto the plateau, shouting and sweeping past Edward and Hastings now, on to the kill of the losers.

Hastings saw Blount again near him. Edward was standing tall and he motioned to Blount and to Humphrey Stafford, who was running toward them. The three of them came up to Edward and he smiled at them.

"Kneel," he said.

They knelt in the snow. Edward raised the sword, and he touched each one of them on the shoulder with the tip of the terrible weapon.

Edward said, "This is the something I promised myself I would do. For gallantry and bravery in the field I dub thee knight, Sir William." Hastings didn't even hear the other words he spoke. He struggled to his feet, footsore and heavy with fatigue. Only his heart was alive, he thought, and he would give it forever to Edward Plantagenet.

But Edward demanded more of his body right away. Although Hastings would have thought it was impossible, nonetheless there was no sleep for him ahead. Edward was going to follow up his victory by catching as many of his enemies as he could.

"It was a tactical error to destroy the bridge," Edward said. "I should not have thought Trollope would be guilty of that." Edward was glad Trollope had died bravely in the field; he had once deserted Warwick, and Edward was glad he had not fallen into the Earl's hands. He swung his horse away from the scene of the deep, swift river in which so many men had drowned. There were red streaks in its black swirls. In fact there was blood in the snow all the way to York, where Edward arrived the following morning in furious pursuit of his enemies. He had been completely victorious—in fact the account of the battle was going to make the King of France quiver with fear—but he had not captured the poor mad King or the she-wolf Queen and her cub.

The city of York had sheltered the Lancastrian forces and the King. When they beheld the first mounted troops with their blazing banners of the suns of York and the white roses, when the ranks parted and Edward rode toward the gates like a conqueror, they opened slowly and within, the city trembled. But bravely the citizens sent their mayor, and in the town square Edward was met by Lord Montagu and Lord Berners. He heard their plea and intercessions briefly.

There was silence in the square. Only the brilliant colors of the banners and the glistening armor set the scene and the ranks of horses, their breath white in the cold.

Edward spoke so all could hear. "We give you our promise of grace for the city."

Lord Berners' face went white with relief. "Thank you, Your Grace."

Edward was somber. "We shall keep Easter with you here." He swung off his horse and the people could still see him because he was so tall. The way was made and Edward went, as he always did after battle, to the cathedral, to the high altar to make his offering. In the dim light, although the candles had been lighted, men watched his bared head; the abbot came to him and blessed him, and the abbot was moved by this young King.

"Father." Edward wet his lips. "My father, the Duke of York —you will help me. You will send a holy man, a monk, and take what remains of him for decent burial to Pontefract. And tonight there will be a mass for his soul. I will come back tonight."

Chapter 2

THE NEWS of Palm Sunday Field had reached London officially on April fourth in the form of a letter from the King to his mother. The first picture of the new King emerged; of one thing the realm was sure. Their young King was a soldier; even in the bitterness of a civil war Englishmen could say with a smile of pride, "I wager the French King is shivering in his boots!"

Rumors continued to flood the city. One was true: that Edward would stay in the north until the country was peaceful and secure for him. Lists of the noble dead reached the city; and among the names listed was that of the oldest son of the Duchess of Bedford, young, handsome, brilliant Anthony Woodville.

At the Woodville manor of Grafton Elizabeth Woodville was dressed in mourning. On Palm Sunday she went to church in the early evening, making her black-shawled way to the village, alone.

During the service she prayed constantly for the safety of her father and two brothers; although she could not know that at that same hour, in the north at Towton Field, in the sleet and dark, the Lancastrian army was still fighting, still it seemed to her later that she must have known somehow, for she was shaken with distress and alarm. She prayed for the soul of her dead husband and the tears came willy-nilly and streamed down her cheeks. After the service she came out into the churchyard, and to cool her feverish head she removed her shawl. In the dim evening light, her gilt head bare, her beauty was so startling that the villagers stared in admiration.

She paid no attention; she stood alone, wringing her hands. An old woman sidled close to her. "The devil will draw your soul to hell," she whispered.

Elizabeth gave a cry of fear. "Witch!" she hissed. She ran, her fringed shawl streaming behind her. The night was darkening, shadows were everywhere and the country wasn't safe anymore; there were scoundrels and ruffians everywhere, people said, and no law in the land and only violence and terror and that horrible old woman muttering curses.

Monday dawned; the life at the manor house went on its prescribed manner, from the early morning milking to evening prayers, and Tuesday arrived. The sun was shining, and it was April and spirits lightened a bit; the children were happy; Thomas and Lionel were playing with their wooden swords, five of Elizabeth's younger sisters played a noisy game of hide-and-seek. Elizabeth fed the baby and put him to nap; then she went out to the kitchen garden, taking her older son by the hand; he toddled alongside of her as they walked about the neatly laid paths.

On Tuesday the first rumors of defeat reached the village. A lone horseman coming from the north brought the tale of a fierce hand-to-hand battle which left the snowy battlefield darkened with blood. More would be following him, he said; the defeated were limping homeward.

At night then Elizabeth Woodville barred the doors. The women of England were bred to keeping the manor in their lord's absence. As a child she had seen her stalwart mother throw open the doors and advance, arms akimbo, on a set of hired knaves from a nearby noble who coveted a piece of land. Staves were set handily in the milking shed so they could be seized to beat off any attack. But no danger was worse than roving bands of unemployed, hungry soldiers, who had left their lord either because of his lack of funds or his death on the field. So she kept watch down the long lane, and as the slow days of the week passed she felt increasing fear, and when at last there came ahead one horseman and then a trundling wagon, she knew why it had taken her father and her brothers so long to get home.

Catching up her skirts she fled down the lane, past the horseman to the lead rider with the wagon.

"Father!" she cried. "Thank God! Thank God in his mercy!" She had climbed up onto the wagon seat and looked at the recumbent figure within. Both her hands gripped the back of the rude seat as she knelt there and looked at her brother's face. She had expected to see him dead. Instead of that his eyes were wide open and he smiled.

"Bit of a nuisance, Bess," he said.

Richard Woodville, who had been driving the wagon, dropped the reins and hugged her. "He's going to be all right, Bess," he said. "But he lost a lot of blood and we were afraid to have him ride."

She felt her father's hand on her head, tugging at her hair.

"Bess, Bess," he said.

Then he paused; his hand dropped to her shoulder and squeezed it. "My dearest daughter," he said. "You don't know how glad we are to be home."

Elizabeth stood up on the wagon seat and looked about now at the men in livery, some bandaged, and she waved her hand.

"Welcome home," she said, her voice trembling. "And all who are hurt or need help come to the kitchens."

After Anthony had been carried up to the bedroom he shared with the other boys, and after she had bathed him and rewound clean linen bandages around the gashed leg and hip; after all the other hurts and wounds had been tended, after dinner, when her father sat writing to her mother at the table, his head bent, the pen flying, the messenger standing waiting, Elizabeth sat by the fire, thinking. Absently she watched her father cut off the unused portion of the paper and fold up the letter he had written in a neat packet and then seal it; she could smell the wax. Under the candlelight her father looked drawn. Well he might, she thought. She couldn't get the picture of the little tired troop coming down the lane. Where now was the fanfare of trumpets, the gay banners, the fresh, dancing horses, the bright, heavy wagons with their load of provisions and tents?

"They charged up the hill in the snow—well, it was really sleet, and I thought for a while we were going to get the better of it." Richard was talking to John and Lionel. "And it went on and on, the hand-to-hand fighting, and then, my God, I saw Anthony surrounded! I've never been so afraid in my life! And not ten feet away from us was the King!"

"You saw him plain?"

"Yes! I ran with a shout to Anthony, and he managed to hobble along, and then I practically lifted him on my hip and to tell

you the truth I ran as fast as I could with Anthony dragging behind me. It was night. In the darkness we got away.

"We stumbled on in the dark, Anthony telling me to leave
him, when we fell over a body. I took the coat off it and wrapped
it around Anthony. We hid in some trees and then Father found
us. He told us later that fresh troops came up, Norfolk's men, and
that the battle was over."

Lionel was silent. Then John said, "They say Edward is in York.
They say he will be coming back though in a few weeks."

Lord Rivers rose and handed the packet to the waiting messenger. He came over to the fire and put his foot up on the
fender.

Lionel looked up at him. "What are we going to do, Father?"
he asked.

Lord Rivers squinted into the flames. "I don't know, my boy,"
he said. He sighed deeply. Then his handsome face broke into
a smile. "I'm going to ask your mother," he said. "Goodnight,
both of you."

Lionel and John stood up immediately and gave a courteous
goodnight. Elizabeth stayed on a stool by the fire after she had
kissed her father. Lost in her thoughts, she sat on.

"We may be attainted, you know," Richard said. "And lose all
our lands, and Father's livelihood."

Elizabeth regarded her hands. "Mother will do something," she
said.

"But the King and the Queen and the little Prince got away."

"You'd not keep fighting for them?" Elizabeth cried. There
was silence. "Would you, Richard?"

"Wouldn't I?" asked Richard. Yet in his mind came unbidden
the picture, vivid, of Edward, mighty sword in one hand, in the
thick of the press of the battle. Richard said, "You know, John,
when I remember, I'm not sure I'd want to go against the Earl
of March again." He grinned. "Pour us some ale, will you, Bess?"
he asked. "If the returning soldier can't have a bit of service from
his females, what's fighting for?"

The day after Easter Lord Rivers sent his son John and an
escort to bring his wife from London, and with the arrival of the
intrepid Duchess the whole household took on its regular tenor.
Lord Rivers thought with amazement that the battle of Palm

Sunday Field might never have happened or be a figment of his own imagination for all the thought his wife took of it. It was almost the second week in April and all the spring chores of the manor so demanding that he said wearily one night to Jacqueta, "All this work—and these may not even be our lands!"

Jacqueta said, "Well, that roof has got to go on the milking shed by next week, Richard, regardless of whose cows are in it. The only thing that worries me is Anthony. He's not getting his strength back."

"Give him time," Lord Rivers said. "He sustained two terrible blows. He lost much blood."

On nice days Anthony was carried out and enjoyed watching April bloom. Spring enfolded the land; the earth became warm again to the searching fingers, the air was soft to the cheek and even the rains were gentle and brought green to the land. In the village the long winter was ending, and men and women could come out of the tiny, bare, cold houses. Soon it would be May!

On April second Edward had reached Durham. News reached Grafton that Edward had beguiled the Bishop of Durham with his charm, that he had made the Bishop his confessor and that he was going on to Newcastle to receive the submission of the city.

"But farther than that he cannot go yet," Lord Rivers said, thinking of Northumberland with its great forbidding castles and the hostile Scottish marches lying so close. But rumors persisted that Edward was in communication with James of Scotland and from all Edward was doing and had accomplished in the pacification of the north Lord Rivers said, "I don't know when that young man sleeps."

"He will turn around and come this way," the Duchess said.

Edward stayed in Newcastle only one day and succeeded in capturing the Earl of Wiltshire, who was promptly tried and executed. Then he turned around and was in Durham on May second, and now began his progress down to London by way of Lancashire, Preston, Manchester, Lichfield, Coventry, Warwick, Daventry and Stony Stratford.

"He is going to be in Stony Stratford two days," the Duchess said. "And you must go, you and Richard."

May had never been more beautiful. Lord Rivers and Richard set forth one May morning, dressed in their finest, with polished boots. They rode to Stony Stratford to seek audience with the King and to tender their submission. On coming into the chamber where Edward was, Richard Woodville hung back just a little. He was not quite sure he wanted to be here. Then he saw Edward clearly for the first time, face-to-face. In both their minds was the last time they had seen each other. Edward smiled his merry smile. Richard went down on one knee.

Lord Rivers said, "Your Grace, we are come to ask pardon and to tender Your Grace our humblest submission and to ask for grace."

"Please rise, my lord," Edward said. "And you, sir." He thrust forward his big hand and Lord Rivers took it with sudden emotion and gripped Edward's hand hard. Then Edward extended his hand to Richard.

Richard Woodville was so surprised that he reacted slowly, took Edward's hand and muttered, "Thank you, sir." Then he regarded Edward with his candid blue eyes, and seeing the smile in Edward's he blurted, "I've never had such an honor before!"

Edward patted him on the shoulder; this boy appealed to him; he'd be a good hunting companion and he would be loyal, and the father was a solid English squire, married or not to a Duchess. Lord Rivers was as English as the sudden spring rain that beat against the roof—no ancient nobility harboring ancient grudges or dreams of glory and quartering royal standards on his pennants; just the man who brought thirty retainers to help the muster in time of war; just the man who saw his fields were plowed and the church had a new roof and that his daughters and sons could read and write.

"Lord Rivers," asked Edward. "What of your son Anthony?"

"Anthony was bad hurt," Richard interrupted, for he suddenly felt a kinship with this man, King or no, and he had been just a few feet away when Anthony was set upon by three men at once.

"I know," Edward said.

"You saw?"

Lord Rivers said, in a manner that reminded Edward of his own dead father, "Now, Richard, if you'll just hold your tongue for a moment, I will explain to His Grace that Anthony sends his felicitations and his plea for grace too. But he is not yet well enough to wait on Your Grace personally."

Lord Rivers knew that their interview was over; there were many men waiting to see Edward; all the time they had been talking, members of Edward's household came to and fro and a secretary was busy taking down the matter they had been discussing, namely, the submission of three prominent Lancastrian names. He waited for Edward to terminate the meeting and Edward did. The King had already made up his mind to welcome this family and to grant the royal pardon. However, what he said was, "Tomorrow, my lord, we shall ride over to Grafton. You will send our message of condolence to your son Anthony and our regards to the Duchess of Bedford."

Lord Rivers and Richard backed to the door, bowed and were swallowed up in the crowd of people who waited to see the King. Out in the sunshine, for it had stopped raining and the sun had come out again, Richard helped his father to mount. He couldn't contain himself.

"He's a true Prince, Father!" he whispered.

Lord Rivers did not commit himself aloud. He was only conscious of relief. He was immensely glad that Edward had been kind enough to accept their submission. Richard did not yet know as much as he did about the horrors and cruelties of civil war. As he rode home Lord Rivers was thanking his Heavenly Father that mercy had been shown. After all, Edward's kindnesses had not extended to either Wiltshire or Devonshire: They'd been tried and executed immediately. What Lord Rivers did not suspect as yet was that it was to be Edward's policy to take his servants from the squires and the middle classes, a policy which would be followed by his grandson Henry and which was going to be fiercely resented by the great nobility, but which in the long picture would redound to England's advantage.

When they arrived home at Grafton, the Duchess was absent. And when Lord Rivers found she had gone to the village to chastise a villager whose part of the common field was left untended so that weeds got into his neighbor's plots, Lord Rivers fumed.

"Why didn't you send the bailiff, the hayward?"

"Because I sent him before and the villain paid no heed," the Duchess said.

Anthony was reading.

"Reading when our whole future was in the balance!" Lord Rivers eyed his eldest son. "You dream, Anthony, you dream!" Anthony sighed and closed the big book which was open on his knees.

"The King sent you his condolences," Richard said. "You should see him, Anthony!"

"I have seen him," Anthony said mildly. "I used to see him every day in London last winter as he passed by on his way to visit his little brothers, the York boys." It suddenly occurred to Anthony that he might have done the same thing himself had his father been absent; he glanced over at Lionel and John who were listening intently.

Lord Rivers recollected that the most important part of his message had been as yet unrelayed. "He is coming! Jacqueta, the King is coming tomorrow!"

The Duchess raised her brows till they almost reached her high coif. "I told you the spring planting was important. He shall see our hay will be ready by June."

After the first flurry of excitement, after Jacqueta had sent to the village for the unmarried girls to come and help the household get ready, after each child had got from his or her chest the proper clothes for the morrow, after the bread had been set to rise, the ale, the best ale brought from the brewery, the finest linen laid out carefully, as the sun set and the household prepared for bed, Jacqueta found Anthony again reading by the fire.

She knew her son very well. "Anthony," she said, laying her hand across the wide illuminated page, "you are not happy."

He sighed. "I am the kind of person who is the victim of his own beliefs and loyalties. For some reason, Mother, I cannot just abandon poor saintly Henry. That's why I fought for him. But my family loyalty comes first, Mother. I should not jeopardize you. Perhaps I shan't meet His Grace tomorrow. I could plead fatigue and pain. I could avoid meeting him thus."

"He would be offended. He is not stupid. He is friendly, but he is not stupid. Do not underestimate him. That is what too many have done."

"I shall see," Anthony said.

"Your face is so transparent, Anthony. Try to be practical."

"What of my conscience, Mother?"

The Duchess snorted. "What of your family, Anthony?"
"I said that first, Mother. Please do not worry."

The Duchess was right; it was true that Edward, riding to Grafton, noted that the hay was ripening well and that it would be ready for June haying. He noted that the village was clean and that its fences were mended and its roofs stout and that most of the villagers had a cow and some animals in the rear of their plot. He noted that in the common fields the strips that divided each man's plots from another were well defined and one man couldn't plow another's oats. He noted that their smocks were clean and neat and the alehouse well kept and brightly shuttered.

At the church the priest waited; at the village green the villagers cast flowers in front of his horse. Edward drew up and spoke with the priest.

The villagers crowded closer to get a look at their new King. The girls sighed. The men stared in envy at this handsome Prince, his jeweled cap on the side of his head. The eyes of the women went from one young man to another—Edward's followers were all young—and returned fascinated to the King. He was speaking with the priest, but suddenly out of all their throats came a lusty cheer.

Edward raised his gloved hand in salute and he smiled. They noted he had no bodyguard, just his courtiers and a few servants; he was content to ride among them, unpretentious, a true King, they thought. When Edward rode on, they ran after, cheering and calling, "God bless Your Grace."

The Duchess had proudly drawn up her family in the hall. With Lord Rivers at her side, then John, then Richard and Lionel, then Anne, Katharine, Margaret, Edward, Jacqueta, Joan, Mary and lastly tiny Martha. Edward did not realize that two were missing. And what he saw enchanted him. He couldn't help smiling broadly. "Madam," he said, "my congratulations!"

His eyes swept down the line. Health and beauty and intelligence in every pair of bright eyes. If every family in England looked like this, Edward thought, the realm would have no troubles.

The Duchess swept him a deep curtsy. "We are honored, Your

Grace, at your presence among us, and you do our household a favor of which we are very proud!"

Jacqueta's charm was never more evident. In the first place, as a woman, she appreciated Edward; as a Frenchwoman she made that fact subtly and wonderfully plain.

Edward raised her up and gave her a quick kiss. Then he went down the line of Woodvilles, greeting each as they spoke their name to him, and Hastings came after him, presenting his companions. It was so beautiful a day that the Duchess had set up trestle tables outside, and the board bore the weight of the food bravely, and the air was redolent with roasting meats and fowl. Jacqueta herself bore the ewer to Edward for him to wash before the meal. It was a splendid day for Grafton; within the house the sounds of laughter and voices sounded very plain.

"It will be successful," Elizabeth said. "Mother is always successful."

Anthony nodded abstractedly. "You should be there with them, Bess," he said.

She shook her glittering gilt head. "I am a widow, Anthony, of but a few months. It would hardly be seemly for me to join in the festive feast. And my husband died fighting for old Henry. I don't want to see him either. You know that."

But she had promised. And Jacqueta knew neither she nor Anthony would break that promise. After dinner the Duchess would bring Edward back into the hall.

The sound of music echoed in the windows and the open doors. Cautiously Anthony got to his feet. He and Elizabeth started down toward the hall; at almost the same moment the Duchess steered Edward, who was followed by Hastings and a few other of his companions, into the open doors.

"Anthony, my oldest son," the Duchess was explaining, "was not well enough to join us at dinner. Elizabeth, my oldest daughter, is in mourning for her late husband, Lord Grey, of Groby."

Edward, whose long strides were carrying him forward, suddenly perceived ahead of him the figure of Anthony Woodville, Anthony, already famous for his chivalry, his gentleness, his wit. He was trying not to limp. At his side was a woman; she held his arm.

Edward took two more long strides. Elizabeth curtsied and

Anthony tried to go down on his bad leg. Edward was sure he would fall; the Duchess gasped and at the same moment Edward had both hands under Anthony's shoulder.

Anthony said easily, "Thank you, Your Grace." Then he said, "I can stand, sir."

Edward released him and Anthony did stand. Then Edward turned his eyes onto the woman. Looking deep into those golden-brown eyes, Edward had a sensation of the most pleasant kind of drowning. The sheer impact of her beauty, her perfect face, her gilt-colored hair, her slim, straight, standing body—if his badge were the white rose, here indeed was the most wonderful rose that ever grew on English soil.

"Lady Grey," he said.

"My daughter Elizabeth," the Duchess said.

Edward was conscious of Hastings at his side and he presented him.

Elizabeth said, "We have met through correspondence. We wrote of a betrothal between my son and Sir William's daughter when she arrives." She smiled.

"You have a son?" Edward asked. He looked at her figure again.

"I have two sons, Your Grace."

Hastings stepped back. Edward's eyes did not deceive anyone, least of all Hastings nor Anthony. He took his sister's hand. "We are unhappy, Your Grace, that we could not join the dinner. We ask your forgiveness."

Edward noted that he did not ask for pardon. Yet he forbore any comment. He had no doubts about Anthony—his face was too honest. So Edward said, "It is our hope that you soon fully recover, sir. It is our wish that you then present yourself at court."

It was a command, of course, and Anthony knew it. "I shall be honored."

The Duchess thought Edward had handled Anthony well. But the shadows were lengthening inside the hall and it was time for the King to ride away. Edward took one last lingering look at Elizabeth Woodville.

"The next time I come I shall hope for your company."

"It shall be my hope also," she said politely.

She raised her eyes; they looked all golden to Edward.

"Good-bye," Edward said.

On this first moment of the meeting and parting her eyes searched his face. "*Au'voir,*" she whispered low.

The soft farewell echoed in his ears. Why had she used French? he wondered; it was like a caress. Elizabeth didn't know why she had said it herself; it was habit, she thought; it was habit among the family to use the expression—her mother always used it to her children; you used it to an intimate, a loved one. Elizabeth glanced at Anthony; had he heard her?

"God bless Your Grace," she said stiffly.

Hand in hand with Anthony she watched him go. Her eyes followed every move of his figure, the even, long stride, the squared shoulders; her ears strained for the sound of his voice. Her fingers were tight on Anthony's hand. Then suddenly she loosed it and ran toward the big doors; standing to one side of them, she watched Edward mount, and she stood there looking up the land until the last rider and last pennant were out of sight.

Chapter 3

ANTHONY WOODVILLE, elegant as always, dressed in dark-blue satin, came down the stairway at Lambeth Palace behind his King. It was June twenty-sixth and he had been at court two weeks. He was fully recovered from his wounds, but his tanned face was pale and his eyes shadowed from lack of sleep. He had never worked at such a pace in his life.

His mind was a kaleidoscope of impressions of Edward; Edward in the privy chamber; Edward at dinner, giving instructions while he ate; Edward, his brown eyes remote as he dictated; Edward laughing, Edward scowling, Edward irritable, being undressed, Edward asleep.

Edward saying, "Peace abroad is mandatory till we have peace at home."

"Rewrite that into French, sir, and give it to my principal secretary immediately."

"It is positively necessary that you pick a faithful man to go to the Lord of the Isles with this bribe money."

"I've heard your father raises the best dogs in England. Please ask him to send two to the Milanese ambassador, Count Dalugo. Fine relations with Italy mean trade."

"The envoys to Scotland will be followed by Lord Montagu with five thousand men for a show of force. The embassy with the safe conduct for the Scottish lords will follow them. These safe conducts should be stamped with the royal seal and in the embassy's hands by tomorrow."

"I shall need a new sword for the coronation as my offering. Mine is too well used. Don't pay more than six pounds."

"These are the names of the thirty men whom I shall honor this Friday before my coronation by creating them Knights of the Bath. I shall wait till the day after the coronation to create my brother George the Duke of Clarence. Be sure enough time is allowed me to do all this with proper ceremony."

"The coronation banquet should be splendid but it is never necessary to waste money."

"On Friday the Mayor of London and the alderman will be dressed in scarlet; they propose to meet me at Lambeth Palace and escort me to the Tower. Four hundred principal citizens of the city wish to accompany them and they will be dressed in green. I tell you this so that you gentlemen may pick another color to ride in procession, if you wish."

And there they were in a blaze of red and green, plus the court and the royal family; for it was Coronation Day. Rivaling the sunny day were the flaming suns of York and the banners with the white rose fluttered from tall lance tips.

London had outdone itself. Every doorway was decorated with garlands of green and flowers; flowers and sweet grasses strewed the streets, flags flew and from every window women waved the colors of the King. Loving hands had embroidered suns and roses on the fluttering standards of the King.

It was Friday. The procession wound its way to the Tower slowly so all could see the scarlet and green of the city's principal citizens, then the magnificent young lords who surrounded Edward, but principally so they could see their young King who would be crowned in the abbey on Sunday. That night, surrounded by his lords, Edward created twenty-eight Knights of the Bath, but what almost brought sudden tears to Anthony's eyes was when one of the young knights to receive the honor was Edward's young, slight brother Richard.

Richard was nine. He was dark and thin; his brown eyes glowed. He stood before his towering brother, and Edward commanded two knights to fasten on the golden spurs; they loomed large on his small boots. Then Edward stepped down to his brother. In his big hand was the new sword and belt, worthy of a knight. Edward deftly girded him, then he leaned down and kissed him.

"Be thou a good knight, Richard," he said softly.

Richard's eyes blinked rapidly to hide the unmanly tears. Edward kissed him again, and even Edward's hardened soldier lords blinked too, hastily. Edward set Richard back then, and the youngest, littlest knight was taken away to bed.

The time flowed on and it was getting too late, so the next morning Edward created the other four Knights of the Bath. When that was done, they, in their white lace hoods and their blue silk gowns, all preceded Edward from the Tower to Westminster, and all of London followed after. And while all these ceremonies were solemn, they were as nothing when Anthony beheld the coronation itself on Sunday. The creation of Edward's other young brother George, who was twelve, the Duke of Clarence; the look on Edward's face when he bestowed a barony of Will Hastings and Will Herbert, his dearest friends—all these vivid impressions faded when the jeweled crown of Edward the Confessor was placed on Edward's head. The Archbishops of Canterbury and York, dramatic in their robes, music pouring through the stony beauty of the abbey, reaching high into its soaring arches, Edward kneeling, Edward throned, with the blessing of God and the saints upon their young King—this Anthony would never forget. Later he hardly remembered the magnificent coronation banquet at all.

On Monday there were more official duties for Edward, and then, as though he were testing him, Edward set Anthony to work on the most pressing problem of any monarch: money.

For there was no money. Money was begged and borrowed. The merchants of the staple advanced a thousand pounds and the bishops did their share. Anthony wrote begging letters to abbots and abbesses, priors and prioresses, and merchants and laymen. And he was instructed to dig into household money to replace horses lost on the field at Towton. Anthony was amused at one entry, the repayment of five marks to Richard Langport, clerk of the council, for a book lost on the battlefield.

The foreign merchants did their share too. In return Edward granted them letters of safe conduct. But the lesson learned had already made a deep impression on him. Money. From the Italian merchants he chose three to act as factors for him. Early that summer three ships left port with the King's goods; Edward was already in the business of shipping and trading.

July arrived; it was hot but Edward was too busy to leave London, so there Anthony stayed. The weeks fled and on the twenty-second of July there arrived news that sent the men who dealt in diplomacy and foreign affairs running to Edward's privy chamber. The King of France was dead! None of the men gathered in the chamber could fail to perceive the implications. The new King of France was Louis, Louis whose banners as the Dauphin had floated alongside of Edward's on Palm Sunday Field; now instead of an enemy on the throne of France Edward had a potential friend.

But Anthony had no idea of Edward's next diplomatic move until a week had passed. That night after dinner Edward had returned to his table; he was conferring with an Italian envoy, who presently bid him good night. The gentlemen of the bed-chamber disappeared into Edward's bedroom to prepare the royal bed, to lay out Edward's bedgown and slippers, to plump up the royal pillows and carefully fold the royal counterpane. Edward was bidding good night to the occupants of the room, and Anthony began to back to the door when Edward said, "We wish you to stay, sir."

"I?" Anthony blurted, in excitement and fierce pride at being thus singled out from all the lords. He glanced around at their faces, for he knew they all remembered full well that he had fought against them on Palm Sunday.

"Yes, you, Anthony," Edward said, amused.

The room emptied quickly. Edward was still at his table. Anthony stood before him.

"Sit down, sir," Edward said. "You speak very fine French."

Anthony sat awkwardly on the edge of a velvet-cushioned, carved chair; he had been fascinated by these chairs, for they were collapsible and came from Venice. He wet his lips. "My mother taught us. We speak French at home."

"You're very modest, Anthony, a quality I find refreshing," Edward said.

"Thank you, Your Grace," Anthony said, not knowing what else to say.

"Anthony, Dr. Hatclyf, Dr. William Hatclyf and Thomas Vaughn, both very valuable and fine Englishmen, have been imprisoned in France by the late King Charles. Margaret, calling herself Queen, had repeatedly asked Charles to deliver these men to her for certain death. Fortunately for us and partly due to our able ambassador's efforts, Charles simply kept them in prison. Now I want you to undertake to travel to France and to offer the new King Louis a modest ransom to show our goodwill. Approximately two hundred and fifty pounds. You will carry a letter from

me to Thomas Vaughn, who will then proceed to King Louis with
a message from me. Thomas Vaughn is an able diplomat and he,
as I've said, will go to Louis. Dr. Hatclyf you will escort back to
me. I am very fond of Dr. Hatclyf."

Edward paused. "Interrupt me if you have questions," he said,
and Anthony again marveled at his easy democratic manner, and
yet Anthony knew how well it served him, for his lords adored
him. Edward was frowning and rubbed his fingers over his brow.

"There is another matter. You will present yourself to Philip of
Burgundy and will speak of a marriage between us and Philip's
niece, Mademoiselle de Bourbon. She is a member of Philip's
household."

Anthony's eyes were wide. "But I—"

Edward waved his hand. "He will refuse, of course. Henry, the
King you fought for, still lives, and Henry has a son, and Philip
of Burgundy will not yet marry one of his nieces to me." Edward
looked down at the parchment in front of him. "When he refuses,
in polite terms, prevaricating as he will, then come to the point
of the business: a year prolongation of our truce, the free intercourse of merchandise and, very important, a meeting to be arranged between our ambassadors and King Louis.

"We must immediately begin to talk with King Louis. The
sooner the better."

Edward paused again. He held up a thick packet. "There are
full instructions here. Read them. We will talk again before you
go. But here is something else." He lifted another parchment
from the table; he rose. Hastily Anthony jumped to his feet.

"Your pardon, Anthony. It passed the Great Seal this morning."

Now standing, the two men faced each other, Edward holding
out the pardon, the Great Seal heavy and official. Edward said,
"We have come a long way in three years." There was the flicker
of a smile on his lips, in his eyes.

He is remembering too, Anthony thought, as it flashed into his
mind, vivid, the first time they had met and stood face-to-face
three years ago. God, what a night that had been! He would
never forget it. He had been afraid and angered out of his wits.
And it had all begun so innocently when his father had taken him
on a trip to the coast to inspect a vessel that the Queen had
wished his father to command for her. They had been asleep in
the cabin when out of the night had descended the daring Earl

of Warwick and his men; rudely they'd been seized and hauled away to Calais; it had been still dark when they had landed, prisoners, shoved around, accompanied by heavily armed men, and in the light of flaring torches they had been pushed into the presence of the Earl of Warwick, who stood and glowered at them.

Contemptuously Warwick had rated Anthony's father. "Squire," he had spit. "You dare to oppose your betters!"

Anthony's father, afraid for his son, returned a quiet answer, glancing at Anthony from the corner of his eyes. Anthony had been only seventeen but he looked older, for he stood almost six feet tall. "My boy," Lord Rivers said, "my boy and I are acting under orders from King Henry." He didn't mention Margaret, the Queen, for he knew if he did Warwick would shout "that evil bitch!" and order them hanged.

"Squire's son and squire," Warwick had ground out, "do you dare talk back to me?"

Anthony Woodville's face went pale with anger. Could he listen to any man so address his father, his own father? The sudden rage that filled him put one foot before the other, his shoulders squared, his eyes blazed, and even though Lord Rivers grasped his arm desperately Anthony would have lunged at the figure of the hateful Earl of Warwick had not another voice, quick with authority, suddenly spoke, and Edward, Earl of March, strode forward in haste, only Edward's legs were so long that it looked as though he were being very casual.

"Good evening, Lord Rivers," he said, coming between Warwick and Anthony.

"To what can we attribute the pleasure of your company in Calais this evening?"

Anthony said, "We were captured! And—"

"Brought here?" Edward intervened. He smiled ironically.

He turned to one of the guard. "Take them away and treat them kind. We won't get our ransom if you are rude."

Lord Rivers seized Anthony's arm and maneuvered him toward the nearest guard. Anthony heard Edward say, "Well, my lord Warwick, allow me to congratulate you on a daring venture. I trust you captured the ship too."

Edward had the same gleam in his brown eyes now as he had had that night in Calais and when he had said only a few moments before, "Henry, the King you fought for," and there in

front of Anthony was his official pardon, being tendered. Light
from the huge ruby on Edward's finger swam in front of Anthony.

"It is kind of you, Your Grace, to give it to me yourself. I appreciate it more than I can ever say."

He knelt, took Edward's hand and put his lips to Edward's
ring. Edward patted him on the shoulder, and when Anthony
rose the King was looking at him with an affectionate smile. Edward held out his hand and Anthony gripped it hard.

"Good night, Anthony," Edward said.

Edward had known that Anthony would learn much from the
magnificence, the rigid protocol, of the Burgundian Philip and
his court. He did. He absorbed it like a sponge, for it suited him.
And his mission proceeded just as Edward said it would; Thomas
Vaughn went on to King Louis as Edward's special envoy, and
Anthony returned to London, escorting Dr. Hatclyf; Philip of Burgundy had hedged politely about marrying his niece, "the Bourbon female," to Edward, but he had listened kindly to agreements
for trade. And when Anthony landed he discovered that affairs
had gone well for Edward in England.

Pembroke Castle had surrendered to Will Herbert and gratefully Edward gave him the custody of the castle and its lands,
and the custody also of a four-year-old boy named Henry Tudor.
But the defenders of the castle were pardoned and Edward's
kindness extended to the Countess of Richmond, little Henry's
mother, who was carefully restored to all her dower rights from
her father and her first husband. In the north Warwick and Montagu were restoring order, and in Calais William Blount had
succeeded in recapturing Hammes Castle.

On September twenty-fourth Edward had granted a safe conduct to the Scottish ambassadors; this was important, for Margaret and the saintly Henry were being sheltered in Edinburgh,
and Edward wanted to drive them out of Scotland especially
now that King Louis was not friendly to them—now that France
would not be a particularly hospitable place for them to go. Edward wanted to get his hands on Henry and keep him in safe
custody; a former King was indeed a liability and a nuisance to
the keeping of the realm; all the little plots and bubbling of rebellion and fomentations in the far counties would simmer down
if Henry were in Edward's hands.

Is it possible it is already November? Anthony wondered. The time had fled. The morning of the fourth of November Anthony dressed in a suit of white velvet that the finest tailor in Burgundy had lovingly contrived for this so handsome, tall Englishman who had been so kind to him, like a true knight, and whose French had been impeccable even to accent. "*C'est incroyable!*" he had told Anthony.

Anthony's valet had finished with his master and was overcome with admiration.

"The other gentlemen of the King will be jealous!"

Anthony smiled, but indeed it was pointed out to the Earl of Warwick slyly that the arrogant young Woodville was more sumptuously dressed than the great Earl himself. And if there were envious eyes cast upon him he didn't note it, because this morning Edward opened his first Parliament and Anthony was completely caught up in the historic implications of this moment in which miraculously he himself was a part.

The Chancellor spoke solemnly on a text which Anthony knew Edward had devised. Leaning forward, he thundered, "Amend your ways and your doings! Amend them, for your King, King by God's law, man's law and the law of nature, has sworn to uphold the laws of this land!"

Then he told them what Edward wanted from them: attainders against the former King and his followers. Next, a legal reform close to Edward's heart: the power of the sheriffs to go to the justices of the peace; and even dearer to his heart, the abolition of livery and maintenance, which allowed a man license to arm his retainers and set them loose on his own errands.

"There can be no law in a land where criminals can hide behind their master's badge!"

Of course there can't, Anthony thought. And evidently Parliament agreed; it granted Edward's three major requests and dealt kindly with many of the minor ones, for it seemed to be greatly relieved that Edward, astute as he was, had not asked them for more taxes.

"Parliament was overgenerous," Edward said, for now began a period in which Anthony worked as a personal secretary. Edward's confiscation, through Parliament, of the great Duchy of Lancaster and the forfeited estates of Lancastrians amounted to a great deal; that was why Edward had not asked for money. He thus rewarded his own followers and kept Anthony busy giving away valuable property into the outstretched hands of the men who had helped Edward, and the patent rolls of that year teem with grants from these forfeited estates.

Nonetheless Edward dictated no less than eighty-nine exemption clauses, for there were many who, Edward felt, had submitted to him or would submit, would be faithful. Carefully every name was scrutinized so that Edward would not unwittingly send back into the Lancastrian camp a potential follower.

This bill of attainder and its eighty-nine exceptions took a lot of thoughtful time, and it was not ready until the twenty-first of December when the laborious work was presented to the King in full Parliament. Edward rose to speak and every eye in the chamber was fastened on his tall figure.

He spoke as he usually did, simply and easily.

"James Strangeways," Edward said, calling the Speaker by name, "and all ye who have come here for the commons of this my land, by your true hearts and assistance I am restored to all that is my right and title. I thank you as heartily as I can with all my heart, and if I had any better good to reward you than my body, you should have it, which shall always be ready for your defense, never sparing. I shall be unto you your very loving liege lord."

A sigh ran around the chamber.

"Now I tell you solemnly that you have done well to pass the ordinance against livery and maintenance, and I tell you even more solemnly that all the lords in Parliament have sworn before us in chamber that they shall abide by it and that they will capture criminals and punish them, even though they be their own retainers and wearing their own badges."

Edward let his eyes rove about the room.

"And we tell you on our oath that criminals will be punished even if they wear our own badge, the King's badge."

Edward sat down and the Chancellor rose and read once more all the laws which had been passed, that they were now the law of the land.

Edward was going down to Greenwich to keep Christmas and Anthony was going to Grafton, but the night of the twenty-first Edward kept the candles burning late. Anthony's nephews, Elizabeth's two little boys, were among those on the list of Lancastrian names whose revenues had been diverted by Parliament to the crown. Anthony was torn by two loyalties. He knew Edward needed the money; he knew the only way the King could pay and reward his followers was by grants of land, and yet it was his sister's living. During a pause in which Edward stretched, rubbed his eyes and frowned, Anthony said, "The ordinance against livery—I thought you might like to see this, Your Grace."

He handed Edward a letter from Elizabeth. It was brief. "And when you come, Anthony, bring crossbows, windings to bind them with, some poleaxes to keep the doors and some jacks. Last night I set the dogs on some men who were trying to steal our barley."

Edward, reading this and remembering the woman he had met, had a picture of those golden eyes flashing with anger as she urged on the dogs. Nonetheless it was imperative for the safety of not only English men and women but for the crown itself that nobles be no longer permitted to arm bands of men and set them roving the country as thieves in the night. Edward knew also that the two small sons of Elizabeth Woodville were attainted; they were on the list right under his big hand. But he only sighed deeply and handed Elizabeth's letter back to Anthony.

But he meant to keep his oath to Parliament. One of Edward's own servants had struck a man in Westminster that day. Before the King left for Greenwich the next morning the offender was punished by the loss of the offending hand. Then Edward issued a general pardon for Christmas and left for Greenwich. Anthony turned his horse's head for Grafton with a cart full of arms and fruit and food for Christmas.

The whole Woodville family was gathered for Christmas. In the confines of their own home they could talk.

"In spite of all he has done," said the Duchess, "I have never heard of so much robbery and crime as now."

Anthony opened his mouth and shut it again. He was appalled by the task of trying to explain to his mother all that had been done and the hugeness of the burdens that Edward was carrying on his broad shoulders. How also to make her understand that most of the men around Edward were young like himself? How explain the fine enthusiasm that beat in Anthony's breast? Anthony, who usually never found himself beggared for words, flung his arms wide. "My beloved Mother," he interrupted the Duchess' flow of rapid French, "speak English! I tell you we have done more than is humanly possible! We never even sleep!"

The Duchess saw that indeed that was true, for her oldest son was thin and pale. "*Mon Dieu,*" she cried. "*Mon pauvre fils!*"

"Speak English, Mother," Anthony shouted.

"Oh!" cried the Duchess. "Are we so English now? Am I a disgrace?" Hands on her hips, she confronted Anthony.

Their father and sister were suddenly convulsed with laughter. Elizabeth doubled over and let out peal after peal of laughter. Lionel, who adored his older brother, giggled in relief that evidently his father found this funny and not horrifying.

The Duchess surveyed her family. "*Zut!*" she said haughtily. "You English are all crazy. And you, Anthony, should go to bed and get some sleep!"

"Later," Anthony said. For there was much to discuss and much to explain. He thought, It has been a quiet Christmas. Because of Elizabeth's widowhood there had been no disguisings, nor dancing, nor music from a happily strummed lute. "Only chess and perhaps cards," the Duchess had decreed, "and perhaps the singing of carols only."

They were all gathered in the big hall, the fires blazing, the manor servants too. Anthony watched from the shadows and listened to the ancient carols. He felt his father's eyes on him, and he looked over and smiled. Lord Rivers was pleased with Anthony, and he was glad that he was happy, for happy he was in a way that he had never been before. Anthony had belonged to the young group of intellectuals who were always discussing life and Lord Rivers was impatient with their theme of "its fleeting uselessness."

When the carols were finished and as each of the young children came to bid their mother good night and to receive her blessing, Lord Rivers stood with Anthony.

Anthony thought, All his life Father has been in the thick of things and now he is not, and yet—"Possess your soul in patience, Father. You knew my lord of Worcester—he is back and sat in Parliament and has been made a member of the council and will soon be Constable."

Lord Rivers remembered the Earl as a man to be reckoned with on all counts, almost frighteningly so, and a mind like a razor.

"How do you like him?" he asked curiously.

Anthony said, "Oh, he has been in Italy for two years."

Lord Rivers thought that this was enough to recommend a man unreservedly in the eyes of the young.

"In Italy he studied at the universities and was at the court at Milan. He says if he ever weds again it will be for love, and love only."

Anthony cast his eyes on his sister speculatively. She was clever enough for John Tiptoft, Earl of Worcester, and she was undeniably the most beautiful woman Anthony had ever seen; even though he was her brother, when he had walked into the house and she had run to greet him that same astonishment came over him, how shining and wonderful her face, the great glowing eyes and dazzling smile and that gilt hair. Anthony didn't realize it, but he looked a great deal like his sister, and now Lord Rivers looked at both of them, his two eldest—they were both so beautiful and so bright and sensitive that sometimes it made his heart ache to see them, for he was afraid that they were too vulnerable to life; I, he thought, can shrug off much. I am just an English squire, as Warwick once contemptuously told me; but they—they are star-kissed. Lord Rivers, who ordinarily didn't use such words, was pushed to poesy only about his children— they have royal blood from the rulers of Luxembourg; they shine like jewels. What have we done, Jacqueline and myself? We have brought into the world thirteen unusual children, and how shall they fare? And these two are the foremost jewels in the crown, although little Lionel was so brilliant that even his mother was astonished by him. Lord Rivers' thoughts drifted on.

Anthony was saying, "Well, Bess, let me try to make it plain to you. Warwick—you remember his remark that there were more books than ever in England and the trouble was people were reading them, you remember that? Well, Worcester says there aren't enough books in England and not enough people are reading them, and that in a nutshell is the difference between the two men."

Lord Rivers bit his lip. The beginning of the struggle between the great Earl of Warwick and the King was as evident to Lord Rivers in Anthony's remarks as though it had been illuminated in a manuscript. Lord Rivers had been in politics and about the court all his life, and he was too clever not to see the shape of things to come. "Anthony," he said, "be careful of repeating gossip. Never discuss personalities of the men like Warwick—to anyone, not even me."

Anthony looked startled.

"You are too trusting, Anthony."

"Father, I am not! I am very circumspect!"

"The great Earl is not for the likes of us to deprecate, Anthony."

Anthony's eyes flashed. Elizabeth said, "Now what do you mean by that, Father?"

"Exactly what I say," Lord Rivers said with authority. "And you had both best bide by it. You have both of you a touch of arrogance from your beauty and your mother's blood, but never forget from my side you are just plain English, the children of a squire." Lionel was listening.

"Oh, father," Elizabeth said.

"He's right, Bess," Lionel said. He was twelve. "However, Father, I have ambitions too."

Lord Rivers laughed. "What are your ambitions, son?" he asked, patting Lionel on the shoulder.

"I should like to be the chancellor of a great university," Lionel said absently, his mind on his chess game. He moved a piece. "Checkmate," he said to his brother John who was staring down at the board.

Anthony also looked at the board. "Give up, John," he said. "By God, Father, he will probably be the chancellor of Oxford before he's thirty."

Lionel was setting up the pieces again. "Want to play, Anthony?" he asked.

Anthony Woodville caught the understatement; their chess games were something Lionel looked forward to all during Anthony's absences. He bowed to his brother. "My pleasure, young sir." He sat down on the stool and stretched out his long legs. It was nine o'clock, the twenty-eighth of December.

At this same moment, in his palace of Greenwich, the young King of England was sitting at a chessboard too, opposite his twelve-year-old brother George; young Richard Plantagenet was watching the game. "I shall play with you next, Dickon," Edward said. Richard leaned against his brother's shoulder, and Edward reached out a big arm and squeezed him. "Have another fig," he said. "You're thin, Dickon. We have to feed you up so you're tough and strong when you go north with my lord of Warwick."

The Duchess of York cast a fond look at her youngest son; she didn't like to see him go, but she knew Edward was right and that he would be properly brought up under Warwick's care and household, and it was fitting that he be under the tutelage of the great Earl, who was also her own nephew. But this Christmas season, while she had so much to be thankful for, was also a heartbreaking reminder of her loss.

The room was silent while George pondered a move. The Duchess glanced over at her blond and pretty daughter who held her lute in her lap.

"Play, Margaret," she said. "It will be good to hear a bit of music."

Edward looked up. He was in no mood himself to hear anything nostalgic or touching; much less would be his mother. "Play something new and gay, Margaret," he commanded. Then he bent his attention to the game so that George would not lose too quickly.

The next morning was cold and clear. Anthony woke early and rolled over and bumped Richard, who was sound asleep. Richard grunted and pulled at the quilt. Anthony yawned, put his hands under his head and stared at the ceiling. He was thinking again about the King. He poked his brother.

"Wake up, Dickon," he said.

Richard groaned. "Why?"

"Because I am going to Greenwich today and I want you to come with me."

"Today?" Richard turned over again and stretched out comfortably. "But you said you were staying for New Year's."

"I'm not, though." Anthony could see and hear Edward, so clear was his vision of the King. Tomorrow Edward would keep solemnly his father's year mind, the anniversary of his death and also that of Edward's brother.

"I must go today," Anthony said. "Get up, Dickon. You will have to pack and see you have the proper clothes. Tomorrow is a day of prayer and mourning for His Grace, and I want you to be there too."

Chapter 4

ELIZABETH WOODVILLE could never remember a longer or colder winter. Even short February seemed to stretch its days with stilly freezings and light, powdery snow, and the days grew dark so early.

In church on Sunday the villagers looked pale and as depressed as she was. When they went home to their midday dinner of thick pea soup she fared little better, for money was short and meat and fowl with which she was usually regaled during the winter had been sold to provide silver. Her mother and father were at court with Anthony and Richard and John. Lionel and Edward were at school. Only she was left at home with the younger children. Thus she was kept eternally busy, and she had almost no one to talk to save Sir William, the village priest, whom she had known as a boy growing up in the village. She remembered the day of the manor court when his father had asked that he be sent to school to learn to be a priest, he was so studious. His father had paid six shillings, and the manor court had sent him away to school. Now he was back, the head of his flock.

He talked over his sermons with Elizabeth, for the Bishop had sent word that he wanted his priests to talk to their parish on the great solid virtues of thrift and industry.

On the first Sunday in April Sir William spoke on the granting of spring as part of the great wonder of God's gifts.

Elizabeth sat in the pew reserved for her family; the rest of the villagers stood, some of the men clustered around the pillars. When Sir William spoke, though, they quieted and the whispers stopped. Today Sir William didn't lecture his flock; instead he told them of the great goodness of God and of all the blessings that he bestowed upon them, his children, and how they should lift their hearts in gladness, for the mercy of God went always with them.

"How petty are your discontents beside the bounty of God's love," Sir William said.

Elizabeth raised her eyes to look at him; he was surveying the standing congregation. She wiped her eyes. It was true, she thought; all winter she had been cross and flailing against her fate, cross with the children, cross with the manor servants, cross with Anthony when he wouldn't help her. Elizabeth bent her head and prayed for forgiveness; it was suddenly very clear to her that she had behaved unworthily and that she had done nothing to help herself, only complain.

"I've been wallowing in self-pity," she said to herself.

"With God's love all can be accomplished," Sir William said.

Elizabeth thought, It is true!

Elizabeth bent her head for the prayer and slipped to her knees, holding tight to the hands of the sister on each side of her. Sir William's blessing fell on her, coming from heaven; her care and trouble fell away and she felt strong and young and hopeful just like the spring itself.

Outside the church she thanked Sir William. The breeze was gusty and blew his robes; the doors of the alehouse were open, and men's laughter and talk sounded plain.

"Come and have dinner with us," Elizabeth said.

He was pleased. They walked slowly, the children scampering ahead. They discussed some of the village problems. Young Henley wanted three acres of uncleared land, an assart on which to build a cot, for he wanted to be married in the fall. At the next manor court one of the Stewards wished to buy his freedom and had the money. He wanted again to tell her father—he would himself when Lord Rivers returned to the manor—how successful had been the permission for the villagers to take what wood they could from the manor forests by hook or by crook; much of the village economy rested on wood, from beechen bowls for porridge to teeth for the harrow and for precious heat.

Over their meal Elizabeth told him, a bit shyly, how much his sermon had helped her.

"All winter I felt old and discarded. Now I feel young and strong."

Sir William smiled at her. But he did not see any way out of her dilemma except marriage. He knew very well that it was difficult for her, who had been a wife for four years, to suddenly become a daughter again. He knew how heady was the taste of freedom. Elizabeth had had her own life, her own two dowered manors, smaller of course than Grafton. Sir William deplored the mercenary aspect of marriage, and yet it existed. Now here was Elizabeth, a poor widow with two sons, and her only dowry her astonishing beauty and her wit. He could not help but feel sorry for her. Before he left he blessed her.

"I shall come to vespers," she promised. She liked the vesper service; the church was usually filled mostly with her own sex. It made the service more of a retreat from the world of men in which she was trying so hard to find a niche.

All of April Elizabeth wrestled with the problem of her position, that of a pensioner in her father's house. She composed in her mind and on paper a dozen letters to the King and then tore them up, for no matter what she said it sounded like a plea for charity, and she was too proud. And then she worried about what Anthony would say or what Edward would think, because Anthony was right there to plead her cause and yet he did not. Her frustration with Anthony grew. Although she had made herself a new gown with the material Anthony had sent, her youngest son, not yet two, would soon be dressed in homespun. She did write to her mother for the sake of little Richard Grey, who was named for her father, to bring shoes and hose for him. The Duchess and Lord Rivers would be coming soon, for the court was moving about with the King.

But never had the spring been more lovely. May came and by the end of May even Anthony arrived; Edward was at Stony Stratford, and Anthony had ridden over to the manor to spend the few days.

All Anthony talked about was Edward and what he was doing. Elizabeth had never felt more provoked with Anthony; it seemed to her he had abandoned all his old loyalties to the family.

Elizabeth could be as sharp as the Duchess. "You act like a woman in love!"

"I ought to slap you for that," he said angrily. "I can remember Mother slapping you for fresh remarks when you were twelve. That's the way you're acting now. Is it necessary for you to retrogress because you're living at home again?"

"Shut up!" Elizabeth spit.

"You exist here in this backwater and aren't even interested in what is going on in the world outside." He turned away and went to the great doors of the hall. Elizabeth looked across the bare boards, swept clean of the rushes, to his tall figure. He looked so handsome with his hunting cap with its gay feather and his light, supple leather jacket. Still angry, he slapped his gloves across one hand.

A servant was holding his roan.

"Where are you going?" Elizabeth called, picking up her skirts and running toward him.

He called over his shoulder. "Hunting."

She could hear his dogs now, coming pell-mell from the kennel. She stood in the doorway and watched him go up the long lane, the dogs yelping, running ahead, and Anthony and his four attendants cantering easily behind. He didn't even turn in the saddle and wave good-bye. A voice at her elbow made her jump. Lionel was saying, "He is going to join the King. I wanted to go."

Lionel watched down the lane till all he could see was dust. "He didn't say good-bye, either."

"He was angry with me," Elizabeth said.

"They're going to hunt through part of our land and the forest." Lionel offered this information thoughtfully, and Elizabeth suddenly turned and stared at him.

"Are you sure, Lionel?"

Lionel looked surprised that anyone could question his phenomenal memory. "Naturally I'm sure, Bess. Why wouldn't I be? It's what he said."

"It is insupportable," Elizabeth said to herself.

Lionel frowned, trying to make this statement intelligible. "They won't trample the crops, Bess," he said. "Anthony will lead them careful."

"I know," Elizabeth muttered.

"If you think, Bess," Lionel said kindly, "you would be able to figure out the ways they will take."

"Yes, I should."

"Of course."

Elizabeth leaned down and kissed Lionel. He was touched. "I'll take little Tommie for a look at the new pigs," he said.

"Not now, thank you, Lionel. I have to bathe and dress him. Later."

Lionel looked after her retreating figure in surprise. She didn't usually bathe Tommie this early in the morning. He scratched his ear and wandered off in the direction of the piggery; he wanted to see the new litter himself. He saw three of his sisters ahead of him, and he hurried to catch up with them.

Elizabeth went flying upstairs. She bathed and dressed both of her little boys; then she sat them on the edge of her bed and told them to stay there. They squirmed while she brushed her long hair and wound it about her head. She surveyed her eyebrows in her little polished mirror to see if they were neatly plucked. She used her rose perfume; she turned her hands to look at her nails—they were shining and clean.

It was a cool morning and she took a small shawl; then taking each child by the hand, she led them downstairs and out through the hall into the big kitchens.

She wrapped a small loaf of fresh bread and a wedge of cheese into a napkin and drew off a small flagon of milk. With one hand on her basket and tiny Richard in the other and with little Tommie scampering ahead, Elizabeth set off down the lane, where the dust from Anthony's horse's hoofs had not yet settled.

"We're going for a picnic," she said, talking rapidly because she was excited. "Won't that be fun? We'll walk through the forest, and in the forest there is an oak tree. There it will be shady and we can have a fine meal, and you may pick flowers and listen to the birds and maybe you will have a fine adventure and see the King come riding through the forest. Maybe you will see the King!"

Presently she slowed her steps. She had been walking too fast. "Poor little Richard," she said, smiling at him. "There is no hurry. We can rest for a while if you want."

As they went along, she was busy going over in her mind exactly which would be the route Anthony would take, and it was not till she had recalled exact all the paths she knew so well and settled in her mind on the most probable place to waylay the royal hunter that she had time to consider whether she was doing the right thing or what she could conceivably gain by it.

She could imagine her mother's horror and her father's rage, but they were older and had stricter standards of conduct than she, the younger generation. All subjects in all kingdoms were not forbidden to petition the King—indeed it was very common —and since Anthony would not help her then she must indeed help herself and her children.

She reached the sheltering branches of the young oak about eleven. The tree was not yet tall enough to have killed the grass underneath it, and it was one of her favorite spots in the forest; it commanded the reach of grassy glen and the pathway through Whittlebury forest could be seen plain now in spring. Later in summer it would be more obscured.

She sank down on the grass and stretched out luxuriously, and every nerve in her body felt alive and trembling. The little boys stretched out too, and Elizabeth took Richard's head on her lap and rubbed his soft hair. She studied his features; he was so handsome a little boy, surely he could not fail to appeal to Edward, who was known for his kindness to his own young brothers and to everyone, truly.

"He is kind," she said to Thomas, "your sovereign lord. All say so. And he will realize he has taken your rightful inheritance."

Thomas said, "What, Mother?"

She laughed. "You must bow when he comes. After we eat, nay, maybe before we eat we shall practice. After you've rested."

In a few minutes they stood. Elizabeth took a hand of each child. "Pretend they are coming through the forest. Then we shall stand straight here, heads up like that, Thomas. And then when he comes closer, I will curtsy like this, and you must both bow to your King. Put your hand here, Richard, and put your head down."

"He'll forget," Thomas said.

"No, he won't," Elizabeth said; she picked Richard up and hugged him.

"I'm starving," she said. "Let's have our picnic."

She spread out the napkins and broke the bread and the cheese. And after the last of the milk had been drunk and the leftover bit of bread and cheese carefully wrapped again in the napkin and replaced in the basket, after that they began their wait.

Richard pillowed his head on his mother's lap and slept. Thomas played with the five toy soldiers his mother had brought along. Elizabeth leaned back against the comforting trunk of the tree, pushing away the doubts that began to assail her, and pushing away anxiety, and pushing away with desperation the look on Anthony's face when he would see her. Then she began to worry about whether, if the dogs were in full hue and cry, anyone would notice her. Indeed not, and her whole venture would be in vain.

Her throat was dry and she wished she had saved a bit of the milk. There was a stream nearby, but it would take a minute to reach it, and then while she was there by the stream the hunt might come pounding through the glen.

"Why did I ever come?" she said aloud in despair. "I should just stay at home and resign myself to a living death!" She felt very sorry for herself, and large tears sprang into her eyes; just at that moment she heard the sound of a distant hunting horn.

She struggled to a sitting position and lifted Richard onto her lap to rouse him. She smoothed back his rumpled locks, pulled his jacket into place.

"Thomas!"

He looked at her, and he rose and came over holding one toy soldier. Elizabeth set Richard on his feet. Grasping the children's hands, she came out from under the shadowing branches of the oak into the sunlight, the sounds of the hunt coming plain now, the jingling of the harnesses and hoofbeats of the horses, and then the first rider came into the glen.

Elizabeth took a backward step and then another. By the time the whole royal hunt had gained the glen she was almost under the oak. A single shaft of sunlight pierced through the leaves and rested on the three gilt-colored heads. Elizabeth's huge eyes were wide as a startled fawn's; she clung tight to the hands of her children. And in the midst of his friends and courtiers Edward reined in his big horse. Anthony muttered under his breath and swung his horse around to come up to Edward's side. Edward raised his hand to signal a full stop; he shook his head at Anthony, and he slid down to the ground and tossed the reins of his horse to Anthony. While the rest of the hunt followed this drama with fascinated eyes, Edward walked across the fifteen feet of space that separated him from Elizabeth.

Edward looked down on her bent head and the little boys' bows. The bigger boy had a red soldier clasped tight in the fingers over his chest as he bowed the way his mother had taught him. On the grass four other bright painted toys lay alongside a basket.

Edward concluded rapidly she had waited here a long time. "Please rise, my lady," he said.

The sound of his voice startled Elizabeth in the stillness. Edward found her eyes, and Elizabeth rose. He towered over her, his broad shoulders in the green hunting jacket blotting out the rest of the hunt. Edward looked at her fully and then his eyes went to the two boys. Little Richard was going to cry.

"Don't be afraid, little one," Edward said quickly.

Elizabeth glanced down at Richard. "Don't cry, Richard," she whispered. "He's hardly two, Your Grace."

"A fine boy for two," Edward said, leaning down to talk to Richard. "Don't be afraid," he repeated. "Certainly no harm can come to a boy when his King is holding him!" Edward grinned and picked Richard up, holding him against his shoulder. He jiggled him up and down.

Elizabeth watched her son's face, and gradually a smile replaced the frightened look and Edward sighed in relief. Still holding the child, he looked down at Elizabeth. "You wanted something from me, madam?" Elizabeth wet her lips; they were so dry she didn't think she could utter a word.

"I waited here," she said.

"So I gather," Edward said.

"Anthony wouldn't speak for me, so I came myself." She stopped and looked up at him appealingly. "I have no living, Your Grace, nor for my sons. I wouldn't want for myself, but for my two boys—it wasn't fair to—I am asking pardon for my two little sons so that they may enjoy your favor and—" She stopped for breath. "That is what I meant to say. I am asking pardon for my two sons."

"What?" asked Edward. "For these two dangerous fellows? You can't be serious!" He kept on jiggling Richard.

Elizabeth didn't know whether to laugh or cry. The hunting dogs were clustered around them now; sniffing, their ears flapping, one of them sat down beside Edward contentedly. "That's my favorite hound," Edward said to Richard. The huge greyhound was licking Thomas' hand. "Well, madam, are you going to answer me or not?"

"Well, I was serious," she began, and then her eyes met Edward's and she smiled suddenly, her wonderful dazzling smile. Her eyes gleamed with humor; here they were, surrounded with dogs and children while the courtiers waited not so patiently, she expected, and Edward still jiggling little Richard, and for a moment they were not subject and monarch but a young man and woman met unexpected in the spring. Elizabeth breathed lightly, holding his eyes. "You disinherited them," she said low.

He said quickly, because there was little time, "If I am brutal it's because I am poor. We shall discuss it further. Tomorrow afternoon at four, right here. A picnic. I'll bring the wine."

"I will bring the meal?" Elizabeth asked.

"Please," said Edward. He sat Richard down. He took her hand, and at the touch of his fingers she looked up at him in surprise and pulled her hand away in haste. Edward bowed slightly, and Elizabeth made him a small curtsy. Edward's horse was brought and he mounted. Elizabeth was conscious of Anthony's angry eyes, of the brilliant colors of the mounted men; then the dogs ran off yelping and the whole hunt followed, and in a scant two minutes there was no one left in the glen at all but Elizabeth and the two children and the five toy soldiers.

Elizabeth didn't know it, but Edward spared her an onslaught of words from Anthony, whose choler was unconcealed during the rest of the hunt. By the simple expedient of asking Anthony to be his bedfellow that night, the King kept Anthony by his side and away from his sister. In the light of a single candle Edward talked about his policy in the north, the necessity of capturing the mighty castles of Northumberland and the northern counties along the Scot border. If Anthony had any suspicion that Edward was going to ask him about his sister he was wrong, for Edward never mentioned her. Anthony at last asked directly what Elizabeth had said, and Edward told him.

"She asked for her sons' manors."

He didn't say anything more and soon he slept, but Anthony stayed awake. In Grafton Elizabeth, in the curtained-off alcove which she shared with her children, hardly slept at all.

Gradually the dawn came. She washed in cold water and made up her bed and went down to the manor's inside kitchen, where she picked out two plump hens and set them to roasting. Then she went out into the kitchen garden and picked cherries. It was cool and misty in the garden. Perhaps it would rain! Back in the kitchen she washed and pitted the fruit, and set it to stew with a bit of honey. It would be such a simple meal for a King. With cheese and bread—it was all the manor afforded.

Elizabeth had reckoned without her mother. The Duchess came bustling into the kitchen, looking for her daughter.

"What are you doing?" she asked, her sharp eyes taking in this unaccustomed foray into cooking.

Elizabeth was silent. She was reminding herself she was a grown woman.

"I am preparing a picnic basket, Mother," she said.

"Two chickens?" inquired the Duchess. "Just whom are you expecting on this picnic?"

Could she have guessed somehow? The Duchess was as canny as a witch. Elizabeth said, "For His Grace, Mother."

The Duchess' mouth fell open, for she had not guessed at all. *"Mon Dieu,"* she muttered. The fruit boiled over and Elizabeth snatched at the pan to get it off the fire. She stood there holding it.

"Elizabeth, are you mad? Put the pot down. How did this happen? How did you make a rendezvous with the King? What have you been doing?"

"Mother, I am fully grown and I went, well, I went to the forest yesterday when he was hunting and I met him."

The Duchess perceived a servant out of the corner of her eye. "Out!" she cried, pointing to the door. "Out!" She turned again to Elizabeth. "Put the pot down!" She took it from Elizabeth and stirred it with the wooden spoon. "It's not burned," she said. She looked straight at her daughter. "When is this picnic?"

"At four."

The Duchess sighed and pulled out a stool and sat down at the trestle table. She pointed to another stool. Elizabeth sat down too, and the two women faced each other across the well scrubbed board. The Duchess was silent for a long time. Finally Elizabeth said, "He didn't give me time to refuse. He just said, 'Tomorrow at four.' If I do not go—" her voice trailed off.

"He would wait there for you," the Duchess said. "So you are at an impasse. Has it not occurred to you to send him a message that you are ill?"

Elizabeth stared at her mother. "No. It didn't occur to me at all."

"I thought not," said the Duchess. "However, it is a simple solution. Shall I send for pen and paper?"

Elizabeth looked down at her hands.

"You want to go, eh? So do all the women in England. Have you thought of that?"

Elizabeth said stonily, "Mother, I have thought of nothing at all but seeing him again today. And you can't stop me."

"Don't be arrogant, Bess." Suddenly she leaned over and patted Elizabeth's hand. "I cannot control your actions, you, my oldest daughter. I only beg of you to remember that if you need me I shall be ready to help. Speak to no one else about this, about Edward. Promise me!"

"I do," Elizabeth said. "I promise."

The Duchess said, rising, "I still do not approve." She swept out of the kitchen and Elizabeth thought that was her last word. It was not. At three, when Elizabeth went down the kitchen walk with the covered basket and a fresh rose pinned in her collar, the Duchess was at the gate.

"A white rose," she said conversationally. "In honor of your liege lord. Elizabeth, I must say you look more beautiful than usual, if that is possible, but somehow you remind me of a white lamb going to slaughter." The Duchess threw out a smile and little laugh along with this, and the sound of it stayed with her daughter as she marched angrily away from her home.

While anger kept her walking fast for ten minutes, her pace then slowed; the basket was heavy. Probably she had brought too much food and he would laugh at her. Would he like the fresh-made cheese? No, probably not. It was just country cheese.

I should never have come, she thought desperately. How foolish I am. What will I say to him? We have nothing in common, I know none of his friends, I know little about the court, for the court of Lancaster, of which I knew a little, was so different. I have nothing to offer him save a country meal.

Meanwhile the June afternoon was as soft and warm as a child's kiss. There was almost no wind and the birds sang.

Elizabeth shifted the basket to her left arm. Although the air was redolent with the smell of fresh-growing grass and wild flowers, she could smell the rose pinned under her chin; it gave off a heady odor, and she kept remembering her mother's taunting remark. The basket was getting heavier and heavier. As she approached the clearing, she could see no one. Her eyes searched the glen and the oak tree; there was no one there.

She set down the basket. Then with hasty fingers she tore the rose from her collar. It pricked her finger; she threw it to the ground and put her foot on it, her head bent so she did not see Edward as he stepped from beside a tree right alongside of her. He had his cap in his hand, and he looked down at the crumpled rose.

He asked, "Why did you do that?"

She was so startled she couldn't answer. She looked up at him helplessly. He leaned down and lifted up the rose, holding it in his big hand. It lay in his palm as though he were offering it to her, and she put out her fingers for it, and both of them saw the drops of blood from the thorns on the tip of her finger. She raised her eyes to his face. The look was so appealing that Edward said, "It hurt you, my Bessie!"

"I was just thinking, when I took it off, that I—that it was presumptuous of me to wear the white rose."

He dropped the rose and picked up the basket.

"It doesn't hurt," she added. "But I shouldn't have crushed it."

Edward, bemused by her sorrowful look, said, "It's not an omen for bad, Bessie. You are the fairest rose in England." He took her hand. "Come with me, Bessie."

Elizabeth felt as though she were dreaming. They walked hand in hand toward the oak tree, Edward swinging her hand a bit.

"You are very kind," Elizabeth said stiffly, thinking she should pay some heed to his compliment. "But you flatter me, Your Grace," she added politely.

At this moment Edward's horse whinnied loudly and Elizabeth jumped. Then she saw the tethered horse and Edward was looking at her once more with a bemused expression. He set down the basket, released her hand and went over to the horse and opened the saddlebag. He got out a leathern wine flask, two silver cups and a woven blanket. He spread the blanket and set the wine on the edge of it while Elizabeth stood stiff watching him with enormous eyes, saying nothing.

He couldn't help smiling. "Do you think I'm going to chop your head off any moment, you little Lancastrian?"

"No, Your Grace."

"Sit, my lady." He waved his hand at the blanket and Elizabeth sat down on the very edge of it, folding her hands on her lap, her slippers peeking out of the edge of her skirt. Edward looked down at her; he sighed a little and sat down himself, then stretched out lazily and put his hands under his head. "Why," he said, "can't you forget, and let me forget for a few hours, that I am indeed the King of England, France and Ireland. I should like to forget the whole damned world once in a while. Won't you let me do that? With you?"

He was staring straight ahead up into the leafy branches of the oak. He could see bits of blue sky through the branches and for a moment indeed he did forget and remembered lying thus as a child, dreaming, on a lazy, hot spring afternoon when he had no cares and the heritage of his birth had lain less heavy and been too far away to worry about. Without turning his head he reached out and captured her hand. "Even when I was a child," he said, "I was told over and over that I was an unordinary child. I was born, as my mother says, to the purple. I used to hate the damned color. So at the age of seven I was dispatched with my brother to live at Ludlow Castle. My tutor told me every day what I should or shouldn't do. To tell you the truth, the person whom I loved the most in those years, outside of my brother, was my nurse. She was French. Her name was Anne Caux. Even now, today, I pray to St. Anne, for somehow I think I couldn't have done without my own Anne. The first thing I did when I became King was to pension her. When I am lucky enough to have daughters, one of them shall be named Anne. Now under no condition do I want you to feel sorry for me. I simply want you to try to understand me a little. Are you listening, Bessie?"

"Yes, of course," she said low.

"Is it so difficult for you to forget that I am the King?"

"Yes," she said. "It is. It is impossible. But that doesn't prevent me from understanding you."

He raised his head to look at her.

"I wish you would keep on talking. I don't mean quite that," she added. "I didn't quite mean understanding . . . I meant I am pleased and happy that you talk to me this way. I will try to understand you."

He said, looking up again at the sky, "Well, I shall never understand you, I can tell that immediately. I haven't the faintest idea what is going on in your head, whereas I'm sure you know what is going on in mine. If I should ask you to lie down alongside of me now, you would probably refuse, wouldn't you?"

"Yes," said Elizabeth hastily.

"Yes what?" asked Edward.

"Yes, I'd refuse!"

He laughed and sat up. "All right. Then you force me to sit up too so I can look at you."

She asked, "Does anyone know where you are?"

"Yes, of course. I cannot disappear for more than a few minutes. Hastings knows where I am. But he doesn't know with whom."

"Oh," said Elizabeth. "Are you hungry, Your Grace?"

"Yes," he said. "For you. But I'll settle for food." He grinned and took up the wine flask, carefully pouring two cups and handing one to her. "Your health, Bessie."

"Yours," she said solemnly and drank a little wine. "Oh, that is good," she exclaimed; she had never tasted anything like it.

She busied herself with unpacking the basket. She laid out the linen cloth and the wooden platters; then taking up the silver bowl she had brought, she went over to the stream, filled the bowl with cool water and brought it to Edward with the finest white-linen napkin she had been able to find in the closet.

Edward washed his hands and dried them. "Chicken!" he exclaimed.

Elizabeth went back to the stream and washed her hands too. Then she came back and set out the cheese and the bread. She sat with her legs tucked under her, looking across the cloth to Edward.

"Will you bless the food, Your Grace?"

She bent her head while Edward said grace. When she raised it, he was looking at her and she suddenly smiled. Happiness flooded her. "This is the first time we've ever dined."

"It won't be the last," he said, his mouth full.

Elizabeth drank more wine, and though she had thought she

couldn't touch a morsel of food she found herself eating. Edward apologized for the amount he put away.

"I overindulge myself," he said. "It's one of my bad habits, I guess."

"You're so big," Elizabeth said. "I should think you'd really need a lot."

"Ah, but I eat more than I need," he confessed.

"You're not fat," she said. "Not at all."

"The chicken is wonderful," Edward said.

She told him they had little beef and that it had been a bad year. They talked about the troubles of the manor and the price of barley and oats, and Edward listened carefully, frowning a bit. Then he said, "I expect it is hard for you to be without a living. I realize that very well."

"I don't want to ask you any favors, Your Grace. Truly I don't. I'm sorry I did before."

"I shall work out something which I hope will be to your liking." He poured out more wine.

Absently she sipped it, for he had filled her cup, and then told herself she had had enough. She set down the cup.

Edward ate the stewed cherries and the pot cheese. When he finished, she gathered up the wooden bowls and washed them and put everything back in the basket. The sun was sinking; it threw its golden shafts on them, lighting the gold in Edward's brown hair. Elizabeth put her shawl over her shoulders.

"Thank you, Bessie," Edward said. "You look so sweet."

"I'm so glad you liked it," she said shyly. Then to her horror, she yawned; she tried to stop it by biting her underlip, but finally she put her hand over her mouth and above it her eyes met Edward's and he laughed.

"Sleepy?" he asked.

"I think it's the wine, but I didn't sleep very well last night," she said with as much dignity as she could muster.

"I never get enough sleep," Edward said, as a matter of fact. "At least I think I don't." He held her eyes. "I think Cupid has sunk an arrow in my heart, Bessie." He sighed. He put his hands on her waist and gently set her back on the blanket; he lay down at her side, then he put one arm across her waist and closed his eyes. "Just for a moment, just for a few minutes we'll pretend we are just anyone in the world. Just a man and a woman."

He was looking at her again, his eyes open, his head pillowed on his arm. "Close your eyes. You look so sleepy," he said, smiling.

She wanted to speak but there were no words to find, and then she realized they were unnecessary. She touched the side of his face with her hand, and then let it rest on his shoulder; she closed her eyes and felt as though she were floating in a heavenly eternal springtime; half awake, half asleep, lying at his side like any man or woman, as he said. He touched her cheek gently with his big hand. "I'm falling in love with you, Bessie."

"I too," she whispered.

When the first coolness of evening came, he propped himself on one elbow and leaned over and brushed her lips with his.

"Wake up, sweetheart," he whispered.

She sighed; she sat up and studied his face. "I wasn't asleep."

"We must go," he said; he held out his hand and helped her to her feet. Without a word he picked up the basket, went over to his horse and took the reins. Elizabeth put her shawl closer around her shoulders.

"Good-bye," she said.

"I'll walk you home," he said, turning around surprised. "I wouldn't leave you here." He frowned at her a little.

Her eyes fell from his, so he turned again and put the blanket and flask in the saddlebag. He handed her the empty basket. "If you carry this I can take your hand."

Leading the horse, they left the glen. The lightness of evening was about them, the sky a pale silvery blue.

"I have one more day in Stony Stratford," Edward said. "Which way?"

"This way," Elizabeth answered.

"Will you meet me tomorrow?"

"Yes, of course," she said.

He squeezed her hand. "Do you want me to bring the food?" he asked.

"I'd rather bring it. I like to prepare it for you."

There were a few stars now. "How beautiful it is," she whispered. They walked slowly. "Where do you go from here?"

"North."

"There's no danger, is there?" she asked suddenly, thinking re-

gretfully how little she knew; she should have paid more attention to Anthony.

"No," he said. They had come to the edge of the manor house;
the path to the kitchen gardens was before them.

"I go in this way," she whispered. A lone dog howled. "Good
night, Your Grace," she said.

"Good night, sweetheart." He still held her hand. "Good night.
Till tomorrow."

She sighed, looking up at him. It was getting dark. "Good
night." He dropped her hand, and she went up the kitchen path.
At the doorway she stood and watched him ride off into the night.

But in the sober grayness of the following morning Elizabeth
Woodville, gathering the few cherries ripe enough for picking,
suddenly felt as forlorn as the small fruit. She went back into the
dark kitchen and sat down at the table, on the same stool she
had sat on the morning before. In front of her was the bowl of
cherries, still wet with dew and as cold as the reality which
pressed upon her. Yesterday, for a few hours, she had been in
love like a girl. But she was not a girl; she was a woman with
two children. Yesterday was something they could never recapture; she knew it as surely as though Edward himself had told
her. Yesterday was a miracle that would never happen again. She
would always remember it; never, never could she forget. There
was nothing she wanted more to do than to meet him again, fix
the meal, walk the path, knowing he would be waiting at the end
of it. And yet it would not be the same. Nothing would ever be
the same again, she thought despairingly. Her mother was right.
I am old enough to know that; I am old enough to know that
when we found each other, just being together was more than
enough, but it will not be tomorrow or today or next week, and
then—he would ride away like he did last night, and I cannot bear
it, she told herself, I cannot bear it. He will have a Queen and I
am too proud.

She went out the kitchen door and threw the cherries on the
ground for the greedy birds. Then she went back into the manor
house, to the table in the small room off the hall where her mother
kept her pens and paper, her private books of the manor and her
accounts. Elizabeth sat down at the table and began to write. She

begged his forgiveness but she was ill. And she hoped he would have a pleasant journey.

She cut off the rest of the paper that she hadn't used, folded the single sheet to make a packet and sealed it with wax. The manor was stirring. Out in the stables she found one of her father's servants and to him she entrusted the letter. Then she went up to her own bed and lay down, staring up at the ceiling.

"I wish I were dead," she said. She couldn't even cry. Her eyes felt wide open and blank. It was the baby Richard who brought her relief. Waking, he climbed up into her bed. She hugged him close, burying her head in the pillow so he wouldn't see the tears that flowed now so freely. But I can't lie here and cry like a girl, she thought.

She made herself get up to dress him and take him down to the kitchen for his porridge. She drank a little ale instead of her usual milk. It tasted cool and refreshing, but her life was over. She would devote herself to the children and she would not disgrace them by bearing a child, an illegitimate brother, an illegitimate Prince; at the thought her eyes filled with large tears again and she blinked them away. From the unwanted, imaginary child she had borne, her mind went again to Edward. He would know her illness was just an excuse and he would probably be angry and annoyed with her. He thought like Anthony, she knew, that life was to be lived and one couldn't abide by the old rules their fathers had laid down. "Much they know. Men. They just think they know everything," she said aloud, and the cook heard and nodded.

"That's the truth, my lady," she said.

She took Richard by the hand and went out into the garden, under a large tree in front of the manor where the Duchess had some benches; the Duchess liked to sit outside, and the benches were covered every morning with woven covers. The sun had come out thinly, and she watched Richard toddle about; she thought she would sit with him awhile before she went in and helped the Duchess with the sorting of the linen. As for Edward, she would never see him again.

She had reckoned without Edward. Edward had a horror of illness. Anthony had had a suspicion of it by the dogged way Edward had got Dr. Hatclyf back from France; he had been insistent about it. Edward thought that Dr. Hatclyf was the finest physician in the world and he wanted him at his side. So Edward, in his immediate energetic way, sent for Dr. Hatclyf, who as the royal physician traveled everywhere with Edward; he had beef broth stewed and some fine Gascon wine poured tenderly into flasks. Then with Anthony and Hastings, he started out for Grafton.

Elizabeth was still sitting on the bench, and she called to her sister Kate to please bring her her needlework. For once Kate complied without arguing. "I don't feel well," Elizabeth told her and thanked her.

In the meantime Anthony was galloping alongside of Edward, for Edward had set a fast pace.

"What's the matter?" Anthony shouted, for all he had known was that he was summoned to attend the King.

"Your sister," Edward shouted back.

Anthony forbore from asking him how he knew; it was something one did not ask one's King, especially shouted over a hard-driven horse. All Anthony could do to take out his frustration was to keep up with his lord's magnificent horsemanship, for Edward rode like a centaur. They pounded through the village, scaring the few grazing sheep, past the astonished eyes of Father William at the church door and up the long manor drive. Elizabeth list-lessly looked up; even at this distance it was impossible to be mistaken; the riders were coming far too fast, and Richard was toddling along toward the oncoming horses.

"Richard!" she cried. She ran toward him and scooped him up in her arms just as Edward brought the big horse to a sudden stop. Ahorse he confronted her, scowling down at her.

"By the mercy of God!" His favorite oath ripped out with force.

"What heedless riding, my lord!" Her eyes flashed. But her face was as white as paper.

Edward dismounted; he stood over her, looking down. "You said you were ill!"

I wish I would faint, she thought desperately; now she was conscious of Anthony at her side, and wordlessly she handed him the baby. At her other side was a man she had never seen before. He smiled at her and put his arm around her supportingly and led her willy-nilly to the bench, with Edward stamping after.

"I am Dr. Hatclyf," he was saying, "and I guess you are my patient. Sit down."

Elizabeth obeyed; she felt she could hardly breathe. Dr. Hatclyf held her wrist; her heart was pounding madly and he nodded solemnly at Edward. Elizabeth's eyes, circled from lack of sleep, rested on him and her hand trembled.

"Lady Grey is having a chill," he said. "She should be in bed."

Elizabeth raised those deeply shadowed eyes to look up at Edward. His face was sober with concern.

"That's what I was afraid of," he said, and their eyes met again. Without a word he leaned down, picked her up and started toward the house.

Her head lay against his shoulder. "I was afraid," he whispered, "that you had caught cold yesterday when we lay on the ground."

Elizabeth felt two large tears puddling her eyes. "Don't cry, sweetheart," he whispered in her ear. "Please don't cry. Smile, for my sake."

"I can't," she said. "I'm too happy."

He squeezed her tight. And at this moment the Duchess appeared at the top of the steps, her face utterly bewildered as she saw first Edward and Elizabeth, then Anthony and a strange man and the yard full of men and horses.

"Madam, your daughter's ill," Edward said without preamble.

The Duchess was speechless for once. "Your Grace," she muttered finally. "This way then, my lord."

She led the way with Kate trotting at their side, staring up at Edward.

"I didn't know Bess was ill." The Duchess flung this remark over her shoulder as she hastened along.

Kate spoke up. "Yes, she told me."

Bless her, thought Elizabeth; that's the first time in her life she has ever remembered what anyone said to her.

"Bess said she didn't feel well," Kate repeated, still watching Edward with enormous eyes.

"You should never have got up," Edward said as he laid her down on the bed in the curtained alcove.

"I wanted to mind Richard." She held tight to his big hand.

The Duchess was putting a quilt over her and getting another pillow out of the chest at the foot of the bed.

"Why didn't you tell me, Elizabeth?" she was asking, but Eliza-

beth was suddenly too exhausted by a welter of emotions to answer. I thought I would never see him again and he is here. The
sentence ran around in her mind. She heard Dr. Hatclyf say,
"Now I want you all to let my patient sleep. I want her to stay
in bed the rest of the day, madam, and not to get up until she
has no more chill. Are you warm enough now, my lady? Or do
you need another quilt?"

Elizabeth opened her eyes. "Thank you, Your Grace. Thank
you, Dr. Hatclyf. I'm warm enough."

Edward said, "Obey Dr. Hatclyf. Now you go to sleep."

The curtain swung to and she was left alone. She lay still. She
could hear Edward's voice in the distance, saying something
about good wine and beef broth. He will leave, she thought, of
course he will leave. But he cared enough to come in haste. He
will leave; tomorrow he will ride away; when shall we ever meet
again? And yet someday, someday, she was sure he would come
riding through the gates again. She closed her eyes and slept.

Chapter 5

ELIZABETH HAD saved all of Anthony's letters. Now they formed a contact with Edward and the court, and by piecing carefully together all the scraps of information contained and by questioning her father and her mother, she began to have a clearer picture of what had happened last winter and what was happening now. To help herself in the beginning she made a list. In her clear hand she wrote:

> *His Grace's Evil Willers*
> Queen Margaret
> King Henry
> Louis XI, King of France
> Scotland

To battle all four on the diplomatic level had been the work of the winter. Therefore she made another list of the monarchs of Europe.

> Philip of Burgundy
> His son and heir, Charles of Burgundy
> Francis of Brittany
> John of Aragon
> Henry of Castile
> Ferdinand of Naples
> The Duke of Milan
> The Pope

"Should you have placed His Holiness last?" Lord Rivers inquired with a twinkle in his eye.

"Father, it is so complicated," she cried.

Lord Rivers frowned. "France is still our principal enemy. The former Queen, as you know, escaped from Scotland, eluding our ships, and landed on the coast of Brittany, where Francis received her with elaborate gifts, which pleased that snake King Louis. Louis then received her himself and promised her men and money for the invasion of England. And she will come too. So His Grace was left with one recourse, which he took right away."

"What?" Elizabeth asked.

"Force," Lord Rivers answered. "The fleet descended on the coasts of France and Brittany. Louis changed his tune in a hurry. You see, Bess, Louis is afraid of Edward, for he knows that Edward would be more of a match for him in the field. All Europe knows this."

"Is it true?"

"Yes, it is," said Lord Rivers. "He is a great soldier. I know. I've seen him. I saw him first when he was only fifteen. He commanded one wing at the first battle of St. Albans and he won."

It was fall. Anthony and the King were in London. Anthony wrote jubilantly that the news from France was that King Louis was afraid; that the threatened alliance between England and Castile filled Louis with horror; he could see in his mind's eye an English and Castilian army invading him through Guienne. "Undoubtedly," Anthony said, "in the end Margaret will come but not with the aid she would have had, and this time we hope to catch her. Warwick is already in the north."

Elizabeth laid down the letter and retrieved a previous one that had bearing. She read:

> I can tell you now that for months ahead His Grace had been assembling a fleet at Sandwich, knowing he might need to put on a show of force against France and Brittany. Reports leaked over to Louis about this fleet, as His Grace wanted it known. Not all the ships were to be used against France though; some were to go on to Ireland, for the Butlers and the Ormondes are fighting there, and some men have to be sent over to enforce the peace. We had one scare. I had accompanied His Grace to Canterbury; it was a dark winter day. I was waiting on the murderers' porch at the cathedral, and the King was at the tomb alone. Suddenly a messenger arrived from Sandwich; ships had been seen. I had to go into the cathedral and interrupt His Grace at his prayers at the tomb. I shall not forget it. Even on that dark day the great ruby, the gift of France, glowed like fire; it was still and cold

within. His Grace was kneeling, and I knelt alongside of him and whispered that ships were sighted off Sandwich. He crossed himself, got to his feet and put his hand on my shoulder. We walked out of the great cathedral together.

We rode for Sandwich immediate, but it was a false alarm; they were merchant ships of the Hansards with whom we have concluded a treaty for trade, for His Grace is very emphatic about the need for trade. At any rate the fleet under the Earl of Kent and one of the Howards descended on the coast of France in four places, and although Louis rushed to the scene he could do nothing. Now there is no talk of war but an embassy, and we doubt here that much aid will be forthcoming to the former Queen. Even the young Charles of Burgundy has seen the light and sent his personal secretary over to London, where we have been busy entertaining him. It is a feather in His Grace's diplomatic cap. But Margaret will come.

What Anthony had written about French aid and Margaret had been vouchsafed to Edward by his spies at the courts of France and Brittany. And it was true. When the former Queen set forth she was accompanied by only eight hundred men, and they had been paid by neither Francis nor Louis but by De Brezé, Margaret's competent commander and her dear friend. On October twenty-fifth she and her ships touched briefly at Scotland to pick up King Henry and then they sailed on to Bamborough on the coast of Northumberland. Bamborough Castle, held by one of her friends, took her in, whereupon the castle surrendered. This news reached London on the thirtieth of October, five days after Margaret's initial landing.

Although Warwick was already in the north bearing Edward's commission of array, Edward left London in four days, pausing only long enough to speak to the council and obtain some money, to send orders to the fleet at Kingston-on-Hull to be ready for his coming and to raise troops. Then Edward left London in such haste that his supplies and artillery would have to follow him.

The country shivered. Margaret's horde of Frenchmen and Northerners had wreaked havoc before. Edward reached York six days later and rode north as fast as possible, sending ahead of him the royal commission of the array of the counties to raise the royal standard against the Scots and the French, who were, as the commission stated, "disturbing the peace of the realm."

Rumors flew in all directions. It made Edward realize that a reliable system of couriers was necessary, and he plotted it in his mind as he rode side by side with Anthony. But when he reached York on the thirteenth of November, he learned for a certainty to his relief that the northern counties had not risen up to aid Margaret and that she, learning that he himself was on his way to confront her, had taken flight into the teeth of a bad storm. She had escaped to Berwick from her sinking caravel by way of a fishing boat, but all the French who had landed on one of the islands had been captured or killed and their leader, the Seigneur de Graville was already on his way to London as prisoner.

Nonetheless Anthony had no rest, for, determined now to recapture and hold the three great Northumbrian castles of Bamborough, Alnwick and Dunstanborough, Edward pushed on to Durham.

They reached Durham on a cold, snowy day. The Bishop greeted Edward diffidently. Did the King know that he had comforted Margaret and taken in Henry? The King did. In cold fury Edward set up his headquarters at the abbey, and he had already given orders for the temporary seizure of the bishopric. The entire possessions of the bishopric were handed over to the comptroller and the treasurer of the royal household, and one hundred and seventy-two beefs and one hundred and seventy-nine muttons from the Bishop's pasturelands made Anthony's stay at the abbey more pleasant for his stomach.

"We shall stay here only one night," Edward said. He had commandeered the Bishop's own chambers; they were paneled and tapestried, and a fire burned on the hearth. The Bishop's accounts, which Edward was reading, showed that he was the possessor of about six hundred pounds.

"This will make it easier for me to forgive him some year later," Edward said. But he passed his hand over his forehead and pushed the papers to one side.

Anthony and the Earl of Kent, who were in the room, glanced at him, for his voice had been low. Edward closed his eyes and rested his chin on his hands.

"That bitch in Berwick," Edward muttered. His big hands pressed against his temples; suddenly he raised his head and looked at Anthony. He said incredulously as he tried to stand up, "There's something the matter with me." He gritted his teeth in the effort to stand, grasped for the table ledge and Anthony was at his side and the Earl at the other. Fear struck deep into Anthony. They got Edward undressed and into the Bishop's big comfortable bed. He was shaking with cold; they piled feather quilts on his big frame and the doctor arrived on hasty feet, his flat, black cap awry.

Edward had pulled himself up onto the bolstering pillows; he felt a little better now that he was recumbent, the dizziness had passed and warmth was beginning to flood through his body. He held up his hand for silence as Dr. Hatclyf was about to speak. His voice sounded more normal.

His eyes were beginning to glitter with fever, but Anthony saw only the wicked humor in them as Edward said, "Anthony, I know you. You are on your way to the chapel to pray and by God's most blessed lady I need your prayers. But don't stay on your knees all night. If I am not well enough in the morning I want you and Kent to lead the portion of men I was going to lead. I want you to go to Alnwick. I want Alnwick Castle badly."

"Aye, Your Grace," Anthony said.

"There are Frenchmen garrisoning Alnwick." It made Edward so angry to think of Frenchmen in the mighty castle that he sat up straight. "Worcester and Grey will attack Dunstanborough, and Montagu and Ogle will proceed to Bamborough."

Dr. Hatclyf went closer to his patient. Edward's eyes were closed. Dr. Hatclyf looked down at his face, motioning one of the servants to hold the light closer. He frowned. Then gently he drew back the quilts, exposing Edward's massive chest and flat stomach. The candle flickered. Edward shivered. Dr. Hatclyf drew back the quilts and tucked them around his royal patient. Edward thought he was burning up. His head pounded and every joint in his body ached. He coughed. Had he been poisoned? He opened his eyes and was about to ask the dreadful question when he heard Dr. Hatclyf say, "Your Grace, have you ever had the measles?"

"Measles!" Edward rolled over. A muttered obscene word came from his lips.

Dr. Hatclyf knew what he was thinking. He had come all the way north to confront his enemies, his rebellious subjects and finally Margaret herself, and now he was struck down by a childhood disease. The only fly in this ointment as far as Dr. Hatclyf was concerned was that Edward would not pay enough attention to his advice. So he began immediately.

"Your Grace, measles can be serious if you do not take care of yourself."

Edward replied with another muttered oath.

"I am going to call the apothecary and give Your Grace a potion. You must sleep and not lie there and fret. Besides, it will make you more comfortable."

Edward coughed again, a nasty, racking little cough.

"How long have you been feeling ill, Your Grace? How long have you been coughing like that?"

"I don't know," Edward said. "I felt tired." He glanced over at Anthony. "You'd best get out of here."

"I've had the measles," Anthony said, which provoked another oath from Edward. But that was the last of his revolts. He sighed and rolled over on his stomach. Dr. Hatclyf gave him something to drink—Anthony didn't know what it was. Afraid of disturbing him, Anthony slept on a pallet on the floor; the candle threw great shadows across the curtained bed; within them Edward slept and coughed. On the pallet Anthony turned, restless, afraid.

In the morning, at the head of one portion of the King's troops, Anthony and the Earl of Kent rode off to bring these reinforcements to Warwick and to lead them to the siege of Alnwick. The morale of the troops was high; both Anthony and Kent were popular; they were steady, competent commanders, ungiven to heroics or cruelties. Two days later they reached the frowning walls of Alnwick, set up the artillery and their camp and began their siege. Warwick himself was at Warkworth, directing operations against all three northern castles. Anthony was glad that he and Kent were alone. From their information Alnwick could not hold out for long; the garrison would be eating its horses soon. They were under Edward's orders not to shell Alnwick unless it was absolutely necessary; the King didn't want the castle in ruins when he recaptured it.

The weeks passed. November became December. Light snow frosted the bare border country; the nights were bitter with the wind from the sea so close. Anthony kept his troops busy cutting wood so that great fires could burn all night for a bit of comfort;

their blazing light was all the cheer available to them. On the tenth of December Anthony received word from Edward that his advices showed the Scots were on their way to rescue all three castles. But the morale continued high and on the eleventh of December John Paston wrote home about the purported coming of the Scots. He was not worried. "We have ordnance in plenty, both for a battle or a siege, and so make as merry as you can, for there is no jeopardy yet."

Edward was sick. His apothecary bill was going to be eighty-eight pounds, which would not be paid until two years later. He fretted, he dreamed, he tossed, his head ached and his eyes burned and he coughed continually. Dr. Hatclyf gave him honeyed wine for the cough, and he grew so sick of it he could not eat and his big frame began to lose weight. But he had his most trusted men in the field. Worcester himself, the Constable of England, was commanding the besiegers at Dunstanborough, and Montagu was at Bamborough. But every day, regardless of Dr. Hatclyf's expostulations he dictated letters and listened to the reports from his spies in Scotland, messengers from London and reports from Warwick and all the others conducting the sieges. And in the back of his head ran the refrain "The Scots will come, and come in force." Meantime he was chained to his huge curtained bed.

The weather turned terrible. It rained, cold, driving rain; it snowed. It seemed the elements were assaulting his troops. He could lie there and vision the drooping spirits of men, wet, cold, weary. And the Christmas season was almost upon them. In the abbey Edward told time by the ringing of the bells for matins, for vespers; ears tuned, he heard the hoofbeats which meant messages; he heard the opening of the big gates and he would wait, impatiently, for news.

The whole operation was like to fail under the impact of his illness, the weather and the damned Scots. He had done his best to make a truce with the Scots and he had almost succeeded. And it was the Christmas season. Surely he could use its help. He sat up and called for his secretary; he might yet pull the fat from the fire; he would use the advantages to his hand; not even Francesco Sforza, the Duke of Milan, could do more.

So in a letter sent out to all commanders the King offered, at this holy season, pardon; pardon not for goods but for life. No blood would be shed; but the rebels within the castles would be brought before him, to the abbey at Durham, in submission to the royal will.

On Christmas Eve the castles of Dunstanborough and Bamborough made an offer of surrender, and on Sunday, December 26, they capitulated. The defenders were brought to Edward at Durham, and before the big bed they knelt and swore allegiance. Edward now had in his hands the principal rebels of his kingdom, the chief Lancastrians. Still half sick, he told himself he would trust them. There would be no slaughtering; for the good of the kingdom he must reconcile all its dissident elements and bring national peace out of civil war. The good Lord had said charity was the greatest of these. The Earl of Pembroke refused to stay. Edward let him go, giving him a safe conduct to Scotland. He had promised them their lives and he would keep the promise. There would be no wholesale executions as there would have been had Margaret been victorious.

But Alnwick held out. The next day Edward wrote to the Chancellor in London that Dunstanborough and Bamborough had surrendered, that the Duke of Somerset, Margaret's chief supporter, had submitted to the royal authority for his life only and that he had received advices that the Scots were on their way to rescue Alnwick. Three days later, worried, he wrote to the Archbishop of York that the Scots were coming Monday or Tuesday, that he should send his clergy in defensible array to Newcastle Moor and that he would be there himself.

But the next day he was sick again with fever and pain. So it was not Edward who appeared riding over the border moor country toward Alnwick and Anthony but Warwick.

Anthony's heart sank. It was pouring rain. Advices from Edward on the nearness of the Scot army and its size had reached them every day, and now arrived the great Earl with footsore and cold, disheartened troops; their appearance made the blast of horns as Warwick approached camp sound as hollow of triumph as the whistle of the winter wind; it caught the draggled plumes of the mounted men and tugged at the flaps of the mended tents. The Earl of Kent was standing alongside of Anthony to receive the Earl. He whispered to Anthony,

" 'Tis the season to be jolly. Falla-la-la-la."

Anthony had written home on the eleventh of December, the

same day as young John Paston, and the letter reached Grafton before Christmas. The news of the King's illness had been rumored but no official word had been received. Elizabeth pored over every word of the letter. She could see plain in her mind the shadowy room that first night of Edward's illness, and she could picture him asleep and Anthony restless on his couch. The rest of the letter told only of the military matter of besieging Alnwick and ended on the hopeful note that the garrison was eating its horses. Elizabeth shuddered; Anthony had said humorously that the garrison being French, they were all hoping they'd soon disgust their fine palates and surrender. Every time the wind was from the west, Anthony said, they'd roast a sheep so the garrison would receive all the wonderful aroma of roast mutton.

Elizabeth took Anthony's letter immediately to Father William, who was anxious for honest news and not rumor; every day he prayed for the King that he should soon be restored to full health; Elizabeth went to church every day through the cold, snowy paths to echo those prayers and knelt at the altar while the candle she had lit flickered as fearfully as her own heart in the cold, dank church. So Christmas passed; with each day it seemed growing more and more cold, with the milk frozen in the pail and the ground hard and uneven to the foot and the fires never warm enough. Nonetheless she and the children gathered ivy and branches, and the Yule log was cut and dragged in, and they were as merry as could be at Christmas for the sake of the children and the villagers. The sprinkling of pretty snow on the trees only meant bitter cold for the men out in the open, and at night Elizabeth turned often in her warm bed, thinking of Anthony on the frozen moors and Edward ill and far away; even Lord Rivers, worried about his oldest son, found it difficult to laugh and be merry for the sake of the three younger boys and eight daughters and his two little fast-growing grandsons.

At Fotheringhay, where she was keeping Christmas, the Duchess of York fretted about her sick son. She tried to remember whether he had had the measles, but try as she would she could not definitely state to herself that he had, for naturally measles could be mistaken for the dreaded sickness of the pox. She tried to have a fine Christmas for the sake of her daughters and young Richard and George. Meanwhile the year was dying and the last of December days were struck from the calendar. On the day before New Year's a royal messenger arrived from London with a package for Elizabeth. Within was a velvet pouch and within that—Elizabeth drew it out slowly—was a white enamel rose, sprinkled with diamonds like dew. There was no message.

She turned it over in her white hands, her long slender fingers caressing it. She knew by its very arrival that Edward must have ordered it long ago; indeed with his forethought, when one of his ships had gone out in the early summer laden with twenty thousand woolfells for trade in Italy, he had ordered his factor to find and bring back such a token. It had been six months since she had seen him. Her mother viewed the gift thoughtfully.

"It is in perfect taste," she conceded. "Not too valuable."

"It is an object of beauty," Elizabeth said, hot reproof in her tone. The older generation didn't understand the importance of beauty; they thought too much of cost and money.

The Duchess knew when she was rebuked and she smiled amusedly. "You're so comical, Bessie," she said good-naturedly. "And when you lump me in your thought with the reprehensible oldsters, don't forget the King's mother, the indomitable Duchess of York, proud Cis." Jacqueta slitted her eyes and set her chin; even the thought of Edward's mother was enough to put her face in battle dress. Then she sighed and threw up her hands in her most Gallic gestures; there was no use worrying about the Duchess of York now; no matter what else there was to distract Jacqueta, Anthony was really never absent from her mind and her thoughts always came back to him, her beloved son. Elizabeth pinned the rose onto her plain collar. Her eyes shone like twin stars. The Duchess suddenly bethought herself how Anthony, Richard, her husband and now Elizabeth were being drawn into and closer under the King's influence. She fretted on the thought. Was it for the best? How could it be in the case of Elizabeth? Then the Duchess' buoyant faith in her own abilities to manage asserted itself. "You're always discontent in the winter," she told herself. "It's time you outgrew it."

The news of Alnwick's surrender reached Grafton through a letter of Edward's to the Chancellor in London, and one of Lord Rivers' servants brought the news; but there was no word from Anthony and Lord Rivers knew the Duchess would worry until she heard from him direct. It was the tenth of January and Anthony himself was standing at the foot of the King's bed. The room had been cleared by Edward and now he motioned to a brocaded stool at his bedside.

"Sit down," he said.

Anthony spoke in a low voice as the tapestries stirred in the winter drafts and sleet hissed in the chimney.

Anthony sat gratefully; he was dressed in black hose and slippers, the laces of his white shirt were neatly tied and over it he wore a furred doublet; he was clean-shaven and he had taken the time to bathe and change his clothes, whereas the doughty Earl of Warwick had stamped victorious into Edward's chamber, still clad in mail and exuding the martial spirit. He had champed and chafed like a horse, Anthony thought. Importantly Warwick had given Edward the news of Alnwick's surrender. Then Edward had ordered all out under plea of weariness; only Anthony remained; Warwick, and even Hastings, hadn't liked it too much. Anthony felt it in their regard, and sensitive as he was he couldn't help misliking it. He wasn't jealous of Edward's regard for others; Anthony was so deeply committed to Edward that he thought he was beyond and above envy.

Edward was thinking that Anthony was indeed a throwback to chivalry. He was a true knight; whereas the others paid but a bit of lip service to the old ideals, Anthony lived them.

As a matter of fact Anthony was smiling, thinking of his own likening of Warwick to a horse and how angry the Earl would be could he read his mind, and he was startled when Edward evidently could, for the King said, "Well, now, you must give him his due, for he had fought hard and well here." Edward paused. "It was a nasty job. From his account. Now tell me what really happened at Alnwick."

Edward leaned back against the white pillows, and Anthony was struck again that he looked thinner in the face, older suddenly over the richly furred bedgown; the brown eyes were a bit remote and illness had made his face more stern. Anthony leaned forward.

"Your Grace," he blurted worriedly, "are you feeling better?"

Edward's smile flashed out, lighting the whole world for Anthony. "Much better," he said. "I intend to leave here in a week or so. I'm so anxious to hear your account, Anthony."

Anthony began. "We had received your advices on Sunday, the latest one, that the Scots were coming Monday or Tuesday, and

Wednesday our advance scouts reported a large army. By Thursday they had appeared, a much larger force than ours, and so my lord of Warwick's troops being disheartened by long cold and rain, he decided to withdraw them to a spot between the castle walls almost and a marsh. Kent and I protested a bit, Your Grace, thinking the position was a trap. But it turned out well—I learned from a private conversation later. Angus and De Brezé, seeing us withdraw, feared it was a trap of some kind for them"—Anthony threw out his hands as if to say they must have been crazy—"and that somehow we were working not to retreat but to attack, and the garrison of the castle then, so near were they to surrender, threw open the gates and marched out right under her eyes. They scurried for the safety of the Scot camp which of course they attained; our guns didn't fire. But either Angus is in his dotage or De Brezé is not the soldier he's reputed to be, for damned if they didn't all march away, the garrison with them. Well, of course, the following day, Friday morning, the few men left in the castle surrendered and we marched in."

Anthony's eyes were as surprised retelling the story as they had been at the anticlimactic end of the siege of Alnwick.

Edward's smile was thoughtful. "Angus is dying," he said. "About De Brezé, I don't know." He said nothing further, only he was storing in his mind his own evaluation of Warwick as a campaigner. Anthony's story was plain, unvarnished truth and that was the reason Edward had kept him here.

Edward said, "Today new writs were issued summoning Parliament for the seventh of March at Leicester. We expect to start for London in a week and to reach Fotheringhay by the twenty-sixth of January." He looked across at Anthony. "How long since you've slept in a warm bed? Share mine tonight."

Since Edward had summoned Parliament for the seventh of March in Leicester and since through sickness he had lost previous weeks, he now moved with his usual, precise speed to accomplish all he wished before he opened Parliament. He had intended to celebrate the second anniversary of his father's death on the thirtieth of December but he had been in Durham and in bed. Therefore he changed the date to his father's month mind, the thirtieth of January, and on the twenty-fourth of the month he left Durham for Fotheringhay.

Up from London came his father's hearse, powdered with roses and golden suns and banners displaying the arms of St. George, St. Edward, England and France. This hearse which Edward had set up at St. Paul's soon after his victory at Towton was covered with a majesty cloth on which was wrought the image of our Lord and images of kings and angels. During this time the Earl of Warwick similarly honored his father, Edward's uncle. His body was brought from its temporary grave after the battle of Wakefield and accompanied by a large cortege of the nobility: Warwick and his brothers and Edward's sister, the Duchess of Suffolk. The Earl's funeral took place at Bisham Abbey.

Then Edward turned his face toward London.

At Grafton, even though the winter cold had settled into the bones of house and villagers and even those to the manor born, there was peace and a curious attitude of waiting. The Duchess was content that both her sons were safe and well and with the King. The fighting was over temporarily. Elizabeth rose each morning to her accustomed tasks, only now she wore always the white rose that Edward had sent at New Year's.

Toward the end of January the Duchess and Lord Rivers went to Fotheringhay to pay their respects to the King's dead father and to attend the costly ceremonies. And when the Duchess knelt before the hearse in the light of the wax candles she remembered to include the King and Elizabeth in her prayers, for she knew well that the King's gift meant that Edward was simply biding his time and that he would act.

Elizabeth knew it too. Looking back on that months and weeks later she realized that she had moved in a kind of curious vacuum, a period of quiet suspension as though there were no time, no hours, no days. There was nothing she could do; instinctively she knew Edward would make the next move on this complicated chessboard.

It was quite late at night when suddenly at Fotheringhay one of Edward's servants appeared at the Duchess' chambers and without a word handed her a letter from his royal master. The Duchess took the folded, sealed packet over to a bench and sat down before she read it.

It was brief and to the point. Edward charged her and her husband, Lord Rivers, to attend him at Shene on the nineteenth of February and to bring her daughter, the Lady Grey.

The Duchess dropped the letter on the flames of the bright fire. And the next day, after she had waited for a while in the audience chamber, she finally found herself face-to-face with the King.

The Duchess looked up at Edward. "You do us great honor, Your Grace. If Elizabeth is well and it is her wish she shall come. The decision shall have to be hers, my lord, for she is not robust for winter journeying."

The Duchess curtsied deeply to make up for her declaration that she would not pander for her daughter. Edward's eyes glinted a bit in sudden anger, then his sense of humor took over and he too bowed as to a worthy opponent. He said easily, "We shall then look forward in any case to meeting you and Lord Rivers."

Two days later the Duchess hurried home. Two minutes after she entered Grafton she laid the King's words before her daughter. Elizabeth said first, "You didn't bring the letter?"

"Of course not," snapped the Duchess. "I burned it!" She shook her finger at Elizabeth. "And if you ever receive a letter you burn it!"

Elizabeth said, "I couldn't!"

The Duchess swore in French. Elizabeth cried, "You don't know what it's like to love a man, you can never, never have!"

The Duchess was so amazed and annoyed by this remark that she started to slap her daughter; she raised her hand and then remembered that Bess was too old to slap. "I don't know what it's like to be in love? I? When I bore you for your father I was in a heaven of love so much that I forfeited all I ever had, my family, my dower—don't talk to me of love! Married secret with secret meetings—" The Duchess broke off as her husband entered the room. In a sudden rush of emotion the Duchess fled over to him, and astonished, he put his arm around her, his eyes going from his wife to his daughter.

"Are you quarreling?" he asked. "What is the matter, Bess?"

It was too much, too much to see her father and mother so close, so loving, "How happy you must have been!" Elizabeth cried, and then sinking down on a stool she buried her face in her hands and sobbed as if her heart were breaking, as indeed she thought it was.

It was imperative, the Duchess thought, that her husband not be informed of the cause of these tears. She removed her husband's arm from her waist and went over to her distraught daughter. She tapped her on the shoulder.

"Bess, Bess, I am sorry. I don't like quarreling. You have been alone too much." The Duchess hesitated. Then she added, "Your father and I have been asked to attend the King at Shene. If you wish, if you wish, mind you well, Bess, you may go with us for a bit of change."

Later in privacy Elizabeth said only a few words steadily and with no trace of tears. "I must go, Mother. I must. I can't hide; I must see him."

The Duchess kissed her good night; thoughtfully, her agile brain busy, she added, "Never, Bess, talk to anyone but me. Never, never say anything to Anthony or your father. This is women's business, not men's."

Elizabeth's fine clothes had been laid away during her period of mourning and during her quiet life at Grafton. Now with excitement she opened the big chest at the foot of her bed. It smelled sweet with herbs, for she had taken care of her clothes; they were precious indeed. One by one her five fine gowns were laid out on the bed, even to the one she had worn when, before marriage, she had for a brief few months been a lady-in-waiting to Queen Margaret.

The Duchess helped her try them on. "Not an ounce have you gained," the Duchess said triumphantly. "You are just like me!"

They needed a bit of change. The Duchess emptied her own chests to find a fine bit of brocade to sew on for a new cuff or to put about a slightly worn hem; she donated a carefully saved bit of marten fur to edge a small cape. The Duchess and the seamstresses worked on petticoats too, adding bits of lace; it was very important for Elizabeth to look as well as she could, for Edward's court was lavish and gay; older people complained about the magnificence of Edward's own personal dress and his expensive tastes, but even though they grumbled at the cost they were fiercely proud of their handsome, magnificent King.

On the eighteenth of February then they set forth, Elizabeth bidding a sudden anguished farewell to her little boys; she seized and hugged them as though she would never see them again, as though she were deserting them. Lord Rivers had given his daughter a fine mare with splendid trappings; he had equipped ten servants in livery and on the trundling carts bearing their needed possessions, including three feather beds, rode four maids. They made a fine display, Elizabeth thought proudly; they were coming to court in fine style.

To think, she thought, it is incredible, but we shall be in Shene tomorrow!

Edward had planned to make a stop at Hertford Castle and then at Sion at the nunnery. Once there he hesitated. The Duchess' words to him had been sobering. Should he make for London? He sent word that he would. Then changing his mind he arrived at Shene the evening before Elizabeth set out from Grafton and set another messenger galloping posthaste to London to advise its citizens he would arrive by water, for he knew that they were planning a triumphant gala entry into the city for him, and in truth he was longing for a sight of it. His audience chamber was crowded the next morning and after dinner, about two o'clock, he was standing in the window overlooking the courtyard when the Earl of Warwick arrived. The whole court was full to overflowing with men wearing the red jackets and the ragged staff, there was a multitude of carts and baggage and Edward thought of the enormous cost of feeding all these people; he decided then that he would set someone who was good at figures on a book of household accounts: what allowances should be made and exactly how much food, candles, ale and even wood should be dispensed by the treasurer of the royal household. Looking at all those men stamping about his court only made Edward think of money. It was all very well for my lord of Warwick to allow any man to come to his dwelling and carry off as much meat as he could stick with his dagger but he, Edward, had to be careful of money. The bugbear of any monarch was taxes. Edward scowled down at the courtyard as it was gradually emptying. Outside the gates the small cavalcade of Lord Rivers was trying to enter. Lord Rivers cleared a path for himself and his servants, then he bade Elizabeth to ride in and from the window Edward saw her. She sat her horse just like Anthony did, Edward thought; maybe Anthony had taught her. The King stood at the window transfixed. She came closer. Hastings came up alongside of Edward.

"What are you looking at, Your Grace?"

"A vision," said Edward absently. Why is she sitting there, he

wondered? But he didn't move and neither did she because Lord
Rivers had commanded her to stay in the saddle while he sent a
servant to find Anthony to come help them and conduct them
to their allotted quarters.

In about five minutes Anthony arrived; Edward saw him help
his mother and sister from their mounts and then they disappeared below him. Edward turned from the window.

Lord Rivers was surprised when Anthony conducted his
mother and sister to a separate chamber. "I thought Bess should be
in with the other girls," he said. "This is very kind of His Grace.
Probably due to you, Anthony." The Duchess shooed them out.
She helped Elizabeth out of her riding costume, one of the maids
found quilts and both women lay down. The cold air and the
long ride lulled Elizabeth into deep sleep.

When she wakened she sat up with a start and remembered
where she was. The maids had brought water, and her mother
was already making her toilet and searching through her jewel
chest. It was necessary that they present themselves to Edward's
mother, the doughty Duchess of York.

Elizabeth's gown was laid out, a rich tawny gown of velvet
with long tight sleeves cut away to expose her neck and shoulders and slit up the front to show her gold-lace petticoats. It
matched her glowing eyes.

Her coif added height; she pulled her hair through it so it
floated from the top of her coif like a golden horse's tail the
color of one in a legend or a fairy tale. She looked so beautiful
that the instant the Duchess of York saw her she provoked an
instant animosity.

"Who's that?" the Duchess whispered. "Jacqueline's daughter?"
The Duchess never used her rival's nickname.

"The Lady Grey," was the whispered answer.

Elizabeth came nearer and the Duchess rested distant eyes on
her.

Elizabeth curtsied deeply. "Lady Grey, Your Grace."

The Duchess nodded. "You are a widow, madam?"

"Aye, Your Grace." Elizabeth stood straight, conscious of
anger. She wet her red mouth with the tip of her tongue. She
wanted to remind the haughty Duchess that she, Elizabeth
Woodville, had made a marriage equal to the Plantagenets themselves, for her dead husband had borne one of the finest names

in the realm, and he had been brave and handsome and she, Elizabeth, had loved him deeply. So she said, "I am the Lady Grey, of Ferrers of Groby."

Her mother intervened. She had also made her curtsy, a small one. Jacqueta cleared her throat. "We are so happy to attend Your Grace," she said, her eyes meeting those of Cecily's squarely.

"I too am happy," the Duchess replied.

"Then we have your leave?" Jacqueta took Elizabeth's arm and they withdrew to one side of the room. Jacqueta was muttering in French under her breath and Elizabeth wanted to smile, but instead she looked about the big room.

It was full of women. Elizabeth reminded herself that this was a court which had no Queen. The majority of the women were young; some around the Duchess were sewing, as she herself had used to do when she had been in attendance on the former Queen. They were playing at cards and chess and there was a set of ivory ninepins. There was an odd air of restraint and waiting in the room, and Elizabeth guessed it was because they were waiting for supper.

"I am hungry," she whispered to her mother. "It must be five."

At that moment the Duchess rose and all the gaily clad ladies followed her; Elizabeth could hear the sound of trumpets somewhere. Suddenly she felt as though she could not breathe. When one of the Duchess' ladies came over to her in the dining hall and showed her where she would sit, she could hardly answer.

She found herself conducted to a long table against the wall with all the rest of the Duchess' women, whereas her mother, in deference to her rank, was placed at a table in the center of the room. Elizabeth, who had been well taught, introduced herself to her companions on either side, then she fell silent. There was a stir in the room, everyone still stood, and then from her distant place she saw the King come striding in, the Earl of Warwick at his side and a host of men following after. Edward was talking earnestly to Warwick; he appeared not to even see the throng of people who now all bowed before him. He reached the head of the main table, the trumpets blew again and Edward sat down.

Everyone followed suit; Elizabeth fastened her eyes on him while his priest blessed the food and the long line of servants bearing the huge platters began their march into the room and around each table. The room was so crowded that Elizabeth had barely enough room between the bench and the wall at her back. She tasted her wine and it was not the same as Edward had brought at the picnic; it was not the same as Edward himself was drinking at that very moment either.

At the table where Elizabeth sat all the women were chattering. She guessed most of them were unmarried and she felt as different as crow among swans. I a widow, she thought. There were three courses and Elizabeth, hungry as she had thought she was, ate very little. She felt very alone and very alien; the Duchess of York obviously had hated her on sight. Yet she was annoyed at being placed among these women, for her own title was far above theirs and she knew the Duchess had done it on purpose. Edward seemed so far away—she could hardly see him —and the stone wall rubbed uncompromisingly on her back. She was thankful when the meal ended and she could rise and bow again as Edward left the dining hall. Then like a sheep she followed the other ladies back to the Duchess' drawing room. She stood there alone.

Within the room there was once more that curious air of expectancy, and the Duchess' musicians began to play a nostalgic tune; some of the women gathered around, one with a lute, and they began to sing. The Duchess sat in her high chair as though it were a throne, some of her women about her on cushions at her feet. It was a pretty scene, Elizabeth thought, when suddenly in the open doorways appeared a group of courtiers.

The room came alive and Elizabeth realized then what they were all waiting for; Edward and the men who would accompany him. With a great sigh of gratitude Elizabeth saw her father and Anthony come purposefully toward her, and when there was one of them on each side of her she smiled up at Anthony, and that was the smile Edward saw as he came into his mother's chambers, looking, searching for the sight of the woman he wanted so badly.

Once again all the ladies bent like flowers of a slender stem and billowed up again. Edward went straight to his mother; he stood at the side of her chair, leaning his arm on the high back, and while he talked his eyes went around the room. Dancing had begun but Edward pretended he was in no hurry; he was his indolent self; he bent down and raised his pretty sister Margaret

to her feet and carried her off in the bouncing morris step, whirling her around and laughing at her. He loves her, Elizabeth
thought, watching his fond smile. He was coming nearer with
Margaret, then he was right before them and he transferred
Margaret to Anthony, saying, "Sir Anthony is a better dancer than
I am." He half turned to watch Margaret whirl off in Anthony's
arms, then he held out his arms to Elizabeth and she stepped into
them. She felt his hand on hers; she was conscious of every eye
in the room and she whispered, "Not too fast, please! I'll miss the
steps!"

Edward grinned and looked down at her.

"I haven't danced for two years!"

Edward stood still for a moment, looking down at her. "Smile
at me, Bessie."

She tipped her head back a bit to look up and met his eyes,
and she was so happy suddenly that the smile she gave him was
glowing with the light of youth and joy and love. The Duchess
felt a stab at her heart; they were so beautiful, so young, they
were perfect, she thought, like a painting; the Duchess grasped
her husband's hand. But Lord Rivers was thinking only of his
daughter. "I'm so proud of her," he whispered. Now they were
off and dancing.

"You lied to me," Edward said.

Her eyes widened.

"You dance like a feather."

"Oh." She breathed a sigh of relief. "I thought you truly
meant—"

"I have waited months to hold you," he said directly. "Months
to behold you even. You are the most fair, the most precious bit
of my whole kingdom. Including Castile." Edward smiled; his
most loyal supporters claimed the throne of Castile for him too.

Overwhelmed, Elizabeth couldn't answer. The music stopped
for a moment, then began again and to her surprise, just as she
saw Hastings, Edward transferred her to him, bowed slightly
and turned aside. She didn't have time to wonder because Hastings was not as good a dancer as either Edward or Anthony, and
she had to concentrate on following his step. She was a bit embarrassed by Hastings anyway, for they had betrothed their
respective son and daughter, and now with little Thomas disinherited Hastings might not wish to honor the contract, although

he hadn't written to her to break it. She didn't know whether to bring up the subject or not. Hastings stood so close to the King that his daughter would be an advantageous match for little Thomas Grey. For her son's sake she should speak; the tiniest frown crossed her high white forehead. Hastings must have noted it, she thought, for he said, "Are you weary, my lady?"

"Oh, no!" She glanced at him, still thinking how to approach the betrothal affair.

"Have you ever been to Shene before?"

"No. I've not, my lord."

"The King's favorite dwelling is Windsor."

Elizabeth tried to think of an answer but Hastings said, "If you've never seen the palace, perhaps you would like me to show it to you." The music stopped and Elizabeth could not help glancing about to find Edward. He was nowhere to be seen. Hastings said, "His Grace has retired, madam, to write a bit in his privy chamber. Parliament opens the seventh of March and His Grace is planning to speak." He put her hand on his arm. "Come along," he said, "I'll show you a bit of the palace."

They were near the doors and obediently Elizabeth trotted along beside him, her golden horse tail of hair flowing behind her. The Duchess of York's sharp eyes watched her go with Hastings. They went down a long hall with flaring torches set in the niches. Hastings opened a big set of double doors; within was dark. "The audience chamber," he said; then he closed the doors and they started off down the hall again. When they came to another narrower corridor Hastings said, "His Grace's privy chamber and withdrawing room are to the left." But he turned right and opened the first door.

There were candles burning within and there was a rug on the floor. Hastings seemed to be waiting for her to enter, so she did and looked around the fairly small room. A fire was burning on the hearth and there was a cushioned bench before it; a curtained bed stood in the far corner; Elizabeth turned around to leave the room when Hastings smiled and bowed and shut the door in her face.

She stared at it in utter surprise. Then a sound made her turn again so sharply her full skirts stood out as though she were dancing. She was facing another door; it was opening and Edward was framed in it; he stepped inside and shut it. She looked at him in real amazement.

"I thought you were writing a speech!"

He laughed. "Bessie, Bessie, you are so innocent."

"Innocent?"

He sighed a little. "Well, maybe that wasn't the right word, although I think it was. I couldn't escort you myself. Hastings did it for me."

"I understand that," she said. "Now I do. But I didn't before." She raised slightly troubled eyes to his and this moment her first dismay at Hastings was born. She clasped her hands tight and looked across to Edward; he was still dressed in the same black velvet, had divested himself of the heavy gold chain and was wearing a furred doublet; but now that they were alone in this small room and he was coming closer to her, for the first time she was afraid. What if he makes love to me? she thought. What will I do?

"You should have thought of that before," Edward said, for he could easily read her mind.

Elizabeth said, "I did. But I didn't think it through. Will you excuse me, Your Grace?"

"No," Edward said. "I won't. Come and sit here on this bench." He drew her over to the bench and she sat while he stood by the mantle, leaning his elbow on it; and to remind him that she couldn't sit when he stood she started to rise. Edward put his big hand on her shoulder and sat her down again. "In the privacy of my own chamber we behave as I wish," he said. There was a slight set and sternness in his face. He was facing a difficult job and he knew it. How to begin? He had never in all his dealings with women used the kingly prerogatives. Women came to him easily; besides that it would have been against his nature.

"I have no intention of asking you to just spend the night with me," Edward said. "You can put that out of your mind and not look as though you wished there was something you could do with your hands, like some infernal sewing. I want you to pay attention to me."

"How can I help it?" she asked. "You are right there—here, I mean." But she looked relieved and she smiled doubtfully at him.

"But I am going to ask you for your love."

The sentence was like a blow for which she was unprepared.

Through her mind went the parallel of the chessboard. He had taken her off guard by surrendering a pawn. "As my liege lord, you have all my love and devotion," she countered, like moving her castle to protect the Queen.

He swept it away. "That isn't what I want."

She raised her head to look at him squarely. But she must make him understand that she would love him the rest of her life; no matter what else he must understand that. "I want to thank you for the rose." She touched it gently. "It is the most precious gift I have ever received and I vow to you I shall wear it for the rest of my life. I will serve you as my liege lord the rest of my life. But what else can I give you in honor?" Her voice broke. She wanted to stand and face him, but she sat stiff, because she didn't want him to think she was so distraught and that it was so hard for her to sit quiet.

"I love you," Edward said.

She gazed at him wordlessly, her great eyes holding his.

"We are not children, we are neither of us inexperienced. I love you and I want you, Bessie."

Her mind was flying about crazily. She seized on one of his sentences. "I am certainly no child and I am older than you."

"That's a *non sequitur*," Edward said, annoyed. "I am a thousand years old whether you know it or not. How old are you, twenty-three? What an advanced age!"

"I am twenty-four."

Edward swore his favorite oath. "In that case our liaison should be perfect, because you're far too old to bear children."

She cried, "But I should bear your child! You know it and so do I. We both have children."

Edward said, "And you wouldn't want my child?"

There was silence in the small room. The fire crackled. He leaned on the mantel, she sat like a statue. Checkmate, she thought, the board is swept clear. She said very low, "There is nothing more that I would wish in the entire whole world." She looked up at him. "But not a bastard child, Your Grace. I can't do it. Not for me but for him." Now she did rise because she couldn't help it. "My child and your child, the son whom we should have—your son—I will not have called a bastard. And have you name him Arthur or Grace."

Edward drew a deep breath.

"Don't speak, my lord," she cried. "Please. Let me finish. I know I'm not good enough to be your Queen, but our children—are too good to be—I am too good to be your mistress."

He said nothing. Elizabeth backed to the door. She curtsied. "Will you excuse me, Your Grace?" She cast him a long look; she would never see him again. In that moment she regretted bitterly her words; there was no comfort she wished now more than his arms around her. I love you, he had said, and she was leaving him. Her hand was on the door and for a long minute she waited for him to speak.

He said, "You may go, Bessie."

Her eyes were swimming with tears; I am leaving him, she thought, leaving him, my dearest beloved. She opened the door and closed it gently behind her.

Chapter 6

WHILE EDWARD had lain ill in Durham the affairs of state had been carried on as usual from his bed, and on the previous December he had sent safe conducts to the Hanseatic ambassadors. So that when he arrived in London from Shene by water and the mayor and magistrates greeted him and the city was gay with a welcome for their King, the ambassadors were already there. This trade treaty was important to Edward.

But the first piece of business was the proclamation for new elections. Parliament would be postponed until April twenty-ninth; he had made the change, he said, partly because of the Lenten season "when all men should devote themselves to purifying their lives to God's pleasure," and because in the shires "the elections had been marked with inordinate fraud and violence. Therefore, no man could come to vote, on pain of imprisonment and forfeiture, to the elections of the knights of the shire unless they were possessed of a freehold in the shire to the amount of forty shillings and unless they came in a peaceable manner."

Edward spent the next two months at Westminster and Windsor. He brought with him the former Queen's favorite, the Duke of Somerset, for it seemed reasonable to Edward that he try to use the royal clemency and charm to win away Margaret's former adherents. He pursued this course even to the extent of making Somerset his bedfellow and advancing him money from the privy purse and restoring Somerset's mother to some of her estates.

The trade treaty with the Hanseatic towns was concluded in March, and at the same time the Sieur de Lannoy and his train arrived from Burgundy Edward determined to treat them as royally as he could, so Anthony and the Earl of Worcester paid almost three hundred pounds for screens, curtains and silk hangings, counterpanes and a magnificent crimson length of gold for a cloak for Edward; one hundred twenty pounds were paid out for cloth, woolen and linen, and the bakers, grocers, fish-mongers, butchers and woodmongers of London were kept busy with orders from the clerk of the Green Cloth.

During this time, as April began, Edward sent for Lord Rivers and set him the task of preparing a household book in which every expense of the King's household would be set down and the amount of reasonable expenditure laid out by rule and rote, down to the last farthing. This was a tremendous task and Lord Rivers applied himself to it diligently. Meanwhile Edward promised the Burgundian ambassadors that he would indeed send his representatives to St. Omer to the Diet in the effort to conclude a treaty of peace and trade with France. Edward, who could be as cynical as any monarch, had tried bribing the Sieur de Lannoy and found him too honest. His ambassadors in Cas-tile returned home early in June, bringing assurances of friend-ship, seventy tuns of fine wine to quench Edward's thirst and a book for Anthony, *The Dictes and Sayings of the Philosophers*. Anthony read it sometimes aloud to Edward when the King was able to snatch a few minutes of rest.

"You should translate it for me," Edward said, for sometimes he had difficulty understanding the French.

Edward opened Parliament in the Painted Chamber on the twenty-ninth of April. He was pleased when the Commons elected John Say as Speaker, for he was a member of Edward's council. Say spoke on Edward's suggestion: *"Qui judicatis terram, diligite justitiam."*

It was a subject close to Edward's heart; he had spent three days sitting in judgment on the King's bench, and it was an ex-tremely important Parliament for Edward because he needed money badly.

But first the laws. To improve the cloth and shipping trade: England's ships were smaller than those of other nations; to en-courage shipbuilding then, English merchants were forbidden to ship in foreign bottoms if there were English merchantmen avail-able; the importation of woolfells was forbidden except from Wales and Ireland, and the clothmakers were ordered to pay their wages in money.

The silkwomen of London received an embargo on imported laces and pins, and the handcraft industry was protected by severe limitations on the import of bonnets, fringes, hammers, daggers, playing cards, tennis balls, scissors, razors and gloves.

Edward sat one day and heard the statute proclaimed that the importation of barley, wheat and rye was prohibited unless the price were high enough to protect the farmer; unless the price of wheat exceeded six shillings eightpence. It seemed so long ago that he had listened to Bessie telling of the low prices of wheat and barley.

As for money, Commons granted the King thirty-seven thousand pounds, excluding those who had less than five marks' value and no landed property or rents; this was granted on June seventeenth and was hastened by the news from the north that Ralph Grey had turned traitor and handed back the Northumbrian castles to Henry and Margaret.

Edward decided to go north himself and he took Somerset with him.

At Northampton, under Edward's own roof, some men in the streets broke in and seized the Duke. Edward, hearing the disturbance, came into the lower hall to find Margaret's erstwhile favorite being dragged out into the street for certain death.

"Hold there," Edward roared, coming toward the melee deliberately, and when the men turned and found the King standing there they released the rumpled Duke and stood quiet.

Then violently they pushed him to the floor at Edward's big feet. "He ain't fit to lick your boots, Your Grace. He ain't fit!"

Edward glanced down at the proud Duke at his feet. The thought flicked across his mind that perhaps Somerset would rather be dead than lying like the wounded animal that indeed he was, blood seeping from a blow to his face. Edward said, "He deserves our royal clemency after submission to us—he deserves it as much as you do."

Because he could imagine how Somerset felt he leaned down and lifted Somerset to his feet like a doll. A muttered roar of anger came from the massed men in the court and in the hall. Edward stepped forward to face them.

"There will be no violence under my roof or in this land," he said pleasantly, "or I'll hang every one of you."

They retreated slowly. But one of them called out desperately, "We only wanted to save you from the likes of him!"

"Aye, aye," they shouted. "God save Your Grace!"

Edward smiled. "There'll be a tun of wine in the square tonight for all."

"I'll be damned," he said to Hastings a few minutes later. "Mercy is a commodity which, if I spend, does not appear to repay me." He scowled. "I know that after almost forty long uncertain years of a weak King the natural ferment of rebellion has sown its seeds deep. But we are going to be master of this realm if I have to have the heads of every dissident noble or rebel, and by the time I am finished there will be law in this land for your children, Hastings. And mine."

The next day in Northampton Edward received the news that Warwick had raised the siege of Norham Castle and that the former Queen had fled without even an escort and had taken ship for France. So Edward turned to Fotheringhay, where he could have some hunting, because he was fighting Margaret on the diplomatic front and that was more important. Peace abroad was the order of the day.

It was summer—a beautiful summer, each day warm with sun, each night an instrument to turn a man's thought to love. But instead couriers came to and fro from Fotheringhay.

So on the first of September Edward's ambassadors in France —and he had sent the Chancellor himself—opened their negotiations with Burgundy and France. Louis proved a shy horse, but when the English ambassadors stopped at the château of the Duke to thank him for the sumptuous banquet he had spread for them in the park Louis was there. The Chancellor of England spoke then with the King of France, and by the twenty-fifth of October the envoys were back in London to tell their King of the continuation of the treaty of commerce with Burgundy, and on the twenty-seventh the proclamation of the treaty of a truce with France was proclaimed which was to endure to the going down of the sun on the first day of October, 1464.

Edward was very pleased. He had made a fast trip to London to see his ambassadors before they had left in September. By the thirteenth he was leaving the city again and on his way north to confront the Scots, who had learned of the peace treaty with France. Thus left alone sailing a lonely vessel through the dangerous diplomatic seas, the Scots decided to use the safe conduct Edward had granted a few months before.

On the third of December Edward rode to York from Pontefract and the parley lasted only a few days. Edward made the minor concession of sending the belligerent Earl of Douglas (his own agent) to Ireland, where he set him serving as warden of Cragfergus Castle, and on the ninth day of December, with the cold winds blowing about the walls of the room, the truce with Scotland was signed.

It was Christmastime. Much had been accomplished. Edward rode back to London. It was Christmas and Margaret of Anjou was a penniless woman living at her father's house: There would be no support from Scotland or France. With the truces concluded Edward could turn his attention to his own realm; fighting had been unnecessary, and sensitive to the grumbling about the taxes he returned to the commons the extra six thousand pounds which were to be levied on the poorer of his nation, those with a living of twenty shillings or more. He thought he could keep Christmas in good cheer.

But the matter on which he had been thinking deeply was brought sharply to his mind. On the day after Christmas word was brought to his private chamber that his current mistress had borne him a child. She was a pretty, gay girl, the daughter of a London silkwoman. Taking Hastings with him he went to see her, and excited by the honor of a royal visit her mother admitted him with much bowing and smiling.

"Merry Christmas, Grandma," Edward said, his smile flashing out; he gave her a kiss. "I don't know which of you is the more fair," Edward said, looking at the bed in which, her hair tied in a big bow, her blue eyes sparkling, lay his current favorite, the child in her arms.

Edward went to the bed and leaned over and kissed her. "We must name her together, Your Grace," she said.

"She is beautiful," Edward said. "What name would you bestow, Hastings?"

Hastings began, "Why, Your Grace—"

"That is the name," came the cry from the bed. "Grace! Say it with me, my lord."

Edward, who had been holding her hand, bent his head. Then slowly he knelt beside the bed. He said, "My little Grace, God bless you and keep you." His voice stopped, and he rose and leaned over and kissed the child's mother.

Outside on the London street, in the cold air, he paused for a moment. Snow powdered the uneven rooftops of the houses.

"Once I told someone I was a thousand years old," he said to Hastings. "Tonight I feel two thousand."

At Westminster, in his privy chamber, he found Anthony waiting to say good-bye, for he was going home for New Year's. Edward said, "Give my regards to your family. Are they well, Anthony?"

"Oh, yes, Your Grace."

"Bid them a happy New Year for me. It surprises me that your sister is not wed yet, Anthony."

Anthony frowned. "I don't know what's the matter with her, to tell the truth. When men approach me to ask if I will present them to Bess, she tells me no; she says her heart is broken in three pieces and she will never wed again." Anthony flung out his hands. "I know she loved John very much, but I tell her she is too young to spend the rest of her life alone."

"Of course," said Edward in an odd voice which made Anthony look at him, for the tone belied the words. Suddenly Edward smiled.

"Go along home, Anthony," he said. "I wish to God I were going with you."

Anthony, who had backed to the door, hesitated. Did Edward want him for something? "I was going to bed early but—"

Edward shook his head. "I, too. I'm going to bed also, Anthony. Good night. Godspeed."

But he was sorry to see him go. He reminded Edward of Bessie: They looked alike, their voices were oddly the same with the same inflections even in stress. In stress. Edward couldn't keep her voice from his mind. "But your child and mine. I can't do it. And have you name her Grace!"

"It might have been her child," he thought. "Her child and mine." A Princess of the realm, a beautiful, beautiful baby, born to be beloved by the whole land, bright-haired and bright of mind. "You were right, Bessie," he said aloud to the empty room.

The great matter of the King's marriage had been resting on Edward for a year. It had been almost a year since he had seen her. Yet the longing for her had not diminished and anyone else was but a brief and unsatisfactory substitute. For months, in his quiet moments, he had thought of nothing else. It had crossed his mind to bribe her with Bradgate, the great inheritance of her sons; he hadn't done it because he knew it would offend her. Even thinking about offering it made him feel slightly guilty, as though he could see the reproof in her golden eyes. Another way was to marry her off; then, he would say, there would be no illegitimate children, Bessie; they will have a fine, proud name. But whose? He had reviewed all the men he could set his hand on, and he didn't want any one of them in bed with Bessie.

The Nevilles, Warwick, the chief of them, were becoming increasingly insistent about his marriage. Of course it was true. He had been assiduous in presenting his kingdom with bastards; it was time he presented them with an heir. But tonight he was tired. His big magnificent body cried for sleep.

"The devil with it," he muttered and called out for Hastings to get him into bed.

On Sunday morning as the first of day grayed the skies four men wearing the King's livery and four men wearing my lord Hastings' livery rode out of Westminster and the gates clanged shut behind them.

The little troop reached Stony Stratford in time for a late dinner and refreshment after the ride. Then with a change of horses two of the riders set out again for Grafton.

At the manor the Hastings' retainer went up to the big doors. "I bear a message to be delivered personally to the Duchess of Bedford," he explained.

He was conducted to a small anteroom off the hall and Anthony, seeing his figure at a distance, thought there was something oddly familiar about it. But then the door closed. The Duchess looked up.

"Lord Hastings!" she cried.

Hastings was wasting no time. "Where is the Lady Grey?" he asked peremptorily.

The Duchess bridled. "She is not here at present."

"Where is she then, madam?"

The Duchess closed her mouth and eyed him. Hastings gave her a long look back.

"His Grace demands to know," he said, and waited.

"The Lady Grey is at church at the vesper service," the Duchess said haughtily, but that was lost on Hastings for he bowed briefly and made for the door. "Thank you, madam," he threw over his shoulder.

Outside he mounted again and rode up to his waiting companion. "At the church," he said, and without a word both wheeled about and made up the long drive at a good gallop. It was still quite light.

Outside the church Hastings dismounted and held both horses, and the tall man in the King's livery went in the doors. There he paused and made the sign of the cross, then he went through the clusters of women kneeling about the pillars to the only pew behind the chancel screen.

Father William was at the altar with his back to his congregation.

In front of the pew there was one figure kneeling on a little red cushion, her head bent and her hands clasped. Edward went down on his knees beside her and laid one big gloved hand over hers.

"My own sweetheart," he whispered.

Elizabeth looked down incredulously at the hand across hers.

"If you pray for me I know God would listen," Edward said in her ear.

Her heart was beating so madly she could not speak; she gazed at him wordlessly, but her eyes carried an unmistakable message.

"You love me, Bessie," he said low.

"Yes," she whispered back. "I love you with all my heart and soul, forever and ever will I love you."

"Then," said Edward, "here, my darling, in the sight of God I am asking you to marry me and be my wife."

There was a rustle in the church behind them as the prayer ended and the women got to their feet. Father William turned from the altar and saw the two kneeling figures in front of him, their profiles turned to him since they were looking one at the other. They still knelt and then in astonishment Father William recognized the King.

Father William's well-trained boys' choir now raised their pure voices; the two figures still knelt, and Father William realized that Edward was dressed in livery and that he did not wish to be recognized. He kept on with the service.

Elizabeth and Edward now realized they could sit and they both slid back into the pew, holding hands, Father William thought with a sudden rush of emotion, like any two young lovers worshiping God together.

It was time to pray again and automatically they both knelt again.

Looking down at them from the altar Father William prayed

for them. "God's blessings on His Grace, our King," Father William said, "and on all those kneeling here to do Him homage, and on all those who love truly may His goodness and mercy follow them, sustain them in time of great trouble and make His face to shine upon them. Amen."

Edward and Elizabeth both rose and then Edward sat down again.

"Let the others leave before us," he said.

The church slowly emptied. Father William went to the doorway and spoke with some of the women, but he wasn't as chatty as usual and so they left and only Hastings was waiting outside with the two horses, and the village women stared at him curiously.

The altar boys were snuffing the candles, a gift of Lord Rivers to the parish church. Father William now went up to his distinguished worshiper.

"Father William," Elizabeth said tremulously and then didn't know quite how to proceed.

Father William said, "You do us great honor, Your Grace."

"If you love me, Father," Edward said, "speak not a word of what you have seen tonight."

"On my oath in my church," Father William said.

Edward smiled; he liked this man. He held out his big hand. "Thank you," he said as Father William took his King's hand and grasped it warmly.

"May God's blessing go with you both," he said.

Edward took Elizabeth's hand; they walked out of the still-open doors, Elizabeth carrying her gay little red pillow.

Hastings saw them coming hand in hand. He glanced about to see if there were any watchers, but the churchyard was deserted and the alehouse doors were closed tight against the cold December night. Edward mounted and Hastings helped Elizabeth up into pillion position behind him. She clasped him tight, her cheek against his shoulder. All the world was nothing compared to this, she thought. Even what he had said was a blur in her mind; only the fact that she was holding him in her arms had any meaning. For these brief moments up the empty village street past the little cottages, down the rutted road to the manor house she would never forget as long as she lived; it was true, what Anthony said, that life was not, could not be a doomed tread to death but the wonder and joy of love and the astonishing beauty of the earth and the seasons, and like a miracle it was all hers tonight. She laid her lips against the rough woolen of his jacket, bestowing her kisses on the rough cloth, her clasped hands hugged him tight.

Edward drew rein and she felt Hastings lift her down. Edward slid down beside her and took her in his arms. "I can't come in," he whispered. Hastings turned his back and Edward wrapped his arms around her and kissed her.

The world turned upside down. They spoke the words all lovers speak, bits of sentences, hurried, because there was so little time.

"May first," Edward said. "I shall write."

"I love you," Elizabeth answered.

"Burn my letters. Promise me." He tipped up her head with his fingers so he could look into her eyes. "Say, I promise to burn—"

"I promise to burn—" she repeated.

"The letters."

"The letters."

"There will not be many. I'll manage to send word through others. It has to be done this way, Bessie. I would not do it otherwise—in secret. But I must."

"We shouldn't do it," she cried suddenly.

"Yes, we should. It is right."

"You should have a Princess."

"With bad teeth and an insane sister?"

He smiled down at her, his eyes brilliant. "Bessie, Bessie," he said. "I need you, sweetheart, I need you very much. *Ergo* the realm needs you, you in your health and beauty and youth and good, sturdy English stock. Bessie, I love you very much but I wouldn't marry you if I thought we wouldn't have children. Kiss me, sweetheart, I have to leave."

Hastings still had his back turned. He was shivering with cold and it was getting dark. He felt Edward's hand on his shoulder and he turned to see Elizabeth running toward the manor house; when she almost gained it she whirled around for a last look. Both men were mounted; Edward waved and then in the gathering night both horsemen disappeared and she stood there peering down the black lane, wondering whether they had come at all or whether it was a dream. Then of course she knew it was not and that on the first of May she would be wed secret to the King.

Chapter 7

It was the New Year. Like all very busy men Edward combined his New Year greeting to his mother and the great matter of his marriage. The Duchess was at Fotheringhay and there Edward sought her, sending ahead of him a gift of ten tuns of Gascon wine for her delectation and some beautiful velvet from the royal wardrobe for her and for Margaret and his two younger brothers and some gifts of jewelry, including two fine ruby rings.

Proud Cis, as both her friends and enemies called her, had indeed a throne room at Fotheringhay, and when Edward entered the room his mother was standing to one side of it alone.

Edward approached his mother, a small smile on his face. "Do I sit there or do you, madam?" he asked.

"Oh, Edward," she said; Cecily Neville never quite knew how to take Edward's humor; in fact she didn't know where it came from. George and Margaret were both so charming and handsome that everyone liked them and Richard had no sense of humor at all; at eleven he was serious and intense. But none of them had Edward's sly humor and her husband hadn't either.

The Duchess sighed a bit as she surveyed her oldest son, her eyes bright with her admiration and her love. Edward smiled back. "Sit down, Mother," he said. "I've something very important to tell you and you'd best be seated. Climb up on your throne and pass judgment on your unruly subject, because what I've got to say won't be to your liking. Now sit down—" The Duchess arranged her skirts, eying him apprehensively, still now, and Edward continued. "I'm going to get myself married, Mother, on the first of May and to the Lady Grey."

The Duchess truly thought she would faint. The whole room reeled around the tall standing figure of her son, the King. She grasped the arms of her chair and her mouth fell open; then her mind took hold of what he had said and she blurted, "You're teasing me!"

There was silence. The Duchess grasped the chair tighter. "Edward!" she cried. "Oh, Edward!"

He didn't answer her; he looked faintly amused as at the antics of a child. The Duchess then grew angry; hot, bitter rage poured through her and she set her teeth. "You must be mad! You have lost your mind over a woman. It's disgraceful, Edward. Are you crazy?"

"Crafty maybe, madam, but not crazy."

He glanced toward the heavy doors; they were tight shut. But, "Lower your voice, Mother. There might be pricked ears outside."

"Edward," the Duchess said, leaning forward and lowering her voice but speaking each word slow and distinct, "never in the history of the realm has a monarch married a poor widow. Never! Therefore I think you are mad. Never before has a King of England married any but a Princess!"

"Then it's time for a change," Edward said. "A long, overdue change."

"I can't believe you're saying this." And she couldn't.

Edward sighed a little. "Mother," he said, "a few months ago Warwick seriously offered my hand, such as it is, to Mary of Guelders, the Queen Mother of the Scots, who was an aging bawd. Mercifully for me she just died. Two months ago it was suggested I wed the daughter of Louis XI. She is four years old. By God's most blessed lady, madam, do you all seriously expect me to entertain even the notion of either marriage? None of you have any idea of statecraft or of politics or of the world as it is today."

"You should marry a French Princess!" the Duchess cried.

"And then throw ten thousand English archers into the field to protect her lands? Mother, I have enough problems right here. The time for spending all our money and good English lives for a piece of war-trodden French provinces is past, forever past. A month ago the Pope asked for military help against the Turks. I prevaricated, pleading trouble in the realm, which was of course true. But I didn't say what was the truth: that no English soldier is going to fight the Turks. Not one! Because it is politically inexpedient and far too expensive. We can't afford it. When I fight France, Mother, it will not be for a province. It will be for political reasons or power or money. Not land. I've got enough right here."

"You are like a rich man who would marry his maiden for wanton dotage over her person. You should marry for state, for great possessions!"

"I have enough possessions to keep me very busy," Edward said, thinking of the Northumbrian castles he was on his way to recapture.

"A great Prince and a poor widow. 'Tis an unfitting thing. A blemish to your majesty, to the sacred majesty of a Prince, who ought to approach the priesthood in cleanliness and integrity and in dignity, to be defiled with bigamy and a wife who isn't a virgin!"

"Bigamy?" Edward frowned, then smiled. "As for the bigamy let the bishop lay it to my charge when I come to take orders—for I understand it is forbidden to a priest but I never knew it was forbidden to a Prince."

"This marriage," said the Duchess, "contains no alliance with other nations!"

"It is not unprofitable. I value the amity of no other nation to be so necessary for me than the friendship of my own. And it is more likely to bear me favor that I did not disdain to marry with one of my own land."

The Duchess was silent.

Edward said, "I am at a point in my mind, no matter what. It has taken me some time to reach it. I know myself out of your rule, but first if outward alliances are thought to be so necessary, so requisite, I will find other means than to marry where I do not love."

"But there are other fine English girls, then!"

"I doubt it not," Edward said. "Even others fully comparable—let them that like them marry them—no more is it reason that any man mislike that I marry where I wish. I want you to take this well. Surely when you speak of the sacred majesty of a Prince —marriage is spiritual. It ought to be made for the respect of God where His Grace inclines the two parties to love, as it is in my case."

His quiet tones could not have told her more plainly that he loved Elizabeth Woodville. The Duchess knotted her hands together.

"What of Warwick? He'll never forgive you!"

Edward's brown eyes looked as though they were trying to see into the future. "I am sure my cousin of Warwick loves me so little as to grudge that I love. Nor is it unreasonable that in a choice of wife I should be ruled by my eye instead of his, as though I were a ward bound to marry by the appointment of a guardian. I would not be a King under that condition to forbear my own liberty. The possibility of inheritance of other lands, which is what he advocates, is, as I've told you, occasion for more trouble than profit. We have already title to sufficient to keep well in one man's days." He spoke a bit ruefully.

"And a widow with children!"

"By God's most blessed lady, I am a bachelor and have some children too, and each of us has proof that neither of us is barren. Therefore, madam, I pray you be content. I trust to God that she shall bring forth a young Prince that shall please you."

But Edward's mother was a woman of such strong mind that she could not give in. "It is my duty to God," she said, "to call for Elizabeth Lucy, who has borne your children. If you promised her anything you may not marry!"

Edward's eyes suddenly glinted with anger. Then he feigned his usual good nature. It was perhaps as well. This marriage he intended must be legal. Any impediment, real or fancied, must be openly disposed of. Briefly he felt sorry for his discarded mistress but he would make it up to her. He said easily, "Yes. Call her, madam. Let her testify before her peers under solemn oath that I ensured or promised her anything." He bowed slightly. Then, because he was really a good-humored and good-natured person, he said, "Wait, Mother. Wait till Bessie presents you with a fine lusty Prince, squalling in his cradle. And, madam, I'll marry your daughter Margaret to the finest Prince in Europe!"

As he walked from his mother's presence Edward wrenched his mind from the thoughts of Bessie and instead reheard his own words: "We have title to sufficient land to keep us well in one man's days." For regardless of the kind way in which he had been treated, Somerset had defected and escaped into Northumberland to join the old King Henry at Bamborough Castle. At Durham the Duke was recognized and almost taken in bed but he escaped, barefoot and in his shirt. Edward confiscated all his castles, lands and titles and handed them over to his younger

brother Richard and placed extra guards around Somerset's
brother in the Tower. There was trouble on the Welsh borders
and constant trouble on the Scottish borders; despite the truce
with France, French and English seamen kept up with vigor their
running sea fights, to the detriment of trade. A French embassy
was on its way and Henry of Castile was sending a confidential
envoy to speak on private matters. In January Edward was so
pressed for time that he rode from Coventry to Worcester in
twenty-four hours. Nonetheless Elizabeth received the promised
letters; sometimes they purported to come from Anthony, but
they came. Elizabeth could see the smile lighting his eyes as he
wrote:

> Henry of Castile offered me the hand of his daughter Isabella.
> We decided finally after long thought to regret. But we were
> very polite in our refusal. We were able to turn down this offer
> with the free consent of our cousin the Earl of Warwick because
> he had got it in his mind I should marry the sister-in-law of King
> Louis. We pointed out mildly that our subjects wouldn't like it—
> the French alliance. The prettiest of the two sisters is named
> Bona. Can you imagine me married to a woman named Goodie?

Elizabeth smiled. Sitting before the fire, her stool pulled close
to the hearth, she memorized the words. "Good night my own
sweetheart. I dream of the nights when I shall find peace in your
arms."

Gently she laid the letter on the flames; the torn pieces flared
up briefly. And the winter days passed.

The letters continued.

> We are carrying on negotiations with the Hanse towns and the
> Master of Prussia; today two envoys were appointed to repre-
> sent us. The negotiations with Scotland are proceeding satisfac-
> torily, but there is so much unrest in the north I have sent
> Montagu with troops to escort and protect the Scottish ambas-
> sadors. Today I signed the treaty of peace on the sea with
> France. Do not forget your promise: Remember what you said;
> repeat after me, I promise to burn all your letters.
>
> Today is the fifth of April and I can hardly believe it. Today
> we empowered Warwick and Montagu to treat with the Scots
> for perpetual peace, but the French ambassador is still here and
> I may keep Warwick in London for a while longer. Now for the
> plans; it is mandatory that there be witnesses not of your family.
> It is our wish that Father William perform the ceremony; don't

you know two gentlewomen whom you could trust? They should attend you. Then perhaps one of the boys of the priest's choir to assist in the singing. Your mother present too, of course. I shall arrive alone just before dawn. I shall be able to stay only a few hours. To celebrate May Day with you. Although I am not an expert on the subject, my studies have convinced me that early morning is most felicitous for making love. We'll see what you think. My most precious subject, good night. By the time you receive this it will be less than three weeks before we will kneel together to take our vows. I love you. Edward R.

It was the last letter. She pressed it to her cheek. She took out pen and paper. Carefully she copied down Edward's instructions, for of late she had been unable to remember anything; unseeing, she bumped into furniture and forgot to eat. So she copied down the few orders and folded them neatly in a small wad, then she put her hands over her face and murmured his name into her palms. Anthony, who was home briefly before going north with Montagu's troops, found her thus.

"What's the matter, Bess?" he asked worriedly. She was so thin.

She removed her hands from her face and mumbled, "Nothing's the matter, Anthony. I'm so happy!"

He looked so astonished that she laughed and he thought she was hysterical. Clumsily he patted her shoulder and she took his hand in hers. "Oh, Anthony," she cried. "I love you!"

"I love you too, Bess," he said, embarrassed. "But I worry about you. I'm going to speak to Mother about you."

He did and he found his mother strangely unsympathetic. But she nodded her head when he said Bessie looked thin as a wand and tense.

"Yes," said the Duchess. "I think she doesn't get enough sleep. The carpenters are coming today. From the village. They are going to build a separate chamber for Bessie, with fine paneling. She is too old for sleeping in the room with her sisters."

Anthony said, "Mother, the trouble is deeper than that. She needs a husband."

"She is perfectly happy, Anthony."

"You're so stubborn, Mother!"

"I know what I'm doing," the Duchess said. "When do you leave?" Anthony stared at her. Usually she wanted to keep him at home as long as possible. He said, "What's the matter with you and Bess?"

"There's nothing the matter with either of us," the Duchess said, wishing desperately she could take Anthony into her confidence. For a moment she almost blurted out the truth. "It's spring and almost May!" She ran from the room leaving Anthony in bewilderment.

"I don't know what's wrong with the women in this household," he said to his father, "but they certainly aren't normal."

"They're just women," Lord Rivers said. "With all your junketing about you have no family life, Anthony. What we all need is a wife for His Grace—all you gentlemen of the bedchamber might as well not be married. And there is criticism of the loose living."

"His Grace is only a man," Anthony said. He didn't add that in Edward's intimate circle the subject of his marriage was not brought up anymore because Edward obviously didn't want it discussed.

"The most important thing now, Father, is to catch Somerset and old King Henry. While the former, so-called King remains at Bamborough or anywhere in the north there will be rebellions and fomentings in the realm."

The next day Anthony rode off; it was a beautiful April day and Lord Rivers rode out himself to inspect his lands because the sound of the hammering and sawing of the carpenters making the new room for Bessie rasped on his ears.

On the twenty-fifth of April Edward gave instructions to the Archbishop of Canterbury to prorogue Parliament till the twenty-sixth of November and three days later he left London. At St. Albans he spent two nights with Abbot Whethamstede, where he made his confessions and asked the abbot to help him pray for guidance and wisdom. Edward reached Stony Stratford on the thirtieth of April and went to bed.

At Grafton the Duchess said good night to Elizabeth Ovedale and Joanna Norries; they were sleeping in Elizabeth's curtained alcove. Then the Duchess cast another glance at the rest of her sleeping daughters and hastened from the room. The manor gates were closed and the house was dark. In the faint night light from the Duchess' bedroom she and Elizabeth carried down the Duchess' *prie-dieu* and set it up in the Duchess' small anteroom off the big hall. In there they dared to light a single rush.

"I could hear Richard snoring," the Duchess whispered to comfort her daughter, for the thing they dreaded most was the sound of Lord Rivers' footsteps and his astonished questions should they be discovered.

"I feel like a thief," Elizabeth whispered.

"Aye, and others will call you thief for stealing the richest prize in the realm," the Duchess said. "You have a hard way to tread that will be immensely difficult, Bess. I pray God you shall be able to do it."

"I love him," she said.

She looked about the small room. She had gathered flowers and the branches of green and branches of flowering shrubs and apples and cherries. The Duchess and she moved the chest from against the wall and set it behind the *prie-dieu* where Father William would stand, and from it they took two pillows and set them on the floor, and on the chest they banked the branches and on the floor too to make a circle of flowers around the improvised altar.

The tall, white wax candles were ready to be lighted in the darkness before dawn. The floor was strewn with fresh-gathered rush; the room smelled like the fields of England in the spring.

"Now you must go to bed," the Duchess said. "Only, my Bessie, do not forget your prayers."

Elizabeth swallowed. She went down on one knee before her mother.

"Bless me, Mother," she said. "Please."

The rushlight flickered. The Duchess placed her ringed hand on her daughter's bright head. "May you carry your husband's love and God's love all the rest of your life, I pray to God, Elizabeth."

The two women embraced. Silently the Duchess and Bessie left the now dark room and crept up the stairway. Bessie entered her new room; the floor was touched with moonlight; here too the rushes were sweet-smelling and fresh laid. The finest, newest linen sheets were on the bed; the Duchess had just finished supervising its curtains and the pillows smelled of lavender.

Elizabeth knelt beside the bed and said her prayers; then for the first time she prayed for her unborn children and for the realm as though, already, without her knowing it, the ermine mantle had fallen upon her. So she closed her eyes and thought of Edward. Did he sleep?

At three o'clock Father William dressed and went to waken the young boy with the clearest voice and the steadiest blue eyes, who had slept in the priest's house that night. When the boy was dressed Father William carefully placed the folded, just-washed choir robe under his own robe, set the boy upon his mare, mounted himself and in the moonlight the gentle horse ambled slowly toward Grafton.

At four Edward roused the sleeping Hastings and said irritably that he couldn't sleep. He commanded to be shaved and Hastings went on slippered feet to waken a body servant. At four thirty, alone, dressed in hunting costume, Edward rode out toward Whittlebury forest to hunt, his big bow slung across his back, and still very irritable, thought Hastings who wanted to follow him but didn't dare. With a sigh Hastings went back to bed but not to sleep.

At four Elizabeth was getting dressed. It was not possible to wear white, but she had chosen a piece of creamy ivory silk that the Duchess had tucked away; Joanna Norries was helping her, a Joanna now trembling with excitement so she could hardly help Elizabeth; her fingers were all thumbs, she whispered, for above all none of them must rouse the house, least of all Lord Rivers.

"A secret wedding," Joanna whispered. She did not yet know the identity of the bridegroom.

"Yes, and you must promise not to breathe a word of it, Jo." Elizabeth whispered back.

Elizabeth Ovedale was downstairs helping the Duchess light the candles, the priest had arrived and the choirboy in his robe stood yawning, watching the two women flutter about the small room like moths.

Father William had cautiously let himself out the door and was waiting for Edward. He strained his eyes to peer through the darkness; he strained his ears to listen for the sound of a horse. He heard nothing. Anxious, the thought crossed his mind that perhaps Edward would not come. Father William had just fetched a long sigh when he saw Edward's tall figure approaching on foot. Father William hurried to meet him.

"I left my horse down the lane," Edward whispered.

Together the two men entered the house and Father William guided Edward to the Duchess' anteroom in the dark house. The floors creaked with Edward's weight even though he went on tiptoe. Within the room the four women waited: the Duchess, the two gentlewomen to attend and witness, Elizabeth; the choirboy was still stifling his yawns.

Elizabeth heard Edward's step. Then the door opened; he stood for a moment on the threshold with Father William hovering behind. For a single moment no one moved. Then Joanna Norries and Elizabeth Ovedale, realizing suddenly who stood in the doorway, grasped hastily at their skirts to make a curtsy. Joanna turned her ankle, the Duchess bowed and the choirboy gaped. Elizabeth moved slowly toward Edward; Father William closed the door. The Duchess' eyes caught the look that passed between her daughter and the King. "They love each other," she told herself. "It will be well."

But there was need for haste. Father William went to the altar, Elizabeth and Edward stood before him. The Duchess bolted the door. The ceremony began. The words swam around the Duchess' ears. "We are gathered together here in the sight of God. . . ." Then "I, Edward, take thee, Elizabeth, to be my wedded wife. . . ."

Edward's tones were firm and clear. Elizabeth's were unsteady. "I, Elizabeth, take thee, Edward . . ." They were kneeling now and the Duchess wiped her eyes; the sweet tones of the boy's voice filled the little room as he helped Father William sing. Elizabeth's head was bent; the candles burned so brightly over the heads of the kneeling bride and groom as though they were lighting their way to heaven, the Duchess thought, wiping her eyes again.

Then suddenly Edward and Elizabeth rose; the King took her lightly in his arms and kissed her; then he with his fingers wiped away the tears from her cheeks. She gave him a tremulous smile; he tucked her hand in his arm and turned to face the little company.

They bowed, but the King went to the Duchess and lifted her up and kissed her and each of the other two ladies, smiling; his affable self, he shook hands with Father William, patted the choirboy on the shoulder and gave Father William a pouch of gold coins. "For the church," Edward added, "and one for the boy."

He himself poured the wine, for the Duchess' hands were shaking; Joanna handed it about and Edward raised his cup.

"To my bride."

The Duchess recovered herself and passed the plate of wafers. Elizabeth looked at them as if they would choke her. "I cannot, Mother," she said.

Edward grinned and slipped his arm around her. He finished his wine and put down the cup. He took her hand and they went to the door, which he unlocked. Then, hand-in-hand, they went down the small hallway. Joanna grasped a handful of blossoms and ran after them and threw the flowers; they scattered lightly over Elizabeth's shoulders. She turned and smiled. Still hand-in-hand they mounted the steps. Joanna sighed and went back into the little room to help the Duchess straighten up and to say good-bye to Father William. Then the Duchess took the two girls back upstairs to bed again.

At ten o'clock Hastings saw the King come riding into the courtyard. His irritability was gone, Hastings noted with relief, but Edward said little, only that he was fatigued. Hastings got him into bed and Edward waved him out. Hastings gave a last look and saw the dark eyes close. Hastings waited for four hours while Edward slept; then he heard the familiar voice call out, and taking an attendant with him Hastings returned to the King's chamber. An hour later the whole of the men with Edward were mounted and on their way to Northampton. Commissions of array had been issued to thirty-two southern counties, and the men were to join Edward at Leicester where he arrived on May third.

At Grafton the Duchess explained to Lord Rivers that Elizabeth was not well.

Anthony had already gone north with Lord Montagu, Warwick's stalwart brother. Anthony knew how important it was to Edward that he meet with the Scottish ambassadors, and Montagu had been sent north to escort them. On the fourteenth of May Montagu, learning that Somerset and his forces were nearby, attacked their camp with such vigor that the rout was complete, Somerset and his followers caught, swiftly tried by Worcester, the Lord Constable, and condemned to death for treason. But the old King escaped. All Montagu found was his cap, garnished with two crowns and fret with pearls and rich stones. Montagu and Anthony delivered it to Edward at York. In gratitude Edward created Montagu the Earl of Northumberland in the palace at York. But there were still the great castles to deliver again to the King, so Anthony and Montagu turned about again and with some fresh troops and the King's great guns trundling, they hastened back to Northumberland. Edward went to attend the diocesan synods at Doncaster.

The Pope was planning to set forth on a crusade against the Turks and he had sent out papal bulls levying a tenth on the clergy of every land. Edward had refused to permit the papal bulls to be published in England, for it would set a dangerous precedent. Nonetheless politically he had to make some concession since the Christian world would look askance if he did nothing. He had puzzled a time over this and finally decided that he would speak with the synod himself and instruct that the tenth could be levied, but it would be payable to himself, the King, in the interests of the crusade. This way he himself could direct the use of the money should it be needed; perhaps it wouldn't. On the third of June he ratified the peace with the Scots, and it was to endure for fifteen years.

On the twenty-third of June Alnwick surrendered and the next day Dunstanborough. Anthony and Montagu wasted no time and on the twenty-fifth were before Bamborough and the rebellious Lord Grey, whom Edward had pardoned the year before and who now defied him behind the embattled walls of Bamborough.

Edward had issued an ultimatum to be given Grey, and Anthony sent two heralds to the castle with it. The King wanted the castle, he wanted it surrendered, and if the great guns had to be fired at it Edward would have a head for every shot, starting with the head of Grey himself. The heralds returned with answer that Grey would fight to the death.

So the great guns of the King, Newcastle, London and Dijon, were hauled into position and fired. But before much destruction was accomplished, a chance shot plowed into the walls of Grey's own chamber, the stones flew into the sea and Grey lay as though dead. Hastily Humphrey Neville, second in command, sent out a herald to surrender the castle, bargaining for pardon for everyone in it except Grey.

Montagu and Anthony eagerly accepted, knowing Edward wanted the castle more than the lives of the men in it. But when they entered it Anthony ran up to Grey's chamber, where he lay, stepped over Grey's recumbent body and looked out of the massive hole down toward the rocks and the angry sea. The wind blew into the room as though Anthony were standing outside on the cliff. He turned and looked down at Grey, who stirred then. Quickly Anthony stepped to his side and drew his heavy dagger from its sheath; then he went to the door and shouted for help. He wanted very much to bring Grey to the King.

They brought the wounded Grey to Doncaster, to Edward, and there brought him to trial. Again the Earl of Worcester presided. Worcester said, "You have brought arms against the King, who trusted you with the keeping of his castles. You have betrayed John Ashley, who was your brother Knight of the Garter, and he is now a prisoner of the French and I warn you you must now be prepared to die. But because the King's Grace remembers your grandfather, who suffered for His Grace's predecessors, you shall not be stripped of your knighthood and the loss of your arms or your noblesse."

Grey was beheaded on July tenth but neither the King nor Anthony witnessed the execution. Edward was attending the synod and he had sent Anthony home to Grafton. And now that Northumberland had been made safe for the second time and the synod satisfactorily concluded with a levy of sixpence coming into Edward's own pockets, other troubles rose to haunt him. He was worried about London where the plague was raging—two hundred deaths a day were reported to him; Louis of France was urging him to send ambassadors of high rank to the Diet at St. Omer; the state of the currency was unsound—there was not enough bullion. He could not go to London so he went to Stamford and called a meeting of his council to consider the state of the currency.

Anthony arrived at Grafton in the middle of July, bearing a letter from Edward to Elizabeth. He delivered it somewhat diffidently. As he gave it to her he searched her face and it told him a good deal. Rumors had been flying about the country for a month, all kinds of rumors. The King was wed. There had been a wedding. In a village a very tall handsome lord had given a boy a gold piece and the boy had helped at a secret wedding. Was that very tall great lord the King? Why did the King turn aside all offers of marriage to foreign Princesses? Why, why did he adamantly refuse to listen to Warwick who wanted him to marry?

Elizabeth took the letter and bore it out of the room. Anthony watched her go with sharp eyes. Later he ambled up to find his mother; she was with the seamstresses and upon a long trestle table was laid out richly gleaming brocade worth a fortune, Anthony thought. "Where did that come from?" he asked.

The Duchess cleared her throat. "What are you doing here, Anthony?" she asked.

"Don't be petulant, Mother. I'm snooping. I'm going to ask you again where that cloth came from."

"I bought it," the Duchess said.

"Where?" asked Anthony doggedly.

"Why where do I buy cloth? In London of course."

Anthony said slowly, "You've not been to London and no one has come from London to my knowledge. I'm going to ask you once more, Mother. That cloth came from the royal wardrobe, didn't it?"

The Duchess dropped her scissors. Anthony leaned down and picked them up. He found Elizabeth in the garden. It was a hot day; August was approaching and the smell of new-mown hay was in the sweet air. He sat down on the bench alongside of his sister and he said bluntly, "Bess, are you the King's mistress or his wife?" He bit his lip; he was thinking what Warwick and all the Nevilles would do and think and say and how bitterly angry they would be if the latter were true.

Elizabeth closed her eyes to capture the picture of Edward plain. What he had said on their wedding morning was far too precious to share. "I need you, Bessie, and I shall not surrender you. I want us to live together like other folk and to keep our family with us like plain people. Do not be afraid, Bessie. How can you be afraid when you have me?"

And she had promised him. She rose and faced her brother. "Anthony, you are a fool. His Grace has been pursuing me for months. He has made me presents. But as yet I am not his mistress and that is all.

"It is," Elizabeth concluded icily, "entirely my affair, not yours!"

She suddenly swished off from him and he was impelled to laughter.

"Don't trip, Bess," he shouted after her. He pushed the

haughty Earl of Warwick out of his mind and made his way out to the kennels to see the new litter of puppies his favorite hound had presented him with. Sitting there on the straw with the puppies crawling over him he forgot about Bessie and Edward and the Earl of Warwick.

Edward was at Stamford. His council was attending him there. On August twelfth he went to Ludlow Castle and summoned the council to meet him in Reading on September fourteenth to further discuss the scarcity of bullion which was troubling the currency. The obvious solution was to devalue the pound, the noble, the shilling, but how to do it without raising a storm of protest? He proclaimed publicly that he himself would listen to all complaints and all possible solutions in Reading in September.

Anthony read and hunted and sat on the manor court and for a full month he knew the joys of life in the summer on the manor. The harvest had been so rich and plentiful that Anthony was afraid that the poor villagers wouldn't have time to harvest their own strips and virgates, so he organized even his sisters to help, and Elizabeth stood in line and handed out the cotton, homespun gloves to the harvesters. But by the end of August he was getting restless. He felt out of touch; he longed to hear Edward's voice, even raised in anger, and Hastings' bray of laughter and even Warwick's gruff commands. He'd even rather be fighting with Montagu. But the country was at peace and only Will Herbert was fighting at Harlech, the one lonely castle that defied the King. He was worried. Had he lost favor with Edward? Had some of his enemies at court imputed any disloyalty to him? There were still many of Edward's gentlemen of the chamber, for instance, who never forgot that he, Anthony, had been an ardent Lancastrian and had fought against the Yorkists on that Palm Sunday that seemed so long ago. So it was with relief that on the first of September a royal messenger was ushered into Anthony's presence; he took the proffered letter, a big smile on his face. Before opening it he bade the liveried wearer to seek refreshment for himself and his horse. Then taking his dagger he slit the seal and opened the paper.

He read quickly. Then he read the letter again. It lay on his lap; he lifted his eyes from it, perceived a servant and snapped, "Advise the Lady Grey I wish to see her immediately!"

He heard Bessie running light steps on the stairs. She came
flying into the room and wordlessly he rose and handed her
Edward's letter. Anthony read it quickly too. Then she too read
it again. What Edward had written was engraved in Anthony's
brain.

> It is our wish that you escort our entirely well-beloved wife,
> our Queen, your sister, to our palace at Reading on the four-
> teenth of September. There will be further advices from us; until
> such time these messages are in strictest confidence between you
> and us. Edward R.

Anthony thought crazily, I am Edward's brother-in-law. Then
he thought, My God, I shall be surrounded by a sea of envy.
Then he said, "Bessie!" She was standing straight in all her wonderful beauty, her face was radiant, her great eyes gleamed. In
a fine burst of romance and knightly spirit Anthony dropped to
one knee. His sister was his Queen.

"Your Grace," he mumbled.

Elizabeth said crisply, "Please rise, Anthony. In the privacy
of our chambers we behave as we wish." She realized she was
quoting Edward and she smiled dazzlingly, her eyes glinted with
humor.

She told him then the whole story of the May morning. Lord
Rivers came in and saw them across the room, their heads together, talking as though they were still children. He smiled
across at them fondly while Elizabeth whispered, "Don't tell
Father yet."

But on the twelfth of September Edward sent another letter
and an additional escort for his Queen. It was morning. The
Duchess spoke with her husband and in an hour from the front
door of the manor filed the Woodvilles; Lord Rivers and the
Duchess, Anthony, Kate and Anne and Margaret and John and
Richard and Lionel. Edward and four younger girls were left
at home.

In front of the manor waited Anthony's and Lord Rivers' personal retainers, body servants, carts with boxes and chests of
clothes, bright painted and their wheels rimmed with steel.
Ahorse and ready, brave in their livery with the collars embroidered with the suns and roses of York, the King's retainers
waited while out of the manor doors came Elizabeth Woodville.

She was dressed in a green-velvet riding dress. Her gilt hair

flowed like a long tail from her high, coifed hat. Anthony
stepped forward, bowed and helped her up into the saddle. The
King's men filed into place about her, their eyes bright with admiration. Then they trotted down the rutted lane.

Elizabeth guided her horse easily over the familiar ruts and
holes. Ahead of her blew two banners with the royal crests. She
followed them, her heart high. Behind her came her family. She
was leading them to Edward.

Edward's council always met early in the morning. On the
fourteenth of September the council had been sitting for three
hours and it was now ten o'clock. At the head of the table Edward lounged in his chair, his long legs stretched out sideways.

"Then, my lords," Edward said, "my lord of Warwick and Lord
Wenlock leave for France, for St. Omer in a few days."

John Say cleared his throat. "Your Grace," he began and
stopped; he looked about the table for assurance. "Your Grace,
your subjects have long wondered why you do not marry."

Edward smiled at John Say; he was the Speaker of the Commons and Edward liked him. "And they fear I am not chaste."

"Aye, Your Grace," Say said and the other members of the
council all nodded, and now that Edward seemed willing to discuss the subject they pressed their point.

"Since my lord of Warwick journeys so soon to France and since
the King will offer Your Grace an honorable marriage, would it
not be wise for Your Grace to empower the Earl to discuss a
marriage contract?"

Edward said slowly, "We are not at all sure that a French
marriage would be welcome to our subjects. Think you what
trouble has ensued with the last two Princesses of France; it was
our misfortune that they graced or disgraced our land." A faint
smile touched his lips as he surveyed his council. He was right,
he was sure, but how many of them had Warwick influenced?
And how much influence did King Louis hold over the doughty
Earl? Louis was like a spider—his arms were long and his
flattery insidious.

There was a general murmur of both assent and dissent and
Edward cut it short. "I grant you," he said, "that we should
marry."

Smiles now greeted him. Chairs were pushed back or pulled

in as each man wanted to speak. Edward motioned to the Earl of Worcester, Grand Constable of England and a close companion.

"It is our view, Your Grace," Tiptoft said, "that Your Grace should consider the Bourbon Princess, niece of Philip of Burgundy."

Edward looked noncommittal and so it was the signal for those who sided with Warwick to push once more the subject of King Louis' sister-in-law, Bona of Savoy.

But what of Isabella of Castile? She had some champions among Edward's council. Tongue in cheek he let them go on. The conversation waxed heated. There was even a banging on the table by one of Warwick's loudest supporters.

But Worcester was eying his King oddly. What was Edward up to? There was an Italianate side to Edward that few of his lords ever saw; Worcester thought, Is he having fun at their expense? He himself didn't mind; he enjoyed Edward's humor and he was utterly ready to acknowledge Edward as his liege lord and to abide by his decisions. He sighed, watched Edward and finally realized that he had been right, that now Edward was going to put a stop to this and say something important.

"What," said Edward softly, "of a good English wife? Let it not be said that we disdain to marry our own countrywomen."

There was a silence. Somehow Edward communicated to his council that he wished no answer. He laid his big hand on the table; the sleeves of his white shirt fell back to reveal his heavy wrist. "Gentlemen," he said, "we shall allay your fears."

In the quiet that followed, Tiptoft wondered whether Edward had been driven into a corner by his council or whether he had dallied with them on purpose. He wet his lips and heard Edward say, "My lords and gentlemen, I am already married."

There was a gasp; only Worcester and a very few others felt no astonishment. "If you have heard rumors," Edward continued easily, "they were true. I have chosen my bride, my Queen." Then he made some concession. "After long and serious thought and prayer I have so chosen." His grave brown eyes surveyed them closely, studying the faces. "Our Queen is English."

Now the Earl of Northumberland, Montagu, Warwick's brother, leaned forward and asked the question. "But her name, Your Grace? Of whose blood?"

"Her name?" Edward's stern face gave warning. "Your Queen," he said, "is Elizabeth Woodville, daughter to the Duchess of Bedford, niece through her mother's blood of the Prince Jacques of Luxembourg and le Comte de St. Pol, the Lady Elizabeth Grey, widow of Lord Ferrers of Groby, my dearly beloved wife, our Queen."

Carefully and with craft that was well hid Edward's keen eyes evaluated each man's face and registered his reaction for further analysis. There he saw astonishment, dismay, disgust, apprehension, a glint of approval and complete and total anger. To the disgust and to the anger he spoke, letting his eyes rest on each in turn. And he said only, "Such, gentlemen, is my good pleasure."

With that warning he rose to his towering height, necessitating a quick rise on the part of each of the council. Worcester said, "Your Grace, allow us to proffer our congratulations and our deep wishes of goodwill and love to our Queen."

"Aye, aye," they chorused, grateful to Worcester for remembering to do what some of them had forgot in the stress of the occasion. For some, even with goodwill, were stunned. Their King had wed with a poor widow! With two children! Such a thing had never, never happened before in the history of the realm, nay in any realm!

It's a new age, Worcester was thinking; in Italy all the force of the new flowering of the Greek classics and of the ancient writings had been welcomed by his eager mind. It's a new age when men can step onto new paths, untraveled roads; the break with tradition has to come; why isn't it best to come in the person of the King himself? Who else can better lead us? His rapid mind had already evaluated Edward's reasons; each of the foreign marriages had deep disadvantages—even Isabella of Castile was offered by her uncle, Henry the Impotent; Henry's nickname made Worcester shudder. He came up to Edward who, knowing his affection and admiration, put his arm familiarly about his shoulder and the two men left the council chamber together.

She should be here, Edward was thinking; she should be here. His own chambers overlooked the courtyard and he walked to the narrow window and looked out.

There was nothing to be seen but the usual coming and going of retainers, their lords, scurrying messengers in all kinds of liveries, two carters delivering from the bakery and the green grocer. Edward turned from the window. The two men were silent and thoughtful. Edward was thinking that his marriage announcement would separate his true subjects from his potential evil willers; there would be those who would resist and even desert him; when he had told his mother that he did not think that Warwick would begrudge him, Edward, his choice of a wife he had not been entirely truthful. Warwick would resist but how much? Edward could hear his own voice saying to Cecily, "I am not Earl Warwick's ward, Mother, to marry where he wishes. I should not be a King under that condition."

It was true that he owed much to Warwick and his swarming relatives, brothers, cousins and nephews. They had fought for him faithfully in the north. But on the other side of the coin did they not owe him such service? They had been amply rewarded; if, in fact, they wanted the reward to be the actual grasp on the tiller while he, Edward, at the helm but obeyed their orders, then he was afraid they were much mistaken, for it was he who stood on the quarterdeck issuing the commands and not they. He hoped it would be not too difficult a lesson for them to learn, and he used the proper nomenclature—them. There were many Nevilles and many Neville supporters. He thought ruefully, I am well-nigh smothered in Nevilles. And as far as the gaining of the crown itself, he had done that himself. For it was he and he alone who had gained the victory at Mortimer's Cross and Warwick who had failed at St. Albans. He, Edward, who had won at Towton and not Warwick.

Worcester was thinking almost the same thoughts as Edward. For although he had served under the Lancastrian Henry, he was now utterly committed to Edward and would serve him to the end of his life. Only as the days passed could they see more clearly into the future. Now all seemed fairly cloudy, all but one thing. For there was a disturbance in the court below and the street was suddenly filled with people following after Elizabeth's little procession. From the window Edward saw her. He sighed and he turned to Worcester.

He said simply, "I love her, Jack."

Chapter 8

EDWARD WAS determined to do things right, as he considered them. He sent his Bessie immediately to the monastery at Reading. He sent royal messengers riding throughout the realm, advising them that their Queen would be presented to them on Michaelmas Day in the chapel at Reading. And during the next two weeks he sat with his council every day as usual; the matter of the currency occupied his mind; so many protests had been lodged against the bringing of old coinage to be newly coined that he ordered new coins to be struck and made Lord Hastings, who was Keeper of the Mint, the man responsible for the whole operation. The new noble gold would be stamped with the rose of York to be worth ten shillings, the half noble worth five. And exchanges could be made at Coventry, Bristol and Norwich, besides of course the mint at the Tower of London.

By the twenty-eighth of September Reading was thronged with the curious, the nobility and members of the royal family. On that night Edward slipped away and joined the Woodvilles at the monastery. When he entered the room Lord Rivers and Anthony were talking earnestly with little Lionel who had arrived for the occasion; Richard and John were playing cards. On seeing their guest all five rose hastily and John dropped the cards; they spilled at Edward's feet and with a muttered oath John leaned down to pick them up.

"Bess's in the chapel, Your Grace," he blurted.

But at that moment the door opened behind Edward and the Woodville women filed in: the Duchess first, then Elizabeth, then young Kate, Margaret and Anne. When they saw Edward they all curtsied, all except Elizabeth; all she could do was to hold out her hands to him.

Edward led her to a bench, seating her on it and sitting down himself. He took both her hands in his big one, slipped his arm around her and pulled her close to him.

"Bessie, Bessie," he said low.

The ceremony on the morrow was all arranged. The King would be seated at the head of the chapel and she, Bessie, escorted by the Earl of Warwick on one side and the Duke of Clarence, Edward's young brother, on the other, she, Elizabeth Woodville, would have to walk down that long aisle to Edward while everyone looked on and take her place beside him.

Edward looked down at the hands he held, her long slender fingers wearing the great ruby ring he had given her on May first, her beautiful hands which her great granddaughter Elizabeth would inherit and pride. On cushions at her feet sat her three sisters, so lovely in their youth; the Woodville men stood each a little different yet obviously stamped as brothers: Anthony with his ascetic bearing; Richard who looked like his father; and John with the flamboyance of his French blood, a touch of cynical humor in his eyes and mouth, John, the opportunist; and young Lionel, the intellectual, whose steady brown eyes regarded his King with such open and unavowed admiration that Edward felt already a brotherly fondness for him. Edward smiled at him.

"Why aren't you in school?" he asked.

Lionel said, "I have been doing so well in my studies, Your Grace, that my preceptor permitted me to come to Reading."

Anthony laughed. "Tell His Grace what you told me, Lionel."

Lionel then explained in Latin with no hesitation; the Duchess' eyes gleamed with pride and Lionel smiled nervously at the King's open approval.

Lionel ended, "If there is any service I could ever perform for Your Grace, I should be honored."

Lord Rivers said, "Lionel speaks for all of us, Your Grace."

Edward thanked Lionel. The thought flashed through his mind that they were not that unbearable of breeds the sycophants but that they manifested openly a real loyalty and respect. And he liked them. He felt at ease with them. They were gay and young and full of fun. They were a heady mixture, like fine French wine, and they had the assurance that comes along with a big family, close-knit and standing foursquare against the world. It was that perhaps, Edward thought, which kept them from showing any signs of servility, although many people were going to dub it arrogance. Deliberately he kept himself from thinking about Bessie who sat still in the curve of his arm; tomorrow their honeymoon would begin here in the monastery at Reading. He rose, then he told the Duchess to take care of Bessie.

Edward was well satisfied. The problem of both the silver and gold currency had been settled, and searchers were armed with warrants at every port to prevent the smuggling of bullion out of the country. The truce with Scotland had been signed and Edward's most competent spy, or, as he called him, agent, was operating in Scotland in an attempt to drive from cover the old King Henry. Henry's most ardent supporter in Scotland had been Bishop Kennedy, but since the Bishop had now resigned himself to the new King of England and was even on Edward's payroll now, having accepted money, Edward was sure that soon Henry would be turned up by one of the agents operating in the northern counties.

The alliance with Burgundy prospered. Brittany was friendly. King Louis wove this way and that like the suave spider he was. Watch him carefully and never underestimate him, Edward told himself. Denmark and the Hamburg wanted trade talks. English embassies were in Milan, Genoa and Venice. Edward's own factors, the three Italian merchants who handled his own shipping interests, had shipped and sold thousands of woolfells for him; the King's personal business was flourishing—he had even taken charge of some of his mother's trade. In a week Warwick's brother Montagu, the new Earl of Northumberland, would go north to continue the talks with the Scots so Warwick himself could go to York and prorogue Parliament until January. It was meeting in York and the King sent no reason to its members excusing his absence; he simply declared it was impossible for him to come to York. Edward turned over in his big bed and thought that tomorrow he would have his Bessie with him.

There are some women who are born with a natural flair for clothes and Elizabeth Woodville was one of them. She may have inherited it from her French mother, but where the Duchess had elegance and taste, Elizabeth, of medium height but with long, beautiful legs, had both elegance and chic. And like such endowed women she was to have it all her life. The likeness at Queen's College, painted at age fifty-three, shows her still slender, still beautiful, still elegant. But it is from the painting at the British Museum that we know what she wore that September morning.

She had hardly slept at all and wakened with the dawn. Kate and Margaret brushed and brushed her hair, helped her into the blue-satin petticoat. By nine they had been ready, her three sisters and Anthony's new wife, sweet, frail Beth Scales (a marriage the Duchess had arranged years ago and from which would come no children), and the two young women who had witnessed her marriage. Their gowns were high-waisted with robings and reverses of fur; they wore gilded Syrian caps, and their hair was passed through the top and floated behind them. They were to carry Bessie's train, three on each side and one behind.

Now they put Bessie into her dress. It was a golden brocade with a narrow garter-blue stripe alternating with the gold, a color worn only by royalty. Its bodice was tight and low, the sleeves long and tight, with robings of ermine across her shoulder. No wonder Anthony had gasped when he had seen the material.

The skirt was full with an ermine border; around her waist was a scarlet sash; around her neck was a pearl necklace; her slippers were satin and pointed. Her hair was smoothed back from her brow; it fell straight down her back to well below her waist and upon her head was set a crown with closed arches, its points finished by fleurs-de-lis. In the picture her hair is pale, pale, golden yellow.

The Duchess muttered extravagant phrases under her breath. There was no doubt that, although the Duchess adored every one of her thirteen children, this one was the most beautiful creature the Duchess had ever seen. She said, "The fame of your beauty will spread through every city in Europe."

It was the fashion then to pluck the brows so that the eyes commanded attention. Elizabeth's eyes looked like great gold-brown stars. And the reason her eyes gleamed so was partly apprehension, for since early morning while she bathed and dressed the whole abbey was stirring with the preparations for the feast of St. Michael, and the chapel was filling rapidly, and Elizabeth could imagine its solidly packed walls as the nobility, the landed gentry, the clergy squeezed in to behold this extraordinary spectacle in which she and Edward were to be the main participants. It was an unprecedented event.

It was ten o'clock. The abbey bells were tolling. Clear and sweet they rang. And Anthony knocked. The Duchess opened the door. She cast one more glance at her daughter. Then she said, "Do not forget, Elizabeth. The finest blood in France, aye, and in England flows in your veins."

Elizabeth knew she was referring to her father. Lord Rivers took her in his arms and kissed her. "My own Bess," he said, and there were tears in his eyes and Elizabeth cried, "Oh, Father, don't! I'll cry!"

Lord Rivers tried to smile.

"I can remember when you were born," he said. "That's the trouble with fathers."

Anthony came to the rescue. "I am going to escort you, Bess. Mother will go first with John and Richard and Lionel. Then Father and I on each side of you. And all the girls with your train."

Thus the procession started on the first lap of the journey. And the abbey bells kept tolling.

The Duchess was glad she had a hand on the arm of a stalwart son. She set a slow pace. She reached the end of the hall and started down the steps. No one spoke.

Elizabeth felt comforted by her surrounding family. She put aside the thought when she would leave them—now she had both Anthony and her father.

Down the steps and through the cloister walk; now the walls of the abbey loomed. The dying month of September presaged winter; the wind was fretful and chill. A few leaves lay disconsolately on the clipped grass. The side door to the abbey stood open and Elizabeth saw her mother and brothers disappear into it.

Now she could hear the organ and the choir. The music poured out, enveloping her physically, stronger than drafts of wind that scurried around the monastery walls. She entered the anteroom; it was very small. Its door was shut.

There were two magnificent male figures in the small stone-walled room. One of them was the great Earl of Warwick and he was waiting impatient and glowering for the sight of this woman that Edward had wed. And now here she was. The rest of her upstart family, part of them, had passed by under his eyes; now here was Anthony and Lord Rivers, both of whom he had lashed with his tongue before. So here now, Warwick thought with relentless disgust, are two prominent Lancastrians, escorting their poor widowed sister. He was damned if he was going to kneel.

Anthony said, raising his voice slightly because the voices of the choir now assaulted the small room, "Elizabeth, may I present His Grace the Duke of Clarence."

Elizabeth smiled at Edward's younger brother. Clarence's face was wreathed with smiles; he had charm which he bestowed on all; it was difficult to resist Clarence. He took her hand and kissed it. "My new sister and my liege lady," he said.

Elizabeth's smile was warm. Then she turned her eyes to Warwick.

"And may I present his lordship, the Earl of Warwick."

Warwick bowed. He ran his eyes over her. Undoubtedly all Edward had wanted was to get into bed with her; it was obvious. And this woman, Elizabeth Woodville, had been clever enough to insist on marriage. Even the most favorite of his oaths failed him now mentally. Edward was too gentlemanly. He had probably never brought to bear the force of his position to attain his ends. Instead he had paid the price of marriage and to this woman with the horrible upstart family, who would swarm over court and county.

"Lady Grey," Warwick said.

"Your lordship," Elizabeth said, receiving the impression that he hated her quite clearly. She drew herself very straight. She lay one white hand on his arm.

"I am honored that you bring me to His Grace," she said evenly.

Anthony's eyes approved the answer, she knew, for he had drawn her to Warwick's side, the door had opened and the Bishop was standing in front of it; there was the unmistakable sound now of people communicating their presence, massed into the chapel, standing, shuffling from one foot to the other in the tiny space each had, scarcely enough room to breathe, pressed back against the walls, pressing forward against the velvet ropes that cleared an aisle, turning to see, craning necks to watch the Duchess and John and Richard and Lionel proceed down the aisle, turning back again to watch Lord Rivers and Anthony enter, looking back to the far end of the chapel to Edward, who

was standing now in front of his big chair; to his right was another chair, empty. Edward was dressed in a magnificent cloak
faced with red cloth of gold; he towered there, a resplendent
King, a man in whom any subject could take pride, indeed the
handsomest Prince in Christendom, waiting now to receive his
bride.

The organ played very softly. Elizabeth went to the door with
her hand on Warwick's arm; ahead of her went Anthony and
Lord Rivers, down and away, down the long aisle toward the
very foot of the throne at which Edward stood. Now at the head
of the aisle she could see him.

Clarence was now on her other side. With a cheery smile and
much aplomb Clarence tucked her hand inside his arm. When
Anthony and Lord Rivers melted into the crowd at Edward's
feet, for Edward stood three steps up, Clarence whispered,
"Now."

Elizabeth put one foot forward. Warwick was no help. She
wanted to withdraw her hand from his stiffly held arm. She adjusted her step to his and the march down the aisle began.

The huge crowd and the swimming faces and figures nearest
the aisle she knew were there and could not see. Her knees
trembled, but she stood as straight and as gracefully as she could
as one step after another carried her forward inevitably to the
man who waited for her. She fastened her eyes on him, clutching at Clarence's arm for what she hoped was regal balance. The
Duchess had told her to remember not to look strained but not
to smile. To do this she breathed lightly through half-parted lips,
and she kept her eyes straight ahead on Edward; but the excitement glowed in her face, and Edward knew as he saw her
clearly now that she had never looked more beautiful, nay, nor
more queenly. She was indeed, he thought, his heart going out
to her, the most beautiful of all the flowers in England; she
walked toward him, proud, serene; her face had a gentle spiritual
look.

The candles burned in their sconces; the music softened; everyone in the chapel, friend and foe, sighed as the drama reached
its climax. For now only five feet from Edward, so that their eyes
could meet, now nearing the altar, the white-robed choir began
a chant and suddenly the chapel enfolded her with all its familiar

wonder and comfort. She looked up at Edward and she was not afraid anymore.

She took the last three steps. The King then moved toward her, coming down the steps. He bowed to both his brother and Warwick, then she felt his hand on hers and she ascended the steps. She stood at his side, looking down over the chapel.

There was a hush. It seemed as though no one breathed. Then suddenly the choir and organ pealed forth, and within the chapel every head was bowed and the whole company knelt in homage.

The Duchess took the occasion to wipe her eyes. When she felt her husband's hand to raise her she looked at once to her daughter. The King and Queen were seated side by side.

PART TWO
The Struggle

Chapter 9

Make we merry both rich and less
For now is the time of Christmas!
Let no man come into this hall
Groom, page, nor yet marshal
But that some sport he bring withal!
For now is the time of Christmas!

If that he say he cannot sing,
Some other sport then let him bring;
If he say he can nought do,
Then for my love ask him no mo,
But to the stocks then let him go!

IT WAS the feast of Christmas. It was the time to laugh at winter, the time for singing and caroling, for dancing and disguising, for games and feasts in halls decorated with the holly and the ivy, the blazing Yule logs on the hearth. And over Elizabeth's first Christmas with Edward there was no shadow.

Their honeymoon had been spent in the seclusion of the monastery in Reading. We know at the end of November they were at Windsor and by the eighth of December at the King's palace at Eltham, for on that same day a royal directive to the King's treasurer commanded him to pay "to our right well-beloved wife, the Queen, the sum of four hundred sixty-six pounds against the expenses of her household for the coming feast of Christmas," and the grand council in Westminster was instructed to grant her manors in the amount of four thousand marks a year. To these Edward added two gifts of his own, his manor of pleasance in Greenwich and his manor of Shene.

On this first Christmas the court could not have been gayer. The glowering Warwick was absent. Instead there was the suave, cultured Earl of Worcester, the most eligible bachelor in the realm, whom all the ladies pursued with lowered lashes and lowered necklines; there was Anthony Woodville and his wife, Beth, who was one of Elizabeth's ladies-in-waiting. There was John Fogge, Edward's personal treasurer of the royal household, and his gay wife, Alice, who was also one of Bessie's ladies-in-waiting; Sir John had served Edward since the earliest days of the reign. The Duchess of Bedford had brought her family and the Duchess of York had brought hers, Clarence, Margaret and young Richard. The court was overflowing with children; they loved the jugglers and the minstrels; they doubled with laughter over the antics of Edward's two favorite clowns; they ran through the halls and the gardens and took their part in the maskings and disguisings; the little girls danced with the King, who moved through all the festivities his ebullient self, he and Elizabeth setting the tenor of the court, as sunny-hearted as only lovers can be. Did it matter that the great Earl of Warwick sulked in his dour fortress of Middleham in the north like the mighty Achilles himself?

Froissart tells us that the palace of Eltham was elegant. And it was elegant just as was the King's barge in which Bessie had left Reading. And now abruptly the honeymoon was over, Christmas was over, it was the New Year; Parliament opened, the court moved to Westminster and Bessie became not only Edward's wife but the Queen.

Bessie had her own court and household. She had her own doctor, her own confessor, her own solicitor, her own receiver general who managed her estates and monies, her own secretaries, her own council. Her brother John Woodville was her master of horse. She had ladies of the chamber and ladies-in-waiting, nurses, governesses, tutors. Besides her own two boys she had Edward's illegitimate daughter Grace, whose mother had died in the plague the summer before. Into her care had been given by Edward's hands his two very important wards, for they had royal blood, the heirs of Buckingham, two boys, ten and twelve. Bessie had her own council rooms and her audience chamber; it was always full.

Would she give her illustrious name and her money to the college that her former mistress the former Queen Margaret, had endowed? Graciously she assented. Graciously she insisted that the college be known as Queens' College to recognize that the endowment came from two English Queens. Never by a chance word offend, never forget—Bessie could hear her mother's advice dinning in her ears and the voices of the men or women who were asking for help, money or time.

"The mayor of Norwich is here in London, Your Grace, and craves a private audience."

Bessie's head ached.

"The young Duke of Buckingham, Your Grace. His tutor is waiting and asks to see you immediate after your council meeting."

"The chancellor of Cambridge, Your Grace, your confessor. He has arrived early."

"At three o'clock, Your Grace, your coronation gown will be ready for first inspection."

And yet to Bessie, as she strove each day to cope with the endless minutiae of the business of being the wife of the head of state, the center and the sun of her life remained her husband; her big, dominating husband; Edward, weary and harassed, Edward irritable, Edward worried; Edward hungry, eating too much, Edward explaining, planning, Edward joking; Edward grinning his sly grin, Edward making love, Edward asleep, his big arm across her naked body, and she would lie still so as not to disturb his sleep which he needed so badly. Only after she was sure he was deep in sleep would her hand steal to caress the side of his face and to thank all the saints in heaven for the wonder of love and a man like this one.

As for Edward himself, he had two principal problems. In foreign affairs France or Burgundy? With which should England ally? And here at home what to do about the Nevilles, not only their chief, the great Earl of Warwick, but his brother George Neville, Chancellor of the realm, Archbishop of York, and John Neville, Lord Montagu, his faithful friend, the blunt, outspoken soldier. And Edward set out to solve these things in his usual methodical way.

But he had other, more pressing and immediate problems. On the night of March tenth while Bessie was wondering where he was Edward was still sitting at his table. For the last two weeks he had been carefully watching a young groom of the chamber, a slender, rakish young man by name David Cholmlay. Edward was alone save for his cleverest agent, Edward Alayn, who was reporting from Scotland.

Affairs in Scotland were proceeding satisfactorily; there was a conference scheduled for early summer at Alnwick. Edward Alayn told Edward that both the Bishop of Aberdeen and Bishop Kennedy had accepted money and the principal noble adviser of the young Scot King was also on the English payroll so the conference should proceed smoothly and to England's liking. Edward wanted peace with Scotland, a peace which would free his hands to deal with the Continent without any fear that Scottish soldiers, reinforced by the French, would come across the border.

But Edward wanted the old King Henry. Henry, wandering disconsolate, probably sick, hiding away in a manor house or a monastery, was not only a thorn in Edward's side but an insult to Henry himself. Sick and alone, he ill became the majesty of a former Prince. Custody and custodial care was what Henry needed; Edward would provide it with dignity. And then the still-ardent Lancastrians, those who were left, could settle down and stop tormenting themselves about the lamentable prospect of their former King living like a fugitive beggar. It was necessary that Edward get his big hands on Henry. The candles were guttering low when Edward sent for young David Cholmlay, who entered the room amazed by this summons.

But Edward knew an adventurer when he saw one. He introduced the two men, and while Alayn explained his mission to David Cholmlay Edward watched his face and was pleased with his quick questions, the small smile that sometimes accompanied the answers. Here was a very clever young man who would bear watching. When they both left him he felt quite sure that between the two they would turn Henry up before the summer, and he yawned and rubbed his hand over his eyes when Hastings appeared with a late-arriving messenger from the Duke of Burgundy. Lord Jacques of Luxembourg, Bessie's uncle, had arrived in England.

The past October Edward had written to Philip of Burgundy, asking the Duke to grant a safe conduct for an embassy to attend Bessie's coronation, and he specifically asked for Lord Jacques of Luxembourg, Bessie's uncle, Jacqueta's brother, for he wished to remind his subjects that although Bessie was of *petite extraction* on her father's side, on her mother's she was related to the family which had given emperors to Germany and princes to Luxembourg. Now Lord Jacques had arrived. Edward thanked Hastings and told him to get to bed and that he was going to do the same.

While Bessie had John in her household as master of horse and three of her sisters as ladies-in-waiting and while Richard and Anthony attended Edward and Edward was soon to make Anthony a member of his council, now at Shene the Duchess also arrived with her husband Lord Rivers and all the rest of her brood, even including some of the Hautes, who were cousins of Lord Rivers'. The Duchess hadn't seen her brother for fifteen years. Arms outstretched, she flew across to him. Floods of French engulfed the room; everyone talked at once.

"And they already love you," cried the Duchess. She waved her arms. "The Londoners! They already nickname you! Lord Jakes!"

With Lord Jacques' polished entourage, with the Woodvilles' fine exuberance added to Will Herbert's charm, Worcester's wit and polish and the Fogges and the Blounts, Edward's court scintillated the way he wished it to. He was immensely pleased. He was immensely proud of Bessie. He loved to hear her quick French and the dazzling smile and laugh. The court danced and listened to music and had dinner outside in April's bloom and everybody was happy except the Earl of Warwick.

However, Lord Jacques bore secret messages and came, he told Edward, on a dual mission; his master, Philip of Burgundy, wanted Edward to join with him in a secret alliance against King Louis; he wanted Edward to join the League of Public Weal, which the other lords of Europe were forming against Louis.

Edward appointed Hastings and Warwick (to appease him) to discuss all these affairs with Lord Jacques. But that night he said to Bessie, "In the long dismal years of Henry's reign it was as though there was no King nor court. A King should provide mightily for his subjects in the way of entertainment to spur national pride. There will be a tournament after your coronation next month but I have decided to have Anthony send a challenge to the famous Bastard of Burgundy, and we shall have a great tournament between the other principal knights of both countries, a great show in which our people may take pride."

It had to be done with all the amenities and protocol well observed. Bessie sought help from her uncle's secretary. One fine April day she summoned Anthony before dinner; it was still morning. Around her chair all her ladies were grouped, eyes gleaming. Anthony came toward her and dropped to one knee; he had removed his cap and he laid it on the floor beside him. Bessie smiled down at him with love and pride while about him suddenly all her ladies clustered.

"Hold him tight!" Young Kate Woodville cried.

Surrounded by all this giggling femininity Anthony, still on one knee, watched, laughing himself as Alice Fogge tied around his heavy, muscled thigh a collar of gold and pearls with a beautiful flower enameled on it.

"I can't get it tied, Anthony," she whispered, and he grinned.

"I'm not going to help you," he whispered back.

She collapsed against him on the floor, giggling, righted herself and finished tying the slender gold collar.

"Let him up," she said, still laughing. "Look, Anthony, there's something in your cap!"

Anthony rose now, wondering whether the tie was going to hold and picked up his cap and the parchment Beth had laid on top of it.

"You are our chosen champion!" they all said at once.

Bessie smiled at him. "It is your solemn duty, sir, to take the message to the King."

The parchment was tied with a slender gold thread. Gravely, in front of all the gathered lords in Edward's audience chamber, Anthony again knelt and presented it to Edward, who untied it and just as grave as Anthony read it aloud to the assembled lords of both realms.

"A deed of chivalry," Edward read, "is expected of you, a two-day encounter, the first day on horseback with spears and swords, the second day on foot with battle-axes and daggers, this encounter to take place in October with a gentleman of four lineages and without reproach."

Edward signified that Anthony should rise.

He did. "Your Grace," he began, "I shall send this enameled

flower and my challenge to a man famous for valor and skill at arms on the Continent, the Lord Antoine, favorite son of Duke Philip of Burgundy, the Lord Antoine, Bastard of Burgundy. Chester Herald shall carry the flower and my challenge to the court of Burgundy at Brussels and present both to the Lord Antoine."

At this the horns blew, the trumpets sounded and everyone went gaily into dinner. Each of Edward's young lords was already planning to challenge a foreign knight and was thinking of the manner in which his badges could be embroidered on the caparisons of his horse.

The court of Philip of Burgundy was the most celebrated in Europe and its protocol excessively strict. Lord Jacques and the Duchess instructed Bessie carefully.

"When Chester Herald presents the flower and Anthony's challenge it will be before the whole court in Burgundy. The Bastard will touch the flower to betoken his acceptance of the challenge. The Bastard will be richly dressed, of course, and he will present the garments he is wearing to Chester Herald, who will then wear those same clothes when he takes his ceremonious leave of Philip's court."

Bessie nodded. "But then—" suddenly Bessie laughed; in her mind's eye she could see a man in a suit which didn't fit.

"*Alors*," said the Duchess impatiently, "Chester Herald must be the same size as the Bastard." She turned inquiring eyes on her brother.

"He is about Anthony's height but heavier," Lord Jacques answered.

It worked out very well even to the time. Chester Herald returned in time to appear before the King and court on May twenty-third. He was indeed wearing the Bastard of Burgundy's clothes, a doublet of black velvet, the slits of the sleeves clasped with gold; thrown carelessly over his shoulders was a long cape furred with sables. Bessie's eyes sparkled. It had worked out very well indeed. She watched Chester Herald in his finery gravely present the enameled flower to the King, and then Anthony came forward and Edward rose from his big chair and fastened the flower on Anthony's collar. He would be England's champion in the great tournament to come, a tournament which would bring foreign knights from all over Europe, envoys and embassies, so that Europe could see how splendid was England, its King and Queen, its court, its people. Edward was very pleased.

But time was pressing him. He had to be in London that evening. Bessie's coronation was on Sunday; he kissed her good-bye and left Greenwich after dinner, riding for London.

There that night and in his Bessie's honor Edward created in a ceremony at the Tower almost fifty Knights of the Bath. Among them were Richard and John Woodville; the young Duke of Buckingham and his brother; young John de Vere, son of the dead Earl of Oxford, whom Edward had restored to his father's honors and estates; John Say, the Speaker of the last Parliament; the mayor of London and three merchants and aldermen who had been helpful and loyal to Edward.

It was the twenty-fourth of May. Edward had left her the day before. Bessie rose early; Edward had bought her three new horses, two bays and a white courser, and they were trapped with cloth of gold from Florence that had cost two hundred eighty pounds. Bessie rode to London. At the foot of Shooter's Hill she was met by the mayor and all the aldermen, dressed in scarlet. They escorted her through Southwark to the Tower.

The roadways were sanded freshly. The drawbridge had been fumigated. At the bridge the wardens presented her with entertainment.

What a sight it was! Her eyes were astonished at the blaze of color. The famous bridge with its double rows of houses and shops, its churches; now on the south side a stage had been erected and its boards painted with ballads. Here she was greeted by a pageant on which twelve weeks' labor, five thousand nails, and ninety-six ells of cloth had been used, white, black, gold, green and red. Eight effigies stood on the stage.

Bessie's eyes grew even larger. St. Elizabeth welcomed her. The city presented her with two thousand marks. And there were smiles everywhere; there hadn't been such a day as this for a long, long time.

She proceeded across the bridge slowly. At the chapel of St. Thomas, the twelfth-century chapel of Becket, the boys' choir of voices was so beautiful that Bessie felt great tears forming in her eyes and she blinked them away rapidly. She passed on. At St. Magnus Church there was more singing. Then slowly with all of

London following Bessie went to the Tower of London as was the custom. There Edward was waiting.

"The whole city is in love with you, especially the men," Edward said.

The next day in a litter between the two new bays she rode from the Tower to the palace of Westminster; all the newly made Knights of the Bath in blue gowns with white hoods rode before her. All the houses were decorated and the streets were jammed; every window was filled with heads like pins in a cushion and flowers were strewn over and before her way. At Westminster Edward forbid any more excitement and they had a quiet supper together; then they went to the chapel. Bessie was wakened at six the following morning, Sunday, the twenty-sixth of May, and for a moment, as happened sometimes to her, she lay wondering if she were dreaming.

She turned over and looked at Edward who was still fast asleep, sprawled over more than half the bed, and she moved over close to him.

"Wake up, sweetheart," she whispered.

He opened his dark eyes and blinked at her sleepily.

"I'm frightened," she whispered.

He reached out for her and drew her closer. "No, no," he said. "Yes, I am," she said.

"Bessie, Bessie," he said, nuzzling her neck with his lips. She heard his muffled voice. "You're only nervous. I was too." He raised his head and grinned. "Get up, sweetheart." He climbed out of bed and put on his bedgown and slippers and stood there watching her do the same thing. When she was covered, he sighed and went to the door but she came running after him for a last embrace. He kissed the top of her head.

"God bless you, Bessie," he said.

At eight the coronation procession formed. The Duke of Clarence, his horse trapped head and body in cloth of gold and spangles, rode first, then the Earl of Arundel and then the Duke of Norfolk.

The well-mannered horses walked with precision, each hoof-beat sounding on the stone like muffled drumbeats.

Then came Bessie. She was barefoot. Her mantle was purple and her long golden, gilt hair fell straight down her back. She walked under a canopy of cloth of gold, borne by the barons of the Cinque Ports, and at each corner of the canopy were gold bells that tinkled. On each side of her were bishops, the Bishop of Salisbury and the Bishop of Durham. On her head she wore a gold coronet.

Step by step Bessie went forward; under her bare feet was striped cloth and now behind her came the Abbot of Westminster and the Duchess of Buckingham, Edward's aunt, carrying her train; next Edward's two sisters, the Lady Margaret and the Duchess of Suffolk, the Duchess of York and the Duchess of Bedford. In Bessie's right hand was the scepter of St. Edward; in her left the scepter of the realm. She went on.

The little bells tinkled. The barons of the Cinque Ports walked in rhythm. Now she was leaving the hall and going through the cloister to the great entrance for state processions in the north transept. Ahead of her the Duke of Clarence dismounted. Ahead was the abbey and a sea of color, for the procession was joined now by all the earls of the realm, the barons, the new-made knights. There were thirteen duchesses in scarlet and ermine, fourteen baronesses in scarlet and miniver, and twelve lady bannerets in scarlet. Now Bessie could hear the bells in the abbey, ringing, ringing.

She passed through the north door and through the choir and to the high altar. There she knelt.

Bessie heard the voice of the Archbishop of Canterbury. She felt her robe and mantle being removed. The Archbishop annointed her and she prayed, prostrate on the floor before the Archbishop, before George Neville, Archbishop of York, who held the holy unction; the two virgins who had removed her mantle were at her other side. At last Bessie rose. The heavy crown was placed on her head.

The bishops conveyed her to the place of estate, the scepters now borne on either side of her while the Archbishop read from the Gospel.

The words swam around in her mind, for she knew she had to go to the high altar again to make her offering.

The Abbot of Westminster took her and Bessie knelt again. The great crown pressed on her temples. Slowly she walked back to her chair of state, and now on each side of her the Duchesses of Suffolk and Buckingham held the heavy crown in place for her during the mass.

She was assaulted by words and color and music and the familiar words of the mass.

The choir and the organ raised triumphant music. She thought, It is I, Elizabeth Woodville. I have been crowned the Queen of my country. The Duchesses helped her rise. Bessie came down from her chair and began her slow walk back through the great hall and to the palace. The abbey bells were ringing and ringing in her ears; she would never forget them.

Bessie retired into her chamber. Now her ladies clustered around her, bringing a basin to wash her feet, and put on her hose. They helped her into a surcoat of purple; and she remembered Edward saying, "I used to hate the color." She looked at its rich folds. But there was no time to think. Two bishops were waiting at the door to escort her into the banqueting hall. The great hall contained four long tables at right angles to Bessie's table, which was at the head. With the bishops on each side Bessie walked to her throne.

The Archbishop of Canterbury and the King's two sisters sat at her table. The Duke of Suffolk and the Earl of Essex held the scepters. The Duke of Clarence brought her a gold basin in which to wash. The crown pressed on her head, heavy.

At the table next the wall sat the mayor and officers and aldermen and citizens of London. At another table sat the clergy and the judges and officers of the King's bench.

The new-made Knights of the Bath and the nobility of the realm swam before her eyes in a mass of brilliant colors. Then the trumpets blew and the procession formed for the presentation of the first course.

There were seventeen dishes borne by earls, barons and knights, and the Constable and the Marshal and the Steward of England riding again their caparisoned horses.

Bessie was offered the platter. I will have to try to eat, she thought.

The trumpets blew again, the horses trotted sedately and dish after dish was borne high. There was a great platter of aspic in the shape of a bear's head.

She was being served; she took her napkin from the hands of

the lady kneeling at her side. Quail and partridge and peacock, cygnet and heron. Fish in a sauce, and crab and turbot and sturgeon. Her head was bursting, she thought. She reached up and lifted the heavy crown from her head and set it in front of her. Then she tried to eat.

The first course was seventeen dishes, the second nineteen dishes and the third fifteen dishes. The King's minstrels played to preface each course as the trumpets blew.

The new plate from which Bessie was served and for which Edward had paid a high price glittered boldly. The wine cup was heavy in her hand. She kept motioning to one of the ladies at each side of her to hand her her napkin. She tasted a bit of fish and some aspic. Then mercifully the plate would be removed and she could ask for her napkin again.

The trumpets blew again and the subtleties were being borne in. The first one was allegorical—the image of the King with St. Edward. Next came the Our Lady, sitting with the Child and holding a crown in hand. Next a great pelican with birds and an image of St. Elizabeth. The subtleties were made of sugar and almond paste. Bessie tasted a bit of it. The custard was a leopard of gold, holding a fleur-de-lis. And Anthony brought her a tall, jeweled cup of Hippocras.

He was her cupbearer today. She smiled at him gratefully. The music kept on, for other lords had provided minstrels too. Her head was beginning to swim. How many hours had she sat at the table? The last of the plates had been cleared. There were still other duties. Bessie's chaplain began solemnly to fold up the table cloth and bear it away. Sir John Howard lay napery before her and again she washed. One of the Knights of the Bath with a platter of comfits served the Queen. Then the mayor of London offered her the gold cup of wine. Bessie thanked him in her clear voice and she returned the gold cup to the mayor as her gift. At last she could rise.

The barons of the Cinque Ports held the canopy over her as she proceeded from the room. At the doors, with her ladies following, she made a present of the canopy to the barons. The bells tinkled as it was folded. Garter King at Arms delivered her largesses of twenty pounds to the minstrels and to Garter King at Arms. Then the new-crowned Queen of England retired to her own chambers.

Edward had planned a tournament the following day at Westminster; he loved tournaments. There were knights from Luxembourg and Burgundy and the stands were jammed; even the belfry had been let to sightseers. Lord Stanley carried off the highest honors and Elizabeth presented him with a ruby ring. And during all these festivities one figure was absent, the great Earl of Warwick. No larger than that was the cloud on the horizon which betokened storm.

Diplomatically well enough aware of Warwick's disapproval of his marriage and to spare his exacerbated ego, Edward had purposely arranged that Warwick should represent him abroad at the time of Bessie's coronation, for coronation or no the affairs of the nation went on. To obviate the impression that he was sending Warwick to get rid of him, Edward sent Lord Hastings with Warwick, and their mission was to treat with Philip of Burgundy regarding trade and with King Louis for an extension of the truce with France.

It was June and Elizabeth was too busy to enjoy the spring, the wonderful warm days and the blooming royal gardens. Her council sat in the mornings in the room next the Exchequer. She had a receiver general for her accounts but even so she made a habit of going over them herself, for her husband was a man of business and she knew his eagle eye would perceive any discrepancy or complain about any overexpense. She had to check John, for instance, her brother, who was her master of horse. The first week in June she was just in time to prevent his ordering a pair of coursers from Castile.

"His Grace has one," John said, in extenuation of his action.

"Let His Grace present us with a pair then," Bessie said sharply.

The position John held in her household was one which eminently suited him, for he was practical and able, and when her household moved every cart was shined and sturdy and everything arrived on time; she never arrived at a distant manor or palace but that her stuff had not preceded her and her feather beds plumped up and ready to receive her tired body. The stables prospered and John had a wonderful eye for horseflesh. He bargained for their food and even their nose bags shined with polish. But though John was handsome and cynical, both Bessie and her

mother were thunderstruck when John told them he was going
to wed the Duchess of Suffolk.

"Why not?" he shrugged his broad shoulders.

"Why not?" the Duchess exploded. "She is four times your age!"

"Not quite," said John. "She is very, very wealthy. I am part
French, madame, and, uh—thrifty-minded."

"I should ask His Grace to intervene," the Duchess cried.
"You're disgracing your family!"

"How can His Grace forbid his aunt to marry?" John asked.
"Be reasonable, Mother. Why shouldn't I have a wealthy wife?"

Bessie bit her lip. If Edward didn't intervene what could she
do? She asked, "What did His Grace say, John?"

John grinned. "I cannot repeat what His Grace said, Bess."

Angry, Bessie pointed her finger at him. "Get down on your
knees, you impudent boy, and tell me what His Grace said!"

John, unrepentant, dropped to one knee. "Oh, Bess," he said,
still laughing at her. "His Grace added then, after the remark I
shan't repeat in front of you and mother, that if his aunt wanted
a stallion that it was up to her and me. May I rise now, Your
Grace?"

"Get out of my sight," Bessie said.

"I need my job, Bess," John said. "I like it and I'll serve you
well."

"For the mercy of God," Bessie muttered, using Edward's oath.
She looked at her mother. The Duchess said, "At least keep him
working, Bess. It would be more of a disgrace if he idled. But
what of children, John? Don't you want children and a young
wife?"

John rose and dusted off his knee. "Later, *ma mere; il y a plus
de temps.*"

Bessie said, "There will be much gossip." She sighed, shaking
her head, and of course she was right. William of Worcester wrote
that it was a "diabolical marriage." But John cared little what
people said; he went his merry, flamboyant way and wed his
Duchess.

And in the manner of the day Edward and Elizabeth had betrothed four of Elizabeth's sisters to prominent names. Mary to
the heir of Will Herbert, Edward's closest friend; Kate was affianced to the young Duke of Buckingham; Anne was married to
one of the Bourchiers and was a lady-in-waiting. Bessie said to

her mother, "We know there is gossip about our betrothing my sisters, but if we did not there would then be criticism of me—and people would say, Look how she forgets her sisters—she is so proud."

The Duchess said, "I shouldn't worry, Bessie. After all, I affianced you and Anthony to splendid names and why shouldn't you help your sisters?"

Bessie pushed aside the glowering face of the Earl of Warwick. She and her mother proceeded to the schoolroom where Master Giles was in charge and then they went out into the garden with all the children for a walk before dinner. Out in the garden Bessie lifted the little Grace from her carriage and set her on the grass. She was eighteen months old and toddling. Bessie took her hand and the Duchess took the other, and between them little Grace took uncertain steps.

Bessie was silent. The clutch of the small hand reminded her that she had been married since May. She had been afraid. Was it possible that she would bear no more children? Edward had laughed at her fears. In May before the coronation one night, when he realized she was truly upset he had said seriously, "Don't worry and fret, Bessie. Surely the Lord in His Grace will bless our love with children."

The words had moved her very much. Now in this garden she had reason to hope. But she didn't dare tell anyone yet.

On the first of July she sought out her physician and sent for her confessor Edward Story, the chancellor of Cambridge.

Bessie's doctor was part Spanish, a man by name of Domenico de Sirigo, and he had studied in Italy.

"The second week in February, I think, Your Grace," he said.

"Speak no word," Bessie cautioned. Under no circumstances did she want Edward to hear the news from anyone but her.

On her knees she told Edward Story and confessed her sins. When the chancellor had shrived her she rose and smiled at him.

She watched him leave her, his robes swishing from side to side and at the door he stepped aside for a groom of the chamber who was bearing a message. Bessie opened it. Edward desired a private supper that evening. Does he know? she thought incredulously. No, he could not. He just wants to sup alone. She ordered the shrimps of which he was so fond, big shrimps—"gross" he called them—and some salmon, smoked, and doves, roasted. White wine for the fish and Burgundy for the sweets and wafer.

He was late. She was accustomed to that. He explained that David Cholmlay's messenger had arrived; Cholmlay was close onto Henry's whereabouts, for the poor old King had crept back into England now that Edward's successful diplomacy with Scotland had made Scotland unsafe. Bessie listened. But her eyes sparkled and her thoughts wandered.

"You're not listening to me," Edward said.

"I am! I am!"

He laughed. "Well, what happened today?"

She leaned her elbows on the table and looked across at him; he put down his knife.

"Bessie," he said.

"Yes," she said. "Yes, sweetheart. It's true."

The King rose, laid down his napkin and came to her side and knelt beside her, putting his arms around her and she held his dark head against her breast.

"In February," she whispered.

"Bessie, Bessie," he said.

He rose and poured each of them a cup of wine, and he raised it high. "To you and our firstborn child, Bessie."

It was not difficult to see how happy he was, as if she had given him the whole world, but she knew how important it was too, for he fretted about the succession; he worried over Clarence. He had sent Clarence to Ireland to try his hand at authority but Clarence was already drinking too much.

But now he was happy and he watched over what she ate, and later when he asked her what he could do for her to show his great pleasure, she asked him for what was most valuable to her —his time.

She said, "I'd like to go on pilgrimage with you."

"Yes," he said, nodding. "Where, Bessie?"

She knew his favorite shrine was Canterbury and it was not as far as Our Lady of Walsingham, although she loved that shrine. "To the shrine of Becket," she said.

Edward and Bessie arrived in Canterbury on the thirteenth of July, two hours before vespers. They were received by the Archbishop Bourchier and a whole procession of monks in green copes. Canterbury was indeed Edward's favorite shrine, and the following day, ceremoniously, he created it a county independent of Kent. Meanwhile Bessie, four hours before vespers, went to the cathedral alone, to the tomb to pray. Ten monks in white copes preceded her into the cathedral. She was there when a messenger, pounding down from London, brought the news to Edward for which he had been waiting. Henry VI had been captured in Yorkshire and was even now on his way down to London.

With his sense of drama Edward, Bessie and the Archbishop, and all the clergy and monks proceeded in solemn procession to the cathedral and Edward spoke to the people, saying their former, sick King would be well cared for. Then the procession went on to the tomb of Becket and the Archbishop conducted the "Te Deum" mass.

And since the Earl of Warwick had landed in England again on the eighth of July Edward, polite as always, allowed him to meet the captive in Islington and to arrest the former King in Edward's name.

"But I'll have to break my promise, Bessie," he said. "We'll have to go back to Westminster. Right away."

He was frowning slightly, wondering if he'd been right to let Warwick handle Henry. And when he arrived in London rather late in the night, tired, he summoned Anthony. He and Bessie and Anthony were alone. Edward sat in his bedgown, drinking wine while Anthony said bluntly, "Warwick's treatment of Henry aroused pity and sympathy for him. He tied his hands with rope and set him on a shambling mule. His melancholy eyes, his thin face, his shabby gown—people wept to see him thus taken through the streets."

Edward's eyes blazed with fury, and he swore an oath that made Bessie jump and even Anthony looked surprised.

Edward rose and pointed at Anthony, motioning him to the table where Bessie's writing implements stood ready.

"Take this down now," the King commanded. He spoke slowly and with force.

"He is to have a chaplain and attendant. He is to be supplied with new garments, with velvet for gowns, supplied with all necessaries. He is to be treated with as much respect as is—" Edward hunted for a word, "as is consistent with his safe custody." Under no condition did he want poor Henry loose again, wandering like a stray soul through England. "And any man, by license of his attendants, may come and speak with him in his apartments."

Edward sat down again. His eyes were remote; he didn't seem to know there were two other people in the room. They didn't speak. Anthony sanded the words he had written; they would go out as a royal directive in the morning. Edward sipped his wine in silence. He was thinking all possible kindness must be shown a former Prince; it would be a blot on the majesty of any Prince to do otherwise; and he was intensely annoyed at Warwick for daring to show such disrespect to a former King.

He would do all he could to show his subjects that Henry was well cared for. And there was certainly no point in harming him or helping him to heaven.

In France Henry's former wife, Margaret, and her so-called Prince were alive and plotting, whispering into the ear of King Louis, sending appeals to their adherents, fixing to stir up a witch's brew of trouble if they could. Margaret and her young son. Well, he and Bessie would have a young son too, soon. For the stability of the realm he, Edward, needed a sturdy young son, a Prince. He set down his wine cup. Bessie was watching him with her big eyes; she looked tired; why shouldn't she? It had been a long day. Worry nagged at him.

"You should take better care of yourself, Bessie, and get into bed."

Chapter 10

"AND IT shall be," was the royal order, "to Her Highness' pleasure as to what chamber she shall be delivered in."

Bessie chose a wide, airy drawing room in Westminster. It was hung with rich cloth of arras, covering the sides, the roof, even the windows, except that over the long bank of windows overlooking the gardens it could be drawn open wide. Bessie retired to this chamber four weeks before the birth of her first child by Edward.

Women served her as butlers, pages and servers who received all needful things at the great doors of the chamber, and Margaret of Richmond, who was directly descended from John of Gaunt and whose little son, Henry Tudor, was being cared for by the Herberts, she it was who supervised the comings and goings and the bringings and taking away.

Edward's astrologer had predicted royalty and a crown for his firstborn. It was a dark January and a bitterly cold winter. Nonetheless Bessie had the curtains of her windows drawn wide every morning so she could sit in her chair and look out and not feel so confined. When she had first retired into the chamber after the festivities of Christmas, she had been relieved. But now, shut up with only women about, after a week she fretted.

"It's not as though it's my first child," she told herself, pacing the long room and scattering the women to one side.

She sewed and she read and she played cards and chess, and she longed for the sound of male voices. Would February never come? But it did arrive on a snowy morning. She took comfort in the beauty of the world outside, placed her hand against the window to feel the icy pane that promised fresh cold air.

Bessie's mother arrived. "I didn't come sooner," the Duchess said, "because I wanted you to be glad to see me!"

Bessie laughed. The Duchess was full of news and gossip. "But I'm nervous, Mother. What if I have a girl?"

"What if you do?" the Duchess answered.

"I want a boy so bad and so does His Grace!"

"Make up your mind to it, Bessie. You'll bring forth what God wishes."

Gifts arrived from Edward every day. A bird in a beautiful cage. An intricate necklace of pearls with a medallion. A letter written late at night. And on February eleventh Bessie's child was born.

The palace knew that the Queen was in labor. Close to Bessie's chamber crept Dr. Dominic, who had foretold a boy for the Queen. Master Dominic heard the cry of a child. Anxious to bring the news to Edward first, he knocked on the door.

He heard footsteps as Alice Fogge approached the door. He put his mouth to the crack. "What hath the Queen had?" he whispered.

On the other side of the door Alice opened it a bare crack. She too put her lips to the crack. "Whatever the Queen's Grace has had in here, it's sure a fool that stands out there!"

Master Dominic retreated in haste. He should have known better than to brave a chamber full of women. And within the room the Duchess was bathing the baby and dressing it. She brought the child to Bessie and laid it in her arms. Bessie's great eyes asked the question. The Duchess said with a smile, "You have borne a beautiful Princess, my dearest daughter."

The Duchess hurried off to Edward and returned with the King. A brocaded stool had been placed beside the bed, but Edward pushed it aside and sat down on the side of the bed and leaned over and kissed Bessie and asked for the baby. She placed the child in his arms carefully, because had he held a baby before? She looked at him, hesitant, but she could not see from his face that he was disappointed.

Her ladies were all gathered in a little knot at the far end of the draped chamber.

He looked up from the baby. "She is beautiful," he said. He kissed the side of her cheek.

Bessie grasped for his hand. "Oh, sweetheart," she said.

"She doesn't cry," he said. "She is so little."

"We must speak her name together," Bessie said. "You must think what name you wish."

Edward looked up from the baby. "What name? I already chose her name. She will be named for her mother. Who is that, I wonder? Do you know your mother yet, little one? Oh, Bessie, say with me, this little one, our firstborn, is named Elizabeth."

"Elizabeth," repeated Bessie. She closed her eyes so he wouldn't see she was crying.

A month before Edward had made elaborate plans for the baptism of his firstborn. George Neville, Archbishop of York, and nine other bishops assisted, and the great Earl of Warwick and the two grandmothers stood as sponsors for the child at the font. And he had planned an equally elaborate churching ceremony for his Bessie.

The ceremony took place in the abbey. And in England as guests of the King was the Lord Rozmital, brother of the Queen of Bohemia, and Edward wanted to impress them with the magnificence of the English court.

First in the procession to the abbey came the clerics with sacred relics, then scholars carrying lighted candles, then the noble matrons and maidens, then the trumpeters, pipers and players of the King, forty-two of the King's minstrels. Edward was inordinately fond of music and the Bohemians were impressed by the excellence of his musicians. After two dozen heralds and scores of lords and knights, then came Bessie herself under a canopy, escorted by two dukes and followed by the Duchess and her ladies.

Bessie's fame and beauty had reached to all corners of Europe and the Bohemians were anxiously waiting their first sight of the Queen. After the religious rites they were escorted back to the hall where they dined at the table with Warwick, two steps down, as Edward's representative, for the King according to custom could not be present.

After the great banquet Warwick took the distinguished visitors to the Queen's dining hall where Bessie sat on a golden chair. Not until she had sipped at her water could anyone sit. And after the banquet there was dancing and the Duchess knelt at Bessie's side.

"Please get up and stretch your legs, Mother," Bessie whispered. The Duchess did. She rose, the dancing continued and finally the King's minstrels sang to finish the festivities.

The Bohemians noted the prosperity and many foreign merchants in London and that the women were beautiful and virtuous; they were impressed with the art of the goldsmith and the clothmakers of the city and with the reverence which his courtiers accorded Edward.

Edward charmed them. His easy manner, the way he shook hands with them, the multiple questions he asked about their land and his lavish hospitality, which included a fifty-course banquet and the handsome lodgings he had had prepared for them —all these impressed them mightily. At the end of the banquet in their honor the King himself hung around their necks gold collars for the knights and silver ones for the rest. Edward offered knighthood to Lord Rozmital and the Bohemian was astonished that such an honor could be offered in a banquet hall and not on the field of battle.

Then the Earl of Warwick feasted them too. He outdid Edward by the amount of courses, for there were sixty courses; they noted the expensive carpets on the floors. And if the Bohemians noted it, Edward did too.

That winter Edward could see more plain the fruits of his policies and the growing strength of a realm which was now freed from wars and settling into a more law-abiding monarchy. His country was beginning to be strong enough to take her part in foreign affairs and to be an important part of European politics. Embassies were in London from Catalonia, Aragon and Castile. The Emperor Frederick sent a herald and then later the Patriarch of Antioch himself. He brought as a gift four dromedaries and two camels, the first ever to be seen in England. Ferdinand of Naples accounted himself a good friend and had sent his favorite, the Count of Monte Odirisio, to draw a league of amity and trade between England and Naples. Edward bestowed the Order of the Garter on the Count. Yet another Italian prince sent an embassy, Borso d'Este of Ferrara. And Edward was considering no less than five offers for the hand of his sister Margaret.

The most impressive offer came from the widowed Charles, heir to the dying Philip of Burgundy, and it kept Edward sleepless at night. For the largest question before the eyes of the King in the matter of foreign policy was whether to ally with France or with Burgundy. Which would be best for the realm and its safety? The choice was not easy.

France was the ancient enemy. King Louis could be trusted not so far as Edward could throw one of his new camels. Louis was struggling hard to consolidate his kingdom; perhaps Edward understood his problems better than anyone else. Louis' brother had joined against him but, of a truth, Louis was more than a match for any one of them, and in his secret heart Edward believed Louis would be as successful as he, Edward, hoped to be. Therefore it followed that Louis would do all he could to hinder Edward, that he would not only shelter the former Queen but help her, surreptitiously or openly as the case might be. He would stick his fingers into the affairs of Scotland, France's old ally, to keep England uneasy. French troops could land in Scotland as they had done many times before. In the delicate balance of power it was England and France that faced each other, each growing in strength, eying one another across the narrow seas. An alliance with Burgundy would keep Louis uneasy, as he, Louis, was hoping to keep Edward. In the King's mind the die was cast, the lot to be thrown with Burgundy, but in matters of diplomacy, as always, the King did not show his hand complete but held out hope and hand to both countries while he bargained for what was best for England. He had one strong card; Louis was afraid of Edward, the soldier. But yet another problem was coiling in the King's mind and that was the growing great might of one of his cousins, the legendary Earl Warwick. Edward had no standing army; he relied on trusted nobles to respond to the royal call for men and troops. He knew well enough his marriage had disaffected Warwick. Warwick was strong for a French alliance; Warwick had been exposed to crafty flattery of King Louis. Edward knew that Warwick made a mighty and useful servant when he resided at his great fortress of Middleham and directed the affairs of the north; no one was better than he at showing the mailed fist at the Scots or the unruly Northerners. He and his brother Montagu had been the strong right arm of the King and he had depended on them. That there was trouble ahead Edward did not fail to see; how great it was going to be he could not tell, for Edward was a reasonable man and he did not expect other men to descend into a great folly. Certainly, in time, they would see as clear as he did. And yet Edward was not blind; if Louis were plagued by a brother who made war on him, so too could the King of England have unruly subjects and even a traitorous brother. All things were possible under the sun and only a strong hand on the tiller would see them safely through the seas ahead. But Edward was not a tyrant and he wanted his justice tempered with mercy; therefore he proceeded cautiously and slowly. There would come a time when he would try to save Warwick's life and fail.

For Warwick indeed was the last of the barons. Born to a huge family, married to great wealth, he had shouldered his way through life brooking no opposition. Had not he made Edward the King? Had not his hands subdued the north and who ruled the north ruled England! When he rode into London, followed by masses of his retainers, did not the people cheer? Of course they did, and why? Edward thought cynically. Because he buys their loyalty, for when the great Earl was in residence in London eight oxen were roasted every morning for breakfast and any man could come to the kitchens and carry off as much meat as he could hold on his dagger. So splendid was the establishment of the great Earl. Edward sighed, thinking about his cousin. Warwick was in London, so he would hear today's news immediately. For Edward had decided to make Lord Rivers his treasurer.

Edward had had three treasurers already and none of them had completely satisfied him, for Edward was remarkably canny about money. Edward found Lord Rivers' household account book impressive; Rivers had the same feel for money Edward did. Lord Rivers had not been able to trade as the King had, but he had bought land and he owned many manors and in effect he was a kindred soul. More than that Lord Rivers was now grandfather to Edward's first child. So to Bessie's and the Duchess' delight Edward created Lord Rivers Earl Rivers and made him the Lord Treasurer of England. The Earl was going to do a splendid job, but that did not prevent Warwick writhing in disgust at the elevation of this lowborn upstart, as he called him. The appointment stuck in his craw; it was a straw in the wind. Instead of the highborn Nevilles in command of the reign there would be a crew of upstarts, low people, and those born to high estate would be shouldered aside by common trash. It was in-supportable! Warwick thought indeed the court was beginning to resemble a barnyard with the King as the important young cock amid the raggle-taggle, while he Warwick, the eagle, was shunt aside. Warwick hated the Herberts and John Fogge and he despised the Woodvilles; he was far too good to even stand in the same room with them, much less sit down with them at table!

Edward had just signed a treaty of alliance with Francis of Brittany to annoy Louis. Now with that alliance as one of his trumps, he commissioned Warwick and Hastings and Wenlock to go to Burgundy to treat with Philip—this was on the twenty-second of March. They were to treat anent a marriage between Edward's sister Margaret and Charles of Burgundy and between Clarence and Philip's daughter Mary, a child of nine. They also had secret instructions to treat with Louis about perpetual peace and to sound out the King Louis about a marriage for Edward's sister Margaret.

Edward hoped this important embassy would please his cousin, the Earl of Warwick.

Warwick and Hastings arrived in Boulogne on the fifteenth of April and spent three days there, first having treated with the Burgundians at St. Omer. Then they proceeded to Calais, where Louis had sent an imposing embassy consisting of the Seigneur de la Barde, who had accompanied Edward onto Palm Sunday Field, the Bastard of Bourbon, Bessie's uncle, Jacques of Lux-embourg, and le Comte de St. Pol, who was the Constable of France.

That was on the fourth of May. And on the twenty-fourth a treaty between France and England was signed, a brief truce to begin June fifteenth and to last until the first of March, 1468.

The treaty was brought over to England and Edward signed it on the seventh of June.

Charles, on his part, would not tolerate Warwick's arrogance.

Edward told Bessie about it. He said, "Hastings was afraid they might actually come to blows! Charles has a fiery temper."

He was sitting holding the baby, whose eyes were fastened on her father's face in wonderment. "She grows more beautiful every day," he said, "and what an intelligent little face she has, and your smile, Bessie." The chroniclers had labeled Edward's preoccupation with his first child as extraordinary. One summer day Bessie came into the room to find that the King had come in and lifted his sleeping daughter out of her cradle and carried her to the big bed and they were both sound asleep together. She had motioned for silence from her ladies and the baby's nurse, and they left the room, leaving Bessie sitting beside the bed watching her sleeping husband and child. When Edward opened his eyes, she reached out for his hand.

He smiled contentedly. "What luxury," he said, "to have a nap on a summer afternoon with my little Bess."

But it was soon fall and he was deep in the affairs of state. Francis of Brittany had, despite his solemn promises to Louis, taken under his wing Louis' rebellious brother, and so Francis thought it would be wise to creep closer to the King of England and sent his favorite ambassadors. And Charles, now afraid of the peace that Edward and Louis had signed, suddenly decided that he must make advances to Edward too and was sending the Seigneur de Gruthuyse as his special representative.

Edward was fond of Gruthuyse and wanted no interference with his reception of the Seigneur, so he sent Warwick to Newcastle to negotiate with the Scots about the breaches of the truce which had occurred. Thus the Christmas season passed pleasantly; Edward lavished gifts upon his new daughter and Bessie was very happy, because by the end of the twelve days of Christmas she could tell the King that she was going to have another baby.

Warwick returned from Scotland early in February, and at his urgings the King granted a safe conduct for ambassadors from Louis. During the winter and early spring then, at the English court were representatives of both France and Burgundy and secretly Edward was amused.

The great tournament between the Bastard of Burgundy and Anthony would take place in the spring; the French in England were not sure how their cause was progressing even under Warwick's obvious help and comfort. Yet Edward, playing his cards close to his chest, sat down one day and wrote to Louis with his own hand and told him he was agreeing to send Warwick to the court of France, and on the sixth of May he formally commissioned Warwick and Wenlock to go to France to treat for perpetual peace.

In April Edward had said to Bessie, "If I don't get rid of them soon, I'll be out of money. Those Frenchmen have already cost me five hundred pounds for food and wine. The Bastard of Bourbon drinks more good wine than I do. A hundred and fifty-two pounds for fine Burgundy wine!"

Nonetheless, for all the wine he drank, the Bastard of Bourbon wrote to Louis that Warwick did not have the influence that he said he did, that he was by no means sure of Edward, that day after day he had fenced wordily with the Burgundians and that this war of the diplomats in London was as important as any field of battle, more so.

Moreover the Bastard of Bourbon, in his creeping about the court, was suspicious that Edward had signed a truce and mutual alliance with Francis of Brittany, although he couldn't be sure, but he was sure about Castile because on his way home, at Canterbury, he came face-to-face with the Bishop of Redrigo, who was on his way to London to conclude the treaty of alliance between England and Castile.

The King had been his usual affable self when the Frenchmen had taken their leave. Edward was cordial, but his mind was evidently on the tournament of the next day when he himself was going to enter the lists against Anthony. As far as the Bastard could see, Edward had nothing else on his mind, but Edward in mail was so large and menacing that he kept bowing and eying him, and after he left the room Edward turned to Hastings and gave him a small smile.

"I hope I frightened the devil out of him," he said, laughing.

That night Elizabeth said to him, "For my sake be careful tomorrow."

She was six months pregnant, and Edward thought she had never looked more beautiful. "Perhaps you should not be present," he said.

She shook her head. "No, I'd worry more if I weren't."

She sat stiff and afraid the next day in the April sunshine.

As the two men from each side of the field thundered forward toward each other, both with visors open, Bessie shut her eyes. Then they flew open at the first sound of the clash of arms.

Both Anthony and the King were using broad swords. Bessie watched with wide eyes; their horsemanship was so magnificent that she was overcome with admiration and suddenly found herself cheering and shouting with all the rest. But when it was over and called a draw she drew a sigh of relief. They both rode to the center stand where the Earl Worcester, who was presiding, called the match a draw, and they took off their heavy gauntlets and shook hands. Bessie could see Edward's warm smile flash out and Anthony bowed deeply to the King and everyone cheered mightily; the banners flew and the sun shone and even the Earl Warwick had a pleasant expression on his face.

One reason Edward had let Warwick go to France was that he was playing the same game with Louis that Louis was playing with him and he did not want the Earl present when the Bastard of Burgundy arrived. Warwick left before the Bastard of Burgundy, whose given name was Anthony, arrived in England. The Bastard had sailed from Sluis, his large entourage requiring four caravels gay with banners and hung with arras. Crossing the narrow seas they were set upon by pirates who called themselves Spaniards, but Edward had no doubt that they were French. Louis was doing all he could to interfere.

But before Warwick had left, Edward had talked with him in private.

The meeting had irritated Edward considerably. He finally exploded, rising to his feet and hammering his big fist on his table as he rose.

"For the mercy of God!" He was about to ask Warwick if he were in his dotage when he controlled his tongue. Warwick's sudden tenderness for King Louis was beyond Edward's comprehension. Instead he said, "We shall never, never send one single English archer against Burgundy to help Louis conquer it! Never! Such a course would be suicide."

He swung around and gazed fixedly at Warwick, scowling. How could he be so stupid?

"France is growing rapidly in strength. It is insane to suggest we do something to increase that strength!"

Warwick was silent. He is set on alliance with France willynilly, Edward thought. He has been seduced completely by Louis, my adversary. What has been promised?

Edward asked silkily, "Has he promised you the lordship of Holland?"

He had hit very close to the mark, and Warwick flushed slightly. Edward smiled his mocking smile, his eyes lighting with a kind of bitter amusement. He thought, Warwick has helped make kings but he's prevented from being one by sheer accident of birth. And he believes Louis would make him the Duke of Holland. The crown. The ducal coronet. So closely is it coveted. Edward said aloud, as though to an empty room, "What fools men are." He threw out his hands. "You are empowered to make a perpetual peace with France. Treat with Louis. If by any chance you promise too much we can disavow it."

He was done with soft words, but impelled by the past and by Warwick's kinship and the friendship shared he held out his big hand. "Do the best you can for the realm."

With that warning Edward let him go. He was still unconvinced that Warwick would turn to outright treason. When Bessie said to him later that the Earl of Warwick didn't realize that there was but one King of England, Edward replied, "Yes, he realizes that there is one King. But he doesn't realize that his name is Edward."

He smiled at her with his deprecating smile. But it was easy for Bessie to forget Warwick. The magnificent tournament was approaching and the lists at Smithfield were ready; tons of sand from the Thames had been spread onto the field and the carpenters had been hammering night and day to prepare the stands for the King and spectators.

The Bastard of Burgundy was already in London. He had come up the river in specially prepared barges and with great formality and pomp was escorted to the house of the Bishop of Salisbury, where even the beds were hung with cloth of gold; the Bishop's servants, bowing low before this magnificent lord and his retinue, put into the Bastard's hands the key to the Bishop's house in Chelsea in case the great lord "should wish a bit of privacy or to try his harness secret."

The Bastard smiled at this thoughtful gesture on the part of the Bishop. The Bastard put away the keys in his jewel chest and then he and his lords went out into the streets just like any men, the servants thought, in a strange city; they went on foot, laughing and jabbering.

At almost the same moment Edward was entering London. The trumpets, the clarions, the sea of people, of heralds, aldermen and noblemen brought forth his smile, his hand raised in greeting. It was proceeding well. His thoughts were on the impressive way he wished this great tournament to go; it gave him immense pleasure to see his London crammed with foreigners; the tournament itself was a matter of prestige, foreign policy and spectacle to his subjects, the which he thought a King should so mightily provide. He looked ahead at Anthony, who rode just before him bearing proudly the sword of state. Then his mind flicked to the Nevilles and the opening of Parliament tomorrow. Through the thickly massed streets they rode to St. Paul's, as Edward always did when he entered London, to make his offering.

The Bastard and his knights were waiting on Fleet Street, jostling for position to see just like anyone else. The Bastard was very tall, so he stood back a bit with his knights in front of him. He was anxious not only to see Edward but the man with whom he had corresponded for a year and his opponent in the list.

"That must be he, my lord, bearing the sword of state!"

The Bastard stared at Anthony, and while he did Anthony sensed it, for he turned in the saddle and his eyes went unerringly to the Bastard. Both men smiled. Anthony rode on; protocol forbade the two to meet.

But the Bastard was pleased with what he saw, and his eyes now went to Edward. The Bastard, the principal knight of Europe, this favored illegitimate son of Philip of Burgundy, renowned for his daring and knightly endeavors, had surrounded himself with young men of his own ilk. They looked across at Edward; then they looked at each other and they nodded solemnly. Here was indeed a King.

They met him the following morning. Edward received them in an audience before his lords, a formal ceremony in which the English lords had time to study and envy the Bastard and his lords, who wore the latest styles from France, and the Bastard and his lords were able to perceive Edward's charm and the genuineness of his smile and the obvious respect and love his own lords accorded him.

That afternoon Edward opened Parliament. Edward had

planned this very carefully that the Burgundians should be witness to the ceremony. The lords and commons were proud to take their seats before a gallery jammed with imposing visitors, and the visitors were impressed with this symbol of English justice and law of and for the people. King Louis called the Estates General but once in his reign and then no complaints were permitted.

The Painted Chamber was as brilliant as its name. The Archbishop of Canterbury rose to open the proceedings with a prayer. And no one in the Painted Chamber, especially the Burgundians, had any idea that right after their audience had been concluded a messenger had brought Edward a letter which had sent him right to his table, and there had had something to eat while he wrote the notes which lay before him now. No one as yet knew that the Chancellor of the realm, George Neville, Archbishop of York, whose duty it was to deliver the principal address this afternoon, had sent word to Edward at the last moment that he was ill.

Edward had shoved aside all annoyance and had set himself the task of preparing a short address. Now, in the silence after the prayer, the King himself rose.

"We welcome you, my lords, my good Archbishop, our much loved and respected guests, John Say, our Speaker, we give you all good greeting. We are unhappy to tell you that our Chancellor is ill and will be unable to present to you his usual address." He leaned on the lectern and smiled his engaging, frank smile. "We are happy, though, to be thus able to speak with you ourselves."

Edward was a gifted speaker because he had a direct and honest way.

"John Say," he alluded to the Speaker, "and ye, sirs, come to this my court of Parliament for the commons of this my land, the reason why I have summoned this my present Parliament is that I intend to live upon my own and not charge my subjects —except in great need concerning the defense of them and this my realm—but not to my own pleasures."

Of course they were pleased. Nobody likes to pay taxes.

"I assure you that I have only your welfare at heart and that I will defend the laws of the land and the whole kingdom with my own life."

They didn't doubt it; they cheered mightily because they knew their King was as big in battle as he was in his fashionable dress, which they could see right before them.

Then Edward reminded them that the Speaker and members of his council would address them and let them know what specific laws he wished, and that they, through their deliberations and through their elected Speaker, would tell him what were their requests and wishes of him.

He added that he would adjourn Parliament temporarily next Wednesday for the weekend so that all of them might attend the great tournament.

Edward sat down.

He could not help but think of George Neville, whose place he had taken. George Neville, who could raise his silken voice to thunder and who could have supplied the colorful drama that Edward wished his Parliament and visitors to see. Was George Neville really sick? Edward had difficulty believing it. George Neville reveled in his own jovian bolts of eloquence before full Parliament. Had he foregone them to warn Edward that he and his brother Warwick stood shoulder to shoulder in the Woodville manner? Edward cautioned himself; he must not prejudge; first he must find out the truth.

If Edward's thoughts were on the Nevilles, the thoughts of the Woodville clan were with their chief pride, Anthony. For whatever people said about the King advancing the Woodvilles and about their undue ambitions and their sophistication and their clannishness, Anthony had been a shining star in his own right, had previously corresponded with the Bastard of Burgundy.

So Anthony's frail Beth and Bessie and the Duchess and all his sisters had lovingly helped with all the paraphernalia with which women's hands could help. The edging of the gorgeous harness of his horse, the blue silken tassels which would fly from his blue satin tent, the feather plumes for his helmet, his long cape of gold tissue.

He wore that cape when he came up to the city for the weekend. He came by river; his horse and attendants were waiting at St. Catherine's. Worcester greeted him and his father rode before him, bearing his arms. Then trotting side by side Richard and John Woodville; behind him, the same blond hair gleaming under their caps, came young Lionel and Edward Woodville. Handsome and vibrant, the glamour of the Woodvilles was out in force; proudly they presented their champion to London, riding slowly through the cheering streets all the way to Holborn. The whole of the city streamed after them to watch their champion dismount and disappear into the home of the Bishop of Ely, where Anthony would spend the weekend.

Young Lionel and Edward slept in trundle beds in Anthony's room, wriggling and excited, and it seemed to Lionel he had just fallen asleep when he was wakened by Anthony. He blinked and grunted.

"It's very early, Anthony," he protested. He stretched. It must be Monday morning, for yesterday he had accompanied his older brothers to church.

"I need my riding boots. I sent them down to be polished, my thigh boots, Lionel," Anthony said.

Lionel grunted again and got out of bed and into his slippers and robe. He was too sleepy to wonder where Anthony was going until he got all the way back into Anthony's bedroom. He set down the boots.

"Where are you going?" he asked.

"To an early council meeting," Anthony said, standing by the sideboard drinking ale.

He had been summoned early and unexpectedly. The others who lived nearer Westminster or in the royal lodgings would undoubtedly precede him. Anthony hastened out.

When Anthony arrived at Westminster there were with Edward: Hastings, concealing a yawn, Blount, Worcester and Will Herbert; John Fogge and Humphrey Stafford, the new Earl of Devonshire, came in right after Anthony. Everyone looked hastily dressed but Edward, who was wearing a ruffled shirt and a close-fitting, brown-velvet doublet, brown hose and soft boots that reached up almost to his hips. A messenger stood at his side and Edward was reading a dispatch. Anthony bowed and Edward waved him to a chair at the council table; Anthony tried to be quiet but the chair scraped.

Edward looked annoyed. Anthony had wondered all the way here what had happened and he guessed it had something to do with George Neville, the Chancellor, because all through the weekend rumor and gossip had it that the Chancellor was not sick, never had been sick, and that he had refused to open Parliament as a gesture of Neville defiance; why should they take part in this Parliament and great tournament when it was for the advancement and glorification of the King and court and the damned Woodvilles? And there was another rumor going about the city that a papal legate was in London to confer secret with George Neville, Archbishop, and it was that rumor which had just been confirmed by the report from one of his agents; it was in Edward's hands right now. The fact that there was indeed a papal legate in the city incognito, who was seeing the Archbishop secret, and the thought that his Chancellor was carrying on dealings with Rome about which the King had no knowledge was alone enough to make Edward suspicious and angry. A great many men's private word for George Neville was "slippery." The dispatch in Edward's hands at this moment was a message from this legate himself, making himself known, and Edward managed to grunt out that according to the policy of the crown he would allow him his usual expenses, for John Fogge to take note of that and the length of the legate's stay. But that was the end of Edward's patience.

He sat up straight, his face dark with anger. Anthony felt as though four hundred years had rolled back and that he was in the eleventh century facing Plantagenet wrath, and Edward furthered the illusion by commanding, "My horse!"

He stood, his hand on the long, gold-hilted dagger at his side. Someone, John Fogge, murmured something about a cloak. Edward pushed past him, wordless. Then he turned his head. "Attend me," he snapped.

Anthony didn't dare speak; he just bowed and hurried to the doors, backing away from Edward to open them and hold them. The two secretaries had already fled out the side doors to hastily summon the master of horse so that their monarch's favorite mount should be ready and saddled by the time he got down into the courtyard.

George Neville, Archbishop of York and Chancellor of the realm, lived near Charing Cross. During the ride there, as quick as Edward could make it and consumed with his bitter anger, he didn't note that suddenly the people realized their King was riding among them, barely attended with but a handful of his lords.

Edward had not time for the amenities; bound on an errand of state his two foremost riders cleared the way; Anthony and Hastings went to each side of him to keep the people away; it was dangerous, Anthony thought, the sheer masses of people pouring out into the streets to see.

"Make way! Make way!" came the shouts from Edward's two front riders; they glanced back over their shoulders to see if Edward were slackening his pace; he wasn't.

"Make way! Make way!"

The crowd broke and pressed against the sides of the buildings. Quiet, they drew aside, but once he had passed they followed, streaming down the narrow streets after this small group of riders with the King in their midst, curious to see what drama had exploded on a Monday morning.

"Make way! Make way!"

The distant shout reached the ears of George Neville, having his breakfast. It almost sounded like Will Herbert's voice, but of course that couldn't be. George Neville buttered his fresh bread, contemplated the color of the wine in the silver goblet. The windows were wide open; it was a lovely warm morning.

"Make way!"

George Neville set down his wine. That *was* Will Herbert's voice. What was he doing acting as a forerider? George Neville's mouth sagged; he gave a kind of gasp and ran to the window. There was only one person that the proud Will Herbert would ride afore to clear the crowds; George Neville clung to the sill and looked down into his courtyard as Will Herbert flung off his horse, rushed up to the doors and beat on them with the handle of his riding whip.

"In the King's name!" he shouted and George Neville, still clinging onto the sill, looked down at the top of Edward's head just as the door to his chamber burst open and a frightened servant cried, "The King is here!"

"I'm too sick!" returned the Chancellor. He rushed over to his bed and climbed in, pulling the satin quilt about him, settling his bedcap which he still wore, his hands holding the quilt tight under his chin.

"Fetch my secretary! Fetch my chaplain! Send for my doctor! Inform His Grace I am in bed! I am ill! Ill!"

He lay there quivering but thinking he had been rather clever not to have rushed down to greet Edward in haste. But he was the kind of man who was always surprised when other people turned out to be just as clever or cleverer than he was. Such a man stood down in the hall below, his brown eyes grim and uncompromising.

"We regret the Chancellor is ill but inform him that we have come. Inform him we have come for the Great Seal of the realm."

Anthony stifled an exclamation. George Neville was then Chancellor no longer; the King was serving dramatic notice on the Nevilles that there was but one ruler in England. Edward stood still and tall, controlling his anger and restlessness; he waited outwardly patient like the motionless tiger before the kill. The Great Seal of the realm could not be entrusted to other hands; George Neville must bring it himself and lay it into his King's big hands. So Edward waited and Anthony waited and Will Herbert and Hastings waited, silent, grouped around Edward, a little to the rear of him. Then the Archbishop appeared at the top of the steps, wearing a little cap now but still in his bedgown.

He indeed looked sick. He seemed unsteady. He bore the Great Seal before him, and a secretary aided him by holding his elbow; the secretary could feel the trembling in his master's arm.

George Neville descended slowly. He came to a stop before the King. Edward lifted gently, reverently, the Great Seal from his hands. Then George Neville knelt, his cap fell to the floor; Edward looked down at his bent head. His face was unforgiving.

"We give you our good-bye," Edward said, and turned on his heel.

The field was ninety yards long and eighty yards wide. The King's stands were higher than the others. It was a sea of color. Edward was clothed in purple with white hose and shirt; he wore the Order of the Garter and carried a baton; he sat with his council about him and below him three tiers of knights, squires and archers; massed on the stairway to the King's stage were officers at arms and the Constable of the realm. Across the field in a wave of scarlet sat the mayor and alderman, and the rest of the stands overflowed with members of Parliament and anyone else who could squeeze himself in.

The trumpets blew and Anthony rode up to the bar with

Lords Herbert and Kent and the King's brother Clarence himself bearing his helmet. At the bar the Lord Constable asked him why he had come and Anthony said, "It is my wish to accomplish and perform the acts comprised in the articles sent to me by the Lord Antoine of Burgundy."

Edward then commanded him to enter the field.

Anthony went before Edward and knelt. Rising, he went to his tent of double blue satin, and the Bastard then rode up to the bar and performed the same ritual. The Bastard went over to his own tent, but he came out quickly and put on his helmet in the view of everyone. The swords and spears had been inspected; they were sent over to the Bastard for him to pick the ones he wanted. By this time everyone was squirming with impatience but there were more proclamations to come. From all four corners of the field the King's commands were read. "That for the augmentation of martial discipline and knightly honor and to the defense of the right of kings and princes and their estates, certain deeds of arms were to be performed, and no man, upon pain of imprisonment or fine at the King's will, should approach the lists or make any noise or demonstration of any kind by which the combatants might either be troubled or comforted."

Anthony and the Bastard now faced each other ahorse. The heralds cried, "*Laissez allez!*"

The two armed men and beasts thundered forward toward each other, the long spears like toys in the grasp of the mailed warriors.

The Bastard was thundering right toward Anthony. The stands were hushed; there was the sound only of the pounding hoofbeats. The Bastard came rushing on. At the last moment Anthony turned his horse's head, and the Bastard's horse veered and struck its head on Anthony's saddle.

Anthony's horse swerved and neighed loud. The Bastard's horse reared high. Then in front of Anthony's astounded and horrified eyes the Bastard's horse fell, its legs writhing.

The Bastard struggled to his feet. Now his horse lay still. And Edward, face set with anger, brought down his baton sharply onto his open palm and commanded Anthony to come to him. In an agony of embarrassment Anthony wheeled his horse. That Edward should believe he had any concealed weapon or that he would take advantage of a horse or strike a horse was unthinkable. With trembling hands he removed his helmet. He dismounted and knelt on the field.

"Your Grace," he said. "I beg permission to take off the trappings of my horse and to show Your Grace that there is nought concealed and no unlawful armor, none, Your Grace."

Still angry, Edward nodded. There was such absolute stillness that Anthony thought people could hear the pounding of his heart and his quick, unhappy breathing. Clumsily he removed his gauntlets. The earl marshal and the constable and the officers at arms crowded around but at enough distance so that Edward could see, and one by one the magnificent trappings that the Duchess had labored over were removed from Anthony's restless horse.

There was nothing underneath but Anthony's war saddle. He raised his eyes to Edward's face. Anthony said, "I beg your forgiveness and yours, my lord," and he bowed to the Bastard who was by now alongside.

Edward then asked the Bastard if he would have another horse.

The Bastard replied it was not the season. So Anthony left the field. He had never felt worse; it seemed as though he had cheated the King and all the spectators and turned a great occasion into a farce. Anthony retired into his tent and sat down, putting his blond head in his hands, and Will Herbert patted him clumsily on the shoulder.

"His Grace was very angry," Anthony muttered.

"Aye," said Will; there was no use blinking the truth. "But it wasn't your fault, Anthony. Oliver de la March told me the Bastard was somewhat nearsighted. He didn't mean to careen into you that way. He misjudged." Anthony knew that Will would tell Edward that, so he sighed and let Will take off the mail and place again on his shoulders his gold cape, and then riding proudly Anthony left the field and everyone cheered, for after all he was the bearer of the colors of the King and country.

Sleep came tardy and reluctant to Anthony that night. Too much wine was forbidden to him, for the solace of the grape would be tomorrow's infirmity. The hours of early morning prolonged themselves until finally it was time to rise.

It was a beautiful day. Once more the stands overflowed and the banners flew and the colors gleamed; today a high air of expectancy communicated itself to both Anthony and the Bastard, for if they had failed yesterday to entertain no one doubted that today they would put on a show no one would ever forget.

And so it was. For if Anthony felt that his honor had been besmirched by the death of his opponent's horse, the Bastard felt he had clumsily committed an error of horsemanship which was a blot on the great escutcheon of Burgundy. So when Anthony presented the weapons once more for Edward's approval, he laid before the King, once again clothed in purple and wearing the Garter, a fearsome array of battle-axes, daggers and spears. The Bastard nodded enthusiastically. As he had said to Oliver de la March the evening before, "Today Sir Anthony fought a horse. Tomorrow he shall fight a man."

But Edward, sensing that each man was more than determined, decided not to permit the use of the spears.

"This is an occasion of pleasance," the King announced, and the spears were borne off the field by Will Herbert and the weapons then presented to the Bastard so that he could have his choice.

The Bastard lifted one of the battle-axes and found it suited to his grip. He balanced one of the long, heavy-bladed daggers. He took his time, laying down one dagger and picking out another, weighing that in his open palm, then shifting his fingers to the grip, pausing thoughtfully while no one breathed and every one fastened their eyes on his magnificent figure, the representative of the most munificent and magnificent court in Europe, the darling of his father, Philip the Good, the man who had fought even in Turkey. Finally the Bastard signified himself satisfied. He bowed and backed away and Anthony now picked out his own two weapons, one battle-ax and one dagger. After he too had performed this ceremony he looked up at Edward and the King smiled his merry smile. Anthony felt much better and with relief and fierce desire to redeem himself he went back to his tent to accouter himself for the fray.

Because of the battle-axes both men wore heavy armor. The heralds cried, the trumpets blew, there was a pregnant hush and then the clash of arms. On foot, in the center of the large field, the Bastard and Anthony put on a spectacle that was to become the most famous duel of their times.

Anthony fought with his visor open. Whether it was a brave show for the crowd or whether he could see better, the King and Anthony's womenfolk didn't know. The Duchess' hands were clasped so tight together that her fingers were sore for a week, while in front of her eyes the Bastard's battle-ax descended in a sidewise sweep into Anthony's shoulder. Anthony stepped back and circled his opponent. And so it went, as they traded blow for blow; massive strikes against the body which would have felled another man hardly staggered the tall broadness of the Bastard.

Once again cheering was forbidden, as it might discomfit the combatants, but nonetheless as each man struck a blow, a sigh like a soft wind went over the field, as though all together had let out their breath; and in the beginning, wary, the two Anthonys circled and crouched, delivering a quick blow and circling away, Anthony's face intent, the eyes narrowed to slits. The Bastard's face was hidden behind the closed visor but Anthony could see his eyes, gleaming like his own.

And then the fight waxed hotter. Perfectly matched, they increased their tempo as though they were playing on instruments; and as though the crescendo of the fighting were perfect timed, like the beat of the drum or the speed of a glissando, it rose and rose and rose until the stands were huddled watching like a beast with thousands of unblinking eyes fastened on the two men as the axes descended time after time. For now it was quite obvious that this was not Smithfield at all but somehow a Roman arena and the struggle was to the death.

This drama the two men managed to convey to the spectators quite quickly. Anthony had come onto the field determined not to leave it; his honor demanded that he give his all for Edward who watched him, Edward, his King and the man for whom Anthony would willingly give his life. If it were necessary he would give it today on the already bloodied field.

Edward's eyes were now as narrow as both combatants' as he watched. He had muttered his favorite oath more than a few times as he realized that yesterday's fiasco had turned into today's struggle, for this did not resemble an ordinary duel, after the first ten minutes it had not; Edward had seen a struggle like this on the battlefield. From his vantage point he could see that Anthony's armor was badly gashed—Edward knew very well the strength of the blows from the Bastard's ax which had caused them.

But the first person to feel Anthony's determination was the Bastard, who was now too completely caught up in the struggle, and they went at each other with fury, complete and unconcealed, as though the mighty god of Mars had taken each to his breast, and the drama exploded in the field and no one could make a sound even if it had been permitted.

The blows were staggering the two men. The Bastard reeled back from one blow, recovered and came at Anthony in a rush which Anthony could not avoid. The Bastard's ax caught Anthony's left shoulder as the Bastard aimed a backhand strike. Now it was Anthony's turn to reel away.

Edward now raised the baton. Neither man would see it; now the traded blows were coming faster as they stood almost toe to toe, defying each other, daring to stand face-to-face and beat upon the other's armored body. Their breathing was so labored it could be seen even across the field as their broad chests heaved like animals, and neither would concede.

"For the mercy of God," Edward muttered under his breath for the last time. "They're going to kill each other!"

So he rose to his enormous height, throwing down the baton to stop the fighting before either the Bastard or Anthony fell dead on the field, but neither man saw the baton or the King rise, and then just as Anthony was raising the heavy ax for another blow, Edward cried out to stop him, using the first word that came into his head.

"Whoa!" Edward shouted.

The ax did not descend. It stayed upright in Anthony's hand. He took a wavering step back, and so did the Bastard, and the spell was broke; they looked at each other and then to the King who was standing, then back to each other again and both of them were perfectly still, stunned by the abrupt end of their contest.

Both men's seconds ran out onto the field; wearily the Bastard took off his helmet, Anthony did the same, and just as wearily they handed the axes to the group of their noble seconds. Anthony handed his to Will Herbert, who was speechless with relief that Anthony was still alive and overcome with admiration at the performance Anthony had put on. And now that it was over the spectators could release their pent-up feelings, and great waves of cheering and shouting passed over Anthony and the Bastard. They both turned their heads this way and that as if to see where they were.

The Bastard raised the visor of his helmet, leaving a bloody mark; Anthony met his eyes; they looked honest and bewildered. Anthony muttered, "I apologize for yesterday."

"It wasn't your fault," the Bastard said, trying to catch his breath.

"I'll never fight you again," Anthony said. "You're too good for me."

The Bastard smiled, for Anthony had said what he was thinking himself. "We'll take an oath on that tonight."

They were suddenly surrounded now by their retinues who had swarmed out onto the field. Will Herbert proudly took Anthony's ax and bore it high, and Clarence tenderly took the helmet Anthony removed from his head. Then with their nobles streaming behind both men went over to the King's stands and stood side by side before Edward.

Anthony raised his eyes to Edward's face, his dented, gashed armor his badge and gift to his King. His broad chest rose and fell, and it would be a moment before he could speak; he could feel the warm, wet blood running down his right arm and trickling onto his fingers; his whole body ached as though he had fought a battering ram instead of a man. He planted his feet wide to keep from swaying, and out of the corner of his eye he noted the Bastard did the same; Anthony could hear his labored breathing, or was it his own?

The trumpets blew as though they were far away, and the heralds announced the King's decision that the match was a draw. Edward's handsome face with its proud smile swam in front of Anthony's eyes, then suddenly he realized that Edward was commanding him to take off his gauntlets and to shake hands with the Bastard.

Anthony drew off the heavy battle gloves, one of his men took them from his fingers and he extended his bloody hand to the Bastard.

"Love each other as true brothers in arms," commanded the King.

There was no need for them to speak, for the few previous

words had been enough. But the Bastard said, "Tonight we shall take our oath never to fight except side by side!" He relinquished Anthony's hand. They exchanged a quick rueful smile, for each was wondering whether he could walk off the field, but they did. The great tournament was over for them; tomorrow they could sit in the stands next the King and watch.

Edward's good humor was completely restored by Anthony's gallant fight, and Anthony basked in the light of the King's approval and the English chroniclers claimed the victory had been Anthony's when the King interfered. Anyway it had been a brave show, and Edward had planned that the tournaments should continue through the next week. The Bastard and Anthony had fought on Friday; Saturday and Sunday they could sit in the stands, and on Sunday night Edward and Bessie feasted all their guests. Bessie had rounded up seventy beautiful ladies and the dinner was held at the Grocer's Hall, and it was very gay.

The Bastard was planning to return the hospitality the following Sunday evening and Anthony was helping him as one of the stewards for his banquet. For the dinner was to be in honor of Bessie, her sisters and her ladies. But suddenly from Burgundy came the news of the death of the Duke, the great Philip the Good. So all the elaborate preparations had to be canceled, and instead of helping with the banquet for Bessie Anthony helped the Bastard make his hurried and sorrowing leave. The great tournament was over.

Chapter 11

THE BURGUNDIANS had been overwhelmed by Bessie's beauty. They repeated what King Louis had remarked with positive awe when he had learned of Edward's marriage. "He married her," said Louis, "for her love and for her beauty."

And was he not to be envied. When she appeared at his side, her hand laid gently on his arm, she was his most perfect complement, blooming with love, her body rich with their child, for Bessie was more than seven months into her second pregnancy.

She herself, her sisters and her court had impelled the gay and lavish dinner they had planned to honor her, and Anthony had told her all this.

She said earnestly to Anthony, "Above all, I want to be a credit and help to my husband. He has so much to trouble him."

Their eyes met and Anthony nodded. Parliament's one request to Edward had been to end the lawlessness in the realm.

"He is more plagued and troubled about it than they," Bessie said. Anthony was silent. One of their father's manors had been attacked. It would have been sacked and pillaged but the Woodvilles were served with enormous personal devotion by those who loved them and Lord Rivers' servants and bailiffs had managed to escape from the house with all its valuables. Anthony had no doubt that it was Warwick's doing, for the struggle between the King and Warwick was now more than a cloud and the rumble of thunder could be heard throughout the land. And as the Lord Rivers suffered and the Pastons, so did others.

Northumberland was a coil of trouble. Its principal peer languished in the King's prison of the fleet, and Edward gave some thought to Lord Percy and wondered whether clemency or harshness should be the order of the day. But he put that thought into the back of his mind as he played one man against the other, for he had bestowed the earldom of Northumberland on his cousin, Montagu, Warwick's brother, the Neville of which Edward was so fond and whom he trusted. It had been Montagu who had helped so much to quiet Northumberland, and now Edward sent him back there to enforce the peace of the realm. Nonetheless he often thought of Percy, for the fierce Northerners responded best to their own lord. Edward gave orders that Percy was to be well treated and allowed him a considerable sum for his comfort in jail.

On the twenty-eighth of June Edward took the afternoon off. He and Bessie and just a few of the court took the children to the Tower to see the King's menagerie. Great was the excitement and astonishment when the King appeared, carrying little Bess in his arms, with Richard Grey clinging tightly to his other hand.

"One with two humps!" cried little Richard.

"They are called dromedaries," said Thomas Grey solemnly. "Look, Mother!"

The keeper of the King's menagerie was bowing this way and that. One of the lionesses was going to have young. "She will bring forth a baby," he told Thomas.

"So will my mother," Thomas said, and Edward laughed. Bessie had Grace by the hand, and she would soon go into retirement before the birth of her second child by Edward. She was wearing a full-paneled dress; her hair was piled on top of her head and covered by a little fezlike cap which had a floaty, gauzy veil. It was a beautiful hot summer day, and the keeper would report to all his friends at the tavern that night how beautiful the children were, and how friendly and kind the King and Queen were with them. And he would also report that it was the veriest truth, the Queen was the most beautiful woman he had ever seen in his life.

That night the first reports of the plague reached Westminster. The next day the first deaths were reported. On July first Parliament prorogued in panic, and the rumbling carts carrying the dead and the rumbling carts of the fleeing wealthy and country gentry all mingled together. In haste Edward sent Bessie and the royal household to Windsor. Bessie did not want to go farther than that, and she picked a set of rooms overlooking the stretching fields toward Eton. On Edward's instructions all clothing was aired and brushed and laid in the sun, all precautions of cleanliness were taken and Bessie had a room set aside with a big bath that was draped about with the finest of imported lawn. Once again women took over the duties of her own household, from carver to server, as for the second time she prepared for the birth of a royal child.

Her ladies—her sister-in-law, Alice Fogge, her sister, Anne Bourchier—were joined this time by Edward's sister, the Lady Margaret. From her two windows Bessie could see the sweet, flowing fields that surrounded Eton. She could not see the chapel that Edward was building. But she had set aside a small room as a chapel for herself, for as she said to the Duchess, "The honeymoon is over a long time now, and I am expected to bring forth an heir."

She was not referring to Edward but to his subjects, for Bessie knew too well that her enemies, which were legion, saw no excuse for her occupying the throne of England at all if there were no males born of her union with the King. It was particularly frustrating because there was nothing whatever she and Edward could do except hope; nonetheless there was another avenue and that was prayer.

"My sins sit heavy on me," she told her mother, who snorted. "I am vain and proud."

The Duchess gave a louder snort, her white fingers busy at the intricate loom at which she worked. She pulled through a shining thread, snipped it off and said, "You'll be just like me, have a dozen or more children and some of them will be male. Be content and happy, Bessie, that you are fruitful and that you will soon present your husband with a beautiful baby."

The Princess Margaret's marriage negotiations to Charles of Burgundy took Bessie's mind off her own disquiets.

Margaret had come before the King's great council at Kingston-on-Thames and approved before the lords the marriage arranged by her brother. Edward himself appeared before Parliament to explain in his frank, direct way that the principal enemy of England was still France and that he had succeeded in making alliances with the countries that ringed France and in making peace in Scotland for fifty winters; and they responded, for it was still the popular feeling that France was the enemy; Edward understood his fellow Englishmen far better than did my lord of Warwick.

It was a fine match. Margaret was pleased with the thought of reigning over the most magnificent court in Europe, and Charles was a romantic, bold figure. But meantime Bessie herself had been matchmaking with Edward's older sister, the Duchess of Suffolk.

The Duchess was well disliked. She was officious and mercenary, and people said her first husband had been killed by her unkindnesses. But there was an heiress born of that first marriage, and now she and Bessie bargained across their sewing. In the end Bessie agreed to pay the Duchess four thousand marks and the Duchess agreed to betroth her little girl to Bessie's son, Thomas Grey.

So what with the bargaining and the gossiping and Bessie's restless waiting, the women's chambers seethed with rumors such as: The King and Hastings had ridden out one night together and returned very late.

Bessie's hands clenched and she threw her ale cup across the room. He had been with another woman! All the ladies clustered around her, praying her to be calm and remember her child, whereupon Bessie flung herself on her bed and pulled the curtains tight until she could scarcely breathe, for it was a very hot day, and so angrily she pulled them again and saw all the ladies whispering together.

"Stop!" she commanded, sitting on her knees in the middle of the big bed. "Stop whispering!"

Edward heard all this with some amusement and some misgivings. His older sister's daughter had been betrothed to Montagu's son. Now she and Bessie had undoubtedly given offense to the Earl. "For God's sake," Edward muttered; if all those women didn't hatch something worse by the time Bessie's child was born he would be lucky. The evening of that day Margaret came to tell him that the Queen's labor had begun.

In the early hours of the morning, the eighth of August, Bessie's child was born and later came the King himself to her bedside. Bessie said, "Oh, my love, I, I—" her eyes filled with tears.

He brushed them away with his big hand across her cheeks. "We shall name her after Our Blessed Lady, who has blessed us with two fine children. Come, Bessie, say her name with me."

"Mary," whispered Bessie, looking deep into his eyes, holding tight to his hand, her voice mingling with his.

Edward planned an impressive christening, and he seemed just as happy to have another daughter. But throughout the realm spread rumor after rumor, and the young, handsome, volatile Duke of Clarence was still the nearest male heir to the throne.

Chapter 12

IN ONE of the paneled rooms which you are not permitted to enter when you go to Warwick Castle today, the great Earl and Clarence were finishing dinner. Looking back over the years it is difficult to apprise the charm which Clarence was said to possess. He was Margaret's favorite brother, for instance, and she adored him. But his winning charm barely concealed a childish egoism; in his cups he turned sullen and mean and his lack of stability was only too evident to both Edward and Warwick and to Clarence's kin. As a matter of fact, Warwick didn't like Clarence very much either but Warwick had tasted power. It had begun its deadly corruption and now he sought to corrupt Clarence too. "That gold-headed bitch," Clarence said, referring to Bessie, "connives to take my brother away from me."

He truly believed it. Warwick doubted it privately. Were he Edward he wouldn't trust Clarence either. So he was weaving a pretty net for Clarence to entrap him. Money was the trap, money and with it Warwick's sixteen-year-old daughter, Isabel. Warwick had no sons, and now at long last after four years Warwick was going to dip his hands openly into treason.

It was early fall and Clarence and he had noted that Bessie's figure was full again.

"She is going to have another in her litter," Clarence said angrily. "She speaks to him in honeyed tones, she flatters and beguiles him, all sweet submission and smiles, and thus she gets whatever she wants from him!"

Clarence had the faculty of annoying even his adherents or the men who were using him. Much as Warwick disliked, nay, hated the Woodvilles, Clarence's words provoked him to say, "I wish to God all wives were like that."

"All she does is push her family upon him and push me out!"

Warwick stared across the table at Clarence with active dislike. "At least the Woodvilles don't wine," he said sharply.

Clarence's eyes narrowed and became mean, and he was about to retort but the name "Woodville" diverted him and he thought of John who had come back recently from Burgundy with a wardrobe which outshone Clarence's. When Clarence thought of John Woodville shouldering his ambitious way through the courts of both England and Burgundy, John with his cynical wit and his way with women, Clarence was moved to such hatred that he almost choked with it. For his brother Edward was amused with John and liked and trusted him and kept him by his side. Edward couldn't have cared less that John had married for money —that was his business. What mattered to Edward was the young, loyal soldier, who had just carried off all the honors in Burgundy for his native land at the festivities of the marriage between the Princess Margaret and Charles of Burgundy.

"You're not afraid of the devil himself, John," Edward had said one day a week ago.

Clarence could see plain the wicked grin on John's face as he had replied, "No, indeed, Your Grace, I'm on very good terms with him."

Now Clarence leaned across the table, his hair falling across his face. "I will kill John Woodville some day."

"You'll need help then. You can't do it alone."

The thought of Clarence facing John in equal combat was farcical to Warwick. "I'll help you," Warwick said low, "but first, first the marriage."

The first bit of treason contemplated was the marriage of Clarence to Isabel Neville, which Edward had forbid; since Edward had forbid it and was negotiating with Louis for a French princess for Clarence, and since Edward's agent in Rome was the only avenue through which Clarence and Isabel could get the necessary papal dispensation, Warwick confided, his voice low, "I have paid five thousand marks to subvert the King's agent in Rome. And he has promised to get the dispensation for us. But it will take time."

Warwick hid his eyes from Clarence's scrutiny. For what he planned was simple in essence. First the marriage. Then the plan to catch the King unaware. And then—with the King in his power —he could dictate terms, for he could say, "I will put Clarence on the throne. I, who have made you King, unless you obey me will place your brother on the throne and my daughter will be Queen, so you, you, Edward, had best behave and behave well!" For Warwick really had no yearning to deal with Clarence; he wanted Edward, a compliant Edward, and Clarence would be the lever. So while Warwick was planning to play false to both brothers, Clarence didn't perceive it yet and thought that the great earl would help him ascend the steps to the throne he so badly coveted and on which he was so unfit to sit.

"How if that bitch has a boy?" he whispered.

Warwick said contemptuously, "A gaggle of females is all she will produce, mark my words." Yet underneath his remark he did wonder too, but all that could be conquered with enough money, enough treachery, enough ruthlessness. He, Warwick, had placed Edward on the throne; he could remove him, threaten him and bring him to terms; he was sure of it. His glance flicked over Clarence with contempt barely concealed. He would use him, just use him until he had tamed Edward. He would force Edward to acknowledge Clarence as his heir, and then his own daughter Isabel would be married to the man who stood to inherit the throne.

"But how will you capture Edward?" Clarence whispered.

"I will," Warwick said. "Never fear, I will. You will see and you must do as I say."

Clarence nodded but his wits, dulled by wine, still prodded at him, as did memory. "I adored him," he said.

Warwick understood—Clarence was deep in the past.

Yet not so deep, for Clarence suddenly remembered a day just last Christmas. Edward had kept Christmas at Coventry, which was unusual, but he had spent the holy season there with Bessie and the family and Clarence because the country about had been unsettled and Edward had foregone the pleasures of Windsor.

The audience chamber had been crowded that day. A French envoy had been present. Edward, with a heavily furred jacket, had spoke with him, and the whole hall had been quiet when Edward had said, "You may apprise your master King Louis," he paused and Clarence could again feel Edward's steady gaze upon him. "Tell him firm that we shall support him against his brother." Again Edward paused; every ear was strained to hear the King's

next words. "His brother, who is a fool, through whom the lords
of France would like to run the country to suit themselves."

There was deep silence in the audience chamber as Clarence's
face had flushed.

Is it true? he thought. Is it true? Am I a fool through whom
Warwick and his lords will run the country to suit themselves?

"Last Christmas—you were not present—" he began and
stopped.

"I was in the north," Warwick said. And then he too remembered. "Last Christmas," he growled, "your brother in bitter jest
sent to my brother, George Neville, a letter from the Pope which
announced that another man, the Archbishop of Canterbury, had
been made a cardinal!"

Clarence wanted to giggle; George Neville had deserved that
prod; but he caught himself in time and didn't laugh, took a sip
of wine and rose grasping the heavy table. But he looked pale
and sick suddenly. Warwick wondered whether it was the taste
of treachery in his mouth, but then he thought it was only too
much wine that had turned Clarence sick.

During these months as the winter held England in its cold
hands Edward knew no facts and had nothing but suspicion that
all was far from well. His agents kept turning up odd rumors
and reports; the Earl of Oxford, whom Edward had restored to
his estates, had married a cousin of Warwick's; suspected of
treason, he turned the King's evidence against two lesser men.
Mountjoy and Anthony with the fleet had recaptured Jersey
from the French, and Anthony was given the lordship of Jersey
although the captain of the castle was also granted rights.
Sporadic rebellions burst forth in the north, as if Warwick were
warning the King he could not do without him to keep order
in Yorkshire and Northampton. Clarence sulked. The New Year
saw Bessie big with child, and in February toward the end of
the month she went once more into her chambers, gathering
close around her the faithful women she could trust and who
would not put forth the unceasing gossip which she had learned
to her sorrow surrounds everyone in the limelight. The Duchess
swept that all aside.

"You are one of the most famous women in the world," she told
Bessie. "Naturally everyone talks about you. Savory and un-

savory tales—you must expect it. Bessie, you are a very good mother and a very good wife." But she was worried herself. Born a Princess, no one knew better than she the intense jealousy of the nobility regarding the advancement of her whole clever, handsome, ambitious brood. Much as she loved them, proud as she was of her thirteen progeny, she knew that Edward's favor toward them made them well hated by the old and ancient names. She knew that they all took their protection from the towering shadow of Edward and that if anything happened to him her husband and sons would be the first to suffer, along with the easygoing Will Herbert, Mountjoy, John Tiptoft and all the men who stood close to the King. The Duchess knew enough about politics too to know that Edward represented the new concept, the King who was in his own person the head of the state, and that all else must be subservient to him. The Duchess' own brother, le Comte de St. Pol, was behaving in France as Warwick was behaving here in England. It had been that brother of the Duchess who, apprised of her marriage to a mere squire, had threatened to kill her. At the time she had snorted with contempt, *"Zut!"* but she understood that that was the way some felt about Edward's marriage to her own beautiful Bessie. And she understood that Louis, in order to pacify her own brother, had made him Constable of France. Yet the Duchess knew that her brother was capable of rebellion against the strong hand of authority and that the Comte might very well end his life on the scaffold and that Warwick might too. But in the meantime whom else might they drag to a bloody death?

If the Duchess was worried, so was Bessie. Not only did the safety of her family worry her but her pregnancy worried her, for if she had a boy there would be an end to Clarence's pretense to being the next heir. Frowning thoughtfully Edward answered her doubts. "I shall never make Clarence my heir, Bessie. If in the ensuing years we have no son, I shall make Elizabeth my heir, as was foretold to me before her birth."

The little Bess was sitting on his lap, clutching one of his big fingers. Her curly blond head didn't come up to his shoulder, but she nestled there happily, looking up at Edward's face as he talked. Edward looked down at her and kissed the top of her head. "You will be a fine Queen, my poppet," he said.

He is so confident, Bessie thought. But he rose and set Bess down and took his wife in his arms. "Depend on me, my Bessie, my sweet Bessie." He had put his hand on her stomach. "I can feel our baby!" He caressed her. "Don't you fret, Bessie."

Bessie's third child was born on the twentieth of March. This time the new daughter was, even at birth, of a startling beauty. Edward and Elizabeth decided to name her Cecily after Edward's mother.

"Every Prince in Europe will be angling for her hand," Edward said. "I think it may be the King of Scots for this one," he added. Once more he planned a splendid christening. Clarence attended full of smiles. The Duchess of York was pleased that the little Princess was to bear her name. But she couldn't resist a remark.

"I'm honored but I know you would have preferred a son."

Bessie retorted sharply. "The King, my husband, likes girls of all ages."

Edward's eyes glinted with some amusement at the sudden fire in Bessie's tones. He and his mother and Bessie were talking *en famille* and when the Duchess heard these words she glanced at Edward with some reproof. Later when she had gone and they were alone, Edward said, ignoring her oblique remark concerning his fidelity, "Above all, I don't want you to succumb to the feeling that just because our children are not male you have failed as my Queen."

Bessie put her hands over her face; she was standing. How could it be that she had been so happy a half hour ago? When finishing dressing it had been such pleasure to see her slim figure and that euphoria produced so sweetly by the birth of a beautiful healthy baby was suddenly swept aside by the Duchess' remark. She pressed her hands against her face.

"Holy mother of God," she muttered through her teeth.

Edward seized her by the shoulders. "That is just what I want you to forego! Oaths and tears and frustrations!"

"I wanted a son!" She shook off his hands. He reached out for her and she stepped back. "Don't comfort me! Don't touch me!"

"For the mercy of God!" His eyes blazed with anger which he controlled with some difficulty. He said, "I want you to love my children, Bessie, male or female. And be proud of them."

Bessie looked across at him. Although his tones were low his eyes betrayed his anger still and they raked across her face and body. She said, her own eyes golden and sullen, "I'm only a woman." She breathed quickly. "And people whisper and mock me. I'm only a woman and I wanted to—" she stopped, glancing at him.

"If you had wanted to be only a woman," the King said calmly, "you should never have married me."

She shot him another glance.

"When you were crowned in the abbey," Edward said conversationally, turning aside to pour himself a cup of wine, "two duchesses helped hold your crown on your head because it was too heavy. Now, Bessie, you have no one to help you hold it save me. And if the time comes when I am not here you will have to bear it by yourself."

The words were worse than a blow. She took a deep breath. "Forgive me, sweetheart," she said. And because in her heart she knew well that for a brief unhappy moment she had indeed rejected her own child, she went over to him. "I should kneel and beg you to forgive me, my lord."

He held her tight, his big arms wrapped around her. "You should beat me," she mumbled into his shoulder.

He said, "Oh, Bessie, my Bessie, forget what people say about you, forget the gossip and the jealousy—for we will have to bear with it for the rest of our lives and even after."

That day had been the first of April, ten days after the birth of Cecily; the next day the trouble began and Warwick's long winter's work began to make itself felt. The first indication was trouble in Yorkshire. There was an ancient almshouse in York which since Ethelstane had had the right to a thrave of corn from every plowland in Yorkshire, Lancashire, Cumberland and Westmoreland. It was called St. Leonard's Hospital and its monks claimed the farmers were not paying. Edward sent the matter before two chief justices and his own council, and it was decided that the confirmations of the hospital's charter since William the Conqueror had proceeded down through to Edward IV and the farmers would have to pay. A man named Robin of Holderness then led them in rebellion, and Lancashire had another Robin, Robin of Redesdale; with both men agitating the north Robin of Holderness added another claim: He wanted the restoration of the earldom of Northumberland to its rightful heir, Lord Percy.

In London Edward pondered this demand while Montagu, the present holder of the title, leaped into the saddle and hastened north to confront the unlucky Robin, scattering his forces and hastily executing their leader. But Robin of Redesdale was a different matter, although Edward had only suspicion and no proof. Nonetheless he decided to go north himself.

While the royal wardrobe made ready a thousand jackets of murrey and blue, with roses, banners, standards and coat armors, and forty jackets of velvet and damask with roses, Edward set out on the fifth of June with Anthony, Lord Rivers, John and his brother Richard to make a pilgrimage to Bury St. Edmunds and Our Lady of Walsingham. At Croyland, in the usual friendly way, he walked through the village streets, delighting the monks and villagers. In Norwich the people called out to him to bring the Queen and he answered that he would.

Bessie was waiting for him at Fotheringhay.

"You will have to go to Norwich with our three daughters," Edward said, describing vividly to her their eagerness to see her.

"We have a whole week together," she said happily.

The thousand murrey and blue jackets were now filled with men whom Edward had raised on the way, and the banners flew and the standards were proud, and during that week the tents and artillery arrived from London.

"But it is a small force, one thousand men," Bessie said.

Edward shrugged his big shoulders. "I shouldn't need more, sweetheart. It's the appearance of the authority." A frown crossed his face. "There should have been no need for this," he remarked, and again his eyes grew remote and thoughtful.

She whispered, "What if Warwick is deceiving you?" She knew he had just sent Wenlock, one of Warwick's agents, abroad; she knew Warwick was at Sandwich, ostensibly to christen a new ship, and that Clarence was with him. "If the King of France cannot trust his brother, can you?" Her breath was coming sharply, for Edward was a man capable of strong personal devotion, and no one knew it better than she. She sat still as a mouse, hardly daring to look at him.

"Clarence has not matured well," he said, unwilling to make

that concession, "but he is not a traitor and neither is Warwick. And I don't want to hear any more about it."

He turned his back and started out of the room, and while for a brief moment she cursed both Clarence and Warwick for coming between her husband and herself she forgot them and ran after him seizing his arm.

"Sweetheart," she blurted. "Sometimes I'm afraid of them!"

His glance was still icy.

"Some of these men with you," she gestured, "the Archbishop of York sent them."

"According to my orders!"

"Well, I don't trust him either. He's another Neville."

She faced him, her eyes steady now in their regard, and he didn't speak. "I know you said you had a pleasant stay with him at the Moor, but he is Warwick's brother and I don't trust him!"

"Don't connive and plot, Bessie."

"I'm not," she cried, stung. "It is they! Not me! I've learned to live with their dislike and all the things they say about me. It is your safety I worry about. You and only you!"

He sighed. Yet he thought rapidly, Is she right? How much can I trust Warwick? Are these just a woman's fears? But Bessie is not given to fear. He said, "Bessie, don't be afraid. I'll be the King of England till I die, and now we have a week, a week in June."

"A whole week," she said, and her brilliant smile flashed out, but still at nights when she wakened, hearing his regular breathing and the movement of the bed when his big body stirred in sleep, she remembered those words. "I shall be the King of England until I die." And then she thought, But how if they kill him? And then she would turn restless and lie there staring into the darkness, afraid to move much for fear of disturbing him, while the days, the seven days of June, slid past much too fast.

Although Bessie's father and Anthony and John were with the King, nonetheless it was like a second honeymoon, and in the evenings they were alone. Edward had time to be the sybarite he was and indulge the side of his nature which he rarely could recognize, for he never allowed his own pleasure to interfere with the practical business of administering the state. But he hid from Bessie the uneasy flow of rumors which reached him.

His mother, for instance, had hastily gone to Sandwich to see Clarence. Clarence was with Warwick there for the ostensible purpose of christening a new ship.

The Archbishop of York, the slippery George Neville, was there too, again ostensibly to bless the new vessel. Odd bits of violence erupted here and there, in Wales, in Yorkshire.

On the last day in June he said good-bye to Bessie. Her head high, she stood in the great window at Fotheringhay and watched him ride away, but after he had left the castle and she could see just the banners waving in the distance, she felt suddenly very alone and very afraid. Edward had told her that he wished her to go back to London, and this she prepared to do the following day. It was a warm July day with hot sun. The household stuffs had been carefully packed, and when Bessie came out into the court she was surprised to see the size of her escort.

Her secretary came bustling up.

"I shall be glad when we arrive in Westminster," Bessie said idly.

"Not Westminster, Your Grace. The Tower of London."

The coldest shiver passed over her.

He smiled reassuringly. "His Grace's orders. It is safer."

Bessie didn't change expression. "Of course," she agreed.

Edward proceeded north. On July seventh he was at Grantham and the following day arrived at Newark, and there the full realization of Warwick's treason was discovered. Anthony had sent out scourers and in the late afternoon two of them returned. Anthony conferred with them and then hastily he sought the King.

Edward was sitting at a table in the window of a house on the main street. His few troops were quartered outside the town. Anthony closed the door behind him and Edward waved him to a chair. Calmly Anthony sat down. He said, "Your Grace, this Robin of Redesdale has many, many more men than was previously reported. His forces have been augmented by troops who seem to be a great part of my lord of Warwick's."

Edward's brown eyes met Anthony's.

"Moreover," Anthony went on, "the men the Archbishop sent are not to be trusted. They will melt away at nightfall, so my own men tell me."

Edward nodded. "What is that?" He gestured toward the paper Anthony held.

Anthony laid it on the bare table. "A manifesto from Robin of Redesdale. One of my scourers was commissioned to bring it to Your Grace. I don't know what Your Grace's feelings are, but I think this was written in Warwick's own hand."

Edward spread out the folded paper. Anthony could perceive no change in his face as Edward read the following words: "That because he had excluded the lords of the blood from his council and that he listened only to the advice of his favorites, Earl Rivers and his wife and sons, William Herbert, Earl of Pembroke, Humphrey Stafford, Earl of Devonshire, Lord Audley and Sir John Fogge, that he should now be classed with England's three deposed monarchs."

If Edward was frightened—and he should have been—Anthony saw no sign of it. Edward folded the manifesto and put it inside his jacket. He rose and said briefly, "The first thing to be done is to ride back to Nottingham immediately."

He wanted to put distance between himself and Robin of Redesdale, who obviously was taking orders from Warwick.

In half an hour Edward was mounted and the men with the King were riding for Nottingham. During the night the Archbishop's men did disappear and it was a very small troop that entered Nottingham.

Edward issued brief orders. "You, my lord," he said to Earl Rivers, "and you John, get to Wales and inform Will Herbert I need his troops.

"You Anthony, get to Norfolk. You'll be safe with the Duke. Acquaint him with the situation as it stands now."

Anthony hesitated. Edward spoke sharply. "For your own safety! I cannot protect you!" For the first time Anthony saw the anger in his eyes and then it was gone. Edward held out his hand to Earl Rivers and to John. "Godspeed," he said only.

They left the room, looking capable and unafraid. Edward turned to Anthony. He gripped his hand hard. "Take care of yourself, Anthony. Take good care, and may God go with you!"

Anthony's face was white. "God save Your Grace," he said. At

the doorway he paused. Emotionally he blurted, "I won't leave
you the second time, even though you order me!"

The faintest smile touched Edward's face. He went back to his
chair and stretched out long legs. He could hear the noise of the
small companies of men leaving; Lord Rivers and John with only
twenty and Anthony with five. Then it was quiet, it was hot, it
would storm, Edward thought. It was July ninth and he already
had paper and pen to hand. He dipped the pen and began to
write.

Edward wrote in his own hand to Clarence and the Archbishop of York, and then to Warwick.

"It is our wish," he wrote in his clear, stern hand, "that you
come to us as soon as possible. We hope devoutly that you are
not of the disposition toward us as the rumors here runneth, considering the trust and affection we bear you."

Sir Thomas Montgomery and a man named Berkely were off
and riding with the letters as soon as the ink was dry. Edward
leaned back in his chair; he was almost alone save for his few
household men, but he was not afraid yet for himself; his fears
centered around the men named in the manifesto—his good
friends.

Sir Thomas Montgomery rode hard for Canterbury. But the
next day, July tenth, Clarence and Warwick and the Archbishop
were in Calais. False, fleeting, perjured Clarence. He had armed
all of his hired retainers and for his betrayal of his brother had
been promised one-half of Isabel Neville's enormous inheritance
and Warwick's help to force Edward's recognition of him as the
heir to the throne.

Clarence thought, It is going to be easy! It was all planned so
well to catch Edward unawares. Even while he was saying his
marriage vows on the morning of July eleventh, he was thinking
about how well the plans were going and how clever Warwick
had been. He was impatient to see the days go by when he
would land again in England, and this time the manifesto would
be openly in Warwick's name and his name and the Archbishop's
name. So the next day the open letter was carried across to England. Sir Thomas Montgomery obtained a copy of it and turned
his horse's head fast as he could and rode back to his King.

Edward read the manifesto quickly. He passed over the accusation that he listened only to grasping favorites and went on to the meat of the matter, and it was this: "We the undersigned, expect to be in Canterbury on Sunday, and we ask our friends to be ready to accompany us to the King with as many men as they can muster."

"Oxford is with them too," Montgomery told Edward. He flung out his hands in a kind of angry despair, for Edward had pardoned Oxford and now he was showing as base as Clarence.

Edward was thoughtful. "Warwick and Clarence never arrive when they say they will," he said, with his wry humor. "If they arrive by Tuesday I'll be surprised." For he expected that by now Bessie's father and John Woodville would have reached Will Herbert and Stafford, who each should be marching already to join him. "We shall start south to join Lord Herbert," Edward said calmly, for all he needed to confront Warwick and Clarence were the troops which would have been hastily gathered up by Will Herbert and Devonshire. Edward was still not afraid.

But now occurred an incident which Edward in his wildest dreams could not have imagined. Will was already at Danbury; he had marched into town first and commandeered a house for his own use; he left his troops encamped on Damesmoor. About an hour later Devonshire arrived with his body of West Country archers, and he found Will and his brother Richard plus their own gentlemen in the finest house in the town.

"I can see there is no room for me here," he said acidly.

"For God's sake," Will said impatiently.

"You might at least have given some thought to where I should stay, my lord," Devonshire said.

"I'm giving thought to my men and to my King," Will Herbert said and turned his back. "And Robin of Redesdale is between us and His Grace."

Devonshire angrily flung out of the room and in a pique started his men to marching again, and before Will Herbert realized it he was out of Danbury and in his sulk he didn't stop until he had gone ten miles; there, still sulking, he pitched camp.

He was aroused by his scouts just after dawn. Robin of Redesdale had attacked Will Herbert and his brother. A battle was raging at Edgecott where Will Herbert was alone.

In panic Devonshire roused his men and went to Will's assistance, cursing himself and his stupidity as he rode, and the same day Edward rode south from Nottingham almost alone to join them.

Robin of Redesdale was lucky. Will Herbert fought bravely, and Robin lost his own son and Neville kin. But Devonshire arrived too late and by that time Warwick's replacements had come up. It was the twenty-sixth of July and Edward was almost alone at Albion. There the troops of my lord of Warwick surrounded him. The battle between Warwick and his King had been joined.

But where was the great Earl? Not here, for he had sent his brother instead, George Neville, the Archbishop of York, clever, cultivated, silver-tongued and enriched by Edward's own generosity; it was he who was riding at the head of Warwick's Northerners and it was he who came into the chamber where Edward was. There was complete silence in the room.

George Neville was conscious of unease. The people of England respected the authority of the crown and above everything else George Neville was an Englishman, so when he came face-to-face with the seated figure of his King he fell awkwardly silent.

He glanced at the standing figure of Lord Hastings, his brother-in-law. Hastings' eyes stared back coldly. The Archbishop then glanced toward the also standing figure of Edward's young brother Richard. Richard's eyes were almost black with enmity, his thin face white. Edward's other gentlemen, for Hastings and Richard were the only great lords left with him since he had sent the others away for safety's sake, stared remorselessly back at the gaudily dressed Archbishop.

It was Edward who broke the silence.

Leaning back in his chair, his indolent self, he smiled a wintry smile. "Good morning, my lord Archbishop. My cousin," his words were more brisk, "we welcome you. Was your ride hot? We have refreshment if it suits thee." He waved a big, negligent hand.

The Archbishop swallowed. He came across the room. Conscious suddenly of the ring of eyes, he went down on one knee before Edward.

"Rise, my lord," Edward said.

The Archbishop did so. He wet his lips. "Your Grace," he murmured. At this Edward rose to his towering height. He ambled negligently to the doors; he could hear the sound and stamp of armed men in the street, and to satisfy himself of their badges and their numbers he opened the door to the street. Uncertain of what he was going to do the Archbishop fumbled in his robes over to his side, but Edward's size blocked the door and Edward stepped out into the bright July sunshine by himself.

His eyes narrow, he surveyed the ranks and ranks of helmeted, red-coated men at arms; the badge of the ragged staff told him all too plainly he was a captive. Careful, careful, he told himself. He stood on the top step, the men nearest recognized the King and a murmur ran through the massed men, and in a moment every eye was on him, standing there, the blue-velvet jacket fitted close over his powerful shoulders and chest. The King smiled down on them and raised one hand in salute, and the Archbishop, peering under that upraised arm like an owl, his eyes round, saw that indeed there were some answering salutes and a low, uncertain cheer. Edward gave a final smile and turned his back leisurely, as though it were his own troops he was greeting, and closed the door behind him, the Archbishop retreating hastily from him, backing away and stumbling into the stairway.

Kindly Edward took his elbow and righted him, smiling down at his cousin. He steered him back into the chamber where his lords and brother awaited. Edward said, "I take it that my entirely well-beloved cousin, your brother, has sent you to me and that he wishes to consult with me."

"Aye, Your Grace," George Neville said gratefully, glancing about again at the gentlemen with Edward. His life wasn't safe inside this room.

"Well, then," said Edward, "as you know, it is always our habit to ride early before the heat of the day. I should think we could reach Coventry before dinner."

Edward had guessed immediately that Warwick would immure him in Warwick Castle, for it was the nearest Neville stronghold.

The Archbishop found his voice now that Edward had made it easy for him. "Aye, Your Grace. My brother awaits us at Warwick Castle." Then he fell silent again; he didn't know exactly how to convey Warwick's orders, and with Italianate smoothness Edward preempted him; he swung around to Hastings.

"I think it best, my lord, since my cousin has brought an escort, that you take the few men I have with me. And you too, Dickon." Edward's brown eyes rested affectionately on the young Richard, Duke of Gloucester.

"I leave you?" Richard asked.

The Archbishop nodded. This was what Warwick had ordered; there were to be no lords or kin about the prisoner. "I'll have your horses brought."

"Thank you, my lord Archbishop," Edward said. He went over to the sideboard and poured himself a cup of wine, his wits working sharply under cover of his sipping.

"We pushed hard yesterday," he informed the Archbishop, who again smiled uncertainly and was leaning on one foot and then the other, for he was anxious to get rid of Hastings. He was grateful that both men were booted and spurred, and no doubt their horses had been made ready. A banging on the door confirmed this and the Archbishop himself hurried to open it, something he would never ordinarily have done; it betrayed his uncertainty and Edward secretly totted this up in his mind. He had only his wits to unnerve his captors, and he must use them well.

The Archbishop turned from the door. "Your mount, my lord Duke," he said to young Richard of Gloucester.

Richard turned to Edward, looking to him for counsel; Edward set down his wine cup, came over to his brother and flung an arm around his shoulders; he walked with him to the door, and when the Archbishop saw that Edward was going to go out with Richard he opened his mouth to protest and mumbled, "Your Grace!"

Edward turned slightly, as if in surprise. "I bid Dickon Godspeed," he said; his big fingers squeezed Richard's shoulder reassuringly and together they stepped into the bright sunlight again; the Archbishop stood in the door behind them, for suddenly he knew what Edward was going to do and he didn't know how to stop him.

Edward descended the two steps into the street; the armed men were massed down the narrow street far as one could see; the small place in front of this house Edward had used last night held Richard's retainers and his personal household. They stood at attention, the roses blooming bright and white on their collars. Edward accompanied Richard to his own mount.

"Kneel," the King whispered.

Richard obeyed.

"God bless you, Richard. I'll send for you as soon as I can." While he was saying this the King raised his brother up and embraced him. Then with his own hands he set him up in the saddle, for Richard was slight for sixteen.

Now Richard unwittingly took part in the drama which the King wanted all these men to see. For Richard didn't want to leave and he, small though he was, sat on his big mount like a soldier and he leaned over and held out his hand to Edward. The King took it and then slowly their fingers fell away, and slowly Richard turned his horse's head.

The armed men moved aside uneasily. Warwick hadn't summoned them to march to take their King a captive. He had given other reasons. Their faces were set and grim; they knew young Richard well, for he had been brought up by Warwick. Their eyes followed his progress down the street and then Lord Hastings came out the doors.

Hastings was popular. Hastings came striding out, and Edward held out his hand again and Hastings gripped it hard. Then he swung onto his horse and with a sharp gesture pulled on the reins to quiet the huge steed. Edward stepped back and smiled. Hastings said in the hush, "God bless Your Grace."

The solemn words fell onto the hush. Then Hastings too, with his few men, wheeled his mount with a great striking of hoofs on the cobbles, and the King was left standing alone in the doorway.

The Archbishop came bustling out. His men looked as though they could already feel the noose around their necks for treason. The Archbishop looked from right to left and saw none but grim faces, for now it was entirely plain that the smell of traitor emanated through his robes. So Edward spoke, "If we're to reach Coventry before my dinner, my lord, we should ride now."

Now his own household men filed out and the King's horse was brought; and then the troops formed an escort around their King and they started for Coventry.

Edward rode easily, satisfied with his opening guns. He knew very well Warwick would have him taken to Warwick Castle, and he knew the Earl would be there soon, but he doubted if Warwick would murder him. Nonetheless Warwick was capable of reckless, passionate acts, and the most extreme caution would have to be used constant. Edward had already decided on a course of action; he would be pleasant, compliant, at ease. Meanwhile he knew he had already won over the sympathies of part of Warwick's own troops. For he bore with him in his own person the power and authority of the crown; Warwick's whole venture showed that he underestimated that power; Edward's strategy would be to prove it without a soldier, without a sword. The Archbishop, clever as he was, had already perceived that power on the faces of his own men. Let him tell it to Warwick.

At Coventry they rode through the town. When the people saw the King they cheered. And then when they saw his escort there was a sullen silence. So the Archbishop hurried Edward on, for in Coventry he could hand over his royal prisoner, riding between ranks and ranks of steel-helmeted men, to his legendary brother.

We know that Warwick and Edward met in Coventry. We know also that Edward knew that Robin of Redesdale was no ordinary rebel but one of Warwick's men, reinforced by the Neville money and by name Sir John Conyers. And while he rode Edward was thinking that King Louis had been caught like this, taken unawares, and that he had been able to extricate himself. Edward pondered on the similarity of Louis' struggles and his own and it was so apparent to him that it baffled him that Warwick couldn't see the truth—that instead of leaning on Louis Warwick should lean on his own King and that what had happened to Louis' adversaries might indeed happen to Edward's cousin, the Earl of Warwick.

But now in the chamber assigned to him Edward was washing his face and hands, and then he held out his arms for his clean shirt, and his valet laced it for him with unsteady fingers, for Edward was served by his own household with deep devotion.

Thus Edward kept Warwick waiting, and when he finally strolled from his bedchamber into his anteroom he found Warwick there alone. The Archbishop, slippery as he was, had had enough for the present.

Edward greeted Warwick as he always did, cordially, as a relative of whom he was very fond. "But you must excuse us, my lord," he said steadily, his brown eyes meeting Warwick's openly, "but I am dressed in black. I am in mourning for my closest, my dearest friend, Will. Had I been there, my lord, there would have been no silly quarrel about a billet, and Robin of Redesdale would have found a whole army and not a split one." Edward looked full at Warwick now. And the Earl answered quickly, thinking to catch out Edward. "We have grievances, Your Grace."

"I'm sure you do, my lord. All my subjects have grievances. If it's not taxes it's trade restrictions. If it's not Burgundy it's France. And, my lord, I've read your grievances. You published them. I've no doubt that to you they are true and important, but we represent all the people and all of England—traders and wool merchants and peasants, gentry and nobility. I hoped I could count on the help of my own kin."

Edward who had been standing now seated himself, and he did not wave Warwick to a chair; he just looked at him.

Warwick was silent. Edward said, "Have you forgot, my lord, that we were companions in arms?"

"You forgot, Your Grace!"

"No," said Edward shaking his head and smiling ruefully, "I never forget. I never forget my own kin. As I have told Clarence many times, nor do I ever forget when a man has been a faithful, loyal subject." Once more Edward looked full at Warwick. "Where is my lord the Archbishop?"

"He is unwell, feeling poorly."

"A pity." Edward shook his head. "And how is your brother John, my entirely beloved John?"

Warwick shuffled uncomfortably and now Edward did wave a hand at a chair. "Do sit," he invited him and a wry smile touched his lips, for his advices had been that John Neville had not joined his brothers Warwick and George in this adventure.

The Earl of Warwick did not sit. No likeness of Warwick exists, but we can imagine the face of this adventurer, as comfortable on the moors and on the seas as he was presiding over a magnificent banquet, this man who had stood at Edward's shoulder and helped him seize a crown; rugged and clever both he was, as clever as the Archbishop and as rugged as his brother John. "I shan't sit," he said grimly, bethinking himself that he was the master here. "You know our grievances, as I tried to say before."

"Aye," said Edward easily. "And when we talk on the morrow I shall tell you mine. But now I too am not feeling well." He stood, his appearance belying his words. "I am going to retire, my lord."

He turned his back and Warwick was left standing there, frustrated, as Edward closed the door in Warwick's face.

A few years before, the winter after Bessie and Edward were married, a dispute from the town of Coventry had been brought before the King and his council and the matter equitably decided. My lord of Warwick, as great lord of the region, had pre-emptorily set aside this just verdict and the magistrates of Coventry had never forgiven him. Now through the town ran the rumor that their King was being held a captive by the soldiers quartered in their midst, and by daybreak even Warwick began to get worried, and so was Edward, for he wanted no impromptu riot which might cost the lives of himself and the Earl.

So he easily agreed to be taken to Warwick Castle, and it was he himself who invited his cousin to ride at his side so the people could see they were as good friends as ever, Edward said in his genial manner.

The Archbishop had already ridden off back to his house at the Moor, for the Archbishop was content to let his brother handle the sword; he had a notion already that he would need his silver tongue in the next few weeks.

When the cavalcade rode up the hill to Warwick Castle, through the village at its foot, the people came out and waved and cheered to see their lord and the King. Just as always, with his usual good humor, Edward signaled a stop and the Earl's troops obeyed the royal command. Edward nodded his head to Montgomery, who was off his horse in a second and holding Edward's big stallion. Edward dismounted and his pleasant, clear tones could be heard in the street.

"We'll walk up to the castle, my lord cousin, to let the people see." Warwick perforce obeyed, trying to smile as genuinely as Edward. And there were a good many cries of A Warwick! But as they slowly made their way up the narrow, steep, cobbled road more and more eyes gleamed with pride at their handsome tall King, and more and more cries came so that when the great gates of the castle finally swung shut on Edward, Warwick was still hearing it, loud and hammering in his ears: "God bless Your Grace!"

Warwick's face was set and dangerous, so Edward did not permit even a glimmer of triumph in his eyes; he turned from the Earl and perceiving the steward of the castle whom he knew, he asked him to conduct his personal servants immediate to his chambers and announced offhandedly that he wished a tub of hot water and then, in his most affable manner confided to Warwick that he must be excused on personal grounds.

For the next two hours my lord the Earl of Warwick paced his own chamber alone. Although he was not yet going to admit it to himself, he kept thinking of the analogy of the man who held the lion by the tail. His blood burned for revenge and yet he couldn't hate Edward, only he hated Lord Rivers and John. He knew he held Clarence in the hollow of his hand, but he also knew he couldn't trust Clarence any more than Edward could, and he really didn't like or want Clarence; he wanted Edward; Edward, obedient, pliant, Edward, the sunny-hearted Prince. He remembered him so vividly at the first battle of St. Albans when, with Edward at his side, he had scored his first victory; in a flash Warwick could see again the tall, smiling thirteen-year-old, precocious, laughing, yet at his side fighting like ten men. Warwick sighed. "But I'll not be a servant!"

The times were out of joint. He strode from his room, searching for his captive King, hurrying his steps. He had held Edward prisoner for two days now and nothing had happened; he hadn't been able to make Edward see his mistakes. And he, the great Earl in his own castle, couldn't find his King. Edward's servants were vague as to his whereabouts; his steward said Edward was in his bath but he was not, for Warwick had just come from his chambers.

His anger mounting, he finally seized a hurrying groom of the chamber and spun him around. Edward's household man held his temper as he had been straitly ordered. He even smiled. "His Grace is in the chapel, my lord." He bowed and went on and Warwick, hastening, was on the threshold of his own chapel when he came face-to-face with his own priest, who unaccountably barred his way. Warwick stared at him in supreme amazement.

But the priest smiled and said firmly, "His Grace is at his devotions, my lord. He cannot be disturbed."

As though pulled backward by invisible strings, the great Earl of Warwick retreated; he had put up his hands to push the priest out of the way, yet he had not and he looked at his hands, the fingers wide apart, and it was as though he saw slipping through them the power that he should have had, for did he not forcibly possess the King? The slightest edge of panic flickered through his body. He sought out two of his captains, and in an hour they were saddled and riding away with grim orders to find and kill the Earl of Rivers and his sons John and Anthony. Although he had no notion of how this stage of the struggle would be resolved, he knew instinctively that at least this day and tomorrow and this week he must do as much damage to Edward's court party as possible. His men had killed Will Herbert, now they were hunting down Will's two brothers; they had caught Devonshire the day before and killed him, and already the violence and blood had spawned more violence.

As always at Warwick Castle men came and went; messengers pounded up the long, twisting castle hill, urging on the tired horses, messengers from brother George in London and Clarence and the mayor of the city and the Burgundian embassy; messengers from the north, messengers from kindred and ally. The news was all bad, for like a ship without a helm England rose and fell helplessly in a violent wave of lawlessness. The London mob stirred and threatened, thinking of loot; bitter Lancastrians seized the chance to strike back at an old enemy; Edward's own adherents, like the Duke of Norfolk, took advantage of the absence of law to arm their retainers and, as in Norfolk's case, to besiege the nearby Caister Castle which his wife wanted. It would take John Paston years in court to recover it.

On August tenth Lord Rivers and John were captured, hopelessly outnumbered, and in order to save the lives of their few servants they surrendered to superior force. There was not even the semblance of a trial. To Bessie, to Edward, to the Duchess mourning at Grafton, it was murder most foul. To Warwick it was great satisfaction; his enemies were dead—that they went bravely to the scaffold didn't move him; he wanted them dead and he had encompassed it. In the next two days, in the same manner, without a trial Thomas and Richard Herbert were caught and executed, and by the thirteenth of August the whole country was beginning to blaze like a fire out of control. And the cry arose, Where is the King? Where is he?

The Duchess was at Grafton with her children. The whole household was in mourning for the Earl and John. The Duchess suffered for Anthony, and her grief over her husband and John was complete and shattering. She was afraid to set forth for London and Bessie because the whole country was ablaze; and roving bands of armed men and unemployed mercenaries and hot-headed Lancastrians who had suddenly decided now was their chance to put old King Henry back on the throne were raising their banners and stalking the countryside; the roads were unsafe and the manor gates barred and locked and defended at night. So at Grafton she stayed and to Grafton Warwick sent one of his men, Wake by name, to accuse the Duchess of witchcraft.

In the great hall the Duchess met her accuser. If Warwick had thought that honest grief over her beloved husband would soften the Duchess he was wrong.

"Witchcraft!" she spit the word at Wake.

Wake had not realized he was to face a Duchess as doughty as this one. In the end he meekly consented to carry a letter for the Duchess to the mayor and aldermen of London; the letter outlined the charges against her, which she claimed they would know were false, and would they deal with this fellow as they should, considering the services she had rendered the mayor and aldermen in London's times of trouble with the old Queen?

The Duchess had written the letter with her own hand. She folded and sealed it, and thrust it imperiously at Wake.

He took it. He bowed.

"Now go!" commanded the Duchess. "See that it is in the lord mayor's hands by tomorrow!"

"Aye, Your Grace," mumbled Wake. He backed to the door. Then the Duchess turned to look at her two fast-growing sons, Edward and Lionel.

"Madam," Lionel said, his voice trembling, "if I can behave like you when I am grown, I shall be very proud of myself!"

If it was a time of trouble and sorrow at Grafton, it was a time of fear and sorrow for Bessie in London. It was Richard Wood-ville who brought news to Bessie. Richard was a cross between Anthony and John. As nonchalant as his brother John, as easy and elegant in dress as Anthony, he had a disarming charm which he wore like a mantle and it never ceased to serve him. He could be friendly with the butcher and as genial at cards with Edward, and a canny chess player so good-humored as to win from his fellow courtiers without incurring any malice. Closeted with Bessie, still in riding dress but managing to look elegant, he told her the truth as he knew it.

Richard said tersely, "A potential state of anarchy exists. If you'll send to the wardrobe for some clothes for me and give me a paper with your signet, I have a plan to recruit some men for a household guard for you. Also I am sure it would be his Grace's wish that you and your household keep the semblances."

Bessie swallowed. "I have met with my council this morning. We are keeping state, Richard, scant though it is."

He said, "I'm proud of you, Your Grace." He knelt and she put her hand on his blond head.

"God bless you, Richard," she said. "And please take care."

But when he returned, now dressed in a blue jacket with roses and a big *E* on his breast, she cried out. The streets of London were full of Warwick's and Clarence's men. "They'll kill you!" she cried involuntarily.

"Not me," Richard said. "Let any man make a move for me, and the mob of London will rise in its wrath! Not only to save my life, Bessie, although I know every tavern keeper in town, but because there's only a spark needed now." Then he said because it was true, "Don't worry over me. It is John and Father whom I mourn." He looked at her white face. She nodded wordlessly. Then she recovered.

"I have a commission for you, Richard. I should like you to bear a letter from me to the Burgundian ambassadors. I wrote it while you were dressing." She handed him the letter with her seal. She accompanied him to her outer chamber, where a few of the men and ladies of her household were in attendance. Composedly she walked to the big doors with her brother, where he bowed deeply and backed to the door. It closed on him and Bessie turned to face the small group.

"When the ambassador of Burgundy arrives, please escort him to our audience chamber. I would wish we had finer wine to offer but we shall do the best we can."

Every eye had followed Richard from the room, Richard walk-

ing forth as though Edward were in Westminster and not Warwick and Clarence. Then every eye went to Bessie. The Queen
had not slept but the shadowed eyes were steady, her step firm;
she looked as chic and composed as though her husband were
not confined in the great castle of Warwick, as though her father
and brother were not bloodily dead, and even when a few minutes later closeted with Alice Fogge Alice broke down into sobs
and hysterical fear for her own husband, she did not lose that
composure. Finally with set lips she sent for her priest and asked
him to comfort the Lady Alice, and she helped him escort the
weeping lady-in-waiting from her chamber. And the time when
she came nearest to tears was when the mayor of London arrived.

"Your Grace." He went down on one knee.

Bessie's great eyes shone with unshed tears.

"We have brought you a gift. The aldermen have sent you
wine for your household."

Bessie said, "We thank you, sirs. Our household and I thank
you very much indeed."

His heart melted like water under the sweet smile she gave
him. He wanted to say, "Courage, madam!" but he didn't need
to; she understood well enough what the gift meant.

"God bless your Grace," he said.

He glanced about the room; the ladies and gentlemen there
seemed just as always and somehow the mayor was comforted.
He would hasten back and tell the aldermen how much their
Queen had appreciated their kindnesses, just as Bessie was at that
moment commanding him to do.

And the children! All the way back to his own home the mayor
kept thinking of his beautiful Queen and the children. Surely
no one could harm them, and then right in front of the mayor's
startled eyes, who should come riding down the street, brave in
roses with a big E on his breast, but the well-known figure of
Richard Woodville. Richard raised his gloved hand in salute and
the mayor responded in kind. He thought, No matter what they
say about the Woodville arrogance, one had to be secretly proud
of them, that you did, and the mayor permitted himself the smallest ghost of a smile, for then he saw that Richard was escorting
the Burgundian ambassadors; they were calling on the Queen
and he could imagine that the Earl of Warwick would not dare to

lay hands on Richard while he was surrounded by the visiting lords of Burgundy. The mayor knew Richard well enough to know that Richard would think it was a fine jest on the mighty Earl and the traitorous Clarence.

The Burgundian ambassadors were greatly perturbed by the sudden conditions in England. They explained to Bessie just how perilous the situation was at present in London. Bessie sat in her golden chair with her secretary, her treasurer and other lords of her household about her, and Richard leaning on the side of the chair in a kind of protective gesture, one arm laid around the back of her chair. The scene was just like a painting.

The Burgundian lords were dressed as magnificently as only they could dress, and the conversation was conducted in flowing French; one of the Burgundians thought suddenly that it seemed incredible that this civilized scene could be contrasted with the reality of the absent King, for no one knew how far Warwick and Clarence would sink into treason, nor how this situation might explode further into tragedy.

It was not necessary to explain to Bessie that Warwick sided with France as against Burgundy, and that they themselves were in London to present the highest honor of Burgundy, the Golden Fleece, to Edward. Nonetheless it was good that they were here, for they would provide a steadying influence; after all, Edward's sister Margaret was their own Duchess. But the immediate trouble was the London mob, which threatened to get out of control. So they told Bessie they were going to apprise the Earl of Warwick that their Duke Charles would not hesitate to send troops to London itself in defense of their safety and to ensure the safety of the citizens of the city.

The chief Burgundian was the Seigneur de Crequy, and he had accompanied Edward north and had been sent back to London when Edward realized there would be fighting.

"So I told my lord of Warwick," he said to Bessie, "that His Grace, Charles, the Duke of Burgundy, will have vengeance if the citizens of London were unfaithful to his brother-in-law. More I have demanded to send a representative to His Grace."

Warwick yielded to this request because he was afraid not of Burgundy but of the London mob. So in the next days, from Warwick Castle, Edward issued a proclamation in London,

Southwark and Westminster, continuing the safe conduct of the Burgundian ambassadors and strictly enjoining his subjects that no person, on pain of imprisonment, fine and forfeiture, should presume to make any "congregations, affrays, riots or robberies"; and for a while this sufficed and London escaped the horror of mob violence. In London Edward's council continued to sit, and life in the Queen's household went on as usual but, as Bessie said, with scant state. And Warwick began to be afraid.

Warwick Castle was too near London. What was he going to do with Edward? Edward spent his days as though he were the lord of Warwick Castle, casually turning aside any remark, seemingly perfectly content, sending out messengers and receiving messengers, sending out writs under the privy seal and signet.

In the confused country Warwick tried to restore order. He had issued previously, under the privy seal, with Edward's consent, a call for Parliament to meet in York, because he knew he had to get the consent of Parliament to accomplish what he wished, namely the attainder of all his enemies who still lived and those who had died; the recognition of Clarence as heir to the throne; a censure of Edward for not heeding his good friends the Nevilles; and a closing of the ring of Nevilles around Edward to hold him a pleasant, pliant King in their midst.

It was August thirteenth, a hot summer night. Brusquely he issued orders, then he strode to the King's chambers.

Edward was pleasant but distant. His eyes surveyed Warwick the same way they had the first day he had confronted the Earl. "My lord cousin," he said low and tiredly, "you come to us with your hands dripping with the blood of my friends and councilors." Underneath the low voice and the measuring eyes was the quick calculation of his adversary. Warwick was breathing hard like a horse, and that reminded him of Anthony. His private advices, which he was getting through the ring of steel around him, told him that Anthony was safe with the Duke of Norfolk and that Richard was in London, openly a King's man, and comforting Bessie. Edward knew all about what Bessie was doing, how the city fathers had sent her wine to comfort her, how the Burgundians were at her elbow, that she and her household were openly in mourning. He had written her to be of the best spirit she could. But now tonight Warwick was obviously distraught.

"Parliament has been summoned to York, as you know. So I thought it best we go tonight to Middleham Castle."

Edward probed. "Tonight?" he inquired.

The Earl nodded. His hands were restless and he didn't meet Edward's eyes. Edward was satisfied that the Earl was afraid to travel in daylight. The sight of the King riding among Warwick's armed men would provoke the people to rescue him. Edward quickly put aside the thought of trying to force Warwick to ride by daylight; again an impromptu fight might result in a dagger in the back.

"I shall convey the decision to my household," he said. Then he asked, "Do you think it will be safer in Middleham for you, my lord, or for me?" He smiled wryly.

Warwick set a fast pace. A forced night march. And as he rode unease gripped him and he scanned the dark shapes of forest and farmland, of quiet sleeping towns, of lonely, lonely rutted roads. He wouldn't breathe safe until he had his royal prisoner at his huge Yorkshire fortress of Middleham from where he ruled the border, the moors and the rough, country men on whose allegiance he could always count; from the halls of Middleham and Sheriff Hutton he could call up the men who would respond to the Lord of the North. Already, despite unease, he felt better when through the dark night, amid the jingling of mail, he rode north. When the moon came up it caught the helmets of the steel-clad troops in their red jackets with their badge of the ragged staff. And in their midst, elegant in velvet, armed only with his gold-hilted dagger, rode the King.

Today Middleham Castle lies in massive ruins. Approaching from the south as Edward did and seeing the castle from a distance with the gentle hills beyond, the country green now in summer, green and yellow with wheat, as the rising sun illumined the fortress walls, wall upon wall, towered at its edges, it was a mighty fortress that could have housed an army, let alone one man. As Edward rode through the gates there was no hint on his face, no clue to his thoughts. While Warwick seemed grim and his face furrowed with lines, the King seemed fresh, as young and strong as the morning itself. He swung off his mount, patted the horse, standing there tall enough to reach an arm over its head and scratch the ears, speaking offhandedly to Montgomery as if it were the most usual thing in the world for a monarch to ride in forced night marches and to lie hidden from his people during the day. He called to Warwick about the hunting here, and all the time under his lazy manner his thoughts might have surprised the Earl. For he was thinking deeply and with his steellike earnestness about the pacification of the north. He realized instantly that even Warwick had not dared to bring his King openly under armed guard through his own lands. In the past the lords of Middleham and the lord of Northumberland had rivaled one another as the great lords of the north. Now the Nevilles controlled the whole of the north and yet it spewed violence and stirred rebelliously still. Would it be best for his people to restore the heir of Northumberland, Lord Percy, who now was kept in rather fine style in the Tower? Yet Edward was very fond of John Neville, upon whom he had bestowed the princely earldom. And it was obvious that John had not joined into this plot. It was on the horns of a dilemma that Edward sat, and as he went into the castle's great hall he was thinking of a way out—that perhaps he could recompense John Neville, Lord Montagu, in some other way, restore the Percys and see if this rudest, roughest part of his country would settle down in a civilized manner and cease riding the moors armed and bent on insurrection of some kind or another. Edward muttered his favorite oath under his breath, and when Warwick spoke to him he wrenched his thoughts from his problems up here and bestowed a kindly glance on Warwick.

The nights were long. Edward's household men guarded the doors of his room. A handful of them and a single barred door were all the protection they could give the sleeping figure of their King, for the crisis was slowly mounting. Warwick had to have Parliamentary approval of what he had done or else he couldn't consolidate the power he had seized; he couldn't summon Parliament to York until the country ceased to seethe.

The last day of August was a day heralding the fall, a golden day with the fresh wind sweeping over the moors of Wenleysdale; Edward stood in the rude window embrasure and sniffed the air appreciatively. Dust on the horizon meant riders and it was not long before Warwick appeared. He bore with him a letter on which he wanted the royal seal. Edward read it without a trace of a smile. It was a letter countermanding Parliament because "so great troubles in divers parts of our land not yet appeased, county elections could not be held."

Edward affixed the seal and raised guileless eyes to Warwick's face.

"The men in the castle tell me that a man called Neville of Brancepeth is arousing the north. Is he kin?"

"Distantly, I guess," Warwick muttered.

"I hear tell that this man seeks to restore the Lancastrian Henry to the throne," Edward went on conversationally.

Warwick swung around to face the King. "Aye! The fool!" For this was not at all what Warwick wanted and this mad Neville of Brancepeth was harrying the north right now. "I have issued commissions of array," he growled, "and I'll have his head for Your Grace before the week's out!"

Defeat was staring at Warwick and he had sent in haste for his brother George; George arrived, magnificent in his Archbishop's robes, as calm as ever, for he knew very well those robes were the mantle of immunity and that Edward would respect them no matter how treacherous the blood ran in his earthly veins. Warwick was not calm. He explained in tones of muffled and amazed anger that the whole north was aflame and his own men would not heed his call to arms.

George Neville thoughtfully regarded his fingertips. "The whole realm is tottering on the brink of anarchy."

Warwick looked at his brother as though he were out of his mind.

George nodded his head. "It's true," he said. "The people want their King back. You made a mistake."

"I made a mistake?"

"Yes, indeed," said the Archbishop pontifically, as though he had had no part in this plot, and Warwick could see even his brother's allegiance was slowly slipping from his fingers as though Warwick were powerless; the whole scheme was falling to pieces and Edward was going to slip away from his grasp too.

"Richard," said the Archbishop softly, "let me go to the King and intercede for you."

The Archbishop arrived at Middleham in the middle of the afternoon. He issued a few orders, and suddenly there were no armed guards at the hallways leading to the King's chambers and there was a noticeable lack of the jingling of arms in the castle halls. The Archbishop found the King just as always, as Warwick had said. "He never protested signing anything," Warwick had muttered as he left, seizing his brother by the arm, trying to explain to the Archbishop and himself how all this had happened and how incredibly the lion would soon be on the loose. "He never protested. He was calm and contained. He signed anything. He never showed anger, only sorrow at the death of his friends. He never raised his voice, he never threatened."

George Neville heard all this. "I will try bargaining with him. For your sake," he added, maintaining the fiction that he never had anything to do with the plot. But his defection paled beside the big question of how Warwick had failed; he still couldn't understand it. The Archbishop trailed out with his retinue.

"Your Grace," George Neville began softly, his unctuous tones recalling all the speeches he had made before for Edward, "there comes a time in the lives of all great princes when they are called by heaven to be merciful and clement."

Edward could hardly keep his lips from twitching. He quickly lowered the lids of his eyes to hide the sparkle in them.

"We are always aware of that, my lord," he said, almost as pontifically as the Archbishop who, knowing Edward well, glanced at him sharply to see if he were jesting.

"I am here and I shall go on my knees!"

"Do not," said Edward equably, "there's no need."

"There is need," exclaimed the Archbishop as though hammering a point of fine religion from his pulpit, "because my brother is asking your forgiveness."

"Ah," said the King. He gazed at the Archbishop thoughtfully.

The Archbishop fidgeted. Wasn't Edward going to reply? Evidently not. The Archbishop coughed. How to phrase the bargain? He coughed again and brought out his fine napkin which he touched to his lips. "Tomorrow, Your Grace, I shall conduct you in state to York. It is my brother's hope that you will then issue under your *own* name the commissions of array and then my brother will set forth to bring you this Neville of Brancepeth's head."

So that is the bargain, Edward thought. He gives me my freedom partial, and I help him raise troops. He wanted to say "Done!" to the Archbishop and see his face but he didn't; he played this game this way so far and he would play it to the end. No force, only guile. He thought fleetingly that Francesco Sforza would be proud of him.

"It shall be a pleasure to have you in my company to York," Edward said pleasantly. "It is a fine day, my lord. May I also have the pleasure of your company at hunting?"

Now he did bend his direct gaze on the Archbishop, who couldn't accept the invitation, for he had to hurry back to Sheriff Hutton to give the word to Warwick; there was no time to waste. But he also couldn't forbid Edward to go out, so he just chewed his lip and then excused himself with great formality. Edward strode over to his bedchamber and told his few household that he was riding out. Montgomery stared at his King in admiration, for in the beginning he had never expected Edward to extricate himself from this trap without any great humiliation.

He wanted to seize Edward and hug him and congratulate him, but instead he fell onto his knees and muttered, "Thank God! For you, Your Grace."

Edward pulled him to his feet. Montgomery then whispered, "Do we escape?" The thought crossed his mind that they could just keep on riding.

Edward had considered this too and shoved it aside. There was no need for flight nor escape; the reins had slipped back into his own big hands, and he would have not even the pretense of flight from his subject, the Earl of Warwick. No, it was Warwick who was going to be humiliated by the failure to control his King, even when he held him prisoner.

"Escape?" Edward said, with surprise. "No, I want a day's hunting before we travel to our city of York."

Edward entered his city of York on September tenth, riding in state. The streets were jammed and in the Archbishop's ears —for he had seized the opportunity to ride at Edward's side to show all the world that he was the King's kin and good friend— the waves of cheering sounded mixed with relief; the canny Archbishop understood that indeed England had wanted her King back. That same day Edward issued the commissions of array, and now men flocked to the standard and Warwick went riding out as usual in his old capacity of Warden of the Marches, surprising his kin, Neville of Brancepeth, by the fury with which he attacked and disposed of both him and his forces. When he returned, victorious, he found Edward at Pontefract Castle at dinner with the Archbishop.

"Well, my lord," Edward said in his open way, just as he always did, "you have done us and the realm a great service."

Warwick had the impression that the last two months had been some kind of dream; he was utterly baffled by Edward's continued ignoring of what had actually happened. He stared in disbelief at his smiling cousin. What, Warwick wondered, was he truly thinking underneath this unbroken facade of pleasant and unruffled calm? What revenge did he actually plan under the smiling exterior? Warwick could get no hint, no hint at all. He didn't know what to do but he now had the distinct impression from Edward that the matter was out of his hands entirely, and in a way it was a relief. Although he had not yet formulated any new plans to deal with his own descending fortunes, given time he would, he was sure, and he had adherents even if his brother was now abdicating, for the Archbishop was riding south the next day.

"Get in touch with Oxford," Warwick had said, "and tell him he had best stay with you at the Moor or else come up here to Middleham with me." Since Edward had pardoned Oxford and that gentleman had joined the plot against him, he could not expect any royal favor.

The following day Warwick awoke to find his royal prisoner gone. "His Grace is hunting," the Earl was informed.

All day long Warwick fretted. Would Edward return? He wished he wouldn't! It would look better to Warwick's adherents to have the King flee from his most powerful noble. But no, indeed, to Warwick's discomfited eyes the whole royal hunt rode back at dusk, gay and with jingling harness, and the same thing happened the next day, for Edward, who loved the hunt, saw no reason to deprive himself of a pleasure he indulged in too little, and each night his smiling face and offhand manner drove his host deeper into baffled confusion and, somehow, humiliation; to see the smiling King return each night into the fold of the wolf made the wolf look silly indeed. How long was Edward going to keep up this pretense? Edward had been at Pontefract since the nineteenth of September, and it was now the twenty-sixth; a full week had passed.

Edward had allowed a full week because he wanted all his

plans to go smooth. So when Warwick roused early on the morning of the twenty-seventh he heard all kinds of noise, unusual at that hour in the morning, and he threw his bedgown over his shoulders and called a servant.

"Lord Montagu, my lord. He has arrived."

Warwick sighed in relief. His stalwart, dependable soldier-brother! "Send him to me!" he ordered.

He waited impatiently for Montagu, washing hastily and postponing dressing, for he expected his brother to appear at the door any moment.

But Montagu did not appear and then wondering what had happened Warwick shouted for his servant to dress him.

"Where is my brother?" he wanted to know.

"My lord is attending the King," was the answer.

Before Warwick could finish dressing the Duke of Buckingham and the Earls of Arundel and Essex had arrived, and they too were attending the King. In fact the rutted road to Pontefract suddenly thronged with men, for the lords Dacre and Mountjoy joined the King at dinner and early in the afternoon, riding with young Richard, Duke of Gloucester, the King's young brother, came Hastings—Hastings who according to instruction had with him a thousand men. At supper Edward blandly informed Warwick that he had decided to return to London.

Now it was Warwick's turn to prevaricate. He said, "Would it not be wise for me to remain here, Your Grace? There are troubled spots and Brancepeth's men, some of them still roaming and doing damage."

Edward agreed readily. "It would be best, my lord. It would be best that you did not enter London with us either."

The slightest frown crossed Edward's face. Warwick would stay here in the north, sulking in his tent. The analogy was obvious. So was the fact that the Greek army besieging Troy had needed their mighty Achilles, and sooner or later he, Edward, might have to call him from his tent. Edward sighed; he had not been able to make Warwick see reason before; would he the second time? Or was the realm faced with another upheaval when he and his most powerful noble wrestled for the control of the kingdom?

And as far as his open refusal, just spoke, to let Warwick enter London with him, that was the only warning Edward permitted himself to utter, for above all he needed a cool and unemotional head on his shoulders; he was not a man to descend to revenge; he was the King, and he was trying to restore order to a troubled land.

Word, rumor, relief and joy preceded Edward into London. Two hundred craftsmen of the city dressed in their blue, the mayor and the aldermen, knights and squires met him. The Archbishop had wanted to be part of the procession, but Edward had sent him word that he would summon him when he needed him, so the Archbishop stayed at his house at the Moor and wondered what was going to happen next. And what happened was that Edward took up the reins of government where he left off, welcoming the Burgundians and accepting the honor of the Order of the Golden Fleece; he replaced the Treasureship with a man of his own, the Bishop of Ely, once more continuing his custom of giving office to the competent clergy and commoners. Edward made his brother Richard Constable of England and gave him the chief justiceship of Wales, for under Warwick's own tutelage Richard was capable and he had proved his fidelity. Fretting in the north Warwick learned all this; he also learned that Edward had bestowed his father's earldom on Anthony and that now there was another Earl Rivers at court, whom Warwick hated just as much. "And the Woodvilles that are left, including his Queen," Warwick spit out the word, "they will all be whispering in his ear that he should revenge himself!"

But Warwick was wrong. Bessie did not need to whisper in Edward's ear. He understood only too well how she felt, for he himself had suffered the same way with the murder of his father and his younger brother. "And Edmund has been my constant companion," he said to Bessie. "We were brought up together. Edmund was with me at Ludlow Castle for company. I should have given anything under the sun to spare you this and to spare poor Will. Bessie, Bessie, if it is any consolation to you I was very proud of you. You were so brave, putting on as fine a show as I tried to."

"I was so afraid! For you, so desperately afraid, for myself too. What would I do without you, sweetheart? What would I be?" As she fastened her eyes on his face she knew best how true was her statement, for her whole life was bound up securely in his and without him she would be a beautiful shadow; there was no doubt in Edward's mind either as he looked deep into her eyes; her love and need for him shone clear and he seized her tight. "I need you too, sweetheart Bessie," he muttered. Then his eyes lightened with his wry humor. "In fact right now I need you exceedingly."

And even had she wished to influence Edward it would have been impossible, for his mind was made up. It was not for nothing he had spent two months as a prisoner, for every minute of the time his mind had revolved unceasingly about the problems which faced him, and soon after he returned to London he began to act on them. So it was on October twenty-third that a tall man dressed in black was admitted to one of the rooms in the White Tower.

It was night. A single candle flickered. The single occupant of the room lay stretched languidly on his bed, and when his door opened he didn't deign to move but raised his eyes and brows lightly and shifted his hands under his head. Then a faint smile touched his lips.

"Why, 'tis the Earl Rivers." He still made no motion to rise, for the man who lay recumbent on the narrow bed bore one of the oldest names in England. It is doubtful that Lord Percy would have risen for the Earl of Warwick, for had not that gentleman received his earldom through the inheritance of his wife? But this royal prisoner bore a name celebrated in legend, and he acknowledged above his princely earldom none but his King. So Lord Percy blinked at Anthony, then slowly swung his feet over the side of his bed and sat.

"Welcome," he said negligently. "There's a stool."

"Thank you," Anthony said, with a slight smile. He sat down and leaned over to Percy and handed him Edward's ring. "I bring you a message, my lord."

Percy frowned. He had not known whether Edward would make any overtures to him; in his immense pride he had refused to make any himself, and therefore in his way he was suddenly grateful to Edward for having done this because he realized that there was a hint of royalty in the King himself making the first move. He respected Edward for that and he sat up straighter, his eyes searching Anthony's face in the uncertain light.

"His Grace offers you life, liberty and goods," Anthony said briefly.

To Lord Percy, Earl of Northumberland, the words came as a terrible shock, for here, immured in the Tower, brooding, he had tried not to think of the cool desolate moors, or the towering walls of Alnwick and the sound of the sea so near. He had tried to forget that he was entitled to sit as a principal peer in Parliament and that he was indeed the Lord of the North. His was a fierce nature and he was as hardy and bold as the country he was bred to. But he was a Lancastrian. His face was somber. How could he, for freedom and Alnwick and his own beloved north, how could he be bribed?

Anthony said, "His Grace asks me to remind you that his father died too in the same struggle. For the sake of the realm is it necessary that the bitter feud be continued? You are needed."

Anthony was thinking that Edward had pardoned Somerset and been betrayed. He had restored Oxford and been betrayed. The list could continue even down to Dr. Mackerell. And yet Dr. Hatclyf served his King faithfully; he himself, Anthony, would die for Edward; his father and John had. Anthony looked down at his hands in their black gloves and then he looked full at Percy.

"His Grace demands only your submission to him and a bond of eight thousand pounds."

Percy said, "His Grace doesn't trust me."

"Why should he?" Anthony retorted.

Percy said, "Aye. Why should he?"

Anthony said softly, "But you trust him."

The words hung in the small room. Percy suddenly stood and went over to the narrow window, cut into the stone. "Aye," said Percy, driving one fist into another. "I do! Why?"

"The answer to that question would take too long," Anthony said. "But the main reason is simple, my lord. You are alive to ponder it."

"Aye," Percy said. "That's true, I am alive. For that alone I am grateful. Please tell His Grace that—I've never admitted it before." He had not taken Edward's ring from Anthony's palm; now he did and in front of Anthony he went down on one knee and laid his lips against the King's ring. "Tell His Grace he has my heartfelt submission." He got to his feet and Anthony seeing no reason to prolong the interview got up and went to the narrow door.

"Also," said Percy, "tell His Grace I consent to the bond." He grinned slightly.

"The papers will be drawn up for you to sign," Anthony said. He saw Percy was suddenly excited and happy, and why shouldn't he be? But did he have any notion of the repercussions that this act of Edward's would have? No, he was thinking only of himself and that was the difference, Anthony thought, between the King and his nobles. Anthony's tone was severe as he said only, "Good night, my lord."

He reported back to the King immediately and Edward rubbed his brow and prepared for the more difficult interview ahead of him. But first, "You were satisfied, Anthony, of his honesty?"

"Aye, Your Grace, I was," Anthony said. "Not that I can swear to it. But I think you can trust him."

Edward nodded.

"His is a more or less open personality, driving and bold."

Edward nodded again. He needed Lord Percy. He needed him in his old capacity of Lord of the North. He couldn't count on Warwick anymore and he couldn't let the Nevilles completely control the north, but it was a risk and no one was better aware of it than the King. That very night, so John Neville would hear the news from no other lips than his, he called the present holder of the earldom to him.

"John," said the King in his frank direct way, "a few years ago I made a mistake. Now I am going to right it, but it will be to your disadvantage and I am sorry."

John Neville, Lord Montagu, the present Earl of Northumberland, looked amazed. His craggy face was full of questions. Had he not been faithful to Edward when his two brothers, Warwick and the Archbishop, had been so conspicuously unfaithful that many would call it treason? His brown eyes looked hurt and wary. But he didn't know what to say so he kept silent.

"A few years ago," Edward went on, "for your fine and sol-dierly aid in subduing our northern counties, we bestowed upon you the earldom of Northumberland, ignoring the fact that the hereditary Earl was our prisoner. Now after much thought we are convinced that we were wrong and that Lord Percy, having submitted to our authority, should by all the rights of God and man be restored to his proper inheritance."

John Neville's stricken face looked back at the King. Edward said, "We shall make it up to you, John. First we are going to create you the Marquis of Montagu, second we have two other plans which we shall confide to you shortly, and we shall in time make other gifts of land. We ask that you trust and obey." Edward rose and John Neville rose too. Edward flung his arm around his shoulder. "My right entirely well-beloved John," he said earnestly, "trust me. As I trust you."

Under the influence of Edward's dominant personality a small smile lightened the grave countenance of John Neville. His eyes were warm. "Aye, Your Grace," he said. And he knelt to show his obedience to the King's will.

Edward put his hand on his shoulder. "Bless you, my friend," he said. He held out his hand and John Neville took it in a hard grip. He went to the door and Edward heaved a deep sigh of relief. All had, to this moment, gone well.

And now to knit up the grievous hurts of his kingdom Edward summoned the other Lord of the North, Warwick, to London and also his brother Clarence. "If anyone can hold out the olive branch," Edward said to Bessie, "it must be I."

"They would never do it," Bessie exclaimed.

"No," said Edward. "But 'they' are not the King of England by birth, by God's law and by man's law. Now it remains to be seen whether Warwick and Clarence obey my call."

In order to implement his call to the two of his kin who had strayed into rebellion Edward summoned all the peers of the realm to a grand council meeting early in November, losing no time, for Percy was released from the Tower on the twenty-seventh of October and Edward had lost three months anyway, during which time his adversary, Louis of France, had managed to attach to himself the fidelity of the King of Castile with whom Edward had been dealing when he had been trapped by War-wick. But Edward thrust aside annoyance at what he couldn't have helped. And if there was a comic side to this affair it was reflected in Louis, for the reports that reached him from England were so contradictory he had no idea what was happening in the kingdom; one day he heard reliably that his friend and ally, that fine friend of France, Warwick, had control of the King and that France would soon reap the rewards, that English armies would soon help him subdue Burgundy and attach it firmly to France; and the next day he heard that Warwick had failed, that he had fled and was in the north alone. Meantime as soon as Edward had returned to London he had sent out the fleet to keep Louis wondering further, and Louis' agents were not astute enough to report accurately: that Edward was too embroiled in his own affairs to think of attacking France. Still the fleet roamed the narrow seas under one of the Howards and Louis fretted and fumed trying to find out exactly what was happening in England; he looked down his narrow nose and even spoke to his Queen about it, the woman he was fond of introducing simply as "my wife."

Meantime Edward's mother had arrived in London in order to speak to Edward about Clarence. She told him how she had gone to Sandwich before Clarence's wedding to Isabel Neville and tried to stop him. Nonetheless she pleaded for him to pardon Clarence and he assured her that he would. He told her openly that he would pardon both Warwick and Clarence, and of course he knew she would not keep the news to herself and that it would reach the ears of those whose allegiance he was so desperately trying to hold, not for his own sake but for the sake of his kingdom. And before he could make known to John Neville, now the new Marquis of Montagu, the rewards for his fidelity he talked to Bessie.

"In order to attach John firmly to our cause I am going to betroth our eldest daughter to his son."

Bessie's great eyes studied her husband; her beautiful little golden-haired princess—she was three—affianced to one of the Nevilles.

Edward said, "I am extremely fond of John, Bessie. He comes of fine stock. His son is a good lad of nine. He has some royal blood. I am going to create the boy the Duke of Bedford." He leaned forward. "Bessie, in case we have no sons little Bess will inherit. John's son would be a most proper consort and draw to his side all his many kin."

"Then you would not consent to Clarence as your heir?" she whispered.

"No," said Edward. "That is one point I shall not concede. I have been practicing as much self-control and restraint as I can, Bessie." He smiled slightly. "But I will never concede that—recognition of Clarence as my heir."

"It looks as though you are rewarding the Nevilles for rebellion," Bessie said.

"No, I am rewarding John for fidelity. And yet it is a sop to the Nevilles so that I am accomplishing two things at once. The nine-year-old Duke of Bedford is Warwick's nephew so we should draw Warwick toward us and away from Clarence." He rose. "It's a dirty game, Bessie, all I can do is play it as honorably as possible—and as far as our daughter is concerned, she could not have a more adequate mate. If I thought other I shouldn't do it—I assure you of that, my own little poppet."

Bessie whispered, "How if Warwick persists in—in—"

"Rebellion," Edward finished. "You can say it. If he does I'll take all his lands, all his castles from Warwick to Middleham and all inheritances and hand them over to John and his son. And thus to my own child."

On the sixth of November young George Neville's charter creating him the Duke of Bedford passed through the great council, but it was not until December that Warwick himself and Clarence appeared in London to sit in with their peers. On the eleventh of December Edward issued a general pardon, and also before that council appeared the Duchess of Bedford to be exonerated of the charges of witchcraft. The Duchess was accompanied by two of her young sons, Lionel and Edward. The council squashed the charges against the Duchess and pondered the punishment for her accuser. "*Zut!*" said the Duchess when it was suggested that Wake go to prison. "And let him live on the King's bounty? No, remove the livery of his master and let him earn his own bread."

Anthony could not help but smile, and yet he knew that those miserable charges of making images and sticking them with pins had originated in the fertile brain of either Warwick or Clarence, and Anthony knew it was no smiling matter either that those two gentlemen looked at his own younger brothers with hatred. Lionel looked a great deal like Anthony and he was up from Oxford for Christmas. Edward was almost the spitting image of

John, already tall and broad-shouldered, and the hands that hung down at his sides were already very familiar with the sword and the dagger and they were big, hard, horseman's hands. A ready knight for Edward, fierce and loyal, stood there by his mother's side as easy and confident as John had been; Anthony could read Warwick's mind as he studied young Edward Woodville: "I disposed of two Woodvilles and here are two more!"

Anthony said to Elizabeth that Christmas, one time when they were alone, "God help me, Bess, but I don't know what will happen. They hanker for our blood."

"His Grace is aware of it," Elizabeth said. "But he believes they will be faithful to him."

"I don't," Anthony said. "What's more, they are trying to subvert Montagu. They are pouring poison in his ears, saying we Woodvilles are the King's favorites and soon all the Nevilles will be shoved aside."

"Lord Montagu has been conspicuously faithful and Edward loves him entirely."

"Ah, but he is a Neville first and King's man second."

Elizabeth leaned forward. "Do you truly believe that, Anthony?"

He shook his head. "God, I'm not sure Bess. I wish I could be. I'm not quite sure."

"His Grace has complete faith in John Neville."

"All we can do," Anthony said, "is pray that he is right."

Edward was praying too that his self-restraint and kindness, the iron hand in the velvet glove, would bring his unruly kin back into line and into the fold. Not only had he been telling the absolute truth when he told Bessie and Warwick too to his face that he needed him, but he was fond of Warwick. He couldn't help remembering so great a knight as Warwick was those early days in battle, in exile in Calais, in the daring sea raids, the whole, powerful personality of a man who thinks he can shape his own destiny and that of others. Edward saw to his sorrow that Warwick was changing from the high-hearted adventurer into the cold-blooded killer and yet Edward would have been less the King he was had he not been tempted to have a few heads himself, but then he would be making the same fatal mistake Warwick had and replunge the country into rivers of blood. So Edward watched and waited, ready to pounce, and the grand council continued to sit and meet during the months of January and February. After all, Warwick had gained much; with his nephew betrothed to Edward's oldest little daughter and his own daughter Isabel married to Clarence, he was as close to the throne as he could get without murdering Edward himself. Yet the Earl was not satisfied; it was almost as though he were possessed by evil spirits; he could not wash the blood from his hands and yet they greeded for more. Restlessly he too waited, dreaming dreams of conquest. He wrote to Louis of France, his great friend, and he did all in his power to attract his stalwart brother to his side.

Day after day he hammered at one point: He took the earldom of Northumberland away from you! And so if you help me dethrone him, I who put him on the throne, you and I will rule England through Isabel and young George, your own son.

Tempting words. John Neville wrestled with his conscience, his real devotion to Edward, his devotion to his brother; thus on a sea of unrest, as though every man sensed the struggle taking place for mastery of the kingdom, the whole country surged and lifted and rose and fell like a ship on the narrow seas between her and France, a France in which Louis also watched and waited chewing on his underlip—for the good of France he would cause as much trouble as possible in England. Louis understood Edward's problems better than anyone else in the world, for he was having the same ones himself, as both of them seized with royal hands for the tillers of their vessels to steer them into safe waters of a strong safe kingdom, united and at peace within their own borders.

New trouble struck right after Christmas. And it began in Lincolnshire, where at Gainsborough Lord Burgh's house was attacked and pillaged. Lord Burgh appealed to Edward.

Burgh was Edward's master of horse and a knight of the body. His attacker was a man named Welles whose father had been killed at the battle of Towton and who had been attainted. But a year ago he had been restored in blood and once again clemency had ill paid the King. Welles had been assisted in his rape of Burgh's hall at Gainsborough by his brother-in-law Dymmock. Edward was striding through treacherous morass, but since he had issued a general pardon he summoned Welles and Dymmock to London. They couldn't give as their excuse for not coming that they'd been dabbling in treason, so perforce they came although Welles left word with his son Robert Welles to hurry to his rescue if his life was in danger.

They arrived in London in February and promptly submitted to the King. Edward had been busy with his great council, but even now Lincolnshire was stirring, from the reports Edward received, and he decided to go north himself and see what was happening.

Meanwhile according to plan Warwick left London, promising to meet Edward with troops, and Welles and Dymmock were granted pardons in the first week of March as Edward was making ready to leave London.

Edward had intended to leave on the fourth of March, but we know from Clarence's letters that he himself undertook to keep Edward in his capital city for a few days longer, so he sent word ahead to Edward that he would like to see and talk with him.

Suspecting nothing, Edward did delay his departure. Clarence arrived and was staying at his mother's house, Baynard's Castle, and there Edward sought him out and found Clarence his usual charming self. The Duchess was present and she was pleased to see her two sons together again. It was Tuesday, the sixth of March. Clarence had gained two days while Warwick hurried to raise troops. He explained easily that he was here in London on his way west to join his wife, who was carrying a child, and Edward congratulated him. Edward suggested they ride together to St. Paul's to make an offering and to let the city see the King and his brother together and the good friends brothers should be. But Edward was not foolish enough to be completely taken in and he did watch and weigh Clarence as best he could; but the excuse Clarence gave, that of seeing Isabel who was indeed nearing her time, was such a valid one with Edward, who never let Bessie out of his sight when she was in the same condition, that he found himself believing Clarence without more than a shred of doubt.

Nonetheless the King was in a hurry and only a few hours later he left London with Hastings and the new Earl of Northumberland, and as night fell he arrived at Waltham and stayed there at the abbey overnight.

That night Edward drew up commissions of array for both Warwick and Clarence, but before they could be sent off a royal messenger galloped into the abbey with the astonishing news that Welles' son, Sir Robert, had announced on Sunday, two days ago, in all the churches in Lincolnshire, that all men should come to join him under the banners of Clarence and Warwick to resist the King who was coming to destroy them. On the heels of this news a child came to the King, bearing a letter from a faithful lord, Cromwell, at Tattershall, saying that men were gathering in great numbers not only in Lincolnshire but in Yorkshire.

Edward stayed his hand on the commissions and on Wednesday got as far as Royston where a personal letter from Clarence was delivered to him. It was such a pleasant letter. Edward found himself believing it and sat down and wrote back with his own hand. But the day before, he had taken the precaution of sending to London for an armed guard to bring Lord Welles and Dymmock to him for questioning. Meantime Edward dispatched the commissions for Warwick and Clarence.

Hurrying their prisoners along, the guards caught up to Edward at Huntingdon. Edward received them with Hastings standing at one side of him and Lord Percy on the other. Edward was wearing a light mesh and mail coat and both Lord Welles and Dymmock found his eyes stern and uncompromising.

Hastily, trusting to their so recent pardon, they confessed that they had known about the insurrection and that Welles' son Robert had acted on their orders. Then they stood silent.

"My lords," the King said, "both of you will die unless you persuade Sir Robert to submit to the royal authority."

Edward studied Welles' face and saw fear. But Welles said nothing else except that he would write immediate to his son; that day Edward went on to Fotheringhay, taking Welles and Dymmock with him. In the back of his mind was looming the figure of Warwick, unplacated and on his remorseless way to treason and death.

At Fotheringhay Edward received advices from trusted scouts that Welles' son Sir Robert was passing through Grantham on his way to Leicester and the letters from his father had been delivered. That day Warwick wrote two letters, one to Welles' son to let Edward pass through and to meet him, Warwick, on Monday night in Leicester where he and Clarence would have twenty thousand men, raised with the King's own commission.

Whether or not Clarence and Warwick had raised that many men was a question, but Sir Robert Welles didn't wait to find out. Instead he disobeyed Warwick's orders and turned back toward Stamford, intending to attack the King's forces and rescue his father. This Edward learned Monday night when he reached Stamford; that the brash young man had not obeyed orders to lay down his arms and come peaceably to his King. So with some reluctance, for Edward did not like war in his own country, the King donned mail and set forth immediately for Empingham where young Welles was and attacked him with his quick ferocity, he and his men descending out of the night.

Welles tried vainly to rally his men with cries of "A Warwick! A Clarence!" But his men had no stomach for fight with their King and they fled before Edward, throwing their coats away as they ran.

The brief battle was dubbed Losecoat Field and Edward's troops pursued the fleeing rebels with glee. It was like a hunt and they stopped only to gather up the discarded arms and liveried coats. It was only too plain that most of the livery was that of Clarence and Warwick.

Edward stayed the whole day, on foot or ahorse, and returned to Stamford late that night. A servant of Clarence had been captured, with him a casket containing letters which told only too plainly that Warwick and Clarence had planned no less than the destruction of the King and the placing of Clarence on the throne. Reading these letters by the light of a tall candelabrum, his mail coat just loosed at the throat, his feet still booted, a cup of wine at his elbow, Edward was left to face the fact that Warwick and his own brother were not only his betrayers but the betrayers of their country. Wearily Edward let himself be divested of his clothes and he went to bed, leaving instructions that when young Welles was captured he wished to question him. And before he went to bed he sent word to Clarence and Warwick briefly informing them of Losecoat Field and commanding them to come to him, to disband the troops they had been raising and to come with only such retinue as their ranks required.

Edward slept. In the bright light of morning he confronted

young Sir Robert Welles and his ally Richard Warren. They found not the sunny-hearted prince but a stern King.

"Your father is dead by my command," he told Welles. "And you, his son, are responsible. Is it possible," Edward asked, "that you did not know the penalty for treason?"

As Edward surveyed the man before him he briefly felt pity. "It could so easily have been avoided had you obeyed our command," he said aloud, and these words broke Welles' reserve. In stumbling words he poured forth the whole tale, how he was to let the King pass and then Warwick and Clarence would throw an army between London and the King.

Edward heard the whole tale through. When it was done Richard Warren confirmed it in more words. "You shall have a trial," Edward said.

Now Edward acted fast. Messengers were dispatched quickly to Calais, where Warwick still held the captainship, with orders that he was not to be permitted to enter, and the same message was sent to Ireland where Clarence held the lieutenancy. Proclamations were sent out that the King was going to keep both his Christmas pardon and his word in every point; he again repeated his promise of pardon for all offense committed before Christmas, but ordered that no one now should make an assembly or a gathering of his people in response to any message unless it bore the Great Seal, the privy seal or the signet seal. Then he wrote to Clarence.

"We have learned," Edward wrote, "that you have labored diligently, contrary to natural kindness and duty, and that proclamations have been made in your name and our cousin of Warwick. But even now if you come to us in humble wise, as a subject ought to come to his sovereign lord, we will treat you according to your nighness of blood and according to our laws, but we warn you that if you delay we will be forced to punish you, for example's sake, even though we are loath to. And we tell you if blood is shed the blame will not rest with us."

Then he made John Tiptoft Constable of England and sent Anthony posthaste to join Lord Howard in command of the fleet, and Anthony took his young brother Edward with him to give him the first taste of sea duty.

On Monday morning, in front of the whole army Edward had with him, an army which one letter of John Paston describes as the goodliest and best arrayed army England has ever seen, Welles and Warren repeated their confessions and were sent to the block. Edward was at Doncaster. And just after the executions messengers arrived from Clarence and Warwick, demanding a safe conduct and a pardon for the Duke and the Earl.

Edward, striving for calm, failed; his face was grim and his eyes were black with anger, and looming large in mail and armor he was such a fearsome figure that the messengers threw themselves at his feet and begged aloud for mercy. Edward managed to get out one sentence. "Not even our ancient enemies of France would ask for such a surety! Before coming to us!"

He paused. Beyond the groveling messengers at his feet lay a pool of blood, the bloodied block and the two figures of the executed men. The example Edward had been forced to make was the result of Warwick's and Clarence's treason. They could send these men to their gruesome deaths and they were too cowardly to face him themselves. They knew better than any that Edward hated executions; that he would much rather heal wounds than open them; that he was too much a politician to send men to even a well-deserved death if it could be avoided. For them to abandon their followers to him, the King, and force his hand made Edward so angry that he had to swallow deeply before he could speak. The messengers waited, the whole army waited, eyes glued to their monarch.

"Go back!" Edward ordered, gesturing with one big gloved hand. "Tell them that their sovereign lord will treat them as a sovereign lord should treat his subjects. And if they can prove their innocence no one will be gladder than we. But if they don't obey my summons now they shall have exactly what they deserve!"

The two messengers still groveled on the ground. "We beseech your Grace," they cried, "to send such a message by a king at arms!"

"Go!" commanded Edward and that was his last word.

Chapter 13

ANNE NEVILLE was fourteen years old. On the morning of April
sixteenth she was wakened out of a deep sleep, lying on her narrow bunk, tucked in tight by her mother's own hands, her dark
hair splayed across the pillow; she sat straight upright in the
bunk and wondered what had waked her. For she was not sea-
sick today. Before she had been so sick. Sick and terrified, terrified from that first day when her father and Clarence had
appeared at Warwick Castle and hurried their womenfolk,
herded really, on a flight to the coast and to a handful of ships
that her father had waiting. They were escaping from Edward.
Anne had had only her heavy cloak and a change of petticoats
and hose and an extra pair of shoes. All that first day aboard
ship she had vomited and vomited, her thin body racked with
the throes of sickness that only the Channel can produce. And
with it came terror, for her father had sailed down to Southampton to try and steal his great ship *Trinity* from Southampton
where she lay.

But Anthony Woodville was ready for such an attack and a
fierce fight began. Anne heard the crack of guns and saw ships
boarded and captured, and finally just before their own ship
would be the next only then had her father given the order to
flee, and then Anne didn't remember any more, for she fainted
and it was at least an hour before her distraught mother could
rouse her.

The next day had been just as bad, for lookouts constantly reported a sail or a half-dozen sails; and if they were small, a
Breton fishing vessel, her father would attack and then there
would be more fighting and more seasickness, more misery and
terror; in between she kept dreaming of her rooms at Warwick
Castle or at Middleham in her beloved Wensleydale.

Despite her terror she got relatively little attention, for her older sister Isabel was aboard this ship too. Isabel was sick and was almost ready to have her baby, her slight figure great with child, her movements clumsy, her face whiter than paper and her eyes two big holes in her face; for Isabel was terrified too, even more than Anne. She was afraid that both she and her baby would die.

But the night before, in the great cabin with her father and mother and Isabel and Clarence, there had been some assurance from her father, for he had said, "All right, madam!" to his impassioned wife, his Countess. "We shall be safe in Calais tomorrow morning." And now it was morning and something had wakened Anne. She sat still on her bunk; then the sound came again and she knew what it was. Gunfire.

The ship was pitching madly. She seized the edge of her bunk to rise. She had slept in her clothes, for she was afraid to get undressed. She shook out her rumpled skirts and began to pull on her long hose when she heard a veritable rain of shots. The ship bobbed restless as a toy and threw her onto the floor while she tried to finish tying her stockings. Then she crawled around to find her shoes and put them on. Carefully she went along the narrow passageway to her mother and Isabel.

They did not even say good morning; her mother cried, "Anne! Go tell your father that Isabel's labor has begun!"

Anne gave one glance at her mother's face and fled.

She discovered her father on deck, clinging with both hands to the rail and staring in unbelief across the water toward the port of Calais. He had been sure he would be received there. With open arms! By his ally and friend Lord Wenlock. Instead he was greeted by gunfire!

Anne made her way to his side; she too clung to the rail while her father shouted for the signalmen and while cannonballs dropped around them into the whitecapped fierce waves and the sailors shouted orders. She watched hypnotized until finally her father roared out to drop anchor while he parleyed with the fort.

The little fleet with its trail of captured vessels hove to under orders which Anne heard even from the other ships, so close were they on the heaving seas. She watched as a boat was slung over; she peered down at it, bobbing like a cork, standing first

on its stern and then on its stem, while the sailors slid down a
dangling rope ladder. She forgot her fear in admiration of their
skill, and in just a moment they were pulling across to the now
mercifully silent fort whose guns still smoked.

Anne ventured to address her angry red-faced father. "It's Isabel! She has begun!"

Warwick turned his head to look down at her. His face was one
big scowl. Anne wanted to cry but she held back her tears.

"What can I do more than I am doing?" her father shouted, the
wind trailing the words from his mouth.

She looked up at him wordlessly.

"You don't understand! They won't let us land! I have sent a
message."

He gestured to the bobbing boat. Then, "Go below!"

She was afraid to go below. Stubbornly she stood alongside of
him and he forgot her; she shivered there in the wind and the
wet, salt spray.

"Is it always like this in the narrow seas?" she shouted at her
father.

"Aye," he looked down at her again. "Mostly." He put his
hand over hers on the rail. He said, "I've written to Lord Wenlock, explaining. I had the letter ready. I've told him he must let
us land."

Although Anne Neville had never been very close to her father, indeed saw him rarely, she felt safer up here on deck with
him than down below where her vivid imagination pictured the
writhing Isabel; Isabel's cabin was tiny and odorful and so Anne
stayed close to her father.

The Earl of Warwick was beside himself with impatience and
frustration. There lay Calais! Where he himself was the captain.
From Calais he could operate like an independent Prince,
which was of course what his nature told him he certainly should
have been. For he was no servant and acknowledged no master.
Had he not said so himself?

The messenger whom Lord Wenlock sent back from the fort
was a competent sailor—no one else could have managed the
climb up the swinging ladder. And this was his message; Anne
heard it in terror.

Barely half a day before, the King's message closing Calais to
his rebel cousin and brother had arrived; the garrison had

chosen to honor it. The Earl of Warwick was no longer the captain of Calais and he would not be permitted to land under any condition whatsoever.

But Lord Wenlock had writ separately to the Earl of Warwick. The letter was duly handed over and Warwick, not knowing what it contained, burst out, "But my daughter! The Duchess of Clarence! She is aboard and she is in labor with his first child."

The messenger bowed. "I shall apprise my lord Wenlock of your words."

Warwick would have liked to seize him and choke him or order him hanged, but he didn't dare.

"Tell Lord Wenlock!" he shouted. But he couldn't control his tongue. "You fool, you knave, hurry!"

Then seizing Anne by the hand he hurried below, shoving Anne in the door of her sister's cabin.

"Help your sister, you're old enough!"

The cabin door banged and he strode down the passageway to his fretful son-in-law. He paid no attention to Clarence; in fact he was heartily sick of Clarence. He tore open Wenlock's letter, ripping the single sheet in half in his haste, so he had to hold the two pieces together to read it.

It was rather ambiguous, as if Lord Wenlock were afraid to commit much to writing, and yet if he had hoped to conceal the import of treason in it he had failed. He said that it would be of no avail to Warwick to enter Calais, for Calais, he said, is a mousetrap. Charles the Duke of Burgundy could easily capture him there. He recommended the Earl of Warwick take refuge in France and he, Wenlock, would be able to help him better.

Warwick gave a roar of rage. He threw the letter on the floor and Clarence went over to pick it up, but Warwick set his heel on it.

"He won't help us!" he said, and he looked so puffed up with hatred that even Clarence thought about Warwick and not himself. What if he had a fit?

"Pray be calm," Clarence managed to say.

"He tells us to go to France!"

"Maybe we should," Clarence said. Anything to get off this heaving ship; there wasn't even any wine aboard.

"Do you realize your wife is in the throes of her first labor?" Warwick shouted.

"You should have thought of that before when you insisted on her coming!"

"You could have refused, you drunken coward!"

This was too much for Clarence. He raised his fist and would have struck the Earl, but there was an intervention; Anne opened the door.

"Isabel's dying," she screamed. "She's dying! There's blood all over!"

Her father took her by the shoulders and shook her. "Your mother didn't send you here to tell me that! What did she say?"

Anne's head bobbled back and forth. "She said to ask for wine and herbs for Isabel!"

"Go back and say I'll do the best I can," Warwick muttered. Then more kindly, "Anne. Anne!" She turned blindly from the small cabin door. "Anne, there's always blood in childbirth. Be more brave. It is perfectly natural."

She stared at him in a kind of deepening horror. She cried, "Why did you bring us? King Edward would have helped us. I know he would. We would be safe with him!"

Clarence and Warwick confronted the child but she had a last word. "He is always kind. He never hurts women."

"I brought you because I have great plans for you, you silly fool," Warwick said, and somehow this terrified her even more and now she did flee. Even with the sheet anchors the boat pitched like a toy boat, and Anne, stumbling down the passageway, reached Isabel's door; even with Isabel writhing on her narrow, disordered bunk, it was at least more of a haven than her father.

Lord Wenlock had had the kindness and presence of mind to send wine back to the laboring Isabel with a final message to go on to France. But the weather was worsening and it was extremely difficult to get sail up without being blown under the guns of the fort at Calais. Further, there was the Burgundian fleet maneuvering in these waters somewhere, and Warwick knew there was nothing Charles of Burgundy would like better than to capture him; besides that Lord Howard and Anthony Woodville were somewhere near enough and all these facts worried him more than Isabel.

But her brief interview with her father had sobered Anne to the extent that she could now help her mother and the woman who attended Isabel. She could help take the soiled linen and replace it with clean under Isabel's body and sponge her legs with seawater, warmed a bit, and hold her head to help her drink the wine; she could even bear Isabel's thin shrieking.

Isabel's child was born dead. But Isabel herself, barely able to breathe, Anne thought, after an hour lay peacefully asleep as if she did not know, as indeed she didn't. Anne's mother bore the body of the infant into Anne's cabin, and there the two women wrapped the tiny limbs in white linen, their tears christening and mourning. Out on the deck the chaplain read the brief service, and Isabel's baby slid down alone into the water of the narrow seas, the brisk staccato waves like snapping teeth. Anne would never forget it, never. She suddenly gave a great sob, and her mother put her arms around her and tried to pull her from the rail, but Anne was staring down into the unrelenting ocean as if she would throw herself into it to accompany the poor dead child.

"Anne, Anne," her mother cried.

Anne turned her head to look at her father. "It is all your fault," she said. "You killed Isabel's baby and put it alone into the water." Then she turned and her mother, afraid to leave her, put her arm around her youngest daughter and led her from the deck.

"Isabel will have other children," her mother whispered. "One never knows why, Anne, but you must remember that women do lose babies. They do, Anne, they do."

Anne didn't answer; her mother tried to give her wine but she vomited it up. By the time she arrived in France she had lost eight pounds and was so thin and frail that even her father was worried about her, for she was an integral part of his plans for his own glowing future, a future which he would carve out even at the cost of his own flesh and blood. Meantime he and his sailors raided Burgundian and Breton shipping; it was not until May first that the Earl of Warwick with his prizes sailed into the mouth of the Seine and dropped anchor. The anchors slid overboard, the flags flew the banner of the ragged staff, almost as though it represented a separate principality, and the Earl of Warwick was back in France, dragging his womenfolk and his prizes behind him, plus his dubious ally, George Plantagenet, Duke of Clarence. He had great plans. He sent word immediate to King Louis that he desired an interview.

Anne and Isabel and their mother went immediately into a convent, where Anne gradually began to recover. She spent day after day in the company of the nuns and in the chapel and in the gardens, where the very sweetness of the French spring helped to heal the wounds she had sustained. During those days she thought more and more of joining the sisterhood; hour upon hour she spent bent over her needlework, learning to do the fine French stitching. King Louis sent gifts of cloth to her and to the other women and even fine French silk to Clarence for a suit. The days deepened into summer and Anne was content; she felt safe. She had been at the convent a scant ten weeks when her father reappeared. It was July eighteenth.

He was very jovial. He was so glad to see all his womenfolk so well and healthy and recovered from the trials of the seafaring life at which a man like him was so at home. In fact those days at sea—and how many prizes had he taken, twenty?—should serve to show the weaker sex just how rugged and male were the lives of their menfolk—a life women could never understand or imagine 'less they'd shared it. And now all was well, very well indeed, and Anne would see why he had brought her with him to France, because he, her father, was going to make her Queen of England!

"Queen of England?" Anne stammered, having a vision of Bessie, beautiful and assured; the last time she had seen Bessie little Cecily had been only a few months old, Elizabeth had been holding the baby and the King had been in the room and Lord Hastings too. How could she, little Anne Neville, take the place of Elizabeth Woodville? And where would King Edward—her thought broke off. What was her father saying?

"You are going to marry Edward, Prince of Wales, son of Queen Margaret of Anjou and Henry VI of England, and since Henry is unfit to rule, I, your father, will guide you and your young husband."

All her life Anne Neville had been taught to fear Margaret of Anjou, the she-wolf, the French Queen, and to fear her for her very life, for women and children had died when Margaret's armies had swept England, women and children and priests. All her life she had been told that the spoiled, cruel, only son of that Queen was either a bastard or he was mad too like his father. To be delivered into the power of those two was like being delivered to ten thousand devils.

"I can't!" she cried. "I can't!"

She backed away from her father, her great dark eyes shining with fear, all sorts of terrible thoughts pouring through her young mind. The horrible thoughts of the marriage bed with that monster boy, Isabel in childbirth and his ruthless, proud mother, scarred by years of plotting and planning revenge, living on hatred; it had rotted her away and everyone knew it.

Her father said, cold with fury, "You ungrateful, spiritless child! I offer you the honor of being England's Queen! I have bartered my soul for you and your children and you whimper!"

He had indeed bartered his soul and he was playing a more dangerous game than he perceived. He had managed to make of himself a pawn between two Kings. That they would destroy him was inevitable, but now sailing free before the wind he was, he thought, the maker of his own destiny and the maker of Kings. And his pusillanimous daughter cringed before his greatness.

"You little fool," he said only. "You will do as you are told."

When he thought of how he had labored for his alliance; in the weeks just past Louis had been so confounded to see him on French soil. Once again Louis had received such conflicting reports from England that at one time he thought Warwick had betrayed him and had nervously called out the ban and arrière-ban because of the fleets sailing the narrow seas.

Next he discovered to his horror that Warwick had dragged his prizes—Burgundian ships—right into the Seine and his sailors were swarming all over Normandy, hawking their pirates' wares and fighting with the townspeople, for if there was one breed in English the French could abide least it was English pirates. Meanwhile all this was happening right under the nose of Charles of Burgundy, who gave out a roar of rage as only Charles could do, provisioned his own fleet and gave Louis to understand that Burgundian armies would be descending on Normandy at any moment.

Louis sent frantic messages to Warwick to move his ships. Move them! Next door in Luxembourg le Comte de St. Pol was making warlike gestures and crying for Louis to arrest Warwick, for he was a traitor.

Louis, reluctant to have any wars on Warwick's behalf but reluctant to lose a valuable ally who would make trouble in England—and this was the basis of Louis' foreign policy—sent couriers racing to Charles of Burgundy. He, Louis, had not known that Warwick had plundered or captured Burgundian ships—of course he hadn't.

Charles was so angry that to receive the French ambassadors he had himself built a gold dais higher than the French lords had ever seen; it was draped in black velvet, which was Charles' favorite dress, and from its high eminence the Duke of Burgundy scowled down upon the French.

Nothing would do but that Warwick be arrested and that all Burgundian ships be returned to their owners; meanwhile the fleet was already at sea and Louis could expect them on his coast at any time. For Charles was after Warwick's blood, no matter where he was—by land or by sea. Anthony joined forces with him and both fleets harried the French coast while Louis vainly called up troops, warned towns and sent couriers flying to all parts of the country, including Brittany, for he was always afraid of Francis of Brittany's shaky loyalty. Louis, who always rushed about his own country so fast his court and messengers often could not find him—now hedged this way and that, offering to come in disguise to see Warwick but above all asking him to move his ships to Guienne, to the Channel Isles, but away from Harfleur!

But the bait dangled in front of Louis' nose smelled and looked so tasty, so irresistible! He received Warwick and Clarence; he and Warwick closeted themselves in one of the rooms of the palace at Amboise after a ride through the Loire Valley with as impressive a retinue as they could muster. Louis was so kind. He made presents even to Warwick's acrobat. He was so kind he presented himself to Warwick at his own apartments. There Louis rubbed his hands with excitement as Warwick's plan unfolded. Louis had no qualms about accepting these plans. They would turn England upside down; not even the enraged protests of his vassals or even war itself could have made Louis, the canny politician, turn aside from such a ploy.

But what of Margaret of Anjou? Louis remembered a letter she had written him some time ago as a fugitive, penniless, out-

cast Queen—but she had written like a true Queen and he had
said at the time, "Look how proudly she writes!" Would Margaret,
thirsting for revenge, accept the help of the man she considered
her greatest enemy? Whose father and uncle and brother she had
gleefully executed and set their heads up on poles while her fine
little boy watched? Would Margaret marry her only beloved son
to the daughter of the man she hated most in the whole world?

Louis' hooded eyes and long nose and charming manner considered the problem, and Warwick said, "Sire, you will be able
to persuade her."

It would take all the arts and wiles of which he had many.
Louis became fatherly. He placed his hand over that of Margaret
of Anjou. He thought her still lovely; her dark eyes were great
pools. "Your former husband is unfit to rule," he said in tones of
regret and commiseration.

"*C'est vrai*," Margaret conceded. "But I will not—"

"*Du douce*," Louis begged, with a slow smile. He sighed and
was silent, only smiling down upon her sweetly. "My lord of Warwick, my cousin"—Warwick was five times removed from true
cousinship—"is a man of whom I am very fond."

Perhaps it was true; Margaret found herself believing it.

"He desires to atone the wrongs which he has done you, to
atone on his knees, to offer you his heart and, more important,
his sword."

"Sword," she repeated. "*Mon Dieu!* I thought you were going
to say soul!" Her eyes blazed; Louis thought her remark comical
but didn't show his amusement. He let her go on. "If I accepted
his sword I should never accept his heart. It is black! And I will
never permit my most beloved Prince to marry a whelp, a bitch,
of his!"

"Madame, madame, such high words!" He shook his head
slowly. "You failed before because your pride and spirit wouldn't
allow you to accept help. Do you not know that I, your King, can
show meekness and love? Humility becomes a woman. And yet—
what are these words we speak? *Vous n'avez pas besoin! C'est
votre fils!*"

She bent her head. "*Oui, oui, je sais.*"

"You do not need help! But to help your son regain his crown
—what would not any woman under the sun do for that? Can it
be that you will not suffer the help of a former enemy and allow

your son to suffer even more? We—you and I and my wife—should be thinking of the young. I, who have just been able to hold my own son in my arms, know a little of what I speak." Louis shook his head and adjusted his rather shabby coat sleeve. "Can you imagine my feelings, madame, when I first held my own firstborn boy a few days ago? Then if you can you must also know that I consider your objections unlike any parent's. Any parent! Ah! Ah!" cried Louis, jumping to his feet and shaking his head in despair. He threw out his hands to heaven. "I call the saints to witness a woman who would not swallow her pride for her only son, her Prince!"

Margaret of Anjou capitulated. Louis' crescendo of fact, fiction and logic swept her along irresistibly, and he was able to tell the Earl of Warwick that. *"Ce marche!"*

And the indomitable Margaret was afire with excitement with the vision of her son, England's rightful Prince, wearing the crown for which he had been born; and then perhaps someday, sometime, she could say, in a terrible voice, as a King of England had once said before her, "Will no one rid me of this man!" She would have to remind them not to kill Warwick in a church.

Louis sought out Warwick in his apartments, knocking on the door and asking admittance, humble as a servant to a great lord. What balm for Warwick's soul! If Edward had behaved like this! For just a moment willy-nilly in his mind came the remembrance of Edward, striding into his chamber to greet him, a casual arm flung around his shoulders. It would never happen again; Edward would never fling open the door and smile his wide smile—that sunny-hearted Prince, his companion in arms and in exile, was forever lost to him.

"Mille pardons," Louis murmured, "do I disturb you? But I have fine news!"

They got down to business. Warwick had letters from both the Earl of Shrewsbury and Lord Stanley; both promised support. Louis pulled at his lip.

"But what of your brother?"

"George is confined to his own home at the Moor, under guard."

Louis privately thought Edward was being very clement and yet, of course, George Neville wore the cloth of an Archbishop.

"And your other brother?" Louis persisted.

Warwick sighed. John was the crux of the whole plot. "I am not sure about John," he murmured.

But Louis was anxious to get rid of Warwick. He wrote: "You know how I desire M. de Warwick to return to England, as much for the good it would do me to see him come out on top in England—or at least that by his means the realm of England might be embroiled in strife—as to avoid the problems arising on account of his remaining here."

It was the twenty-second of July. In her rooms in the palace, when she woke every morning, Anne Neville faced the dawning day with terror. If she could have fled she would, but this was France and she had nowhere to run and no one to help her. The Countess, her mother, tried to comfort her, but the Countess herself was shocked by the brutality and cynicism of the union and could do little to aid her daughter; both women, frightened and sad, escaped from the court to the chapel or closeted themselves in their bedroom, hiding vainly from their fate. Warwick came to fetch them that night. Louis kissed Anne and the Countess; Anne stood tremblingly by her mother as Warwick himself went to Queen Margaret and knelt at her feet. Anne's eyes fastened on the face of her future mother-in-law; sitting haughty and stern (and wicked, Anne thought), she kept Warwick on his knees for fifteen minutes but to Anne it seemed an hour at least. Her legs shook and her color came and went; finally, seeing her distress, Louis himself assisted her to a stool. Then when Warwick finally was allowed to rise he looked over at Anne; thus prompted she stumbled to her feet awkwardly and licking her lips in dismay came toward her father and toward the seated Queen and the eighteen-year-old boy at her side. His eyes roved over her and Anne stared back at him in open horror. Margaret was surveying her coldly and with disdain. Anne curtsied. The Queen flicked her with another brief glance. Then Margaret said, "Ah, my lord of Oxford." Oxford went down on one knee and she leaned forward and raised him up. "You have suffered much thing for my cause," she said warmly, and she had given little Anne Neville to understand only too clearly that she had nothing but contempt for her.

"Like a little lamb to slaughter," said the French pityingly. In the great cathedral at Angers Anne Neville was formally betrothed to Margaret's son, and she had to take her oath on a bit of the True Cross, which was called the Cross of St. Laud d'Angers. She could barely get out the words. This cross had terrible powers and anyone who perjured themselves would die before the year was out; while she was taking her oath Anne prayed to her patron saint over and over to spare her and to help her and, if she did die, to help her attain heaven. Maybe it would be best to die, she thought; maybe God would strike her dead right here in the great cathedral. After the oath-taking—and even Louis took the oath, and her father and the dreadful woman her father now called Queen Margaret instead of that bitch, that she-wolf—outside in the bright sunlight and the hot July day Anne was informed that she would join the Queen's household but that her mother could come with her. The dispensation from the Pope for Anne's marriage had not yet arrived; mercifully she did not have to take her place in her husband's bed. Warwick was annoyed about this, for he wanted the marriage consummated; Anne Neville, hearing him say this, raised her shadowed, fearful gaze to his face, her last illusions swept away; she had wanted to think that it was indeed for her own good and honor that her father had acted thus, but now understanding his unseemly haste to put her in bed with that arrogant, swaggering boy who talked of nothing but cutting off heads and making war as though he were the god of battle, she saw very clearly that she was nothing but a pawn to him and not a daughter at all. In the back of her mind was the picture of the real King with his own children and how loving and kind he was, and it was upon that man, Anne's sovereign lord, that her new husband spoke gleefully of murder. Day after day, as a part of her mother-in-law's household, shrinking away from the sight of the former Queen and avoiding meals, Anne Neville grew more thin and more pale, and on her knees in the chapel every day at matins, at vespers, she prayed for the life and soul of her sovereign lord, her cousin once removed, Edward Plantagenet.

On that same day that Warwick left Anne and her mother with Margaret he hurried back to Valognes to get his ships and men ready to invade England. Clarence was there at Valognes too. Early the preceding morning a ship had docked at Calais and Lord Wenlock was informed that the small party of ladies aboard was conducting one of their number to join Isabel. Obligingly

Lord Wenlock gave them escort and safe conduct, and the small party—there were two ladies and four serving women—arrived at Valognes; after a suitable interval for refreshment after travel one of the ladies and her waiting woman appeared at Clarence's chamber and were duly admitted to the Duke's presence. Whereupon the lady bowed, turned to her plainly dressed companion, who was lazily lifting the clumsy traveling veil from her golden head and removing her cloak to show her young figure, and said formally, "Her Grace, the Duchess of Buckingham."

"Kate!" Clarence couldn't believe his eyes. "Kate!"

Kate Woodville smiled; she went toward him holding out her hands. "I come to you straight from His Grace." Edward had chosen Kate Woodville for this journey for a number of reasons. One, that she was high-spirited and daring; second, that her young husband was a good friend of Clarence; and third, because Edward could trust her and Clarence knew without a doubt that he could trust her too. Kate's loyalties were all too obviously with the King. And besides all this Kate was bright and quick. With her golden head practically touching Clarence, she offered him Edward's pardon.

"You should return to your own family," Kate said earnestly, her huge blue eyes and her red lips open just a bit so that Clarence could catch her sweet breath. Clarence muttered under that spell, "Do you forgive me, Kate?"

Kate said, "At first I would have said yes only because His Grace wishes me to forgive you and I honor my King above all men. But I realize now that you have been led astray like a boy, by your wicked cousin whom you looked up to so much. How could you, George?"

"I don't know," he said.

"Well, he has cast you aside now and taken up with the Lancastrians. How even they stomach him I do not know."

"Will you have wine, Kate?" Clarence asked in a bemused voice.

It was somehow such a relief to be sitting talking to Kate; it was like being home again, even if it was with the Woodvilles. Clarence had hated John, for John was everything Clarence would have liked to be, and he had hated Lord Rivers as an upstart and he had been fiercely jealous of them. But nobody could dislike Kate.

"I'm sorry, Kate," he said openly.

She sighed. "I want to forgive you and I do, but you can earn everyone's devotion and love by returning to the allegiance of your own family and your own brother, who loves you."

Clarence was silent. Only he knew the extent to which he had injured his brother—"who loves you," Kate said. And only Clarence truly knew how when they were young he had envied him; his mother had always put Edward first and then her baby, little Richard, and he, Clarence, had had only Margaret. Clarence's thoughts roved sulkily.

Kate said, "You were not even asked to go to the betrothal ceremony at Angers, were you?"

"No," said Clarence. But Warwick had promised him the whole great duchy of York and held out the temptation that if little Anne Neville and her young husband Edward did not have children, then he, Clarence, would be the heir to the throne. Kate guessed what he was thinking.

"You don't for one moment believe that if Anne Neville did not have children that the so-called Prince would not divorce her or kill her and wed another, do you? George, one of the reasons His Grace sent me to you is because your life is not safe!"

Fear, bribery, old loyalties, Kate had been instructed to play on them all. Was she succeeding?

"Certainly," Kate went on, "you can take your place more proud as His Grace's younger brother than you can as Warwick's second in favor son-in-law!"

She rose and went over to the window; from that vantage point she tried to study his handsome, selfish face. She said softly, "I am sorry about Isabel's baby."

Everybody lured him with promises, Clarence thought, but nobody kept them; he had forgotten all about Isabel's baby.

"Why don't you come home, George?" Kate whispered.

He glanced at her and for a moment his face was open and sweet. "I want to come," he was whispering too. "But how can I?"

"Are you afraid?"

"If I desert Warwick—" he let the sentence dangle. Didn't she know that Warwick controlled all the ships and their crews? "I couldn't openly desert him," Clarence said, and Kate understood it would be another betrayal with which Clarence's paths were strewn. He seemed afraid and brusque suddenly as if he wanted to get rid of her. He whispered, "Tell the King's Grace, my brother, that I repent my actions against him. And that I will—I will—try to help him."

That was the most she could get now, she was sure, and probably as much as Edward expected from her. For Edward knew surely his own brother's disabilities; the King was now trying to pry away one of Warwick's supporters and only that, although Edward had an affection for Clarence because, as he told Bessie, he could remember him as a child and they were of the same blood and that was a difficult thing for Edward to forget, easy as it was for Clarence. Kate kissed him good-bye; he seemed untroubled by any thought of how she was going to get back to England, but Edward had arranged it well and Kate was to return on the same ship she had come on, with the excuse that one of Isabel's ladies had been taken ill and wished to return to her native land. Kate left Clarence, busy in her own mind with remembering everything that had been said so she could report it to Edward.

Kate returned to England, right under Lord Wenlock's unsuspecting nose, the third of August. Edward had already ridden north, for Warwick's friends in the north were keeping it aroused and Yorkshire Lancastrians had been bidden by the Earl to foment and fight as much as they could to draw the King northward. But to Warwick's and Louis' disgust and dismay, the English and Burgundian fleets had established a close blockade of Warwick's ships and the coast of Normandy, and August passed by with Warwick's sailors close to mutiny, demanding money, roaming the streets of the French towns, making as much trouble as possible until Louis himself, in a fever of impatience, came to see the Earl. During that month Anne Neville and her mother lived with the she-wolf Queen and her cub, but Anne slept each night in her own narrow bed and woke each morning to thank the Virgin for her help and to wonder whether the perjury she had carried in her heart when she had sworn to love her new husband would make each day her last on earth, and to also wonder if it wouldn't be best. Margaret's dark eyes surveyed her with contempt; how could this frail, trembling girl make a good wife for her only Prince? It was impossible—this marriage; Margaret thought with satisfaction that she would probably die at any time and with any sickness. She treated Anne Neville as though she were not there at all.

So the ill-assorted band waited, and as always luck and nature finally took a hand. Just when Louis thought he would have to push Warwick out of France to satisfy Charles and le Comte de St. Pol, a huge September storm was forming in the Atlantic; it burst with all its fury into the narrow seas and the Burgundian fleet and the English fleet were forced to seek safe harbor. Before they could reassemble, Warwick and Clarence with their sailor pirates and aboard French ships with the Admiral of France sailed for Plymouth and there they landed on the night of September thirteenth. Anne and Isabel, the Prince and all the ladies remained in France under Louis' protection until their native land was made safe for them by the sword of Warwick. Edward was still in Yorkshire and as soon as he knew that Clarence and Warwick had landed he started south, anxious to confront them. He sent word to the Marquis of Montagu, his sturdy loyal John Neville, to meet him at Doncaster. In London Bessie had just redecorated a large suite of rooms at Westminster for the arrival of her expected child. Edward sent couriers flying to her to enter the Tower and this she did with her mother and her whole household. Edward was confident as always; he was even rather confident at this point that Clarence would desert Warwick once he, the King, confronted them. Edward reached Doncaster and learned that Warwick, with Shrewsbury now and Lord Stanley, had reached Coventry, but Edward also knew that Montagu was close at hand. After dinner that night Edward's musicians played and neither Anthony nor Lord Hastings could see that he seemed worried, only anxious to get this business over with, it was so distasteful to him. Warwick was undoing all the work that he and Edward had accomplished in the first five years of the reign, which made Edward sick at heart. The old Lancastrian banners were waving again to put a bit of royal woolsack on the throne, so these nobles could rule and make havoc out of the order and sanity Edward had tried to build. Wounds which he had tried to heal were ripped open; for an insane ambition to govern England himself Warwick had abandoned all the old ideals and had even sunk so low as to accept French help, a thing which no loyal Englishman could ever forgive.

Just a few miles away the Marquis of Montagu with most of

the army made camp. In the last two months he had received many communications from his brother; he had read them all and torn them up. He sat alone in his tent after his meal, drinking a little warmed ale, for the September night was cold and damp and there was a fresh wind springing up which ruffled the canvas, and there was rain in the air, he could smell it. Outside the tent his officers and his men had lighted big fires; they were his men truly, for he was Warden of the North, was he not? And had he not ridden these marches unceasingly the past six years on the King's business, and what had he got for it? A new title.

John Neville pondered. "Join me," Warwick had implored. "Have you forgot your own brother? Have you forgot it is the Woodvilles the King loves, not you? Join me and the three of us shall stand together as we did in the old days!"

But in the old days they had had Edward too. The face and features of the King came before John Neville unbidden; the Woodvilles were with him now while he, John, labored in the north marches, more in the saddle than out. Last summer he had pounded down from the north to find Edward and report, and where was the King? The royal party had gone on a picnic, pitching silken tents, gay with color, by the riverbank where Edward's musicians played and the wine flowed and the women were beautiful. It was true Edward had been glad to see him. But John Neville had felt out of place, bitterly uncomfortable beside the Woodvilles and the suave Earl of Worcester whose witty words John Neville never understood.

Tonight John Neville pondered anew. Join me, called his brother Warwick, join me and all will be the same again. It will never be the same again, John thought. Never. After all I have done he has taken the earldom of Northumberland away from me.

He left his tent and called his officers to him. He told them he was going to make a speech to his entire army. There before them, with the fires burning low, illuminating only a little the faces of his men, he spoke, his voice laden with bitterness and jealousy; as in a rush all the repressed jealousy overwhelmed him like a vitriolic tide.

"He has forfeited my allegiance!" he cried. "He has taken away my earldom and given me a title! And given me a pie's nest to maintain it with!"

The men around the campfires sat stunned. John Neville was too good a commander and he knew his men well enough to know that he would have to act fast or not at all. For if he gave them time to think, he might not command the men he had been empowered to raise in his King's name. He cajoled.

"He has forfeited my allegiance and forfeited yours! Join the Lord of the North with me!"

There were few answering shouts and Montagu cried, "I'll pay you double. You'll have coins jingling in your pockets. And any man who doesn't march with me I'll punish!" He hesitated. What other threat could he use? "I command all to put out their fires. I command all to follow me." Then he added, "As you love me, help me. I am your lord. Not the Percy. Follow me and follow the true Lord of the North, the famous knight, my beloved brother, the Earl of Warwick! As you love me and love your land, follow me!"

Such an impassioned plea to fall from Montagu's lips further stunned his men. It was true that the men of the north were ruder, rougher and happier to follow their own lords into battle than the distant King in London. Nonetheless the smell of treason is never pleasant. The man they had served had been so conspicuously loyal, and on the border there was a long tradition of keeping faith.

At the edge of the camp a boy whom Edward had spoken to once at Middleham slipped away from the campfire and threading his way to the horse park took a docile mare and galloped away saddleless.

Montagu's officers and lieutenants, hearing the commands, began automatically to obey, to order the shovels to ladle out the earth onto the fires, to saddle up the horses, to roll up packs and to set the whole army marching on the road to Doncaster. But others went also to the horse park, carefully saddling up, for greater speed.

In Doncaster Edward was asleep. He had already sent orders to Montagu to bring the large force he had raised for the King and had taken to Pontefract, and at the same time he had sent an urgent message to Charles of Burgundy to keep his fleet at sea in order to prevent Warwick from escaping from England and into France in case he fled again. So the King slept.

Through the night then a boy galloped, hands fastened on the mane of his horse, holding lightly the rope by which she had been tethered, and he was the first to reach the quarters of his King. There the sentries refused to let him see his King; only the up-raised voices roused the sergeant of the King's minstrels. An-noyed, he wanted to know what the trouble was.

"Lord Montagu!" the boy cried. "He is coming to capture His Grace!" The sergeant of Edward's minstrels needed no more than those few words; he grabbed the boy by the arm and together they ran for Edward's chamber, the boy answering astonished questions as they ran. All they could hear—the roused household, Hastings and Anthony—was, "Must see His Grace!" and the ser-geant of musicians, of whom Edward was very fond, took the liberty of bursting open the chamber doors and rushing to the side of his sleeping monarch.

Edward sat up in bed; someone had seized a torch along the passageway and its light showed Edward sitting, naked to the waist, his brown hair rumpled, his dark eyes fixed on the boy.

"Lord Montagu has deserted you, Your Grace!"

Edward didn't believe him. It was too incredible. His well-beloved John, his rugged honest cousin, a betrayal like this—Ed-ward's face set, and Anthony now at his side picked up Edward's bedgown and slipped it over his shoulders and Edward stood, the robe hanging from the shoulders of his powerful, naked body. Then he slipped his arms into it and tied the cord at the waist; his eyes swept the crowded room, for Hastings and Anthony had rushed in and young Richard, Edward's brother, his dark gaze fixed on his brother. Richard Woodville stood at Edward's other side, servants and soldiers were crammed in the doorway and halls. The boy threw himself at Edward's feet and cried, "I swear it is true, my lord! I swear it is true!"

Edward reached down and patted the dark head and lifted up the boy.

"He made a speech in front of the whole army!"

Edward held him by the arms studying the obvious truth of the words; how could he have misunderstood? And now a deeper, more assured voice from the doorway spoke as its owner pushed his way through the path that was hastily cleared for him, and Anthony saw immediately it was one of John Neville's trusted lieutenants. This man removed his plain, steel battle helmet, and he knelt before Edward. "Your Grace," he said, "the boy speaks true. Lord Montagu has deserted. He comes with his whole army or much of it—some fled, some are coming to join you, but not enough, Your Grace, not enough."

Edward had put his arm around the boy as if to comfort him like a father.

The room was silent, waiting for Edward to speak. In the silence the enormity of Montagu's rebellion became horrifyingly plain to Anthony in its fullest implications. Edward's most trusted lieutenant in the north, the soldier whose devotion he had never questioned, the man to whose nine-year-old son he had betrothed the most precious of his possessions, his firstborn daughter, his dearest love, his baby Bess—his entirely well-beloved John had betrayed him.

The single torch flickered. Edward was rapidly assessing the situation. Montagu had many more men than he, and coming from the south was Warwick with his raggle-taggle of pirates and the unruly stragglers, the unemployed soldiers who would follow the ragged staff for a bit of fighting and plunder, the vagrants, the dissident elements of any realm, plus the die-hard Lancastrians who were still willing to take up the cudgels for the poor, mad King living so quietly and peacefully in the Tower of London, he and his French Queen and their swaggering son. And here in this room were his closest adherents, and they would all die fighting and England would go down again, gasping, while rivers of blood ran until King Louis could set his armies marching across her prostrate form. A last stand might be heroic, but it would scarcely do good. Now for the first time in my life, Edward thought briefly, but for these few men I am alone. And Anthony, watching his face, Anthony more sensitive and intellectual than the others, felt an electric excitement; instead of being afraid his heart lifted with a kind of expectation, for he sensed something else in this man he adored, something besides the King he had come to know so well. Anthony realized that here before him stood the supreme adventurer; one had only to glance at his face to know it and feel it.

In that moment Anthony felt briefly sorry for Warwick and Montagu, for the outcome of the whole struggle Anthony knew at that moment was never in doubt; he would stake his life on it; indeed he had already done so, for he had no illusions about his fate should he fall into Warwick or Montagu's hands. And he realized too that Montagu had made a mistake that Edward would never have made; he had announced his decision to his men and had thus given his adversary warning of his intentions. Edward would have set his men marching without telling them and fallen upon his prey.

Anthony felt no fear at all during the quick night retreat across a sleeping England to the sea, a retreat carefully covered by Edward's scourers on all sides; Anthony felt no fear at all until, at dawn, he beheld the sea.

He had never seen the Wash so nastily angry. He should have been warned by the increasing gustiness of the wind, coming unimpeded across the marshes and the sea, straight from the ice packs of the north; the windmills were rattling noisily; in some remote age Anthony thought this part of England and Yorkshire must have been connected with Holland.

The wind blew. Edward supervised the embarkation, but he put himself and his young brother Richard in Anthony's hands when he crossed the Wash, taking an oar himself and letting Anthony man the tiller.

Looking back later Anthony knew it was the most perilous part of their journey, and yet only two boats were lost and some of those men hauled dripping and frightened into nearby boats, which maneuvered carefully to drag them aboard, for the danger of capsizing in the wind and current was very grave.

At King's Lynn were the larger vessels Edward needed, for by now none of them doubted that Edward was making for Holland. There were not enough ships to embark all the men; Edward could not descend on Holland with too many men; he couldn't feed them once he got them there. With care he selected the ones who would go with him, those of Montagu's men who had ridden off to warn him or joined him on the march; they would suffer if they fell into Montagu's hands. Men like Anthony and Hastings, who would find only death with Warwick and whose lives rested in Edward's hands. His own personal household. His younger brother Richard. Meantime Hastings had been instructed to pay the men; they were drawn up rank after rank and Hastings told them to disperse, flee back home and remain loyal to their King until he needed their services again. Once he had done that a small boat rowed him and Richard Woodville out to Edward.

Richard knelt on the windy deck. Spray flew over the high sides. "Your Grace," he said, "I shall stay in England."

Edward looked down at his blond head. Was it safe enough for Richard?

Richard answered the question himself. "I can survive," he said, his grin lighting his eyes. "You need me more here, I think."

"Get to Bessie," Edward said. "Give her what comfort you can." He reached out his big hand and the two men paused over the handshake for Edward to say, "God go with you, Richard. Take every care and precaution. That is a command."

"Aye, Your Grace. I vow it."

The sails were being hoisted; Anthony's commands rang out; Richard was up and over the rail and sliding down into the bobbing boat; windlasses were raising the anchor, the white sails filled and bellied taut; the King leaned on the rail watching the shore of England gradually fade into the bleak October skies. He wrapped his marten-lined cloak tight around his big body, his thoughts as deadly and determined as the viciousness of the sea winds.

Despite the winds Anthony sent lookouts up the masthead. The narrow seas could be as dangerous to Edward as the land, for pirates roamed them and Frenchmen and the Easterlings. Edward's small vessels were in good hands though and Anthony managed to avoid any shipping until the coast of Holland was under his lee, and at exactly this time sails were spotted making toward their small fleet with all sails set. Anthony glanced despairingly at the shore; the damned tide was out. They couldn't land and the shores of Holland presented themselves in a sea of mud.

Anthony swore. There was nothing to do but go in shore as close as possible and cast out the anchors, and this he did. Satisfied with this maneuver the Hanse ships did likewise, and it was evident they would just wait till the tide came in.

Edward commanded, "Swing over a boat and get ashore, and tell the Seigneur de Gruthuyse we need aid!"

Edward didn't know it at the time but luck was with him. The Seigneur had just returned to Alkmaar. Aboard his own big ship of war he issued from the mouth of the harbor and the Hansards fled. After the Seigneur's warm but sad welcome of a fugitive King and his assurances that he would house and take care of

Edward's fifteen hundred followers, Edward prepared to go ashore in Holland. But he did not forget the master of his vessel. He took off his fur-lined cloak.

"Thank you," the King said. "And in better days you shall have another and better reward."

Thus in his blue-velvet doublet and hose and without a penny in his pocket Edward set his big boots on Dutch soil; it was October the second. On that same day the news reached London that the King had fled.

Chapter 14

ACCORDING TO Edward's instructions Bessie had left her big, freshly decorated chambers in Westminster and had gone to the Tower with her whole household, the children, their nurses and governesses, her council, her treasurer, her lawyer, even her carvers and cooks, the Duchess and the younger Woodville children. Bessie had already sent word to the aldermen and the mayor of London to arm the guard and man the gates and defend the city and its women and children and peaceable citizens, and this had been done. Without the city walls roamed the unruly Kentishmen and they had already plundered the beerhouses of Southwark and within its gates the city trembled. But now came the news that Edward had fled before Montagu's superior strength, and the mayor hastily called another council meeting. It was agreed that while they would protect and defend the city against the mobs outside its walls, they couldn't very well keep Warwick and Montagu out, and it was also a question of how long the city could defend itself. Bessie quickly decided on her own course; she gave orders to pack as much household stuff as possible in chests and boxes; and within a matter of hours she, England's Queen, was at the postern gate of the Westminster sanctuary.

Behind their beautiful Queen were ranged her children and her household. "We seek sanctuary with thee," she said in her clear voice, and the abbot of Westminster blinked rapidly and bade a clerk to bring the sanctuary book, and in her own hand Elizabeth signed her name and those of her children. Bending over, pen in hand, she wrote, "Elizabeth, R., the Lady Elizabeth, the Lady Mary, the Lady Cecily." At this moment Cecily in her governess' arms let out a loud wail.

Bessie turned her head to look at the child. Then she continued.

"Thomas Grey, Richard Grey, Grace Plantagenet." Grace had escaped from her nurse and had run over to the Queen and grasped her skirt. Absently Bessie reached down and took her hand. "My other household will register themselves."

She looked around. "Mother," she said.

The Duchess came forward holding the hand of her youngest child, the small Martha, who at eight bore all the promise of being a typical offspring of the Woodville tribe. The Duchess now took the pen and signed and Martha called to her older sister.

"Bessie," she cried. "What will happen to us?"

"Nothing," Bessie said. "Take Grace and just wait patiently. The lord abbot will show us to a chamber presently, but don't be afraid, Martha, don't be afraid." She smiled calmly; the abbot kept staring at her, and the monks and the clerk who held the book; servants were crowded in the hallway; even the scullery boys had sneaked up from the kitchens to look at their Queen.

Bessie was wearing a long voluminous cloak which she saved for this time of her pregnancies when they occurred in the cold months. Striving to keep her face sweet and calm and her smile ready, nonetheless her heart was cold with fear. The baby she was carrying was big, the kicks lusty; she had a little over three weeks before its birth, and the events of the past weeks had taken toll in sleepless nights and worry over her husband, the hasty move to the Tower. Now not only fear but weariness gripped her whole body and her legs trembled; she slipped her hand under her cloak to rub her distended belly as if to quiet the restless child within the womb. "Be still a minute, poppet," her mind whispered to the unborn child. But she still stood, as the rest of her household filed past, with a smile and word for each and some questions for the men bearing boxes.

"If that came from Lady Cecily's chamber please put it with the other girls' chests, for they shall have to share a chamber. And their nurses' boxes; you'd best put them all together."

Her watchful eyes counted the boxes, reckoning swiftly if they had brought enough and trying to remember if there were enough warm clothes, for winter would soon be upon them and where would they get enough wood or even enough food?

Her white teeth bit at her lower lip. Food! She hadn't as yet thought of food! Now rapidly she tried to count how many mouths she would have to feed, for she couldn't ask the monks and the abbot to sustain all these people. The Duchess put her hand on her daughter's arm.

"We shall find ways, Bessie," she whispered, guessing that Bessie had thought of ever increasing new problems.

The abbot now took charge. He offered his arm and gratefully Bessie took it, and he led the way to the finest chamber that the sanctuary offered; it opened onto a small inner garden, as did his own study, and it had a small fireplace; there he escorted his Queen and sat her down on a bench.

"I wish I had a pillow," he said, bending over her.

"I brought pillows, Father, and bedding," she said.

He sighed. "Pray do not worry," he said then. "Your Grace shall be safe with us. This is sanctuary."

"I never quite knew what the word meant before," she said low.

"I will pray for Your Grace," he said to comfort her.

"Nay," she cried, "not for me! For him!"

She turned her golden eyes on the abbot and now the fear shining in them was very plain, and he saw she feared not for herself but for Edward and he took her hand. "When you are ready or settled," the abbot said, fumbling for words, "I shall be right over there." He pointed through the windows to another door into the garden. The leaves lay on the path and blew against the stone walls; a few late asters bloomed. The abbot quoted; "'Come to me,' Jesus said, 'all ye who are heavy laden,'" and he would have continued but Bessie's eyes filled with tears and she said, "Please, Father!"

The Duchess had been busy. She held out a cup of wine. "Drink this, Bessie," she said. "The children are hungry and there will be bread and cheese and milk in a moment."

The abbot hid a sudden smile. He said formally, "I would like to ask Your Grace and your mother," he bowed to the Duchess, "to sup with me tonight. I shall look forward to your company." He went to the door, his robes swinging, but his mind was busy too. How were all these people to be fed?

"You must drink some milk, Bessie," the Duchess was saying. "Are your feet wet?" They had come up the river by barge to the sanctuary. "You must not catch a chill."

Bessie looked down at her shoes as if they were not her feet or part of her body. "They're not wet," she said. Obediently she sipped some of the wine. "I would go to him if I could," she whispered, glancing over at the children around the table; her little Bess and Mary sat side by side, their curly blond heads almost the same level on their bench. "But I do not dare attempt it nor—" her voice trailed off, for she suddenly realized that her mother, her indomitable mother, looked strained and pale; her husband, Edward, was presumably safe in Holland, whereas Jacqueta's had died so recently and so bloodily. Bessie remembered Edward's earnest tones: "When you were crowned in the abbey, Bessie, two duchesses helped hold your crown on your head. The time may come when you will have to bear it by yourself." If she came to him he might be disappointed, even angry; she knew that the other prominent members of Edward's government had taken sanctuary also, a great many of them in St. Martin's le Grand. She knew too that she was a symbol; in London she was an important symbol, for in her care were the Princesses of England; she knew too that the talk of the town would be concerned with her doings and that, in her way, she could help Edward more here than anyplace else, even at his side in exile. But most important she knew he would come back. It was so obvious to her that she didn't bother to list the reasons; as a matter of fact neither did the Earl of Warwick; he knew too that Edward would return and that someday he would have to face his King.

Bessie turned to her mother. "I've never seen such strong, thick walls," she remarked. "We may not be too comfortable but we shall be safe." She smiled her brilliant smile. "I believe too, mother, that there is a midwife in every sanctuary."

The troops of Warwick and Clarence were almost upon the city when a gentleman rode up to the barred gates. His cloak was folded behind his saddle and the big *E* on his jacket, worn thus boldly, made the men at the gates automatically throw them open, and as he passed through one of them said in amazement, "It's Sir Richard Woodville!"

Richard doffed his cap; he was accompanied by ten men who would have followed him into hell. Once in the city they dispersed, having decided on a different meeting place each night; Richard stabled his horse at the Crown and went on foot through the narrow streets to the shop of a butcher, by name John Gould.

He asked to see Gould and was ushered up the outside staircase to the room where Gould was having his midday dinner. Richard wiped his boots and came into the room and sat down opposite the butcher, who staggered to his feet in astonishment at his visitor. Richard grinned his wry grin and told Gould he had come for a job.

"Have you an apron which would fit me? I'll work for nothing." Gould opened his mouth and shut it again.

"There'll be no danger to you, my man," Richard said airily. "As a good King's man you should be happy to supply my sister, the Queen's Grace, with meat. I'll help deliver it."

Gould pushed away his plate; he wasn't sure he was hungry.

"When His Grace returns you'll be a hero," Richard said idly.

John Gould looked full at Richard Woodville, whose eyes were at once merry and direct. "I'll do it!"

Richard grinned more widely and Gould filled him a plate of beef; then he fell to his own food again, dipping his bread in the gravy. In the England of John Gould's day, contrary to the Continent, there were no limits a man might not aspire to had he industry and courage; John Gould never enjoyed a meal more and he confided that to Richard Woodville, who assured him it was the same with him too. Below in the street they could hear shouting and commotion. Richard was very hungry; he had not eaten a decent meal since he had stood on the beach and watched Edward's little fleet disappear into the gray seas; he interrupted his eating just long enough to say, "It sounds as if Warwick has arrived."

John Gould nodded; they both kept right on eating.

The following morning, in a neat apron, Richard drove a bright painted green cart, bearing the name "J. Gould," and he was accompanied by one of his men similarly attired. They were approaching the sanctuary, which was near the palace, and drawing toward St. Margaret's Church they suddenly discovered they had unaccountably became part of a procession taking the old King Henry to Westminster. Some rude remarks were directed to Richard who answered them in kind, and everyone on the street joined in. There was a great deal of shouting and gesticulating until finally, collapsed with laughter, Richard left the procession and entered the churchyard. The big roomy building at the end of the yard must be the sanctuary; the church in the form of a cross stretched about and around it.

Richard swore lustily as he heaved the half beef to his shoulder. One of the monks reproved him but made way as Richard staggered into the kitchen door and was directed to the buttery, a room with big hooks, onto which Richard slung the half beef.

"I'll be back with two muttons," he said. "One at a time though."

"Two?"

He disappeared from view, in fact he seemed to vanish, but attention was diverted from Richard by the appearance of his companion who took his time about bringing in the two mutton; he whistled cheerfully and had a good many questions to ask and in the meantime Richard had found his sister.

He came up to her from behind and whispered, "Your Grace," so when Bessie turned he was on one knee, his head bent, and for a moment she didn't know who he was. But the Duchess, perceiving him cross the room, was not fooled for a moment and she said in a strangled tone, "Richard! Richard!"

Whereupon Bessie said incredulously, "Richard!"

Richard was now on his feet and he hugged the Duchess and kissed Bessie.

"Mother remembered my name!" he said to Bessie. "Usually she calls me Lionel—Anthony—oh—Richard."

The Duchess swallowed. "I often had a John in there too," she said, and her eyes filled with tears. She said, "I pray you, Richard—" then she couldn't finish and Richard led her to a stool and sat her down.

"Everything will be all right, mother," he said. "Anthony is safe with Edward and they won't harm me, I swear they won't, and you don't need to worry over Lionel or Edward. They're safe in school."

The Duchess understood from his words that he had not come to stay with them in sanctuary but that he intended to walk out the same way he had come. Richard confirmed that with his next words. "Each week I shall bring the meat and as much news as I pick up. Bessie, you must tell me if you have any needs, for the best way you can aid His Grace is to be well and healthy and have a healthy baby. On nice days you should get outside there in the garden."

Bessie looked out the window; the rain was beginning to stream down the walls. She asked for the news or gossip.

"They have put old Henry in the chambers you redecorated for your confinement, Bess," he said. "That has its ironic side. They've tumbled the royal sack of wool off his shelf. It's pathetic. But the gossip is that already Clarence is grumbling and that Montagu will be sent back north, for they don't trust him!"

Bessie said, "He sold his soul for his pie's nest, as he called it!"

"And it is rumored and seems to be true that the price Warwick paid to King Louis was to promise that he would send English armies to fight *for* France! *Against* Burgundy! And that then my lord of Warwick will be the Prince of Holland. Bessie," he said, "it is so mad a scheme it has no chance of success!"

With that she must make what comfort she could; it was all Richard had to offer. She didn't try to prevent him from going, knowing it would be useless. It poured rain that day and the next, and weary and fearful she spent the two days resting in her bed where she was warm. But then the weather turned bright and October was its cheerful self for the rest of the week, and she was able to get outside in the garden with the children.

But outside the sanctuary walls a rising tide of sympathy and interest in the Queen lapped at the very walls. Every day there were gifts laid at the gates and at the kitchens; the church itself was crowded and the subprior had never counted so much money in the boxes. From the outside the sanctuary looked like a prison, so square and massive and gloomy was it. Only the church, spread-eagled about it, lent it any comfort. The third week of October it rained constantly; the skies were always a deep gray and the little garden was a sodden mass of leaves and dead flowers. That week Richard did not come and the Duchess and Bessie now had a new worry: Where was he? In prison or dead? That week Abbot Milling sent word to my lord of Warwick that the Queen was approaching her time and that he deemed it necessary that someone should be sent to help her; he suggested the Lady Scrope, who had attended Bessie before. And this suggestion was brought before the council and the council approved, and even paid Lady Scrope ten pounds. She entered the sanctuary the next morning, and Bessie met her and wrote her name in the sanctuary book herself.

Lady Scrope brought word from Richard: He was safe but being cautious as Edward had commanded him. Lady Scrope found that Bessie and the Duchess had applied their time to making the sanctuary a passable home for the children. There was a schoolroom and classes were conducted. The Duchess taught French. Bessie read to the children at an appointed hour; the abbot taught mathematics and even tiny Bess was in his class. There were games and music and singing. When Lady Scrope first looked into the schoolroom and saw all the children sitting still on their low stools, her heart jumped into her throat; Richard Grey, who was ten, was reading aloud from a French fable and the Duchess, her head on one side, was correcting his accent.

"Martha will translate now," the Duchess said as Richard handed the book to Martha. "Now the little ones listen and pay sharp attention, for this is a funny story about a fox."

Bessie closed the door gently. They were in Bessie's bedroom. It was two o'clock and midday dinner was over. In her crib slept the Lady Cecily; she was eighteen months old.

Lady Scrope had brought her into the world. She went over to the bed and looked down at the sleeping child. The closed lids hid the hazel eyes; her golden hair curled tight around her head, and Lady Scrope gently touched the tiny hand with its pink fingers.

"She looks like an angel, doesn't she?" Bessie whispered. "She is a good and happy baby too." Then she said, "Oh, I am so glad you are here!"

Lady Scrope bit her lip. "Your Grace," she said, "if they hadn't sent me I should have come whether or no."

Bessie looked into her steady eyes. "Thank you," she said tremulously. "It might be a bit beforehand but I would wish you to stand as godmother to the new baby."

Lady Scrope said firmly, "It is a great honor!" But she was thinking how sad and forlorn this was; the other births had been such happy occasions with scores of pretty women about and, of course, the near presence of the King. Lady Scrope didn't know what kind of solace to give or what words to utter that might help and suddenly Bessie, sensing this, said, "I cannot think of two godmothers more wonderful for a child to have than you and my mother!"

Lady Scrope drew a deep breath; she thought, Edward would be proud of her! So she said, "Well, that's a fine compliment.

Now you must tell me exactly what we have and what we need, for by the look of things we don't have much time."

There wasn't much time, for October was slowly dying. The first of November was the first day of winter; cold, sharp wind blew itself against the five-foot-thick walls; it whined all night on All Souls' Eve and was still blowing just as fierce the first day of November. Late that night Bessie wakened with pain.

The candles were lit and the finest wine, which was a present from an unknown donor, was poured. The Duchess sent for the sanctuary midwife to help Lady Scrope and herself and the other women. Midnight came and went and in the early hours of November second, Bessie's child was born. Bessie lay back on the fresh pillows Lady Scrope put under her back and shoulders. The Duchess had taken the baby; the room seemed to be filled with its cry. Bessie's eyes were closed but she could feel the air on her bare arms outside the quilts. "It is cold," she whispered. "Don't take long with the bathing, mother."

"A big, healthy baby," Lady Scrope said with satisfaction. She was holding a cup of wine for Bessie to drink; there was a smile on her face and Bessie frowned slightly; Lady Scrope was putting a bedgown on her and Bessie sat up to slip her arms into it. This was the time when Edward would have come into the room; if she kept her eyes closed and put out her hand she could almost feel his big hand around hers and his arms slipping under her back and his kiss on her lips. She opened her eyes slowly. I must not weep, she thought, I must not! What was her mother saying? She sat straight up in the bed. Was something wrong with the baby? "Send for the abbot," the Duchess had commanded.

Bessie cried, "What is the matter? Is something the matter with the baby?" She threw aside the quilt and started to step out of bed. The Duchess was carrying the swathed newborn to its mother. The Duchess said, "Here is your baby, Bessie! He is going to be very tall!"

Bessie received the baby into outstretched arms. The eyes were closed and the hair was Edward's color, a soft brown touched with gold. Slowly the blue eyes opened; in wonderment Bessie studied the features; was there resemblance? She was sure there was. The Duchess and Lady Scrope were smiling and weeping. Bessie kissed the side of the cheek.

"Your father isn't here," she whispered. "You'll have to make do with your mother."

The Duchess said, "I told the abbot to ring the bells!"

Bessie's eyes never left the baby; she must say the name. "Edward," she said quite firmly. "Edward, my son."

The Duchess took the baby. "Little Ned," the Duchess said, carrying the baby over to the readied cradle. She tucked the fine, woven woolen blankets around the child. Then in a circle she and the ladies knelt around the cradle to pray for and to bless the newborn boy, their little Prince. Outside in the cold November night the church bells tolled, and when the people sent to know what had happened, the monks told them that their Queen in sanctuary had brought forth a boy, a son.

PART THREE
"Arrivall"

Chapter 15

EDWARD WAS reading. He was wrapped in a heavy cloak, his feet on a brass foot warmer; through its holes the coals gave a wisp of heat. In front of him on the heavy table lay an illuminated book; priceless it was, as were all the books in the Seigneur de Gruthuyse's library, and the long room was beautiful too, with its mullioned windows, its dark paneling, its tables covered with glass; underneath lay the books and manuscripts. It was also bitterly cold in the room; Edward's breath came white.

He turned the large page carefully. The door opened.

"Good morning, Richard," he said. "Come sit down and put your feet on this." Edward moved his big feet to one side.

Richard put out his hand to see if there was any heat; then he put his feet up.

"There's nothing colder than Holland," Edward said, "except to be out on the seas now." He waved a big hand. "But I take pleasure in these books. I have already ordered some and I swear someday I'll have a collection like this."

His enthusiasm didn't reach his younger brother. Richard muttered, "This filthy climate."

Edward said, "Get a woman to keep you warm, boy." He grinned and saw that Richard looked glum and cold and unhappy. Edward sat up straight, putting his feet on the floor; he saw it was time for a lecture.

"Richard," he said, "there is never a time which cannot be employed well and to advantage in some way. I am learning a great deal. I have reread Plato and Horace and Cicero. I have read Caesar and the Greek philosophers—and my faith, the beauty of these pages!" Edward's enthusiasm again got the better of the lecture. "Well," he continued, "there should never be an hour

you cannot profit from." Then he said, "Richard, compose yourself. It will not be long now."

Now he had got Richard's attention, complete. The dark eyes
were intent and excited; he licked his lips.

Edward raised his hand from the page. "Patience, my boy,"
he said, sighing. "Patience is one of the virtues so difficult to learn
and so deadly when employed."

Richard cried, "How can Your Grace have patience when your
enemies"—he breathed hard—"have pushed you out of England?"

Edward's narrowed eyes surveyed him. "And you would have
rushed back unprepared?"

Richard's face was white and unpleasant to see. Edward said,
"A Prince should learn to control passion."

He was thinking of the months past, he saw so clear the dilemma he had presented his brother-in-law, Charles of Burgundy; there is no guest more politically distressful than a
deposed monarch to whom one is related through one's wife.
Penniless and with fifteen hundred men he had landed on
Charles' shores. Now instead of an ally in England Charles had a
liability at home. Edward thought cold-bloodedly that Charles
had been very clever, for he had sent his trusted ambassador,
Commines, immediately to Calais to say to the English there that
his treaty of peace was with England; not with a King but with
England, the country.

"But you are sheltering Edward, the late King," Wenlock said
testily.

Commines followed his Duke's instructions. "The late King Edward is dead," he said blandly.

The lie made Edward smile when he had heard Charles' diplomatic maneuvering. Charles had gained some time, and Edward stayed dead for a few weeks while Charles moved his pieces
on the diplomatic chessboard and reiterated that his treaty of
peace was with England.

It was King Louis' turn to protest now. Couriers made haste to
ride from France to Burgundy; King Louis was properly outraged.

"You are sheltering the late King of England! In faith, it is
cause for war!"

Charles protested. "Our advices tell us Edward is dead." He

was a bit sad to relate the news. "Our treaty of peace is with England."

Both monarchs kept their eyes across the narrow seas on what Warwick was doing while Edward, closeted in the Seigneur de Gruthuyse's library, devoured his books.

"And just how would you have crossed the narrow seas, Richard?" he asked. "Like our lord Jesus?"

He had had to give Charles time, time to see that his best recourse was to help his brother-in-law, Edward; time to see it was best for Burgundy to have a friend on the throne of England instead of the Warwick he disliked so much, who was a danger, who would indeed send English troops to Burgundy if he could and who would receive part of Charles' domains, namely Holland, for successful English aid.

When it became quite obvious to all concerned that Edward was quite alive Charles received him at court.

"Trade has stopped between our two countries," Charles said.

Edward knew what that would mean to English merchants. It was axiomatic that Warwick would hardly be popular with the merchants. He shrugged his big shoulders; he came to the heart of the subject.

"I am anxious to return to England before Margaret of Anjou arrives. If possible."

Edward knew that on paper the government of England looked quite impregnable. There were the three mighty, wealthy Neville brothers in all their power, ringed tight around an ill, mad King, the Nevilles now suddenly aligned with all the Lancastrian devotees. The former Queen and her son were waiting for safety's sake in France, but soon they would make their triumphal entry into England. And there was Clarence, drawing to his side the Yorkists that were left—so what room was there for Edward?

"They are all mad dogs in the same kennel," Edward said wryly. "There is that much chance for peace." He actually regretted what he must say next, for he was ashamed of Clarence. Yet his brown eyes met Charles' steadily. "I have assurances from my brother that he will be at my side." Another betrayal, Charles thought cynically; this time Clarence would help Edward; Warwick hadn't given him enough. The wealth promised was not enough and the prospect of the throne was still aglimmer in the distance. Charles wondered whether Edward would ever be able to trust Clarence and came to the decision that he would not.

Then Edward said, "I have secret advices that as soon as I leave your shores Louis will seek peace with you, my lord, and that it will be to your advantage. Louis is too clever to depend on Warwick."

Charles agreed absently. Yes, he thought. I shall say the thorn between us is removed; King Edward has returned to England and you and I, your most loyal vassal, may sit down to talk. That is what he would say to the French ambassadors in his most lofty tones from his high, high throne.

Charles said, "You shall have ships. The Seigneur de Gruthuyse shall arrange it."

But he was thoughtful. Was it possible for Edward to succeed? Was the venture too risksome? Charles said, "The Milanese ambassador remarks that it is easier to go out the door than to get back in by the window. They—the French—hope you will leave your skin there."

The faintest smile touched Edward's lips. "I know, my lord."

Charles rose. "God go with you."

Edward thanked him. Then, "I must say good-bye to my dearest sister, your wife. I thank you and God keep you, my lord."

Back in Holland, in the cold library, Richard blurted, "But it is the tenth of February!"

"And I read?" Edward looked up, for his eyes had strayed back to the page of the open book. "I should not have kept you in suspense, Richard. I plan to leave next week, on the nineteenth to be exact." He rose to his feet, for he had an appointment with the Seigneur. As he walked to the library door he put his arm around Richard's shoulders. "I am anxious to see my son," he said. "I believe I am quite as impatient as you."

Warwick had learned one lesson from Edward: that to keep the peace pardon might be better than bloodletting, so he issued a general pardon before Christmas; Richard Woodville, after some soul-searching, decided to apply and went boldly to Westminster and gave his name and his pardon actually passed the chancery on the eighteenth of December. Richard then was free to roam the London streets with impunity.

Richard stored impressions like a squirrel.

All along the waterfront ships swung at their moorings, forlorn, the tall masts bare of sail, the docks deserted. Former Lancastrians swarmed around the halls of Westminster, begging and suspicious. All over London the ladies' heads were close together as they gossiped about their Queen and the new Prince. The ladies of London wanted their handsome King back and told their husbands so, and Bessie's doings were all that enlivened the winter in London. During the winter days George Neville, restored as Chancellor, made pontifical speeches entitled, "Return, O Backsliding Children," and they had clothed poor Henry in purple and set him in Westminster.

London swarmed with the French and the French merchants, whom the Londoners disliked to the point of hatred. Warwick was trying to satisfy Louis of France by making good his promise to help Louis with English troops in Burgundy. As for John Neville, Lord Montagu, he was so suspect to the Lancastrians that Warwick had to send him back north. So when Richard Woodville met him early in January he was surprised. The two men came face-to-face outside of St. Paul's. Montagu held out his hand.

Richard stepped back. "Well," he said. "My right entirely well-beloved John." His eyes blazed at Montagu, for as a matter of fact his usual good temper had deserted him and all he was conscious of was the desire to put his big right fist in Montagu's face.

But when Montagu heard the familiar phrase that Edward had always used for him, he looked so suddenly stricken that Richard felt pity for him; so Richard took a deep breath and told himself Edward would not want him brawling with Montagu on the street. He cleared his throat and said, "I thought you were at Middleham, my lord Marquis."

"I've come to see about—well, we need men at arms," he blurted.

Richard grinned. "You can't have my sword to fight alongside of Frenchmen," he said. "Fight against 'em, yes, but not with them," he chuckled. "I guess that's the way a great many feel, my lord, isn't it?" His eyes were sharp and calculating.

"There's no need for me to answer that," Montagu said sternly.

"No," said Richard, "and there's no need to tell you whom I'm saving this dagger for. The talk around London is that you betrayed His Grace out of fear of your brother. But I don't believe that, my lord. If I believed it, I'd try to frighten you into changing allegiance when His Grace returns."

Montagu said, in a breathless rush, "He won't dare! Set foot in England!"

Richard laughed. "You suffer delusions, my lord Marquis. My deepest sympathies go with you." He bowed and turned on his heel, fully expecting Montagu to seize his shoulder and spin him around and Richard was ready. But no hand fell on him and Montagu stood where Richard had left him. The possibility of Edward's return was something Montagu did not want even to contemplate. The treason he had accomplished already sat heavy on his conscience, and he shrank from the prospect of facing Edward himself in battle with all his heart and soul. What had been accomplished in a moment could not now be undone in years, and from that treason he had got nothing, nothing at all, not an extra penny, only virtual banishment to the north to keep the peace. And yet now he pushed all that aside, and what was truly troubling his honest soul was the enormity of the betrayal; every day he knew he would give anything to retract. The web in which in one hasty, passionate moment he had entwined himself was gathering him closer, and like the chorus of a Greek tragedy his own voice was telling him there was no way out; he was doomed inevitably by the forces which he himself had set loose. His mind coiled about what he should do, but he had set his feet on a path from which he could see no reasonable turn. Miserably he stood outside St. Paul's long after Richard had left him.

Edward had not been entirely truthful when he had implied he had spent all his time reading. With his usual bent for business and diplomacy he and his small court had accomplished a great deal. An alliance with the Hansards, for instance, and a promise of future trade—this procured Edward a number of well found vessels to transport his men to England, and since Edward was a cautious soldier they were to remain for fifteen days off the coast in case a retreat should be necessary. Anthony had succeeded in his negotiations for two English ships; it was they who had been running messages back and forth from Holland to England to Edward's supporters there. Francis of Brittany promised and gave aid in the shape of a fleet which harassed the French and succeeded in capturing a load of merchandise designed for sale in England; Louis had wanted earnestly to show the benighted English that they would be better off trading in France instead of Burgundy.

Edward had made friends with a number of the most powerful and wealthy of the merchants; they helped with loans and money, and the merchants of the staple in Calais were only too anxious to help since it was becoming increasingly clear that Warwick's policy did indeed involve war with Burgundy, so that Louis might march in.

How much faith Louis had in Warwick no one knew but him. He could not lose much if Warwick failed. The English are so pigheaded, Louis thought. They would rather fight with France than trade with her. Warwick sent Louis word that he did not dare announce the mutual defense alliance with France until the Prince arrived; it would be best for the Prince to announce that when France fought, England was committed to helping out. In London when this was bruited about, the mayor heard it—some of Edward's dispatches had reached his ears too, and the mayor of a sudden fell sick and took to his bed. It was the twentieth of February.

On the nineteenth Edward had left Bruges, intending to go down to the coast by water. Instead, with his good humor, knowing the people liked a procession and grateful to the Hollanders for their kindness to him, he walked from Bruges to Damme and thence to Flushing by boat.

On the twenty-seventh of February Warwick hastened down to Dover to wait for the arrival of Queen Margaret of Anjou, her son and his Anne Neville, his wife the Countess of Warwick and all those who were accompanying them to England. The weather could not have been worse. The winter winds seemed to come straight out of an icy hell. The shores were lashed by great and thunderous waves and the whole Channel was a seething mass of foam and wind-driven spray. Each day for four days Warwick stared across the heaving water which implacably refused to recognize the plans of mortal men. Warwick left for London with the sound of the sea wind howling remorselessly

in his ears; he returned to a London that was quiet like the lull
before the storm, a London which somehow had learned its King
was coming. The mayor was unaccountably still sick; the French
ambassadors had hurriedly left. They were going to brave the
Channel the next day and be captured ignominiously by the
Bretons. Richard Woodville had left the capital with as many
men as he could muster; they had slipped out at night. In haste
Warwick himself bade good-bye to poor King Henry and galloped for Warwickshire to raise men to repel the invader.

As for the invader himself, the weather was just as bad on his
side of the narrow seas and the howling winds prevented the
running up of even a close-hauled jib. In increasing impatience
which he never showed outwardly Edward waited nine whole
days before he dared embark his men; that same morning, by
agreement with Lord "Jakes" of Luxembourg, Edward set sail for
England and a lieutenant of Lord Jakes made a raid on Calais in
order to keep Warwick's ships there quite busy.

On the morning of the twelfth of March Edward saw the shores
of Norfolk, for the Duke was faithful. Leaning on the rail he ordered a boat ashore to reconnoiter and wrapped in his cloak he
waited for its return.

The news he received was bad. Norfolk himself was in prison
in London and Oxford was hovering nearby with a good many
men—too many for Edward's small force of fifteen hundred.
Worse, the weather was gathering itself up for another winter
storm; under his feet the deck was heaving like an unruly horse.
Nonetheless they hung out what sail they could and steered
north for the coast of Yorkshire.

The storm came. All that night, below in the big cabin Edward
heard the thunderous sound of the water hitting the decks.
Plunging and rolling against the winds and the black night, close-
reefed, his few ships were scattered by the violence of the storm.
So that when he reached Ravenspur, the mouth of the Humber,
he gave orders to disembark whatever the reception might be,
and with Hastings and five hundred men Edward set foot on his
native land, his realm.

He was worried about the rest of his men. It was with relief
that he learned that Anthony had landed up the Humber at

Paul and that Richard, his brother, on the coast several miles up from Ravenspur. By the next morning both of them reached Edward's camp. One boat had been lost; and it was carrying horses.

The wind was still blowing. The safest way for Edward was south, but that meant they would have to take to the ships again to cross the Humber, and Edward knew his men were sick of their dangerous and close quarters aboard ship; worse, people might think he had fled. In a perfectly ordinary tone he gave the astonishing orders that they would march directly north to Kingston-on-Hull. The perfectly accoutered troops made a fine show, Anthony thought. But there were so few of them! On the right lay the Yorkshire moors and forbidding Northumberland. To the south lay Pontefract Castle where Montagu was reputed to be lying with men and arms. All that day as he rode Anthony kept scanning the countryside; gray and cold was the March day and yet it was as though the land slept. Undoubtedly there were roving bands of armed men whom Warwick had instructed to keep out his greatest enemy. Sometimes Anthony caught a glimpse of men in the distance but they melted away, and at the midday stop he knew he had been right; they were being followed and spied on. A few men came into the temporary camp and looked about with curious eyes for their King. Hastings, in charge of the royal purse, passed some money into their hands and they disappeared again, riding away across the moors. Kingston-on-Hull kept its gates shut tight and Edward gave the signal to pass by.

Sentries paced the small camp that night and the fires burned fitfully. The whole north was uncommonly quiet. Anthony pictured Lord Percy in Alnwick; it was he who controlled this country. In an hour he could gather enough of his men to sweep down on Edward's small force and annihilate it. Anthony stirred restlessly in his sleep and in the morning, early, when he woke it was still dark.

He made his way to Edward's tent to see if there was some office he could perform for his King and he found Edward washing.

When he had dressed, Edward came out into the still-darkened skies. "Look," he said, "stars!" His smile flashed out. "It's going to be a nice day. Maybe we'll see sunshine!"

Edward put his hand on Anthony's shoulder. He said, "It was a risk, Anthony, but it has passed. The people know. My quarrel is not with them but with my great rebel. And if Lord Percy were going to betray me he would have been here by now. The North is quiet. 'He that is not against me is with me.' Who said that, Anthony?"

"Caesar, Your Grace," Anthony mumbled.

"Of course," Edward said. "I've read so much in the last weeks I'm getting muddled as to who said what. However, Anthony, I am not insensible as to the dangers to which I am exposing you, all of you." He gestured to the now aroused camp. "Therefore, this morning I put a feather in my cap, a plume rather. It is a ruse I employ that has been employed before." Hastings had appeared with Edward's cap and now firmly attached to it was the ostrich plume that was the emblem of the young Prince, Margaret and Henry's son. It fluttered bravely on Edward's cap. He bowed to Anthony. "I have returned to England, sir, to claim my dukedom, which no man can gainsay, for I am the heir of York."

A ruse that has been employed before, Anthony thought. Employed by Henry of Bolingbroke, he who became Henry IV, the grandfather of the present Henry. Anthony was struck suddenly by the similarities. Henry had landed at Ravenspur also when he had come to depose the rightful King. Now seventy-two years later the heir of York was returning. So, ahead of Anthony, all the way to York rode Edward with the ostrich plume bobbing in his cap.

They could see the city in the distance. Anthony felt excitement mount as the gates opened and a few riders spurred horses toward them. It was the recorder of York who greeted them but not pleasantly.

"The city will not admit you, Your Grace," he added.

Edward said mildly, "My father had a great many friends in Yorkshire."

The recorder was silent. Then he said, "Do not attempt to enter York."

But the King was firm. "We come to claim my just rights, the dukedom of York. I come as a loyal servant to King Henry and his son, the Prince." With that Edward gave the orders to ride on. But when he got to the city gates they were shut tight.

The ostrich plume was brave and conspicuous. Edward signaled the horns to blow. A narrow gate opened and two men came out to greet the King. "I come for my truest rights as a good subject of King Henry," Edward said. "I am the heir of York."

This was indisputable. The two men, Clifford and Burgh, exchanged glances. Then they looked at the orderly troops. They bowed. "Your Grace may enter the city but not with your troops," Burgh said diffidently.

Edward smiled as though it were an ordinary thing for him to enter a city unaccompanied. "We need no troops among good friends," he said. Anthony's heart sank to his boots, he said later. But he betrayed no emotion and within a few minutes he was riding with Edward and fourteen other men through the gates of York. They clanged shut behind the small party. It could be a trap from which they could never escape. Anthony glanced up at the gate as he passed through; it was the same gate that had borne its awful burden when Margaret had executed Edward's father, the Duke of York, and Margaret had crowned the head with a paper crown. Anthony tried to match Edward's smile and his aplomb, and so he too raised his hand in greeting.

"King Henry," Anthony cried, "and His Grace, the Duke of York!"

They had ridden but a short way before there were answering cheers. Now suddenly the streets were crowded with people. Edward's smile and easy manner were hard to resist. Swarms of people followed behind now as Edward rode straight to the cathedral. When he emerged waves of cheering engulfed the small group. Some citizens came to speak with them; Edward was affable and friendly. The mayor invited them to dine and by the end of the dinner Anthony heard the mayor say, "But your men, Your Grace, have they provision for the night?"

"I would appreciate anything you might do for them," Edward said. "They are in my care, for most of them fled with me six months ago."

"Open the gates," the mayor cried out to one of his henchmen at the doors of the chamber, startling all the diners. "Command the guard to open the gates and we shall receive His Grace's men!"

That night Anthony slept soundly in a good bed but he was

roused early because the King was making ready to ride on. He was making for Wakefield and Sandal Castle, one of the castles of his dukedom, and he reached it without incident through quiet country. Hastings whispered to Anthony, "It is almost as though—since we have been unmolested from the beginning—it were great folly to attempt what others did not attempt."

Anthony whispered back, "And also His Grace's great personal courage."

Hastings nodded. They were riding into Doncaster and the memories of leaving it in haste that night six months ago were strong in the two men. This time it was very different, for the people cheered and the dean of the chapel with eight-score men joined his King; and at Nottingham, brave in armor and with six hundred men, Sir William Parr and John Harrington rode pell-mell to kneel before Edward.

Now this day Edward sent out scouts and foreriders and learning that Oxford with about four thousand men was at Newark swung around to try and force him to fight, but in the night Oxford fled at two in the morning, and when Edward arrived the birds had flown.

Edward went on to Leicester, and there the men that Hastings had paid off six months ago came with fluttering banners, three thousand men to swell the King's forces. This time Anthony's heart pounded with excitement as he aided the King to inspect the troops, to talk with the officers, to make sure every foot soldier and every horseman was properly equipped. In his excitement that day Anthony did not notice that Edward Plantagenet was not wearing an ostrich plume in his cap, and that day it was learned that Warwick was at Coventry with six or seven thousand men. In orderly array Edward reached Coventry on the twenty-ninth of March.

My lord of Warwick was huddled behind the walls of the city. From its ramparts he could see the steel-helmeted troops, the bright banners, and he could hear the clarion call of the horns and trumpets. And in the center was a mighty banner with three blazing suns. It was advanced and Edward rode forward; the horns blew again. At last the time of reckoning had come.

From under that mighty banner a messenger bowed, mounted and spurred his horse toward the city. The message he bore was

plain and terse. "The King desires his great rebel to come forth
and determine his quarrel in plain battle."

Warwick retreated to one of the inner rooms of the house
where he was staying. That very morning he had received comforting word from Oxford that he was on his way and comforting
word from Clarence that he too would soon join him and not to
fight yet. For all that comfort the Earl of Warwick was uneasy
and unhappy. Why had his brother Montagu let the King pass?
Perhaps he had not enough troops. Perhaps he knew that only
Lord Percy could really command the troops of the north and
Percy had sat still. In a sudden agony of indecision and fear
Warwick did nothing, and for three days Edward waited outside Coventry, partly to unnerve his great rebel and partly to finish his review and refreshment of his troops; some of them had
ridden hard and long and many of them had tramped miles. Two
things were thus accomplished at once, for when Edward left the
fields outside of Coventry he left a badly shaken foe and Edward had talked personally to every officer and to his men. He
marched directly to Warwick and took possession of the castle,
and he entered Warwick as the King; he summoned a council
meeting and sent forth proclamations under the signet.

Around the council table sat John Say, Lord Mountjoy, Edward's old friend, Hastings, and Hastings' brother, Anthony and
the King's brother Richard. And gay, young Richard Woodville
was also permitted to stretch out his long booted legs under the
polished table. And if any had thought that Edward's ignomini-
ous flight or his enforced exile had changed his policies in diplomacy, they learned that they were wrong.

"I did not think at the time that my great rebel would challenge me in the field before Coventry."

Edward's sentence hung in the room. Then, because his great
rebel was kin and Edward had such strong feeling for blood re-
lationship, he added, "I am not making an aspersion on his personal bravery. It is deeper than that, his indecision."

Richard Woodville was all for forcing a fight and John Say
watched him with some amusement, for he knew that Edward
would propose a parley, and so he did, for others on the council
proposed it also. Edward's terms were simple: the Earl's life and

the life of all his people and followers, pardon for life only. To prevent bloodshed.

Would those words reach through the thick veneer of pride and power with which his adventuring had clothed him so imperviously? Edward said, "We must be prepared for failure. I list four reasons. One, he has sworn on a piece of the Holy Cross to Margaret, Henry and King Louis." Edward never referred to Louis as Louis of France, only King Louis, as though he were King of a nonexistent country. "Second, he may despair of an honorable continuance betwixt us. Third, Oxford and some of the other hotheads may refuse to negotiate. Fourth, does he hope to escape to Calais and France in case of not getting the overhand of us? He is certain of Calais." Edward rose to his feet. "We must be prepared for any of those contingencies, unhappily so." But now there was to be a pretty and heartwarming scene, on the surface at least, to be presented to the troops and the people. The councilors were already in their martial dress, the troops were all ready to take their part and even the King's minstrels were waiting, already in song. While the Earl of Warwick waited at Coventry eight miles away, well aware that his sovereign lord had taken possession of his most precious and mighty Warwick Castle, while he was waiting for the troops Clarence was bringing, a fine four thousand men, the King rode out of Warwick Castle, preceded and surrounded by councilors and nobles and his minstrels onto a fair field at Banbury. There the troops were set in fair array and with many banners displayed, banners of many nobles, and in their center the great sun banner. The King dismounted and the troops stood at attention, and with Anthony and Hastings and his young brother Richard and a few others Edward began to walk toward another host of men similarly drawn up half a mile away.

To be in England when April's there! Could there be a fairer field than this? Edward's heart went out to his country at that moment even more than it did to the handsome man who came toward him, also on foot, his fair head bare; he too was almost alone save for a few noblemen who kept looking ahead at the figure of their King. The sound of the King's minstrels followed Edward and the standard-bearer held the flag of St. George high and proud; then the trumpets blew up and Edward was standing right in front of his brother Clarence, and Clarence went down on his knees.

There was silence. Then Edward lifted him up and embraced him.

"Forgive me," Clarence said, his lips trembling slightly.

Edward hugged him and set him back to look at him.

"There never could have been any outcome but this," Clarence blurted.

Anthony heard the words. Swiftly he assumed that Clarence meant no force could resist the King.

Edward took the words differently. "Not if you love us as we love thee." He smiled. "Now greet your brother, Dickon."

"Welcome back into the fold of your own family," Richard of Gloucester said, and held out his hand.

Clarence took it but his glance was a bit sharp. Then he too smiled. "I received more letters from our sister Margaret than she has ever written in her life!"

Anthony thought, I shall never trust him. He made arrangements to meet his brother here and he was still sending messages to Warwick; had anything happened to the King, he would have joined Warwick—to the last he left open two avenues and in either case he would have betrayed someone. Today it is the Earl of Warwick; tomorrow it may be—he shook Clarence's hand and his eyes rested on the handsome face. Then he stepped back because he knew that the shaking of hands was the merest formality between him and Clarence and that Clarence would always be his unspoken enemy.

But Edward was happy. He and his brother strode along together while the minstrels of both men played and sang, and more trumpets blew and the sun shone palely on the young green of the land; then the whole company turned and proceeded slowly while Edward inspected and received the homage of Clarence's men and the shouts of welcome roared in their ears. Finally everyone returned in martial array to Warwick Castle.

Warwick did not see the triumphal return but he could imagine it. At Coventry Oxford had arrived and now his faithful brother Montagu was with him, a Montagu curiously subdued and morose. Nonetheless Warwick felt better with Montagu at his side and his spirits rose a bit, for if they could just keep Edward from London and if they could just catch him unawares—

perhaps Easter Sunday they might even catch him at his devotions—anyway the worst that could happen was a flight to Calais. He began to gather courage now that Montagu was here and he said so; Montagu looked at him oddly and thanked him in a low voice.

"What can befall that it is so terrible?" Warwick asked. "Long faces won't help."

"Death is better than dishonor," Montagu said.

Warwick didn't believe that for a moment and looked at his brother as though he were mad.

"I'm not able to live with myself," Montagu said suddenly, unburdening his heart in a rush of words. It was a relief; he drew a great sigh. "My boy is only ten."

Warwick said, "His Grace would not harm your son."

The two men faced each other; Montagu suddenly felt the hot tears in his eyes and he was bitterly ashamed, but emotion buried him in his sorrow helplessly. He brushed his hard hand over his eyes. "No, he wouldn't. He wouldn't harm him. But there are others who would, and I find myself with them." He turned and went to the door. "I'll not leave you, Richard. The die is cast and I cast it. But I see nothing ahead but death."

He closed the door; Warwick was trembling; he leaned his fist on the table to steady himself.

Then he reminded himself he had another brother. He sat down, reached for pen and paper and wrote to the Archbishop. "George," his imploring pen scratched hastily, "keep Edward out of London. Provoke the city against him. I will come, I vow it!"

Messengers were galloping to London. Warwick's letter reached the Archbishop on Palm Sunday and Edward was indeed in church. He had reached Coventry and had gone to church as he should, in procession, with the people following after in devotion, craning and standing on tiptoe to see their King ahead of them. The service had come to the place where the veil was drawn up before the rood, that all should honor it with the anthem "*Ave*" three times. Edward was kneeling at a pillar of the church and directly in front of him was a closely boxed statue of St. Anne, of alabaster, shut up and enclosed according to the rule that in all churches in England all images were hid from Ash Wednesday to Easter Day in the morning.

And then suddenly the boards around the statue gave a great crack, which the King saw and all other people. Then the boards closed and opened again completely as though it had been a thing done by violence, and the image stood open and in the sight of all. Edward bowed his head and thanked and honored God, and he offered to St. Anne. Anthony couldn't take his eyes off the alabaster statue. It was a miracle, he thought. He felt free of any doubts; the way ahead had been blessed by a saint and he too bowed his head and honored God. The next day Edward reached Northampton and left behind him a goodly company of spears and archers and behind riders. On Tuesday, April ninth, royal messengers galloped off with a personal letter to Bessie at Westminster sanctuary and other letters to Edward's true lords and servants. That same day the Archbishop, heeding his brother Warwick's plea, called at St. Paul's with all the lords of King Henry's party. They placed the poor King on horseback and paraded him about the city. The sight of the ill King had the opposite effect of the Archbishop's intentions, for all any could feel for Henry was pity. The mayor and aldermen in a hastily convened council decided against trying to obey the Archbishop and the absent Warwick, their might was too little to resist the King, there would be harm and much bloodshed and, the most cogent of all, too many people within the city would have aided Edward, for they loved and respected him.

So on Wednesday the Archbishop told himself he had done his part. He had helped his brother to the best of his ability. It was not his fault the people didn't respond to the man Warwick called Henry VI. After a fine dinner the Archbishop sat down in his comfortable chair and smoothed out the heavy, expensive paper he always used. It was a bit drafty; he tucked his robes about his knees and sipped gratefully at the fine Burgundy in a goblet studded with jewels. He sipped as he wrote to Edward Plantagenet that he earnestly desired to be admitted once more into the King's Grace. This missive was sent secretly to the King.

He was none too soon, for on Thursday Edward entered London. His friends had already seized the Tower. Out of the sanctuaries poured the lords of his government; the King came and rode straight to St. Paul's, thence to the Archbishop's palace.

George Neville in his robes knelt at his King's feet and begged forgiveness.

Edward was in a hurry. Briefly he accepted the forgiveness. The Archbishop presented Henry to Edward as though his head was already on a platter and as though he, the Archbishop, should be thanked for the whole business.

Edward held out his hand stiffly to Henry and the former King took it; then suddenly embraced Edward. "My cousin of York," Henry said. "I know I am in good hands now."

The poor soul, Edward thought; they have made him a pawn, and that made Edward bitter and angry that they should dare. It would be prison for the Archbishop. It was less than he deserved; Edward waved him away and Edward rode straight to Westminster.

There his first duty was to go on his knees in church and this he did, making devout prayers and thanks to God, to St. Edward and to St. Peter.

In the sanctuary Bessie waited, each minute fraught with high excitement. The children, the ladies, even the servants were dressed in the finest they had, pressed, cleaned and mended. Abbot Milling himself tried to keep order in the schoolroom; it was impossible. In vain Bessie admonished that all must wait quiet till their father came; they wanted to go out to meet him and to see and she gave in. They went to the outer rooms of the sanctuary where they could see the courtyard. But that would not do and in the end they went out onto the steps of the church. The April sun shone. It shone brave on the sight of the King and the attending lords; it shone on the brilliant color of both attendant and clergy. Bessie stood on the top step. She saw him. He was about to dismount. She picked up her skirts and went down the steps; behind her were massed her household and the children, waving, crying out to Edward, in their hands the homemade pennants and banners. Bessie descended to the bottom step; across but twenty feet he was and then she could not wait any longer and she ran toward him, her feet barely touching the pavement, letting go her gown to outstretch her arms so when she reached him he was almost afraid she would fall and he seized her and lifted her off the ground, wrapped in his arms.

"My love, my love, my love," she was crying into his shoulder.

Around his back her arms were tight, feeling his closeness with such joy, such pure dazzling happiness that she was afraid she would embarrass him by too much emotion; she buried her head in his shoulder as she hugged him. He was whispering, "Bessie, Bessie!"

Then he sat her on her feet. Remembering where they were the King smiled on all. He placed her hand in his arm. Now she saw Anthony, who had removed his cap and knelt; Bessie held out her hand and kissed him and Richard next and Hastings.

Edward had reached his daughters now, and each was held high in their father's arms and hugged and kissed; and then the whole company, the children going ahead with their nurses, and then the King and Queen, with Bessie's hand tucked into Edward's arm, and all the lords and clergy following, all streamed into sanctuary, where Edward paused to greet and thank Abbot Milling. The abbot led the way to his godson.

The Duchess was waiting in the baby's room. She too was kissed by Edward as he approached the bed where his son was waiting, for he had had to be moved from his cradle; at five and a half months he was too big and active. He was sitting up, his fat hand grasping the side of the crib; his eyes round with wonder at this mass invasion of his privacy. Edward approached slowly; at the side of the bed he went down on one knee so his face was level with his son's and the two regarded each other. Edward held out one finger and his son took it, his fingers tight around the big forefinger. Then Edward stood and Bessie lifted the baby and placed him in Edward's arms and their eyes met above the child's head. "Oh, Bessie," he said helplessly. He kissed the child, speaking low. Then he held him high for all to see, the sturdy, firstborn son; the Prince gravely regarded the whole room, his eyes returning to the familiar face of his mother and then to the unfamiliar face of the man who held him.

"He does not cry," Edward whispered to Bessie.

She whispered back, "He's not used to people yet."

"Look at his eyes," Edward said. "How intelligent. And how big he is, Bessie! He is wonderful, the most beautiful boy I have ever seen! Look, he is smiling at me."

"He has your smile," she said, with such love in her voice it trembled.

But Bessie knew that the time for talk would be later. "We are ready to leave," she said, and Edward nodded.

"I am taking you to my mother's," he said.

"After he had kissed and comforted the Queen," wrote the chroniclers, "and her ladies, then he went to his firstborn son and kissed him, the King's greatest joy, a fair son, a Prince."

They knelt side by side at divine service that evening. Bessie reached out for his hand; the touch of his shoulder against hers —she kept glancing at his profile to make sure it was really he. The thought of the morrow when he would ride away "to confront his great rebel" she tried to push aside as he had commanded or else commit his cause to the lord Jesus. It was Holy Thursday, tomorrow would be Good Friday and regardless of the council meeting summoned for tomorrow morning she and Edward would go to early mass together.

Their room at the York mansion in London, Baynard's Castle, was new to Bessie. It was small and intimate; Bessie had never stayed in the house before. The color of the hangings was soft with age; the floors shone with polish; there was just a bit of carpet by the bed.

But the Duchess had gathered some sprays of greening bush, and the candlelight shone on the heavy silver plate that held a few wafers and carved goblets for wine. Outside the river lapped rhythmically at the stone landing stage and the walls. It was a night she would never forget.

"You leave tomorrow and if you did not come back—"

He cut short the whispered words. "Don't say that!" he commanded. "I must come. And you must have faith, Bessie!"

When the earliest dawn streaked in the windows they were lying wrapped in each other's arms; Bessie's hair had come undone from its plaits. Edward got up, the spring morning air cold on his naked body, and opened the curtains and looked out at the weather. That roused her and she opened her eyes and smiled at him dreamily; the edge of the sunlight turned her hair into purest gilt.

"Were I a poet," he began, putting on his robe; he came over to the bed and she held out her arms; he gathered her up close, brushing her hair back from her forehead with his big hand, touching the side of her face tenderly. "Thank God for you, Bessie," he whispered.

He was at the council meeting by eight, saying briefly they would discuss "the adventures which were likely to come." It was one of his typical understatements. His true lords out of sanctuary would resume their former posts; the government would go as smooth as it always did when he left London. Extra soldiers and guards on the gates, the Queen and Prince and his daughters under heavy guard in the Tower. As for the old King, he would take Henry with him; on no account must he fall into the hands of those who would use him for a front for rebellion or a wish to run the country to suit themselves. He himself would leave London before noon to confront Warwick. He ended by saying he was glad to be able to tell his council that King Louis, of the nonexistent country, had signed a peace treaty with Charles of Burgundy two days before, and couriers had brought the welcome news to Edward.

On that same previous evening, Thursday, the Earl of Warwick had received that news too through his capable spies. That same evening, a servant of the Archbishop had brought the news that the slippery George Neville, Archbishop of York, had submitted on his knees to Edward, and he was now in prison in the Tower but secure of his life and hopeful of full pardon later.

Warwick greeted these defections from him and his cause with pure rage. That King Louis should have dared! That he should have forced Warwick into a course of friendship with France and war with Burgundy: it was this foreign policy that had brought anathema onto his brief watch at the helm; it was the swarming French and their merchandise and the ships moored at the empty docks which had disillusioned London with his reign. For it was a reign. Warwick dragged out a piece of paper, pulling it toward him like a sword to hand, and similarly he took up his pen, wielding it like a branding iron. In this mood he wrote to Louis a letter searing and vengeful, a letter such as has seldom been written to a monarch. Betrayal and lies; dishonor and peasant craftiness—of these was Louis guilty in his dealings with a true friend! All the mean low acts of a lowborn, all the things that Louis' own father had accused him of—they were all true. He, the Earl of

Warwick, was ashamed he had ever sat down at the table with a man like Louis. He, Warwick, had remained firm to the commitments between himself and Louis, and Louis had betrayed him. Warwick sealed the letter with his stamp violently just as his brother Montagu came into the room.

"He used you," Montagu said, and then he understood that Warwick knew it now and that that was what occasioned the bitter anger. "What are you going to do, Richard?"

But now Montagu saw that his anger would sustain Warwick in the path to which he was now committed, on which he had set his booted feet so many months, nay, years ago. Automatically and as encased in his heavy armor on the field of battle, he would set forth on the last march. Even now he was full of plans.

"We shall issue forth from these walls"—he referred to Coventry —"tonight. Even now the Queen and the Prince and all my faithful lords, like Wenlock, will be landing in England. We shall catch Edward and maybe catch him unawares. We are freed of Louis!"

Warwick had issued out of Coventry and his army was toiling down the road to Northampton. On Saturday he was a mile or so out of Barnet and there he made camp. He was hopeful he might catch Edward unaware on Easter Sunday morning. There were convenient hedges and ditches; they made a natural dike and barrier about his men. He set up his field guns, for he had a good many, while he knew Edward had very few. As night fell he ordered the guns shot; he thought with satisfaction that they would keep Edward at a distance if he were approaching. But Warwick's system of outriders and spies was not as good as Edward's. Warwick and Montagu and Oxford did not know that their guns during the night were over-shooting the whole of Edward's army; that it was drawn up much nearer than they supposed. Edward's men had been forbidden to enter the town of Barnet; they were forbidden to speak or make any noise; they lay silent as an everlasting grave under the barricade of shots which fell past them. A mist came up; it lay heavy and thick over both armies. In the damp Warwick's guns functioned well for those days, but the shots whistled harmlessly over the heads of Edward's men. And there were no answering guns according to Edward's orders. And if Warwick expected to catch Edward unaware on Easter Sunday, it was the other way around, for at four in the morning the first heavy rumble of Edward's field guns tore the mist apart; Montagu rolled out of his cot as a cannonball landed against the walls of his tent. Very, very near sounded the clarion call of trumpets and Montagu, sitting straight up, knew that Edward with his customary ferocity in battle was springing out of the night and the fog against his sleeping foes.

Montagu was almost fully dressed; he sent the two men in his tent flying out with orders, threw open his chest and dragged out a battle jacket to wear underneath his mail. He put it on. Then regardless of the haste that was necessary he stared at it. How had he brought it? Where did it come from? For a long second, while about his tent was all the noise of men awakening under fire, raucous voices and yells and men running, he looked at the blue jacket with Edward's badge.

He stood still. I'll wear it, he thought. And over it he put on his mail, picked up his helmet and dashed from his tent to find his brother. With Edward advancing rapidly upon them they drew up in three battles, Oxford commanding one wing, Montagu the other and Warwick the center. Edward's guns were still firing when out of the fog appeared the first troops, protected by a hail of arrows. Edward's strategy had been the correct one, and in the end he had also all the luck.

The mist was so deep that the two armies did not confront each other exactly; one end of Edward's wing was overreached by Oxford, and Oxford's men, swarming through the hedges in the deep fog, soon overwhelmed the men whom Anthony commanded. Anthony swung his forces about to face Oxford more directly. An arrow found his arm, and he tied it briefly with a scarf, but he and his men were being pushed farther and farther back as Oxford's banners with the streaming stars now surrounded them almost completely. Anthony regrouped his men in a circle; the fighting was hand-to-hand; they were backed against trees, against hedges, anything to hold the line and protect the center, and in this way the whole wing swung about. Those who were cut off from Anthony fled toward London and Oxford's troops wheeled and went after them. That was Oxford's first mistake.

On the left wing Montagu was in a like fix. Edward's wing overreached his and in the mist troops poured over his position in overwhelming numbers. Like Anthony, Montagu was forced to retreat and regroup and in this way the whole battle line, obscured in fog, swung about.

But in the center, Edward did not know this. Under the mighty sun banner Edward wielding both battle-ax and heavy sword, a towering implacable figure in mail, was hewing his way forward and forward, his figure appearing out of the mist, then obscured again. Surrounded by his lords and yeomen, he swept like an irresistible tide and Warwick's whole center fell back, back.

Hedges were cut through; the gaps were filled with the men pouring after the King. On the left wing Anthony's line steadied and held; too many of Oxford's men were pursuing his fleeing troops. On the right Montagu was unable to hold, and Hastings and Richard of Gloucester, commanding that wing, were folding it back against its center, and Edward was there. Warwick now attacked the center with the forces held in reserve. When the swirling mist permitted he could see that sun banner coming nearer and nearer. The collapse of Montagu's wing was already apparent, for Hastings and Richard did not turn and pursue; instead they came relentlessly forward in a curve that caught and held Montagu and his men like a noose.

Two hours of hand-to-hand fighting had gone by. Oxford, now perceiving his mistake, rallied his men and tried to get back to his former position and sent his banners racing ahead of him. The banner of the streaming stars. It appeared out of the mist. To the men in Warwick's center it looked like the great sun banner and within a matter of moments the whole wing collapsed.

Behind them was the sun banner and in front of them was the sun banner! In front of them was the King. The center line wavered; Warwick screamed and tried to rally them, but it wavered and then it broke as men turned and fled from the unbroken line of helmeted men, from Edward and his knights coming steadily forward like a bristling wall of steel. The mist parted; the mighty sun banners shone forth clearly. For a moment the Earl of Warwick stood uncertain; then he turned and ran too toward the horse park.

Edward shouted orders; two yeomen of the guard raced forward. Warwick ran on, but now from the wings Edward's troops poured onto the horse park. Before Warwick could reach his horse, before Edward's yeoman of the guard could reach Warwick to save his life a long dagger was raised, hands seized Warwick, ripped open his visor. The dagger plunged into his throat. By the time the yeoman reached him, his body was stripped of the mail and the rich weapons, and all they could do was to cover it with his torn cape and wait there for further orders from the King he had betrayed. The King whom he had served so faithfully had betrayed him. When Louis finally received Warwick's letter he knew he was dead, and he would shake his head in pity and with a small sigh, but what would you? Rebellious nobles, Louis knew, always came to the same ends.

The King followed his two yeomen into the horse park, running, sword still in hand.

"We were too late, Your Grace!"

With the tip of the sword Edward laid the cloak aside and looked down at the body of the great Earl. He was silent; he had failed to save him, as he failed before to save him from his great folly. From the edge of the horse park two men appeared carrying another man whom they laid down next to the Earl.

"The Marquis of Montagu, killed in plain battle, Your Grace."

The mail had been stripped from the body. The blue jacket was stained across the chest almost entirely with blood, but it did not conceal the badge. Edward closed his eyes against the sight. "My God," he muttered under his breath.

The sun was shining bright now. It was eight o'clock in the morning. Edward reckoned swiftly they could reach London that very day, Easter Sunday. Edward leaned the bloody sword against a tree trunk and went immediately about the business of the wounded, as he always did, and the men who served him were used to the sight of the King bearing a wounded man in his powerful arms toward a waiting cart.

At eleven he was ready to go back to London. Behind him and his lords came the trundling cart with the bodies of Warwick and Montagu, to be displayed in London in open coffins at St. Paul's so all men could see that the cause of the King's great rebel was truly and irrevocably lost. My lord of Oxford was not among them; he had escaped. And he would fight again another day.

The sun was shining bright at Weymouth too after a morning of mist from the sea. On the deck of her ship Anne Neville watched the shores of her beloved England come closer. The spring wind was a bit sharp, but it had the wonderful tang and sweetness of April in it; only two weeks and her heart lifted with the promise of May to come. They waited so long in Honfleur and even now the passage had not been easy, for the weather was unpredictable and the spring storms had left the Channel a churning mass of unruly water.

When Anne and Margaret and her Prince stepped ashore at Weymouth, the Duke of Somerset and John Courtenay, who called himself Earl of Devonshire, awaited them with quite a retinue. The news they had for Margaret was not good. Warwick had been unable to keep Edward out; he had been in London and had left the city to confront Warwick. They must all pray that even by now Warwick had overthrown the former so-called King Edward. They knelt to the Prince and Anne and pledged their allegiance; they all wore ostrich feathers in their caps. The Prince accepted their homage and vowed himself more than ready to fight and kill the usurper Edward. A few minutes after these fine words had been exchanged, a suitable dwelling was offered the Queen and her son and Anne, and after the rigors of their crossing they retired into the prepared chambers. The next morning the true news of Barnet Field arrived.

Queen Margaret was wild with anger and dismay at Warwick's stupidity. He had had a chance to kill Edward in open battle and instead he had got himself killed, about which she cared nothing. "He failed me," she cried bitterly. "I knew he would!"

But Margaret was afraid too. Not for herself but for her son. For regardless of her suspicion and dislike of Warwick he did represent a bulwark against Edward, and now that had been swept away. All that stood between her and Edward were her old lords and servants; would they be enough?

"Of course, they will!" Somerset answered her unspoken thought. "Courage, madam!"

"I've always had enough courage," Margaret said. "It's wit that Louis said I lacked. Wit to stop this endless fighting." Her mind wandered a bit and went back into the past. "I never could abide the Duke of York since the time when he tried to betroth his oldest son Edward—he was only two—to the daughter of the King of France! Such impudence!"

Somerset was silent. Why was she raking up the past? She was getting older, he thought.

"He presumed. That's why I hated him. And Henry and I had no children for so long. He considered himself the heir to the throne."

Louis had pointed out, "But he was the heir, madam, and you should have placated him and worked with him."

Margaret shook her head as if to shake loose the memories of the days when indeed she did control England. Somewhere along the way she had made a fatal mistake. And yet look how many men would rally to her cause!

"We shall raise Somersetshire, Dorsetshire, Wiltshire, Devonshire and Cornwall to your cause, madam!" The hereditary Earl of Devonshire was speaking; he had shared her exile. "My old followers will rise up for you, madam." Then he remembered and bowed to the Prince who was looking at him sulkily. "And you, my liege!"

The Prince thought that these men seemed interested only in his mother and his father whom he scarcely remembered and whom he secretly despised. He adored his fiery mother but he thought sullenly that more attention should be paid to him. After all, it was he who would rule England.

Jasper Tudor, who had also shared the Queen's exile in France, was anxious to leave the meeting and do something. "I suggest you go to the abbey at Cerne, madam. I shall go into Wales where I know I can raise men for our cause."

So it was decided. Yet Margaret insisted on keeping her son with her. He is only in his nineteenth year, she said to herself. Until we have an army I shall not let him out of my sight.

They took their leave of her with a good deal of fanfare after she had been properly escorted to the abbey. Only Jasper Tudor had a contrary thought in his head; it occurred to him that his twelve-year-old nephew Henry Tudor would make a better King than the young son of Margaret of Anjou.

Edward had spent the whole morning seeing to the wounded and speaking with them. Next with Anthony, Anthony whose gashed arm was in a tight sling against his chest, he reviewed the artillery and guns and the troops, and he had sent for fresh men from all parts; they were to meet him at Windsor where on Friday he would keep the feast of St. George.

Anthony was not going to be allowed to march with him this time. His wound was still too fresh, too bloody and too painful. Besides that Bessie needed him. Anthony was placed in charge of the Tower with a capable complement of troops; he would guard not only Bessie and the children but the old King.

Edward's capable spies had reported the first movements of the Lancastrians; they were drawing west to Exeter, Glastonbury and then Bath. Edward traced on the map his route and where his dispatches would be coming from; he would march directly west, keeping London between him and his foes so that he could intercept them whichever way they turned.

"Had they gone eastward," he said to Anthony, "I should have made haste to encounter them as soon as possible for the sake of London. But it looks as though they are circling to the northwest and I want to intercept them at Gloucester, Tewkesbury or Worcester."

Edward reached Cirencester by Monday and emptied the town for the safety of its people and lodged his troops three miles outside, but the Queen's host turned aside to Bristol, anxious to avoid Edward, so he pushed on to Sudbury and went to bed, having lodged his van in a protecting valley and he himself on Sudbury hill with the main body of troops.

At three in the morning his spies reported. Margaret and her soldiers were at Barkley, making for Gloucester.

It was imperative that Margaret be kept out of Gloucester and not find shelter behind its walls. Edward summoned his council and dictated a letter to Richard Beauchamp, commanding him to keep the castle and town well protected; he added that he could expect the Lancastrian host before noon and that he, Edward, would soon come to his rescue and comfort. This letter was sent by two of Edward's most faithful servants. The letter reached the city just in time, for the Lancastrians appeared before Gloucester by ten in the morning and demanded admittance.

Richard Beauchamp refused; the walls were lined with archers and they presented too formidable a sight to attack. Nevertheless Jasper Tudor pretended he was going to assault the town, thinking Beauchamp might then give in. But hails of arrows greeted even the semblance of attack and reluctantly Tudor turned back,

reluctantly because they would have been safe ensconced behind the stout walls of Gloucester. They trailed off toward
Tewkesbury.

Jasper Tudor was worried. They had traveled thirty-six miles
in foul country, country all broke up into lanes and stony ways
and between woods, and all without good refreshment. The
greater part of his troops were footmen and now they straggled
along, weary and unhappy. But they reached Tewkesbury that
night, and Jasper picked out a field in a close at the end of the
town with the town and abbey at their backs. He felt fairly safe,
for in front of him and his troops were lanes and hedges, deep
dikes, hills and valleys. It would be, Jasper Tudor thought, a right
evil place to approach.

It was a hot day. Edward had swung about, dividing his men
into three sections, advancing banners and marching toward
Tewkesbury in plain, open, fair country. At Cheltenham he signaled a stop. He was five miles from Tewkesbury and his men
needed food, drink and rest.

Edward, as a soldier, was the most capable commander of his
time. Methodical, always well informed by his "espies and afore
riders," he never outstripped his supplies nor overwearied his
men, and whenever possible he met the enemy on his own terms.
He was doing that now; forcing a fight before they were ready;
even though they were well entrenched, the enemy troops had
traveled too far in an attempt to escape confrontation earlier,
and they had marched not over the "fair plain country" as Edward had but by the stony byways and the thick forests, the
clumsy, footsore way.

Nonetheless the next day's fighting would be upon entrenched
troops because he didn't dare let them get farther north—the restless, prone-to-rebellion north where there was the remnant of
Warwick's men, the uncertainty of Lord Percy, Earl of Northumberland. Would the appearance of the former Queen and her
Lancastrian Prince shake the fidelity of the proud Percy? Edward
knew all too well the roiling emotions caused by this struggle; if
he managed to keep his own emotions under control it was sometimes by dint of great effort, and he thought that there were
many who would succumb to the pull of old family loyalties; if
he himself were tempted certainly others were too. Let Margaret

get to the north and the whole of Northumberland might burst into the signal fires of border rebellion.

The men rested and ate—thank God it was warm—and they in this plain field in the bright sun lay sprawled on back or stomach, savoring the good English ale and the meat and bread. The King was conferring with the newly returned spies and was listening to the quick reports: "The streams were so roiled by the passage of the carts and carriages that there was not water, neither to drink, nor to refresh and wash with." "They are undisciplined troops, Your Grace. There is no true line of march." "They accompany each their own lords. For the most part they are footmen." While he was listening his eyes roved over the lounging troops, well accoutered, confident; confident because of him— Edward knew that his own personal courage was legendary. He would lead his troops on foot in the center of the battle, and they would follow zestfully.

So when they had finished their stout meal the trumpets blew, for it was time to take the field. Drawn up into companies, divided into three battles, Edward's troops now moved forward in battle formation to confront the enemy; the field guns trundling lazily with a company of archers marching smartly behind. The foot and the van were protected by mounted troops, the dying sun fell on the helmeted, marching men; the array of banners, from the great sun banner to Hastings' blue banners, and their heraldic designs caught the last rays of the sun.

Early in the hours of Saturday morning, just after midnight, Edward appareled himself for battle. Fires burned and the banners were displayed by their bearers. Trumpets blew up and the King committed his cause and quarrel to God, the Virgin and St. George. And now they advanced directly upon the enemy.

Shots and a sharp shower of arrows was the herald of the King's campaign. And while the guns roared and bucked steadily Edward himself rode at the head of a group of two hundred spears, to the right hand of the Lancastrian field; a woodslike park it was, and he hid the men there in the trees with orders only to keep a good eye on the corner of the wood. The officer in command was a good one. "You'll see when you are needed. Wait until then," Edward commanded. Then he swung about and trotted silently off into the night.

He left his horse and it was led away to the horse park. The

trumpets blew raucously, and Edward and the center battle began to advance directly upon the entrenched camp, using battle-
axes to rip away the encircling hedges, jumping over the dikes,
while arrows kept pouring into the camp.

Edward gained a plain bit of ground, Richard of Gloucester
following. There swarming troops waited for him.

The battle was joined. Edward's men were close behind and
around the tall mighty figure of their King. Inch by inch they
gained ground, still protected by flights of arrows.

And then the Duke of Somerset, "annoyed by the gunshot and
the arrows, led his men by an unknown way through a narrow
lane to the close where Edward was embattled. There he set
fiercely upon the end of the King's battle."

Edward saw Somerset. The chronicler says; "Then the King
full manly set forth upon them, entered and won the dyke and
hedge, and was upon them, with great violence and put them up
the hill."

Slowly Somerset was driven back; with satisfaction Edward
saw he was withdrawing close to the wood where he had left
his two hundred hidden spearmen. Richard was at his side. Edward still came forward; the Lancastrians pulled back, and now
out of the woods the two hundred spearmen charged. With the
King in front of them and an unexpected attack from the side,
Somerset's line broke in panic and the place to this day is known
as Bloody Meadow.

Hastings' men were behind and around him now, and through
ditches and dikes and hedges they came and the Lancastrian
lines wavered and broke.

Edward had permitted his anger, his usually controlled emotion free rein this morning. His attack had been so sudden and
ruthless that the Lancastrians had had barely time to get the
women out of the camp and the Queen and her ladies to a religious house. He had fallen on them with the fury of a monarch
toward his rebellious nobles. Devonshire lay dead, Somerset's
brother and Lord Wenlock. There is a tale that Somerset himself
killed Wenlock, because he was "standing still," and that Somerset, reviling him for a traitor, struck his brains out with his
battle-ax.

The sun was shining. The field where Edward stood was empty
of the Lancastrians save for their dead or mortally wounded.

With his huge sword in hand Edward knighted no less than forty-three very brave men. In the bloody meadow those men knelt and received their knighthoods for valor on the field of battle, and then still in the heat of violence and anger Edward, naked, bloody sword still in hand, turned once more to pursue his fleeing enemies. To Tewkesbury Edward now pursued and to the doors of the great abbey and church itself. He kicked them open with one big foot and with sword in hand was framed there in the open doors.

There was deathly silence in the church. Men crouched behind the pillars and were stretched out on the stone floors. Through the stained-glass windows the beautiful light fell upon chancery and choir where the huddled figures of the wounded and defeated waited for what seemed like instant death at their King's own hands. There they were, Somerset himself and at least ten of his lords, clinging to the altar. Under the helmet Edward's face was terrifying. The priest who moved toward him was shaking with fright, for Edward was within the church now and behind him were crowded the menacing figures of mailed soldiers; like bloodthirsty beasts their eyes devoured the figures of their enemies cowering before them.

Edward saw the priest coming toward him. He glanced about himself; the sunlight through the windows threw what looked like red blood on the floor before him. But Edward was too angry to move back and out of this holy place. He watched the priest, his eyes blazing. Then the priest said, "Your Grace. In my hands is the Holy Sacrament."

Edward stepped back.

"You have entered the abbey *violente manu.*"

Edward looked down at his gauntleted hands and the bloody sword.

"Your Grace," said the priest, because he had faith in Edward's sanity, "God has accorded you the victory. Lay down your weapons. I shall take you to the high altar to give thanks to God."

The King looked down at his hands again. His sword he handed to the nearest soldier, who backed out the doors as Edward motioned him. Then he took off the heavy gauntlets and bared his head; his hair was rumpled and untidy. He looked at the priest and then he knelt suddenly.

"Forgive me, Father," he said.

The priest in his heart thanked God, for the overwhelming anger that had brought Edward into the very abbey itself was now spent, washed away by the sanctuary itself, the priest was sure, and the presence of God within it.

Edward rose. The priest led him through the huddled men to the high altar and now other of the brotherhood of monks followed behind, so they made procession and they sang and the King went before the high altar and knelt. Edward barely heard the priest's words over his head. When he rose and turned and they all went through the choir and down to the doors again and out in the sunlight, Edward said, "Father, you may tell them in there," he gestured, "that they have my full pardon, save for those who were the leaders. They will have to be tried properly by the Constable of England tomorrow." So the King left the church and went out into the street, Church Street, and on to a fine house which still stands. The battle of Tewkesbury was over.

Edward did not preside at the trial of Somerset and five of his lords the following day; he entrusted that duty to the Constable and the Earl Marshal of England. The Prince had been killed in battle. He was buried in the church at Tewkesbury, his arms and his helmet with the curling ostrich plumes laid to rest under the stones. Edward had forbid any despoliation of the bodies; there would be no setting up of heads on poles. The executed men and the dead were buried in the churchyard with proper ceremony and respects, and Edward himself hurried on to Coventry to rest and refresh his troops and to reassure the city, for dispatches reaching him from other parts of the country were hardly reassuring.

London was embattled. For the Bastard of Fouconberg, Warwick's nephew, whom he had placed in charge of the fleet, didn't believe his uncles were dead and he had managed to raise all the dissident elements in Kent and Surrey; even the Mayor of Canterbury, Warwick's friend, was at his side.

Anthony, the mayor of London and even the King's council had attempted to talk sense to the Bastard. Firmly he was refused admittance to London. "His men are raggle-taggle that want to put their hands in rich men's coffers," the mayor said. He sent an official letter, reminding the Bastard that his two uncles were buried; their bodies had lain two days in St. Paul's, the mayor added. His only hope was to submit to the King, the King who had already dispatched fifteen hundred picked troops to London.

"King Henry!" shouted the Bastard in reply. And he set his men to burning the outskirts of London. The fires burned at Southwark and at the bridge. But the news from the north was worse. There King Henry's old sympathizers were reputedly gathering in great numbers, "making commotions," Edward wrote, "intending the destruction of the church, of us, of our lords and all noble men, and to subvert the weal public of realm." He scowled as he laid down the pen. Meanwhile where was Margaret of Anjou? He sent William Stanley to scouring the countryside. He tried to sweep from his mind Margaret's obvious and sorrowing spirit; she was a ghost, a ghost from the past; he didn't minimize her suffering; she had lost her only child, her son, struck down in the field of battle, a bitter ending for Margaret's pride and love for him; she had been guilty of much against his family but she had forced this upon him, this long drawn-out battle of wills and of bodies. He shoved her suffering out of his mind, for reports had reached him that the proud Percy had left Northumberland and was riding south.

Edward stayed at Coventry from the eleventh to the fourteenth of May and on the morning of May fourteenth Lord Percy, almost unheralded, arrived, for he came as a noble should come to his sovereign lord, attended by only a few men. And when he came into Edward's presence he knelt. He came, he said, to assure his King that the north would remain quiet and that he bore only requests for pardon. Warwick's men, flying north from Barnet, had come to him to ask him to appeal in their name to the King.

The city of York asked for grace and pardon.

Northumberland, standing very tall, still had to look up a bit to meet Edward's eyes. Edward said, "Your plea is granted, my lord. We have no wish for further bloodshed."

"Aye, Your Grace," Percy said, relieved. "I know it. I—" he hesitated. "We thank you."

"Go home," Edward said. "And see that peace is preserved hereafter in that part of our realm."

That same day Sir William Stanley came to report that he had found the former Queen.

"She is in a religious house down the river from Tewkesbury," he said. "They took her there by boat just before the battle. She gave me one message for Your Grace and that is that she is at your commandment."

Edward was extraordinarily busy. "Bring her to me," he ordered.

Sir William rode back immediately with an armed guard. Margaret had with her but two faithful women, so Sir William was surprised when he saw a third small figure wearing a veil from which enormous dark eyes appealed. "My God," he thought. "Anne Neville!"

She looked a reed of a woman; her face white and tragic, even more so than her mother-in-law's. The Queen entered the carriage and sat in the middle of the seat, a lady on each side of her. There was no room for Anne. But there was a strip of barewood running behind the driver's seat, and Sir William aided Anne there; she sat quietly, her hands folded in her lap, her eyes downcast so she would not have to look at Margaret of Anjou.

The carriage jolted over the rutted roads; the spring rains had taken their toll of them. There was no conversation. The Queen remained stonily silent and so did her ladies. The Queen's head was covered with a white veil that came down over her forehead. She stared straight ahead and Anne darted a glance at her, then lowered her eyes quickly. She has lost her dear son, Anne thought; I do indeed pity her. Even though she mocked my father even in death. The events of the past two weeks had been so shattering to Anne that they all blurred together; these few women had accompanied an army which was fleeing before the King's troops and she had shared the forced marches, the lack of food and even water; and in the end they had fled in the night in a small boat down the river before the sound of guns and the whine of arrows and the shouts of men and the sounds of trumpets in the night. The small boat into which hands had pushed her in the black dark had rocked dangerously and it was only after they reached the small convent that Anne realized with surprise that she was still alive. Anne stepped out of the boat, the last person to leave it. There was a little nun standing to her side and Anne clutched at her as her knees gave way, and the two of them went down in a huddled heap. Anne hurt her ankle and she lay there, supine.

Hands lifted her and led her into the little dining room set aside for the abbess. There they removed her soaked clothes and gave her a gray habit.

"If I could wash," she whispered. She looked down at her hands; they were soiled with grime. "We have traveled for days and nights."

The abbess was with the Queen. The young nuns brought her hot water and crude soap. Then they undid her tangled hair and brushed it.

"You are the first ones who have been kind to me," Anne said pathetically, and one little nun was so moved that big tears shone in her eyes. They brought her soup and she drank it obediently; then they put her to bed in a small, cell-like room with a single, small window. Anne said, "If you do not mind I should like to stay here with you. I have nowhere else to go." She closed her eyes; maybe they would let her stay; maybe she could earn the habit she wore; it was clean and seemed to lie about her body comfortingly; she would find safety and peace here. At the side of her bed the two young nuns were kneeling and praying for her; a sweet peace swept over Anne. She opened her eyes. "You have made me happy," she whispered.

Four days later she had had to say good-bye to them. They were just country girls and she knew that they regarded her as being from another world, the daughter of the great Earl, the sister of a Duchess. "But I'm not truly," she thought. "I don't want to leave. If I could I'd stay!"

The young nuns appealed to the abbess. "Let her stay, Reverend Mother."

The abbess was a kind woman. "But—the King has commanded that these ladies be brought to him." There was no help for it; Anne must go.

It was with reluctance Anne took off the gray habit. The nuns had brushed and mended her dress and washed her stockings. It was a May day but Anne shivered as she stepped into the carriage and sat on the hard seat. Suddenly she became aware that her mother-in-law was actually addressing her. "They told me you were sick, Anne. I hope you feel better."

They were almost the only kind words the Queen had ever spoke to her and Anne stared at her in childish amazement.

"Anne," said the Queen then, "do not forget you are the Lady Anne. Your father would not wish you to forget it."

The Queen lapsed into silence and Anne pondered her words. Then the Queen spoke again, almost as the walls of Coventry closed around them. "Adversity should strengthen and harden thee; it always has me until now. Now," the Queen said, not moving a muscle of her face and her eyes stony black, "now my spirit is broken."

Anne swallowed, for she didn't know what to say. "I am sorry, Your Grace," she whispered; she leaned forward and touched the Queen's hand as it lay listless like a hurt bird on her knees. "I am sorry for your grief, madam. I too grieve."

Margaret straightened her shoulders. "You are young," she said. "You will grow strong again and forget."

They were entering the streets of Coventry. Margaret said one final sentence. "Sit straight, Anne. The people are watching. You are my dead son's bride. Sit proud for his sake and for your father's." And these words, like the ones by which she had nourished her son for eighteen years, now did give Anne strength too, and she realized suddenly what it was that had drawn men to Margaret of Anjou and made them fight for her. Anne thought she should say so. She contented herself with three words. "Thank you, madam." Thus she rode through Coventry and to the King.

So now when they were brought to the presence of the King Margaret took Anne's hand and they advanced together, Margaret's two ladies hovering in the background. The King was seated; at each side of his chair stood his brothers. Anne's eyes went to Richard with whom she had played and quarreled when she was a child. She saw his familiar face and sent him the smallest smile, but somehow she saw he looked entirely different and she averted her eyes quickly, for his own were appraising her and it made her uncomfortable. I look awful, she thought suddenly, with a young woman's vanity springing up, and she resented the patronizing look he gave her for they were equals in her mind. Then Margaret and she curtsied before Edward and Anne, rising, now let her eyes rest entirely on the King.

"We are, Your Grace, entirely at your commandment," Margaret said in her lovely accented English.

Edward said coldly, "The fact that you are my prisoner, madam, is entirely of your own doing."

Margaret spoke no word but made a brief curtsy.

Edward's eyes flicked her. This was the woman who had had his father's head severed from his body after his death. But he would not harm her.

He went on, "You and your two women, madam, will be placed in a sanctuary until we go to London, then at that time you will accompany us."

This was dismissal. Margaret took a backward step; but Anne stood still.

"Your Grace," she said, "if I have offended I did so in obedience to the orders of my father, Earl Warwick. I have no wish nor desire to do aught but ask for grace and pardon."

Anne spoke clear and with a sudden resolve which she knew the Queen's bearing had uncovered for her. Edward now smiled at her. Clarence smiled at her too.

Edward said, "My Lady Anne, we bear you no ill will. It is our thought that you will be best off with your sister and mine, the Duchess of Clarence. Preparations have already been made to send you to her."

But Edward had too much on his mind to make much ado about a few women. He gestured to Clarence, and her brother-in-law now stepped to Anne's side and together they left the presence of the King. As they went Anne felt eyes on her back; she was sure they were not Edward's but his brother Richard's and the hand on Clarence's arm trembled slightly as she left the room.

From the windows of her room in the Tower, looking straight upriver, Bessie could see the ships of the Bastard of Fauconberg at St. Katharine's.

She knew Edward's men were on their way. The mayor and the aldermen were manning the gates of the city themselves. At Aldgate she could see the fires they had set.

It was night. She was more worried over Anthony than herself, for he had his arm straitly bound and now, at the head of five hundred men, he was issuing from the postern gate of the Tower to fall upon the rebels at Aldgate. While the fighting raged Bessie and the Duchess waited in terrible suspense, but Anthony by his surprise sortie had taken them off guard and driven them back, and the next day the whole unruly crowd withdrew to Blackheath three miles away.

But Edward was coming. The news dispersed the Bastard's followers and they fled back home. Early on the morning of the twenty-first the mayor and the recorder and diverse aldermen rode out of the city to meet Edward, and the grateful King stopped his procession and knighted the mayor and the recorder and some of the aldermen for bravery and fidelity. Then they came on into London.

Edward's brother Richard was at the head of the procession. The trumpets and clarions blew. The horses stepped smartly and there were more than three thousand mounted men. At Richard's side rode Will Herbert's son. Edward would have wished it were Will himself. So many had been lost to him. Next came Hastings and then Edward. Behind him in a chariot seated with her two faithful women came the former Queen, Margaret of Anjou.

Edward rode to St. Paul's and then going to the altar made his offering; in his big hand he carried the torn and stained banners of the Lancastrian nobles, symbols of his victory, the tattered remains of a lost cause. Margaret was sent to Windsor Castle. The Prince was dead. Somerset was dead. Exeter Edward had spared and sent to the Tower. Oxford and Jasper Tudor had escaped, yet as always if his enemies were powerless to do him harm Edward forgot them. There remained the Bastard of Fauconberg and Edward was now in no mood to quibble; he made up his mind to set forth in full strength after the Bastard the next day.

So while he met his council and received various eyewitness reports on the Bastard's conduct and those who had helped him, his mind was weighing a great matter: the peace of the realm and the former King and his French wife.

He had an early dinner alone with Bessie. He saw his son and held him and kissed him and played with him, marveling, shoving all thoughts and all decisions away. "I am just a staid husband and father," he said to Bessie. "For one hour and one hour only."

That meant he would not see her later. Bessie leaned forward to let her son clasp his hand around her finger and play with the huge new ruby ring Edward had given her.

"He wants to eat it," Edward said. "You can't bite your mother's new ring even if you are a Prince."

Bessie said, not really hearing his words, "But my love—" she hesitated.

"I must see Anthony and must see my brother Richard."

"Oh," Bessie said.

He set his son in her arms. The baby yawned.

"That is very impolite," Edward said, "to yawn in your King's face." He grinned, stood up and fetched a long sigh. "I shall always remember you, Bessie," he said, "when I am away from you, like you are now, so beautiful with your child in your arms."

Bessie started to rise but he put his hand on her shoulder. "Stay with my son," he said. "Let me go."

He said to Anthony, "So they shouted for the old King."

Anthony replied, "It's just a name, Your Grace. It's just a rallying cry."

Edward said noncommittally, "So it is."

The candles were burning. There was a knock on the door. Anthony rose and opened it; the slight figure of Richard of Gloucester stood outside in the hallway where there was more light from the flaming sconces. Richard looked elegant and sleek in black velvet. He was unarmed and unjeweled save for a heavy dagger with jewels glittering in the hilt.

Richard was polite but cool; he didn't like Anthony Woodville very much; he was jealous of him and his closeness to the King.

"Thank you, Anthony, and good night," Edward said.

Anthony backed out the door and it closed. He was conscious of unease and for a moment he stood outside the closed door, lost in thought. He could hear no sound from within, so he shook off his feeling of uncertainty and portent, and when he paused again at the turn of the corridor, where two halberdiers stood motionless, he looked back. The door was still closed.

Within the room the candles flickered over Edward's face. His brown eyes were blank. "So it is on my order that this is done. The blame rests with no one but me."

He was thinking, My most admired contemporary, the late Duke of Milano, Francesco Sforza, would laugh at me, for what is one politically expedient murder? A trial cannot be risked for I've no charge, no valid charge. This poor meek man is paying for his grandfather's seizure of the throne, the glittering throne, and the unspoken word made him think Richard's almost black eyes seemed to glitter. Was it with triumph? Edward scowled. Was Richard eager while he himself dreaded the hour to come? Would Richard actually do the deed himself? How would he, Edward, ever know that?

"What must be accomplished in the next hour," Edward said harshly, "must happen to a man who a few short weeks ago embraced me and said he knew he would be safe with me. Therefore, it is my command that it be quick and merciful, one single thrust, if possible, unseen by my victim." That last self excoriating word Edward used to express the guilt he felt.

"It is ten o'clock, Richard," he said. "I shall expect you back here before midnight."

Richard nodded and yet he himself, as Edward had guessed, did not understand why Edward hesitated.

"To crush the seed," he said.

"How Italianate of you," Edward said. "You forgot to add for the peace and safety of our realm."

It was ten minutes before the hour when Richard returned. Edward was undressed and in his bedroom and Richard said very little, only that his orders had been carried out to the letter.

The King nodded. "Good night," he said.

Richard backed to the door and Edward followed him. He did not usually do that and Richard was surprised, for it was as though the King were actually hurrying him. Richard saw that he was right and that Edward must have had an appointment, for Richard heard a light laugh and then the opposite inner door of Edward's chamber opened and a woman stood there; she was in a loose pretty gown with her hair caught back in a bow; in one hand she carried a lute and in the other a goblet of wine. Richard knew who she was; she had been Hastings' mistress for a short time; Richard didn't know that the King had had her. Her name was Jane Shore and she was the prettiest, gayest harlot Richard had ever seen.

The door closed in his face as Edward said good night. Richard thought, After he orders a murder he seeks a whore. He was filled with emotion and emotion that contained both revulsion and jealousy. And if Edward could have answered his thoughts

he would have said cynically, "And why not? Sinners are best off
with sinners."

Edward did stay in London only one day. And he pursued the
fleeing Bastard of Fauconberg with mounted men. Promptly the
Bastard deserted his followers and fled to his ships, only to dis-
cover that his men had mutinied. In panic the Bastard offered his
submission to Edward.

The King wearily accepted it. He was sick of blood. He had no
faith that the Bastard would be anything but what he was now;
potential betrayal was ahead but he would deal severely when
it happened. The next time the Bastard would face trial and
execution. For now, there had been blood; there had been enough
for any reign already. In fact Edward was so weary of it that
when Oxford finally came into his hands he would imprison him
and not ask for his life. For on Wednesday King Henry's body
was brought from the Tower. It lay in state with priests and soldiers in honor around his body. Edward gave orders for a solemn
funeral and burial at the Abbey of Chartsey. It was the twenty-
sixth of May and England was as lovely as only the green spring
could make her. Edward was at Canterbury and his courts were
sitting to try not only the mayor, who had aided the Bastard of
Fauconberg, but numbers of commons who had joined his preda-
tory march on London.

The mayor was sent to the Tower, his life spared. The punishment which would fall upon the others was dear to Edward's
heart, for it would be punishment by fines and not by blood.
Money was more satisfactory to a King.

The long campaign of eleven weeks had ended. He had come
virtually alone back to England and by the greatest of good fortune he had met his enemies separately, although he thought
that was their weakness—that they could not get along together,
that they were mad dogs in the same kennel, as he'd told Charles.
He had met them and destroyed them. Tomorrow he would re-
trace his steps back to London and to Bessie. Now, this morning,
he stood alone on Murderer's Porch at the cathedral. Then he
entered the nave and went alone to Becket's tomb to pray.

In London that night Anthony was working late, bent over
sheets of manuscripts. Before they had left Holland Edward had
instructed one of his secretaries to write an eyewitness account

of his "Arrivall" in his country. This account had been handed to Anthony to condense and make ready in three copies; these copies to be sent abroad, one to Burgundy, one to the Lord Gruthuyse; Edward wanted them dispatched immediately; the messengers were waiting. For once again what was happening in England was not fully known in Europe and once again Louis was eying the narrow seas nervously, one minute receiving reports that Edward was dead and the next minute that he was readying a fleet. The candles flickered over Anthony's head. "Write an ending," Edward had ordered.

It was a fine eyewitness account, Anthony thought. It would be impossible not to recognize that the writer had actually been there and it was not laced with falsities either. Frankly the author told how no men had come to Edward's side when he had first landed, and why Edward had gone to York, and how he had worn the dead Prince's ostrich plumes, and how Hastings had passed out money and bribes. And the battles were carefully recounted, how Oxford's men returning to Barnet Field were mistook for Edward's own because of Oxford's emblem of the stars with streams. Anthony cut carefully, keeping as many facts as he could while shortening the document. Now the end. Anthony wrote:

> So, with the help of God, he escaped many dangers by his knightly and noble courage, winning two great battles, putting to flight great assemblies of his rebels. They were, it seemed, afraid of the very courage and manhood that rests in the person of our sovereign lord. Whereby it is faithfully believed that with the help of God, which from the beginning never failed him, that in short time he shall appease his subjects throughout the realm; that peace and tranquillity shall grow and multiply. [Anthony crossed out "and multiply."] from day to day, to the honor and loving of God, the increase of our King's singular and famous renown, and to the great joy of his friends, allies and people.

Anthony laid down his pen and handed the sheets over to the copyist. "Three copies," he said. He yawned and rubbing his still-sore arm said good night to the three clerks. The "Arrivall" of Edward IV back to his kingdom was now history.

PART FOUR
Edward and King Louis

Chapter 16

"Now is the winter of our discontent made glorious summer by this sun of York." One hundred and more years later Shakespeare opened a play with those lines but Edward would have deemed them an overstatement, for it was going to take more than months and more than years to knit up the wounds of civil war. The labor ahead of him was gargantuan.

The former Queen was given into the custody of Edward's sister, the Duchess of Suffolk; for the first few months she was kept at Windsor; she was permitted to keep Lady Vaux with her and two other women, the issue rolls show woolen and velvet cloths brought to replenish her wardrobe and her expenses were sometimes as much as a hundred shillings a week.

The Duke of Exeter was Edward's brother-in-law, and guilty as he was Edward sent him to the Tower; he could have his life but not his liberty. As for the only heir of Lancaster who was left, young Henry Tudor and his uncle Jasper Tudor fled to France, only a storm blew them ashore in Brittany and they found themselves the "guests" of Francis of Brittany. Since no one from Edward to Louis to Jasper Tudor could trust Francis, none of the principals were happy about this except Francis who, perceiving he had a fine pawn in his hands, insisted gently that they stay and did not permit them to leave his domains. The Bastard of Fauconberg was pardoned and sent north with Richard of Gloucester to assist in the keeping of the peace in the North.

But there were pleasant duties too. One was the rewarding of the people who had helped "his Elizabeth." Money and pensions were showered on her doctor and the children's nurses. The Abbot Milling was called to sit on the privy council and elected to the bishopric of Hereford. As for John Gould, who had supplied

Bessie and her household with one beef and two muttons weekly, he received at Edward's hands just what he wanted: leave to load a royal ship with hides and tallow to be sold abroad.

On the twenty-sixth of June Edward's seven-month-old son was created Prince of Wales and a week later borne high in his godfather's arms, Abbot Milling now Bishop, in the Parliamentary chamber; all the temporal and spiritual lords who were in London took the oath of allegiance to the baby Prince as the undoubted heir to the throne. Although little Edward needed his nurse, Alice Welles, more than anyone else, the King's little son had a chancellor, his godfather, Abbot Milling, a steward and a chamberlain; he possessed already the Duchy of Cornwall, the Principality of Wales and the County of Chester, and his three uncles were empowered to administer his affairs, together with Lord Hastings, until he reached his majority.

It was a beautiful July. "What I dreaded within the sanctuary," Bessie told Edward, "was not the fact that thieves and murderers were part of the sanctuary too along with us. It was the lack of fresh air and the confinement and the worry the children would get sick. But they hadn't. They were all well."

Edward, in the garden at her side, thought again how perfect their marriage was; June's sunny days had taken away the pallor she had had when he had first seen her that spring, and she was beginning to bloom like a rose, he thought, with the child she was carrying.

As for the field of foreign affairs, Edward was now undisputably the King of England; even Louis was disposed to be friendly; Charles was momentarily grateful because he knew that if Warwick had won Barnet Field he would have had to go down on his knees to Louis; Francis of Brittany had helped Edward and the Hansards were waiting for their treaties of trade.

On his faithful young brother, Richard of Gloucester, Edward bestowed the great Chamberlainship, which post Warwick had held, and the wardenship of the west marches. Included among those duties were immense grants of land—all Warwick's vast estates in Yorkshire and Cumberland, including the great castle of Middleham, where Richard would live and there he would keep the peace of the north with Lord Percy. Richard was not yet twenty but he had proved his fidelity and his ability.

A pardon was extended to John Neville's young son who had

been in Calais, and the Archbishop of York, George Neville, was released from the Tower and confirmed in his robes; he was one of the lords who knelt and pledged allegiance to little Edward, and he had been permitted to return to York and take up his duties there.

But there were unrest and seethings in a country so lately released from its struggling. And day after day Edward struggled to take up the reins of government into his hands once more and to deal with the multiplying problems that beset a King on every side.

Early in June Anthony came before him with a petition to be allowed to go to the Holy Land to fight the Saracens, because he had vowed it when they were abroad. This request, when he needed every man at his side, drove Edward into sudden black anger. He brought his mighty fist down onto his table and Anthony retreated in panic. For one wild moment Edward was pure Plantagenet: Anthony could imagine him calling a palace guard.

"For the mercy of God," Edward exploded. "Who is your master, the Pope or me!"

Anthony begged forgiveness hastily.

Edward was still outraged. "You are the only one of my son's advisers who is able to help now!" Hastings was in Calais, Richard in Middleham. And Edward had no faith in Clarence. "The administration of his estates is only one of your jobs. Shall he grow up penniless?"

Anthony again asked Edward to forgive his thoughtlessness. Edward was still scowling.

"Your request is denied," he muttered quite unnecessarily. "And I have no need of impractical and thoughtless councilors."

With this warning Anthony left the room much chastened.

That day his temper was not further improved by Clarence. Clarence had heard that Richard had asked Edward for Anne Neville to wife. While he listened to Clarence's complaints Edward wondered if Clarence realized how stupid and selfish he was. Possessor already of vast estates his mouth was now watering with Anne Neville's share of her mother's inheritances, and he was desperately jealous of Richard being endowed with Middleham. In effect he wanted all of Warwick's vast holdings and Warwick's Countess' holdings too. In towering impatience Edward suddenly got to his feet and said he would hear nothing further,

nothing at all. "You hold still the lieutenancy of Ireland," Edward said coldly, "and we are not at all sure you either deserve
it or can administer it!"

But he was not through. From his height he surveyed Clarence
with eyes that were both angry and pitiless. "I warn you, George,
that you will regret any act of bad faith with every drop of blood
in your veins!"

Clarence backed away like a snarling dog. And Edward
wrenched his mind from his brother; Edward was both an ex-
porter and an importer and he had scheduled his next hour with
his Italian agent, for he was anxious to set his financial affairs
rolling again, his ships to furrowing the seas; it was one of Edward's foremost policies: that a nation needed a strong monarchy
and a wealthy King and that was one reason why the administration of his son's estates was such an important consideration in
his mind and why he had reminded Anthony of it.

Clarence slunk home to Isabel, who was not able to give him
much help. She knew that it was because of Clarence that her
mother was still in Beaulieu Abbey. From its walls she had writ
many piteous letters and to everyone it was a mystery why Edward kept her there, for it was not his custom nor was it typical.
The Countess had even petitioned Edward's little daughter,
young Bess. The letter was answered by young Bess' secretary;
young Bess already had her personal staff. But then it began to
be plain to all that it was to mollify Clarence that the Countess
was not permitted her freedom or to recover her estates. Edward
realized cynically that the only way he could bind Clarence to
him was by bribery. Isabel said, "But, my lord, we have so much!
And my mother—"

Anne Neville twisted unhappily in her chair. Poor Isabel, she
thought; she looks as though she won't live out the day; even I
look stronger than Isabel, and she wished she could do something to help, but she knew if she as much as opened her mouth
Clarence would turn on her, outraged.

Clarence said, "I was promised all your mother's estates!"

"His Grace never promised that," Isabel said steadily. "And you
know it."

My God, will he strike her? Anne wondered. She got to her
feet and went over to Isabel, her slight figure rigid with sudden

hatred for Clarence. "My sister is going to have a baby," she said. "And you're upsetting her."

Clarence roared, "Don't you dare talk to me that way! And you may address me as I deserve."

Anne licked her lips. "And how would that be?" she said aloud, her eyes black with mockery, for Clarence had a sure way about him of making even the mildest person fight him. "Why don't you go to your wine bottle and leave us alone?"

Isabel stared at Anne in astonishment at her courage. Anne said, "When I think of my mother and my sister why don't you do something to help?"

Clarence had one of his swift changes of mood. He even smiled. "I am trying to help you, little Anne. You will see. I am going to try to protect you from the attentions of my brother too."

Anne said, "It is not because Richard is your brother. It is not Richard. It is that I am not ready for marriage."

I am like a little bone between two angry snarling kennel dogs, she thought. She wished desperately she could put her plight before Edward but she didn't see how she could; she made up her mind to see Bessie.

Anne sent a letter to Bessie and her private audience was scheduled for three mornings hence. But before she could keep it Richard of Gloucester himself appeared, elegant, slight, smiling. He didn't encounter Clarence because he had planned it that way, and he took Anne outside into the garden. There, seated side by side on a stone bench, he told her he had asked Edward for permission to marry her.

Anne deliberately took refuge in childish shyness. Her eyes on the hands in her lap, she told Richard she was not well, that she had suffered much and that she didn't think she would make anyone a good wife.

Richard put his hand gently over hers. "I am determined to have you for my wife."

For my money, Anne thought. For my mother's vast estates.

"We were happy as children. We can be happy now."

Anne said, "You have changed, Richard." She turned to look squarely at him, searching his face as if to see what the change had been and whether she was right.

His eyes fell from hers. She said low, "Please give me time to think, Richard." She took refuge again in her youth. "I am but sixteen and I am not strong. Let me recover a bit." She tried a small smile and an appeal of her eyes.

With this he had to be satisfied. He had to go north but he would be back soon.

Bessie listened quietly to Anne's plea for her mother and for herself: She wished not to wed yet. She tried to explain to Anne that Edward was going to make no hasty decision about the Countess' estates because of the delicate balance between his two brothers. As for the marriage: "The King, my husband, does not wish to personally interfere between his two brothers, wishing instead that they will settle their difficulties without his being an arbiter." Bessie paused. "It would be best if His Grace did not lean this way or the other, for he does not want to make more trouble in his family." Poor Edward, Bessie thought. What he wishes is impossible.

"My Lady Anne," she said, "His Grace is going to suggest that a commission of lords or lawyers listen to his two brothers' pleas so that a court should settle this quarrel between them."

Bessie felt sorry for Anne. She thought, If Richard had said plain, "I love her," Edward would have listened. But he made no such plea. Bessie thought, How lucky, how fortune has smiled on the two of us. It is right and fair that I should have Anne Neville, Richard had said in effect. For all I have done. The greatest heiress in the kingdom, I deserve her.

"And perhaps he does," Edward had said, frowning. It was impossible for Edward to completely understand. He felt vaguely sorry for Richard. "It is a materialistic age we live in," he said to Bessie.

"A plague on both of them," he added testily.

"So you see, my Lady Anne," Bessie concluded, "His Grace will not interfere."

Anne sat very still. She seemed so young. Bessie said, "Many women are contracted early in life. You will have children. You must remind yourself that it is a fine marriage. And Richard is the Duke of Gloucester; there are many women who would be happy to marry him."

Anne Neville sighed. Bessie thought there is something about

Richard that I don't like either and yet I shouldn't dare say so. Wordlessly Bessie nodded her head. "I can't help you," she said honestly. "I can't interfere. His Grace is very, very fond of Richard, a brother whose fidelity has shone so bright. In contrast," Bessie added boldly, implicating Clarence's treachery and selfishness.

"I understand, Your Grace," Anne said. The future loomed before her in all its bleakness. Her mother in sanctuary under guard and she living in a house with Clarence while two men contended coldly for her wealth. She would almost rather Clarence had it but then how would she exist, she and her mother? She was under no illusions about Clarence; once he got his hands on her inheritance she could look for not even a room under his roof, she was sure.

"You are very young," Bessie said. "It is hard to be practical when you are young but you may have to take a practical step."

"Yes," Anne said. "Yes, I may."

But she was not ready yet. Even in two weeks she was not ready. Richard was returning from the north; Edward had arranged that his brothers, as Bessie had said, argue their case in front of their peers and lawyers; Edward was disgusted. Richard wanted to marry Anne and Clarence opposed this because he, and he only, through his wife Isabel should inherit all of the vast Beauchamp and Warwick estates. Richard was coming back and it was four o'clock in the afternoon. It was September and rain beat against the windows and Anne Neville was suddenly conscious only of fright, the same kind of fright she had suffered in France. I can't do it, she thought desperately. She fled out of her room and into the chamber where Clarence was dining, even without knocking.

"You'll have to help me," she said. "You'll have to get me out of here!"

Clarence leaped to his feet in excitement. "Of course!" he cried. "Of course I will, Anne!"

So the world tasted a little sweeter to Clarence that week, the world which he usually found so sour and disappointing. In fact he actually found himself looking forward to Richard's visit. And when it came he was supremely ready; his face had lost its usual sulky look, although when he beheld Edward's favorite brother his twinges of jealousy couldn't help but show.

"The Lady Anne?" he said, in answer to Richard's direct question. "The Lady Anne?" Clarence asked, prolonging the suspense with relish. He looked about the room as though expecting her to materialize.

Richard said, "Where is she, George? I want to speak with her."

"Oh, indeed," said Clarence. "I expect you do. But I doubt if she is here. I mean I haven't seen her about recently. I don't believe I have."

Richard's eyes grew dark and menacing. "What do you mean?"

"Mean?" asked Clarence. "Why, I mean I haven't seen her. I don't think she is with us anymore."

"You don't think she is? Don't you know?"

Clarence grinned. "Not really. I hear you had more trouble with the Bastard of Fauconberg."

"Yes, I did," Richard said. "So I ordered his execution." His brilliant eyes looked straight at Clarence. "May I speak with the Lady Isabel then?"

"No," Clarence said. "She is not well. She is expecting a child." Clarence knew that Richard liked to believe he was very prim and not given to Edward's lusty loins, as he called Edward's earthiness. "How is your son? How is your own bastard?" Clarence gibed. "It's a wonder to me you didn't order him strangled in his cradle to keep faith with your reputation."

Richard turned and left the room. The big door closed on his elegant figure and Clarence was left standing; the faintest bit of fear pricked him. Richard was odd, there was no doubt about it. Clarence went over to the sideboard and poured himself a cup of wine; he poured it very full and had to sip it before he could carry it over to his chair.

Richard was very efficient. And his commands were very brief. What he wanted his henchmen to accomplish was simple; the Lady Anne was hidden somewhere, probably in London; his servants were to find her and find her quickly. He made a brief list of Clarence's adherents and friends; the hunt was to start with those names. And all sanctuaries were to be checked for her whereabouts.

The hunt was on. But Anne didn't know it. She was sitting on a kitchen stool, her slender hands already red from their unaccustomed labors; her long hair tied securely in a kerchief, her waist encircled in a large apron which fell all about her almost to the floor.

Kitchen work began early and ended late. In her narrow bed on the top floor in company with ten other women she slept dreamlessly every night, for she was doing the simplest of tasks, the washing of the pots and pans, the scrubbing of the tables and the stoves and even sweeping the stone floors, for she could not be entrusted with the making of pastries or the concoction of a jelly.

None of her fellow workers knew her identity. "I'm from the country, from Wensleydale," Anne had said, making her Yorkshire accent as thick as had been her favorite stableboy's. I truly am from the country, Anne thought. Here in the kitchen of a London town house it was difficult to imagine the moors of Yorkshire. She had sat down for a moment to eat a bit of black bread and cheese for her supper. The smell of stewing fish was strong; two weeks ago it would have turned her stomach, and it was with some surprise and confidence that she realized she was hungry; the black bread tasted good and so did the milk she sipped with it. And she felt perfectly safe and secure in the warm kitchen. No one would dream of looking here for the heiress of my lord of Warwick. Anne stretched out her legs and wiggled her toes.

"Here, lass," said the cook, breaking off a piece of pastry. "I rolled this extra."

Anne bit into the sugary goodness. "Um," she said. "It's heavenly." There were some crumbs still in her palm and she bore them to her mouth and licked her hand clean of them.

Her hand was still at her mouth when the door burst open.

The kitchens of this house stretched back toward a small courtyard, which opened onto an alley. Two men now stood on the threshold of the long, low room; it was raining outside, and they stamped their cold feet on the stones and looked carefully at each aproned female in the kitchen.

The cook was outraged. She waved her wooden spoon and made to hit one of them. "Get out of here!"

The first man pushed her aside. "Interference with the Duke of

Gloucester will mean prison," he said shortly. His eyes roved about the room; the badge of the boar was obvious on his sleeve, so all knew he was telling the truth. "Now answer truthfully. Which one of these women has been recently come here?" But his eyes were already on Anne and in desperation she saw that he knew who she was; he was just waiting for the cook to confirm it.

The cook hesitated. She didn't want to give Anne away. But what could she do? And what trouble was the little lass in? The cook tried to help. "You're not taking away any of my helpers! Nay, even for the Duke! What has she done?"

He didn't answer; his eyes were studying Anne.

"You're not going to put her in prison?" the cook cried. "She's not done nothing!"

There was silence. To the cook's amazement the intruder now bowed to Anne. "My Lady Anne," he said. "My master has sent me."

Anne felt despair. How if she refused to go! Then Richard himself might come. Her hands clenched. She lifted her head proudly as she rose.

"And your orders once you had found me? What were they?"

"To escort you to sanctuary. To St. Martin's le Grand."

"Very well," Anne said. "I shall go." She turned to one of the youngest girls. "If you will fetch me my cloak, please."

She stood still; there was no sound in the kitchen; the women gathered about her protectively although they knew they could do nothing to help, but still they clustered close.

Anne's new-made friend brought her cloak and her small bag. Without a word Anne reached in it for her odds and ends of chains and pins. These poor hardworking girls had befriended her when she was friendless. With big bright tears in her eyes she put all her pieces of jewelry on the kitchen table. "There will be something for each of you, with my thanks," she tried to keep her voice even. She pulled from her finger her only ring. "For you," she said to the cook.

Then Richard's henchman wrapped her cloak about her shoulders; she didn't dare turn and look back but she went out the door into the slanting rain and cold. Within the kitchen the women gathered about the table. The youngest girl cried and the cook said, "Ah, the poor young lass, how kind a great lady."

"She wanted to stay with us." They couldn't comprehend exactly what had happened but it was a great exciting and heartbreaking event. Lord Vernon's dinner that night was burned.

That summer the plague had raged in London. Too busy to leave Westminster Edward thought he must have swallowed about ten pounds of medicine, to say nothing of the rest of his family, but all were well and when Bessie and he told the court she was carrying another child, he announced they would all go on pilgrimage to Canterbury with all the court. Such a procession had never been seen before, there were so many great lords and ladies and of course the King and Queen.

The September days were sunny and warm, and the countryside greeted them with pleasure. When he returned to London Edward issued a general pardon, and even John Fortesque, Margaret of Anjou's devoted and wise friend and counselor, applied for pardon; and as he was indeed too wise and honest and valuable a public servant, Edward asked him to write publicly the right of the house of York to the throne and made him a member of his own council. So many men applied for pardon that the lists covered thirty-five sheets of parchments and included all those who had fought at Tewkesbury or Barnet. Only Jasper Tudor and the Earl of Oxford remained, one in Brittany, the other in France. Before Edward had permitted George Neville, Archbishop, to return and take up his duties in his diocese of York.

During October and November he signed another treaty with Louis, knitted up the strands of friendship between him and Charles and between England and Brittany; hassled with the Hansards, saw with satisfaction that despite the winter seas, the port of London was busy as usual and James of Scotland was disposed to be friendly. In the north Lord Percy had taken the oath of allegiance to Richard and Richard had vowed to be Percy's "good true lord." But much that Edward accomplished was overshadowed in his own peace of mind by the continuing quarrel over Anne Neville.

The two warring brothers had presented their respective cases before three courts and their peers, and every time judgment was refused and passed on and Edward knew with certainty that the whole mess would be tossed into his lap. Nonetheless he resolved to have a merry, festive Christmas. He and Bessie had spent the previous Christmas far apart, his loyal lords had passed the season either in exile or sanctuary or even in prison; the whole country had been deep in the gloom and apprehension that comes with uncertain rulers. This Christmas they would celebrate at Westminster and it would be a fine reminder to his subjects that he was their King again.

On Christmas day then he and Bessie walked together, both of them crowned. Bessie's glittering diamonds matching her starry eyes. They proceeded to the White Hall with all the court coming after and kept their estate, and there music and a mass at which the Bishop of Rochester officiated. After dinner there was more music and a play, which must have been quite elaborately staged as it cost Edward fifty marks.

New Year's Day Bessie and Edward again went in procession, Bessie wearing the great collars of emeralds which had been Edward's New Year's gift. And on Twelfth Day they both kept estate in White Hall again and they entertained the mayor and aldermen and many merchants to dinner. Bessie wore again her great collar of emeralds but she said to Edward that her crown was uncomfortable and she had difficulty walking straight to keep it on her head.

"After all," she said, "I am six months pregnant."

Edward grinned. "Don't wear it then, sweetheart," he said indulgently.

They had managed to ignore the frosty looks between Richard and Clarence and to take great pleasure together in Christmas. On the morning of New Year's Day Edward had come into Bessie's room to bring his gift. She was sitting in bed with the children presenting their gifts at the bed rail and the little Prince holding tight to the rail with both fat hands, looking with wonderment on the array of beautiful boxes and gay ribbons, boxes full of sweetmeats and painted hoops and toys and even an illuminated book for his father that little Edward was not permitted to touch, only look. There were big brass bowls of holly in the room and his mother was laughing and talking; Edward couldn't get her attention so he opened his mouth to let out a large wail when his father picked him up from behind. Edward's mouth closed on his cry and he turned his head to see who held him.

"It's just your father," Edward said, and his son's eyes studied him; then Edward hugged and kissed him and wished him a Happy New Year, and tucked him in bed alongside his mother, and that is when he gave her the collar of emeralds. He had gift rings for his daughters and for the Duchess and for his mother, and for little Edward's nurse, a magnificent bolt of material for a gown which had cost the enormous sum of ten pounds, it was so beautiful.

New Year's Day was a cold and clear day, and after dinner Richard of Gloucester went to pay his respects to the woman he wanted, at the sanctuary of St. Martin's le Grand. He had a pearl chain for Anne with a beautiful pearl and diamond cross suspended from it, and it was nestled in a jeweler's box from Florence. Richard was dressed in white velvet; Anthony Woodville had a habit of affecting white velvet, and much as he disliked Anthony Richard did approve his taste in dress. Richard was fond of wearing little jewelry save for one magnificent piece; on his velvet cap he wore a medallion with one huge diamond in its center, surrounded by four square-cut emeralds almost half an inch square, with four pearls tucked into the corner of the piece.

Anne had had eight weeks in which to assemble her thoughts and set herself in readiness for this encounter. News had filtered into the sanctuary from outside its cloistering walls and she knew of the arguments pro and con of the King's two brothers.

Oddly enough, she thought, had it been Clarence she didn't want to marry Edward would have listened. But it was impossible to plead with the King that she wanted no part of his faithful young Richard, because he would have little sympathy. Nor could she point to another man; if she could the King might listen. But untouched by love, alone and confined, she knew that as the daughter of an attained rebel, she was at the mercy of the Duke of Gloucester and the only weapons that she had were that she was a woman. This frail girl now summoned all her strength of will, all the strength of mind of her mighty ancestors; she would never have her father's flamboyance and spirit but it could still burn low and steady in his daughter.

Isabel had sent her pretty red woolen for a gown, which she had helped the nuns make. It was gay and suited her dark beauty. She had gained some confidence too. She realized that there were few girls who would have fled from Richard disguised as a kitchen maid; now that she had done it she was aware that she did indeed have some of the spirit of her legendary parent. When Richard saw her he was aware of the subtle change in her too. He attributed it to the dress, and he was conscious also suddenly of her femaleness, her very thinness; the bony beauty of her body suggested a barely concealed sexual excitement. Anne Neville curtsied deeply to the Duke of Gloucester. He took her hand to raise her and his touch sent a shiver through her; she didn't know whether or not it was pleasurable.

They sat side by side on a velvet-covered bench. Richard presented his gift; Anne thanked him politely and regretted that she was in no position to have bought gifts for anyone, even her dearest mother; she had been able to send her only a few handkerchiefs, embroidered by her own hands.

Does she reproach me for her mother? Richard wondered. He was wearing a ring and he twisted it about his finger absently; Anne was to become used to this familiar habit. He said, "It is Clarence who keeps your mother in Beaulieu. The King, my brother, is trying to pacify Clarence." Anne cast her eyes down on her ringless hands; she was silent. And impelled by the silence Richard whispered, "I will do all I can, Anne. I truly will."

For a moment he had sounded just like he used to when they were children and she smiled at him gratefully, suddenly feeling more rapport between them and she was grateful for it. "Oh, Dickon," she said, using the old familiar nickname, "if you could my lady mother would be so happy. And so should I."

"Anne," he said, "I will take you to Middleham."

She sighed deeply. "I would like that," she conceded.

"There is much that needs to be done, Anne. Your father has neglected Middleham in all his plans."

"Oh," said Anne turning concerned eyes on him, for she loved Middleham. "When do you go back?"

"Not until I get our marriage settled," Richard said. "I want to marry you, Anne, you know that. Edward has promised to aid me and he will speak with Clarence himself now. Since the courts would not decide for either of us, His Grace the King will have to decide and it will be in our favor, he promised me."

Anne turned to look at him as he spoke. His dark eyes were serious and honest and there was an appeal in them to which she responded.

"Dickon," she said, "we are cousins."

"Not first cousins."

"No, but we shall need a dispensation. Isabel and Clarence did."

Richard now fondled the hilt of his dagger rather nervously. He didn't want to wait for a dispensation and he wasn't going to wait. "We'll marry first," he said. "I wait on no man, Pope or not."

Anne said, "Dickon, you sound like a tyrannical spoiled boy."

Briefly his eyes flashed with anger, then it subsided. "We won't wait, Anne," he said flatly, "just until we get Edward's permission."

Anne felt a little uneasy; one minute he was her old childhood friend, the next minute he was an unexplicable stranger. He was shoving his dagger back and forth into its sheath, his fingers around the hilt.

"Is it my money you want or me, Richard?" she asked.

She had sounded just like her father. Richard's eyes were bright and the answer was suddenly true, he thought. "I want you, Anne," he said.

But he did have to wait. Five weeks later, early in February, he went with Bessie and Edward and Clarence to Shene, where Edward was seeing to rebuilding, and Edward used this time to persuade Clarence to agree to the marriage. Clarence was surly.

"I'll agree to having her as my sister-in-law but I won't agree to any partition of her lands."

Edward thought coldly that after all he could free the Countess of Warwick and let her give every blessed acre to Anne. But he said, "So be it then." Clarence was rewarded with the earldoms of Warwick and Salisbury and the great Chamberlainship of the realm, which had been Richard's. Clarence did surrender some lands to Richard in the north since Richard already held Middleham and Sheriff Hutton. Richard seemed satisfied; Edward doubted if Clarence would ever be satisfied until the crown was placed on his head, and this thought troubled Edward more deeply than his stupid brother realized.

Richard left Shene hastily, and without sending word ahead reached Anne in sanctuary early in the morning.

"We may marry," he said breathlessly.

He had taken her hands in his and they were icy cold; it was bitter outside. She shivered and drew back her hands.

"We can marry now," Richard said.

"Without a dispensation?" Anne asked, troubled, uncertain.

"Do you want a big wedding?" he countered.

She shook her head. It would be in bad taste with her father recently dead and her wonderful uncle John and her mother in sanctuary. And most of all she shoved out of her mind her child-ish dreams of a marriage, a big gay wedding at Middleham with all her friends and her father's friends; she had often thought about it. The King would come and she, Anne, would have a white brocade dress, falling straight, edged with pearls and rubies and a flat square train and the chapel would be full of flowers and her own confessor would say the words over her and her love's head; and then there would be feasting and dancing. "I used to dream of a big wedding," Anne said simply. "But along with a lot of other childhood dreams that has disappeared too." The simple way she said it affected Richard of Gloucester. All the happy wonderful days in Middleham suddenly were alive again. He went down on one knee before the standing Anne and took her hand and kissed it.

"Marry me today, Anne," he said. "If you please."

Anne laid the tip of her fingers on his dark head. Was she older and wiser than he? "As you wish, Richard," she said.

"I hope to God they'll be happy," Edward said. Ten years ago he had been twenty; it seemed a long time ago. He was a bit nonplussed by Richard; he couldn't understand why he had not waited for his dispensation; it seemed like such a hole-in-corner affair when it was not necessary. Maybe it is his youth, Edward thought, and yet he had never said frankly, "I love her." Edward lifted his massive shoulders.

"They seem so very young," Bessie said. "But they both love Middleham. It should be a suitable marriage."

Edward said flatly, "She is too frail for children." Richard's

motives could easily be mendacious but Edward often shoved
unpleasant suspicions from his mind; he didn't want to be suspicious. He knew well enough that Richard was ambitious; let
him be ambitious then in the north, like the man who had trained
him, Anne's father. If he couldn't be King, then he could be
what Warwick had been; maybe that's why he wanted Anne,
Edward thought, to recapture and relive the legendary figure of
the great Earl.

"It suits him," Edward said. "He'll be happy there and he will
accomplish much." As far as children were concerned he and
Bessie had plenty, but he wanted to get her back to Windsor
soon, for it was more pleasant there than anywhere else to await
the birth of her baby.

Bessie went into retirement the second week in March; she
was growing impatient at these enforced seclusions. Edward did
the best he could; he sent a pair of puppies, a beautiful chess set
from Italy, handcarved and gilded; she had Anthony's book on
The Dictes and Sayings of the Philosophers which he was translating; it pleased her to help and she and the Duchess tried to
copy Anthony's style.

Her baby was born April tenth. Edward and she had decided
if it was a girl to name her after Edward's sister, the Duchess of
Burgundy, who had helped him and of whom he was so fond,
so the new baby was christened Margaret. Spring enfolded the
land once more and once more Louis was weaving and spin-
ning a web of intrigue.

Not more than two weeks after Margaret's birth advices
reached Edward that the Earl of Oxford, aided and abetted by
Louis, by George Neville and indeed even by the sulky Duke
of Clarence, was plotting against the peace of the realm.

Edward had been on very friendly terms recently with George
Neville. He had been the King's hunting companion and dinner
guest; on his knees he had sworn allegiance to the little Prince.
He had even been informed that the King would come to his
home, the Moor, to stay and hunt for a few days. George Neville
got out the plate and valuables he had hidden away and prepared to entertain Edward when instead he received a summons
to attend the King at Windsor. There he was promptly arrested
and sent at night to the coast and from there by ship to Hammes

Castle for internment. With some cynicism Edward seized his temporal goods, had a crown made out of the Archbishop's miter, and gave all the plate and jewels to his little son, the Prince of Wales. He summoned Clarence, who was both uneasy and evasive; there was no doubt in Edward's mind that he had joined in the communications between Oxford and the Archbishop, but if Edward had proof it is lost. Peremptorily he dismissed Clarence from his presence. As for Oxford, he was in France, making raids on Calais and on English shipping; Louis' motive of course was simply to keep Edward busy at home so he could not cast longing eyes on France. For the largest single plank on which Edward's foreign policy rested was the inevitable confrontation of his principal enemy, Louis, and Edward was now ready to load the bombards and to begin to fire the opening salvos. So out went the writs and Parliament was summoned to meet in early fall; all summer embassies and ambassadors came and went from other lands. The most important of these would be Edward's host in Holland, the Seigneur de Gruthuyse, who had helped Edward so much during his exile.

Le Seigneur's entertainment and his lodgings were left to Bessie, and these arrangements took much thought and threw a good deal of light upon her.

Careful instructions went out first to the towns and men who would greet England's guest on his landing and who should meet him and what he should be fed and how the townspeople were encouraged to make him welcome.

It was a glorious, clear, golden fall day when Gruthuyse arrived at Windsor, where Hastings greeted him, presented other noblemen of Edward's court and then immediately took him to Bessie and Edward. After the greeting he was taken to three great chambers set aside for his use, and after he had refreshed himself Bessie and Edward appeared again quite informally and they all had dinner together quietly in his rooms.

After dinner Bessie asked him if he would not like to meet her ladies and her children, and they walked together side by side to Bessie's chambers.

Gruthuyse was charmed at the informal picture. Bessie's ladies, pretty and young, were playing at *marteaux*, a game with balls as small as marbles and ninepins of ivory. There was music and dancing. Edward danced with his little daughter Elizabeth. Gruthuyse was charmed. The children, he thought. The little Princesses curtsied and smiled, little Cecily still holding one of the marbles in her hand.

Gruthuyse did not dance. "You are weary," Bessie said. "We should send you off to bed. Before breakfast tomorrow we celebrate the mass of Our Lady." Her dazzling smile accompanied these words and Gruthuyse, sturdy Dutchman that he was, had the same pleasant sense of drowning that Bessie's smile could produce in men.

After mass the next morning Edward presented Gruthuyse with a covered cup of gold that Bessie had chosen as a gift, for it was a unique piece, she thought; it had a large piece of unicorn's horn on it, carved, instead of the usual jewels.

"After breakfast," Bessie said, looking as radiant as the morning, "I want to present to you my son."

Gruthuyse glanced at her face as the little Prince was brought out by his chamberlain. He walked with all the dignity that a little boy who was not quite two could muster. Bessie was so proud of him that her eyes were enormous. Small Edward bowed and held out his small hand.

"His Grace, the Prince of Wales," his chamberlain said. This was Master Vaughn and it was quite clear Master Vaughn was also so proud of his charge that he could hardly contain it.

Edward bowed again. He told his mother and father good morning. Then formality was abandoned and Bessie lifted him up and kissed him; then taking his hand in hers, with Master Vaughn coming behind, they all went outside to the little park.

The horse which awaited Gruthuyse out there had been the subject of a long search by Bessie and she had asked Edward's advice too, so the upshot of it was that Gruthuyse received Edward's own horse and to accompany the gift, a royal crossbow, the string of silk, the case covered with Edward's colors, in velvet, with his arms and badges embroidered on it.

They had dinner in the lodge at Windsor and after dinner some hunting. It was growing dark. Bessie said, "We wanted to show you the gardens and the vineyards. Is it too late?"

Gruthuyse didn't think it was too late. He and Bessie and Edward strolled through the gardens and the vineyards which were

Edward's special joy and pleasure. They walked back across the park toward the darkening castle.

"Now we usually hear evensong," Bessie said. "His Grace is fond of this part of the day."

That first day Bessie had planned should be mostly in the open air with the informal meal at the lodge, and Gruthuyse had seemed to enjoy it. The second day of his stay was to be more formal, and so Bessie was giving a banquet in his honor in her own chambers.

The tables were arranged in threes. Gruthuyse and his son sat at the same table with Bessie and Edward, the little Princess Elizabeth sitting next her father. The Duke and Duchess of Buckingham sat there too, Kate Woodville being as charming and pretty as ever; Hastings sat with them and Anne Bourchier, Bessie's sister. At a side table sat some of Bessie's ladies, all on one side so they could be seen. The room was not large enough to contain another table, so in the next room the rest of Bessie's gentlewomen and Gruthuyse's attendants sat together at another long table.

There was music of course. After dinner the tables were cleared away and the dancing began, and the little Princess Elizabeth danced with her cousin the Duke of Buckingham. At nine o'clock the festivities came to a close with the King's minstrels.

Once more, informally and with grace, Bessie and Edward, accompanied by the prettiest of Bessie's ladies, including her sister Kate, conducted Gruthuyse to three chambers.

The three chambers Bessie had labored over. Carpets covered the entire floors. They were hung with white silk, which made them pleasant and airy. In the first chamber the bed was of the best down Bessie could obtain, with sheets of white linen and a counterpoint of gold, furred with ermine, a canopy of cloth of gold and curtains of white sarcenet, while the pillows were Bessie's own.

In the next chamber there was another great bed, all hanged and in white, a couch with feather beds and a cupboard. In the third room Bessie had prepared baths, covered with tents of white cloth.

On the cupboard had been displayed green ginger, comfits and goblets of gold in which to drink the hippocras. Gruthuyse did indeed permit the Lord Chamberlain to undress him and prepare him for the bath and later partook with him of the comfits and the wine. Bessie and Edward had said good night.

Edward had wanted his hospitality to Gruthuyse to be as fitting as the debt he owed him, for no man had ever found a stauncher friend than he. Edward was particularly pleased.

"The chambers were beautiful, Bessie."

"I wanted him to see the way we lived too," Bessie said. "And the children and the gardens."

Edward said, "Everything was perfect and most of all he enjoyed it, I could see. You made him welcome. Going with him to show him his rooms and going to bid him good night."

Edward was escorting his guest the next day to Westminster, for now the formal part of the Seigneur's visit began.

Edward opened Parliament the next day, the sixth of October. This was a very important Parliament for him; it signified that he, Edward, was indeed the only and sole sovereign lord of the realm; it was the first Parliament since his return and it was to be witnessed by the Seigneur de Gruthuyse. But perhaps even more important he was now going to state openly that the ancient enemy of England was Louis, and Louis alone.

But first the Speaker, with Edward sitting in royal robes with the cap of maintenance on his handsome head, had to bring his hearers up-to-date.

So he began by thanking God for the safe return and mighty overthrow of his enemies by their sovereign lord himself. Then, "Our Queen, how we commend the womanly behavior and the great constancy of our Queen in time of great sorrow and trouble when His Majesty was beyond the seas, and the great joy and surety of this land in the birth of the Prince!"

The Speaker then thanked the Lord Gruthuyse for his great kindness and humanity that was shown to the King when he was in Holland.

The Speaker even mentioned Clarence, but briefly as Edward had told him. Then he went on. Who was the instigator of all our inward troubles? A man called Louis. Yet His Majesty had made sure and certain alliances with Burgundy, with Brittany and with the King of Aragon and even with Scotland, and he warned the lords and commons that if those dukedoms were denied the help they sought against Louis, they might cease to be England's friends and become her enemies or they might be overthrown, in which case the King of France would be mightier than ever. Not only would England's commerce, especially her vital trade with Burgundy and the Low Countries, be destroyed but she would be surrounded by powerful adversaries and forsaken by her friends.

The Speaker, plus the Archbishop of Canterbury and other of Edward's council, spoke, pointing out that Scipio, when the Romans despaired of defending their country against Hannibal, instead went to Carthage and won his victory there. For all nations knew through long history that an offensive war was better than a defensive one and the place to fight was never in one's own country but in the enemy's; these were true and tested maxims which no man could deny, nor wish to deny. It was obvious that to keep French armies from England English armies had to go to France.

So what was their King asking? Nothing less than taxes for war on France.

Chapter 17

EDWARD KNEW the temper of his people pretty well. The Lords of Parliament were so aroused that they even voted a tenth tax upon themselves.

But what Edward's subjects didn't realize was that part of these speeches were political ploys and that the King himself had no intention of setting out to wage war on French soil until he was sure of both of his allies, Brittany and Burgundy, and sure of peace in Scotland; and he wanted to settle his affairs with Denmark which were at their lowest ebb. Closeted night after night with ambassadors going and coming, with secret instructions of which many have never reached the light of day, October and November weeks went by and Christmas was coming, and with that December came the first loss that Bessie and Edward had to face together.

On a bleak, cold December morning Bessie was called to the bedside of her last child, the little Margaret scarce eight months old. White-faced nurses and ladies clustered around the child.

"A sudden raging fever and a cough."

For three days Bessie kept her vigil beside her baby. Edward could scarcely bear to enter the room and scarcely bear to leave it. Helplessly, in the very prime of his manhood, he watched in agony his little daughter's struggle to breathe, and every once in a while the little plaintive cry for help from the infant went to the King's heart and the bright tears would come into his eyes as he knelt beside her bed, praying.

"Oh, my God, Bessie, I can't stand it!"

The Princess Margaret died the third day of her illness. Edward decreed that she be placed in a tiny tomb alongside of her greatest ancestor. It was just before Christmas. Bessie and Edward knelt there together in Westminster Abbey at the altar end before St. Edward's shrine. The tiny sarcophagus of gray marble which Bessie picked you may still see, nestled close to the tomb of Edward III.

That winter Bessie had a new worry, a woman called Jane Shore.

It was inevitable that the King would find Jane sooner or later. The prostitute with the heart of gold, the lilting laugh, the quick, sweet mind and the everlasting favors of the body which she can so lovingly and gaily bestow, this legendary prostitute who never exists did exist in Jane. It was as though she had sprung fully panoplied from the loins of Eros.

Bessie had never seen her; she was afraid to. First there were only rumors about Hastings' latest harlot. Then came the whispered reports that the King had taken his pleasure with her one night. Then it came to Bessie's ears that men who couldn't get to her own ear were petitioning Jane for a kind word in Edward's ear. Bessie did the only thing she could then, send for the Duchess.

The Duchess stopped first at Oxford to see Lionel and then with her train of carts and servants arrived at Westminster. When the Duchess first saw her daughter she thought she had been sent for another reason.

"Why, Elizabeth," she said. "You're going to have another baby!"

There were others about so Bessie tried to smile. "Not till August, Mother."

"Congratulations, my dear," the Duchess said warmly. But her quick eye perceived instantly that something was wrong, and of course the Duchess guessed that the only thing which would truly worry Bessie was Edward. What has he been up to? the Duchess wondered. She shoved women out of her mind; for all his attractiveness to women Edward had been a pretty good husband, the Duchess thought. Never had he brought another woman to court; never had he embarrassed Bessie by casting longing eyes on another titled gentlewoman and his court thronged with them; never had he installed a woman in any royal palace, a woman whom others would openly call his mistress. The Duchess suspected that his forays into the manly art of seduction had been, as she put it, *"Pour le sport."*

When the Duchess thought of the famous Philippe le Bon of Burgundy, who at his deathbed had passed from the world with his swarm of mistresses and his wife in the same chamber, much like the old cock and all his hens, the Duchess thought Edward had behaved pretty well. So she was unprepared for Bessie's revelations.

"Does she live here openly?" the Duchess asked, her mouth a perfect round of amazement.

"No," Bessie said. "Evidently she comes and goes. She has a husband of course."

"Her talents must be prodigious," the Duchess said. "I'd like to wring her neck." Her eyes were speculative and Bessie had the wild thought her mother actually would wring Jane's neck if she got the chance.

"They say she is sweet and kind and witty and gay."

"No doubt," said the Duchess. "He would hardly be interested in a disagreeable whore."

"She is fairly well educated. She reads and writes."

"In bed?" asked the Duchess.

Bessie said, "Mother, she is more dangerous than you think."

"Pooh," said the Duchess. She was silent a moment and then she said, "Bessie, you and Edward have been married for almost ten years. You know each other better than anyone else in the world could possibly know. Your husband loves you and you adore him. Now you must overlook the peccadilloes of the male. He has been a good husband."

"What shall I do, Mother?" Bessie leaned forward, her golden eyes wide and brimming.

The Duchess smiled. "I just said Edward is your husband. Do what any wife would do."

Bessie whispered, "But he is the King."

She truly worships him, the Duchess thought. "Bessie," she said, "you are the Queen."

Edward had been turning over in his mind the idea of installing the little Prince, his son, in the castle of Ludlow in Wales, just as his own father had done. Wales was turbulent. But the loyalties of the Welsh were almost legendary and Edward wanted them diverted to their own little Prince. His son, sturdy and brightly intelligent, was a little boy who could easily win hearts;

all he had to do was smile. Edward's mind was also revolving about a council for Wales; the Prince's council could thus act in a dual capacity. So Edward was thinking that if Bessie had another son—and her baby was due in the summer—it would be easier for him to part her from young Edward. They had never parted with a child before; always the children were raised right within the royal household. Bessie, it seemed to Edward, was like the French in this respect; they were never happier than when their sprawling homes contained just as sprawling a family, complete with aunts and cousins. He knew he would meet a storm of protest when the time came for him to part her from her son.

"You look pale," he said. "Were you outside today? You should walk in the gardens. It is you I have made them beautiful for."

How can he, she thought, pretend to be so loving?

"It was too cold."

"But you have your marten cloak that you always wear."

"It's too old," Bessie said.

"It can't be," Edward said. "But I'll send to Gratiani tomorrow. There's a ship due."

"Have you emptied the royal wardrobe then for your mistress?"

Bessie turned to face him, her eyes holding his, hers angry and Edward's momentarily astonished.

Bessie seized the opportunity of his amazed silence.

"There is a sentence of yours, my lord," she said coldly, "going about the court, repeated to one of your cronies. It goes like this. 'I have had three mistresses, which in diverse properties diversely excelled: one the holiest, one the wiliest and one the merriest harlot in the realm.' I gather this Mrs. Shore is the merriest!" Bessie had guessed from what Anthony had said years ago that Elizabeth Lucy was the holiest harlot; she didn't know who was the wiliest and evidently she was never going to know and neither was anybody else for that secret was with Edward. He himself was hunting for something to say, and this allowed Bessie to cry, "Oh! If I were only a Duchess I would pay you back!"

This remark struck Edward as funny and involuntarily he grinned, whereupon Bessie, as the outraged wife bearing a child, confronted with an unrepentant beast of a male, burst into tears.

"Don't cry, sweetheart." He came toward her and she turned

her back; he took her shoulders and then slipped his arms around her and kissed the back of her neck. "Please don't cry," Edward muttered, trying to turn her to face him. "It is only you I love Bessie," he said; he tried again to turn her but she kept her feet planted firmly on the floor, so with his hands on her waist he lifted her. "I wouldn't cause you any tears for all the world."

"I can't always be gay," Bessie sobbed. "Wives can't."

"I know you can't," he said. "Tell me you forgive me."

"It's because I love you so much that I cannot bear to think of you with—in—"

"Bessie," he said, "I love only you."

She studied his face.

"My own sweetheart," he said. It was what he had always called her from the very beginning. "Bessie, we are very fortunate, do you realize that?"

She nodded. Already she had a scapegoat—Hastings. It was always Hastings who drew him away and into bad company. But she didn't say so aloud; Edward loved Hastings entirely.

"It worries me," he said earnestly, "for you to be upset when you are pregnant. And I do want you to walk outside and get fresh air."

"I will," she promised. "My cloak is warm. It isn't really old."

"We'll go now," he said. "We'll fetch the little girls and go out."

Bessie threw a wan smile at him. She drew a deep sigh. He smiled and hugged her. And walking beside him a few minutes later, her hand in his arm with the children scampering ahead, she knew she would try to forget Jane Shore as though she were nonexistent and unimportant. "The ship," she said, "you spoke of a ship. If there are figs or fruit on her I'd like to send some down to Lionel and Thomas at school."

Edward was still feeling a trifle guilty, especially since he had no intention of foregoing Jane's company when he desired it. Bessie's mention of her oldest son started a train of thought in his mind which had been there previous.

"I'm going to make Tom the Marquis of Dorset, Bessie," he said. He knew nothing would please her more and he was rewarded by her sudden and ever dazzling smile. Edward could still receive that pleasant drowning sensation.

"Your eyes are pure gold stars, my Bessie," he said wonderingly. Her happiness was contagious and suddenly and once again the world turned a sunny place, the light spring wind with the hint of rain confirmed the wonderment of the coming spring; Edward's heart lifted with her hand in his.

"And do you know, Bessie, I think this time you're going to give me another son."

He had never predicted before. "You do?" she cried, stopping to look up at him.

He nodded. "My gambler's instinct," he said seriously. "The odds are greatly in favor of a boy. Come on, Bessie."

Obediently she trotted along at his side, for his strides were long and he was excited by his sudden sureness. His brown eyes were gleaming. "We'll name him Richard, sweetheart, for your father and mine."

And even though he had not renounced his lovely Jane, actually his fidelity in the coming months was all too obvious to Bessie. Never had she seen her husband so tied to his affairs at home and abroad.

Slowly, slowly his big hands began to untangle all the woven threads of internal and foreign policy.

Oxford was loose, hothead that he was, he and his two brothers; with help and ships from Louis they were harrying English shipping. Edward would have welcomed their actual landing on the coast of England; he could deal with that easier. The Scots were beginning to negotiate; they at least inferred they were sorry they had sheltered Oxford temporarily and gave as their excuse that he had possessed a safe conduct from their King, which had now expired. Edward held his temper and offered to meet the Scottish ambassadors and send his own safe conducts for them. He was working on a marriage alliance and eventually he would succeed. Oxford had told Louis that he had the seal of a Duke among his adherents and so Edward, if it were true, did not doubt that the Duke was Clarence; in fact he attributed much of the unrest in England to the activities of his brother, for even people who were his own faithful adherents were uneasy in their minds about what Clarence might do or whom he might attack. As a warning Edward released the Countess of Warwick and sent her to her daughter Anne at Middleham. Clarence would know if Edward chose he could restore the Countess to all her rightful inheritances and this might give the shifty Clarence something to think about. "The King's brothers are quarreling," John Paston wrote, "but he, the King, means to be bigger than both of them." Edward's ambassadors to the Hansards were having rough going of it. Charles of Burgundy was beginning to be more difficult; he was having delusions of grandeur, Edward thought. It was said he called his lords together every day and lectured them at length. He was also beginning to truly earn his nickname—*le Téméraire*. What would he do next? his friends and allies wondered. What extremes might he attempt?

Edward, competent soldier that he was, wanted no rash military actions against France until the stage was well set, and any abortive attacks on Louis would not only be rash but laden with the risk of failure which would bring all Edward's long-range plans into ruin. War with a foreign country was an undertaking which necessitated far-reaching strategy and was not a hastily conceived, ill-laid venture.

And to keep his subjects well aware that their King's all-seeing eye was upon them Edward, as soon as the spring rains ceased flooding the roads, spent the whole summer moving around, taking the Speaker Alyington and much of his council with him and his family. During June he and Bessie were at Ludlow, Coventry, Kenilworth Castle and Leicester. During July Bessie was with him at Nottingham, Stamford and Fotheringhay. In the middle of July he sent Bessie to Shrewsbury and he joined her there the second week in August.

On the night of the sixteenth of August Edward wearily dismissed his council as the clock was striking; it was nearly midnight. They had been dealing with unemployment and begging, and Edward was so perturbed about the itinerant begging that his latest proclamation forbid even pilgrimage without the great seal and assurance that the would-be pilgrim had enough money to finance his trip; even students had to have the permission of the chancellor of their particular school to travel about, and by royal commandment idleness was forbid and work was the order of the day. Edward went to his chamber trailed by a few of his lords. He permitted himself to be undressed and he was standing in only his hose and unlaced shirt when there was a knock on the door.

It was opened by one of his gentlemen, and they were astounded to see the Duchess of Bedford, as merry and sparkling as ever, even if it were one o'clock in the morning.

The Duchess paid no mind to Edward's undress. She bowed and smiled. "The Queen, my daughter, just wished me to inform Your Grace that she has just brought forth a child." The Duchess paused. "Her labor was a scant hour."

Edward took a step forward; he said nothing; he waited.

The Duchess laughed. "If you would like to come with me, Your Grace, your newborn son is waiting to see you."

It seemed to Bessie that that summer marked a new part of her life. For almost nine years she had been a wife and a mother and a wife to a King; now imperceptibly she was to become a Queen. She was ready now to stand as a symbol and Edward thought so too. The country was serene compared to the years of struggle, and the first indication Bessie received of her new status was to be sent the next month along with Edward, the little Prince, to Wales to make a progress by herself, to let the people see her and their sturdy little Prince, to win hearts and allegiance and to remind the people they had a royal family. Edward couldn't be everywhere but Bessie could take his place.

It was with great pride of accomplishment that Bessie set forth. Edward would be three in November. Nonetheless his mother had chosen for him a tailor who was undoubtedly an authority on fashions; he was French, and with her affinity for clothes—Edward smiled a bit at his wife's choice. So for my lord the Prince: a doublet of purple velvet, a doublet of purple satin, two doublets of black velvet, a bonnet of purple lined with green satin to go with the purple velvet doublet, and two bonnets of black velvet lined with black satin; for state occasions a gown of cloth of gold upon damask. There was no doubt that the little Prince was dressed in the height of fashion.

But of course no matter what Edward was dressed in, his unfailing appeal lay in his sturdy height, the bright intelligent eyes, the ready, wide smile and the picture of vibrant health. When Bessie set forth upon her journey to Wales, accompanied by the Speaker himself, now a member of the little Edward's council, and ten more members who had been added to the council for Wales (which was a new departure), and with her ladies—her two sisters, Kate and Anne—and all the attending servants and

chaplains, they made a fine show. But Bessie's own heart burst
with pride and love when hand in hand with her son, she walked
with him to the waiting carriage.

Politely, as he had been taught, Edward stepped to one side to
let his mother enter first; then he climbed in himself and seated
himself next his mother. Edward stood in the courtyard; his heart
beat fast; he had never in his life seen a more wonderful sight;
he had to turn away quickly, for it aroused an emotion which he
knew would bring the sharp tears into his eyes. He cautioned
himself to stay steady but he could be permitted a final farewell.
Rapidly he walked over to the carriage.

"Good-bye, my own sweetheart," he said. "Good-bye, my son."
He held out his big hand and the Prince grasped it in his small
one.

"Good-bye, Father," he said.

"Take good care of your mother," Edward said.

"I will, Father."

Edward couldn't resist; he leaned over and hugged the child.
Then he stepped back. The first horsemen were wheeling out the
big gates; at them Edward turned and waved, and his father
gave an answering wave. He thought, Whatever I must do to keep
my realm safe for him I must do it, and whatever I have done I
am sure it has been right.

Bessie and the Prince were accompanied also by judges. The
disorders in Wales, coming now under the royal eye, would be
stopped by orderly trials; offenders would be indicted, punished
and fined; the men who had suffered under the wave of lawlessness would be able to confront their despoilers and justice would
be done. It was a beginning. Although some of the people were
afraid to accuse their enemies for fear of reprisals, the sitting
judges and courts brought a measure of sanity and order; the
presence of the Queen and the Prince and their entourage
brought the show of royal power and civilized laws which were
to be obeyed. The business of the judges doubled and tripled as
faith in their jurisdiction grew. Although it grew slowly it grew,
and Edward was very well satisfied. As for Bessie herself, the very
actuality of being in Ludlow, the castle where Edward himself
had grown up, brought a curious pleasure. It was as though, along

with her own little son, her own Edward, the King strode at her side and she could imagine vividly her husband as a boy.

"He was always precocious," his mother had ever told her. "Always." She had been told of Edward's letters protesting the strictness of his tutor, Sir Richard Croft. Sir Richard still served Edward faithfully; Bessie knew his craggy face well with its jutting brows and stern mien; he had fought at Edward's side at Barnet and Tewkesbury; Edward had the power to command lifelong fidelity which he himself cherished and nurtured with his own fidelity to his loyal lords. Bessie could imagine well Edward's fretting under the constant and burdensome regime which had been imposed on the young Edward, whose family considered him the true heir to the throne. And even at ten he had had a taste for food. "If you'll send me Master Bank to Cook and wait, I'll send you back one of the men here," he had written his father. "And there is no use my practicing daily with the sword and spear. I've learned it. I think I should be permitted to hunt more and fish."

In her bedroom at Ludlow, which was the same one that Edward had used, she slept in the same big bedstead. She could see him so plain, sitting at the table after dinner, for after dinner he had had to go back to his studies, his head bent; in the winter, the candles lighted, his big feet would shift restlessly and the young brow would be drawn in concentration as he mastered his sums and his algebra and cast longing eyes out the window as the afternoon waned—he would much rather be outside ahorse. "Although I had plenty of physical exercise," he had told her, "that was part of the regime too. It wasn't ever what I wanted to do, I thought then. But it was no use, my protesting. Sir Richard kept me at the sword and spear and my favorite, the battle-ax, and the feel of armor, and of course that is what is responsible for this." He thrust out his naked arm. "My tirelessness in battle, as my enemies dub it." He grinned his wry grin.

But Bessie and the Prince and the council had done a good job in Wales, so when she returned he was ready to tell her the experiment had succeeded. Edward planned a permanent council for Wales, his son's council, and he explained to Bessie that since Edward was almost three the time had come when he would have to take up his residence in Wales as befitted a Prince. Edward expected a storm and he got it.

"But he is only three!"

"I know," Edward said.

"Edward!" she implored. It was only the second day they had been back together. She was holding her baby Richard.

"You have little Richard," Edward pointed out. He leaned forward. "I promise you on my oath that I will never part you from Richard. Richard may be brought up right within the household."

Richard was now three months old. His legs were kicking rhythmically back and forth like pistons and he was making little noises of contentment and trying to look around the enormous room.

"But to not see him every day— But—"

Edward said, "To me he is our precious son and God's gift and our dearest treasure, but this is what must be."

Bessie was silent, her face looked so sad that Edward cried, "Bessie, he will come back on holidays, on state occasions, many times! You won't be parted forever!"

She looked down at little Richard, whose round eyes were surveying her with interest. Then another thought occurred; she could see plain the stern eyes of Richard Croft; she knew Edward regarded him highly. She said, "But who will take care of him? Who will—" she sighed; she knew Edward would lay down strict rules for the upbringing of the most important boy in England. "Who—" she broke off; she almost didn't want to know who would have her son's charge.

But now Edward was on sure ground, for he had given this matter a great deal of sober calculation. "Who? Bessie," he asked, "can't you guess? Who is most fitted? Who is the gentlest knight?"

Bessie's eyes filled with tears; they ran down her cheeks. "Anthony!" she said. "Oh, thank you, my lord. I thank you from the bottom of my heart!"

"Anthony is the logical choice, Bessie. He is nigh in blood too, although I should never trust my son to Clarence, more's the pity."

It was the first time that he had openly accused Clarence to her in so direct and damning a fashion, for who could sink lower than to be mistrusted when it came to a three-year-old boy? It made Bessie shiver. But Edward shoved Clarence out of his mind and began to read to her his own drawn-up instructions for Anthony and Alcock, the Bishop of Rochester, who was to be the Prince's teacher and president of his council for Wales.

"He is to rise each morning at the same hour, convenient to his age," Edward began, "hear matins in his chamber and go as

soon as he is dressed to chapel to attend mass. After mass, breakfast, and after breakfast to give his time to the learning his age
suffers him to receive. At dinner he shall be read stories, noble
stories as behooves a Prince to understand and know." Edward
looked up from his parchment. "This reading, Anthony is the best
judge. He will know exact what to read."

Bessie's head was swimming. Edward grinned. "If I could do it
he can, sweetheart," he continued.

"After dinner he is to return to his studies and learning. For at
least an hour. Then sports and exercise till evensong, which of
course he will attend. After supper then is the time for play and
all disports as can be devised for his recreation. Eight o'clock is
to find him in bed with the curtains drawn."

Bessie said earnestly, "Command that those who attend to putting him to bed are merry and make him merry. It will not be
hard, he is such a joyous little boy." She bit her lip.

"Please don't cry, sweetheart," Edward begged. "I'll command
it: that he be put to bed happy and smiling. And around that
bed watch is to be kept all night and every minute."

"What about a doctor?" Bessie said worriedly.

Edward nodded. "Here it is, what I wrote: 'A doctor and a sur-
geon always in attendance on his person. So that disease shall not
rob the King of his precious son and most desired treasure.'"

"And what of his servants and attendants?"

"There will be no swearing, no ribald words used in his presence. No brawler or hothead, no drunkard employed. Anthony
as his governor will keep strict watch over his staff and any man
found wanting will be dismissed. Bessie," he inquired, "what
would you think if we sent his half-brother Richard with him?"

Bessie smiled. "Aye! To have his kin. And Anthony loves Richard. He has always regarded Richard almost as a son, as Richard
never knew his own father." She raised her eyes to his face. He
knew that, of course; there was nothing now they didn't know
about each other or what had happened before they had met. All
the tangled threads of living now were entwined. She leaned
forward and touched his hand. "Oh, my love, you were right
when you said a month ago or so how fortunate we are, the two
of us."

"My Bessie," Edward said, "I know it. And let us plan to have
Edward with us at Windsor for Christmas."

Chapter 18

THE SNOW fell gently over the moors of Wensleydale, drifting down upon the battlements of Middleham Castle. Within all was in readiness for Christmas; the hall festooned with pine, holly and ivy, the great tables scrubbed, the meats and fowls ready for the oven, and both the castle bakers and the village bakery ovens glowed far into the night. The jugglers had a new act and tight green hose, and the minstrels had been practicing the carols. In the village the napkins and bowls and eating knives and spoons were polished and clean and wrapped in a clean napkin, ready to be carried to the castle hall in anticipation of their lord's largesse, the Christmas meats and sweetmeats; the villagers would eat as much as they could out of these bowls and be permitted to take them home full with a loaf of bread in their napkin.

The household of the castle had been increased by Anne's mother. It had been a wonderful day for Anne to see her mother. She had spent much of November overseeing the making of new gowns for the Countess and new petticoats and her shoemaker received fourteen shillings for new slippers.

"You should give my mother jewelry," Anne told her husband, "for she has so little left," and Richard smilingly assented and had sent to London for gift rings and a gold chain with gems for his New Year's gift to his mother-in-law.

Although Richard was always anxious to oppose Clarence, whom he hated deeply, and Clarence had opposed Richard's espousing the cause of the Countess and installing her in Middleham, nonetheless Richard was glad to have her on another count. Anne was pregnant and she was so slight that every time Richard looked at her he was filled with fear and dismay, and the Countess' presence was reassuring. "Look at Isabel," she said to him in private. "Isabel has just had a fine healthy daughter." The child had been born in August, the same month as Bessie's little Richard. "I will have two grandchildren this year," the Countess said. She was used to dealing with moody men; hadn't she been the wife of the Earl of Warwick?

As for Anne, the birth of Isabel's baby had been a good portent, she thought. She told herself she was seventeen now and stronger; all summer long she had been in the open air, and now with her mother here—a baby for Christmas. It was the morning of the twentieth of December, and she was talking to her young cousin, Montagu's son, whom Edward had pardoned and whom Richard had taken under his wing. Anne had been glad to have him here too; it made their little family just a bit more of a family, although sometimes she thought rather despairingly that the three of them were like the flotsam and jetsam thrown upon the shores after the ship had foundered. I mustn't think like that, she knew it; it wouldn't be good for her baby, her own baby, someone who was entirely hers to love and to cherish and whom she would love entire and never use, nay, nor do anything which did not consider only the welfare of the child. When she recalled that she was indeed the Duchess of Gloucester and that all over the country women would envy her, it was almost with surprise that she realized this, for she knew now that all she had ever wanted was for someone to love her. Now be thankful you have your mother, she counseled herself, and your little cousin. He is only twelve and you are all he has. It was obvious to Anne Neville that she and her husband were not in love.

Two days later Anne's baby was born. And after it was over, the long, long hours, young as she was and unknowledgeable as she was, she knew she could never have another baby. If she conceived one she would die or else the child within her would die. Her mother was astonished that she was still alive. She folded the quilts around Anne's thin shape on the bed; the fire burned bright and the candles looked cheerful; but there was no sound in the room. The attending women and the midwife moved silently and shaken about their tasks, carrying away the basins and the stained linens. The midwife muttered to herself that they should all go to the chapel to thank God for the tragedy so slenderly averted.

"I seen the hand of death," she whispered to the young woman she was training. "I seen it plain for both of them."

Slowly Anne came back to life, she thought. She lifted her hand and looked at it; her mother was watching her.

"I am at peace," Anne whispered. She tried a small smile.

"You have a son," the countess said, trying to keep her voice steady, for she knew if she broke down it would upset Anne further.

"Please bring him," Anne said. Her great brown eyes looked like shining wells of love and the Countess stumbled to her feet. When she brought the baby and put him in her daughter's arms she said, "Anne, you are the most good person of any I've ever known. May God bless you, my daughter, and your little boy."

Anne scarcely heard her but with her usual politeness in any circumstance she said she didn't deserve such a compliment, while her mother showed her how to hold the tiny infant. "With your hand under his head, Anne. He is so little."

"I am little," Anne said tenderly. "Little or big or ugly or handsome he will always be my greatest joy, I know, Mother. He is a miracle."

"Richard is here," the Countess said.

Anne could hear his voice. He was saying, "The baby, is he all right?" His voice had its familiar nervous pitch, the intensity with which Richard blurted out a question important to him. It crossed Anne's mind languidly that he hadn't asked for her, yet it didn't disturb her, for it was something she had always known in her heart. But now they both had a new little human being to adore and to share together and it should draw them close in mutual love, and Richard would adore him too; she was sure of that. Proudly she raised her eyes to Richard's face. "I'm not going to let you hold him yet," she said.

The couriers went racing proudly to the King to tell him and Bessie that Richard of Gloucester was the parent of a boy, a boy named Edward in honor of his uncle the King. Edward sent back his congratulations and a magnificent gold cup as a christening gift. But Clarence remarked that it was the little son who would pay the penalty for Richard's cupidity in wanting Anne Neville. "The poor little thing will probably never live out five years."

Isabel heard these words with such deep revulsion she couldn't answer. Clarence was slowly and very surely alienating his whole family. Only Edward kept trying to placate him and show him the error of his ways but even Edward was beginning not only to lose patience but to grow angry. His voice was stern and ominous. "When you forget that I am your brother, remember never to forget that I am your sovereign lord. You are lucky to be a Duke. Were you French, you should be simply *monsieur*, and I can make you that, Master Plantagenet!"

Surrounded as he was by conniving nobles and foreign Princes and Kings, must he also be burdened with a brother whose fidelity was not only suspect but whose treason had already been open? I'd like to take the law in my own hands, he told himself, but he would not, he knew. And what occasioned his warning of Clarence was that Oxford had landed on St. Michael's Mount with a few followers, and Edward knew that Louis had helped him and that Clarence was implicated, although he had no proof.

Nonetheless Edward was glad that Oxford had foolishly shown his hand and was on English soil. Harrying the seas, he was a menace to Edward's shipping, and of course the merchants raised loud cries of alarm and why didn't the King do something? It was far more difficult to catch a fleeing sail than it was to bottle up Oxford on the Mount where he had stupidly placed himself within reach of the King's justice. Edward commissioned young Will Herbert to go rout him out and sent him armed with a pardon for all who would desert Oxford.

This didn't suit his lordship's high heart at all; he was well ensconced on the rocky island with plenty of food, but the safety of his men within and the plenitude of food didn't help; the promise of freedom and pardon was too juicy a lure, and one by one and two by two his men deserted him. The game was up. Oxford threw himself on Edward's mercy and unaccountably he received it. With pride young Will Herbert brought his illustrious prisoner to London. Edward was grim.

"Pardon for your life only," he said. He forbore to talk to Oxford; he had been pardoned and restored before. Edward sent him away to Hammes Castle to prison. He confiscated all Oxford's estates; but he did allow the Earl a decent allowance in jail and two servants and a chaplain. Oxford was out of the way and Edward promptly forgot him, but he didn't forget King Louis, the man who had helped Oxford.

Europe was seething. Louis wove more plans than a spider has legs. Having failed with Oxford, he was trying to seduce the King of Scots and so was Edward; Edward was dangling a marriage alliance in front of James' nose, meanwhile feeding English gold into Scotland and into the pockets of James' recalcitrant lords. Louis was undoubtedly in touch with Clarence, holding high the prospect of dethroning Edward and placing the unstable Clarence on the throne of England. Louis knew that only a fool like Clarence would swallow such bait, and all Louis was trying to accomplish was to keep England stirred up in a cauldron of uncertainty. The next move on Louis' part was a masterstroke. He offered to make a marriage alliance between his brother, the Duke of Guinne, and the only heiress of Burgundy, Mary. The thought sent a shaft of fear through Edward. Why the devil didn't his sister Margaret bear a child? A male, his own nephew, who would be the heir of Burgundy? "Charles must be impotent," Edward growled. "He's got a strong young wife, my own sister, to produce an heir for him. I'd like to send over a stalwart English archer to creep into her bed."

The danger in the marriage that Louis had proposed was that Louis' brother could very well be Louis' heir, for the little Dauphin, Louis' only boy, was sickly and hunched. Were the Dauphin to die, which might happen anytime, then Louis' brother and Mary of Burgundy would control and ally their respective domains to the danger of England. Faced by that alliance what would Edward do? The confrontation between him and Louis loomed ever larger. It must be; it was coming. There was no way out; ahead was war with France.

But no matter what Louis had done to hamper Edward and no matter what Edward had done in reply and return, the two monarchs, eying each other across the narrow seas, still continued to receive and send embassies. They were curiously alike. Both monarchs revered the memory of the same man, the great Duke of Milano, Francesco Sforza, the man who with his own strong hands, plus a marriage, had molded for himself a dukedom and kept it. Not only had he kept it, he had made his court one of the most glowing and civilized in Europe and Italy. This canny adventurer, the clever, clever man who was never at a loss for words or deeds, represented the ultimate ideal to both Edward and Louis while around them seethed the plots and counterplots of rebellious nobles, of conniving brothers, of vassals who coveted power.

It began to seem to Edward that there were never enough

hours in the day; there were fewer than there had ever been. But the winter days bore fruit. James of Scotland signed the peace treaty; his son was affianced to Edward's daughter Cecily, Cecily who looked most like her mother and who was the most startlingly beautiful of Bessie's daughters. The Hansards under Dr. Hatclyf's tender tutelage and physician's tact, signed the treaty of trade and Christian of Denmark sent gifts and goodwill. Two treaties of trade were signed again with the Italians and Edward's own ships continued to bring him gold and more gold as his individual enterprises were crowned with success. The scramble for the throne was proceeding apace in Spain. Louis espoused the cause of Alfonso, but Edward threw the weight of England on the side of Isabella and Ferdinand and it was going to be the correct choice.

But the news from Burgundy was bad, for Charles was embarked already on his suicidal course; instead of readying his armies and waiting for Edward he had begun the siege of Neuss and instead of fulfilling the articles of his treaty was on the Rhine with his men and not ready to attack France in concert with the English.

Edward, of course, was too canny not to have foreseen this difficulty with Charles. Early in April he had sent Anthony to Neuss to try to talk sense to Charles. Now Anthony was back. Anthony had come up from the coast that morning. Anthony had seen the concentration of ships in every port; there were fifty-five hundred bottoms waiting to transport troops, horses, gear, provisions, the latest engines of war, field guns. Everything was ready, including the flower of English nobility and their well accoutered troops; everything was ready and was as efficient as only Edward could make it. And yet when Anthony remembered what Charles had said and what he had to report to Edward, his brown eyes were troubled; he had to tell his King some unpalatable facts. And how to begin? To Anthony's eyes the scenes at Neuss had been incredible. He brought out one sentence.

"I have never been exposed so often and with so many men to such a web of double-dealing!"

Edward laughed. "You amuse me, Anthony," he said. "And by God I need amusing." Since Anthony was hesitating Edward said, "I gather that Charles refused to leave the siege of Neuss even when you delivered my ultimatum—that I would not come either to France."

"Yes," said Anthony miserably.

"You didn't fail me," Edward said. "It isn't your fault. It is Charles'. He is wildly impractical and impractical Dukes always lose their coronets." Edward ran his hand through his hair. "We shan't be able to save it for him. Perhaps."

"Almost all countries had an envoy at Neuss. Even the Pope had sent a legate to implore Charles to make peace with the Swiss. Christian of Denmark sent a delightful Bishop. He was the only one I could talk to honestly. The others—my own uncle—" Anthony was referring to le Comte de St. Pol who was Constable of France. "Even my own uncle, whom Louis sent to urge Charles to sign a treaty of peace with him, broke faith with Louis and offered to let you, Your Grace, enter Amiens. He told me to tell you this secret if you would pledge him the county of Champagne."

Again Edward laughed. "He is fond of wine." He didn't tell Anthony that in the secret treaty he and Charles had signed the two of them had disposed of le Comte's holdings between themselves; Anthony was very naïve, Edward thought, and le Comte de St. Pol treading in dangerous waters now that Edward had proof of his perfidy toward Louis. Edward had a prodigious memory and he stored away these facts carefully under his smiling exterior.

"So all your efforts were vain. Charles will not leave Neuss and he has broken our treaty." Edward announced this matter-of-factly and Anthony nodded.

Edward rose. "It is far too late in the game for me not to invade France, Anthony," he said. "Remembering that we—as other creatures in this world—are transitory. We have even already made our will."

He was still frowning slightly when he arrived in Bessie's chambers. She greeted him in French because he had been speaking only French with her for the last month; he wished to impress the nobility of the Continent with his ease in the language.

But tonight he spoke in English.

"Bessie, I intend to be in Calais with all of my army by June twenty-second at the latest."

Bessie thought of her son Thomas Grey. He was seventeen and old enough to take his place at his stepfather's side. Bessie knew what Anthony had reported but she didn't look worried and said calmly, "Aye, my lord." She took another stitch.

"Put down your sewing and take up your pen. I want you to write a letter for me in French. To King Louis. And I want you to say this."

Edward paused and watched Bessie go to her writing table. Then he began. "I want you to say that we are coming to France to demand the surrender of the kingdom. We are coming for the purpose of restoring the ancient liberties of the church and the people—to lift the heavy burdens now oppressing them."

Bessie glanced up at him and saw the small smile at the corners of his lips.

"I want you to imply, Bessie, that we have no other ends but the lifting of the burdens of the oppressed and enriching the people of France. And we demand surrender, for war is foolish."

Bessie wrote a sentence hastily and rewrote it while Edward gave her time.

"War means devastation and famine and death."

Bessie carefully picked out these French counterparts.

"Devastation and death! And to the country we consider our heritage! We should do nothing to destroy those people—if we can help it. Those people who are so dear to our heart. It seems best then to demand a surrender before we use so reluctantly our army."

Bessie wrote and rewrote, her gilt head bent over the paper. Time passed. Edward poured himself some wine and poured Bessie a cup which he set at her elbow and leaned over to see what she had written.

"Don't look! Wait till I finish."

He paced across the room, deep in thought; the candles flickered. Bessie's pen scratched on, and finally she drew a deep sigh and settled back in her chair to reread what she had written.

She handed the sheet to Edward. A slow, approving smile was her reward.

"It's perfect," he said. "Perfect. Bessie, you have a more subtle style than Anthony. *Quelle finesse,*" he added and made her a low bow.

Chapter 19

THE LORD Commines, he who had served first Charles of Burgundy and now served so well a greater master, King Louis XI, this man from whose journals we have learned so much took the letter from Louis' hand. Louis' lords were about him; in an anteroom the English herald who had brought the letter cooled his heels under the hostile eyes of armed guards. Commines read the letter once, twice. His eyes gleamed. "No Englishman could have written this."

Louis slowly read the letter aloud to the intimate group with him.

"The style is too fine for an Englishman to have written it," Commines repeated.

Louis looked puzzled. Was it some kind of trick? But no, it had been brought straight from Edward, the tall English King who now waited, one foot on French soil, a glittering figure in armor, while France lay before him. He had already landed; Louis hadn't known for four days that he had landed, so well had the English fleet kept the narrow seas. Only yesterday had Louis known and then what had he done? He, Louis, had ordered his own troops into Picardy to lay waste the slow-borne labors of the fertile fields of his France so that the feared and hated enemy should find the cupboard bare. But Commines had said sorrowfully, "The reports show he, Edward, is well provisioned and needs no provisions from us."

Louis raised his thin hands to heaven. "Ah, Holy Mary," he cried, "even now, when I have given thee fourteen hundred crowns, thou dost not help me one whit!" Louis' unshakable belief he could bribe the saints in heaven was beginning to totter. And yet—the letter. The letter! His mind, his searching mind, had memorized the letter. But he didn't dare write back. No, he didn't dare.

"Send that Herald to me!" he commanded.

The English herald was a bit nervous, a strapping young man, well and befittingly dressed as a proper herald of England, a collar of roses white about the blue-velvet doublet. He was grave and intent; Edward would have been proud of him.

Louis began gently, "I know your master comes to France to please the Duke of Burgundy and the English people." He paused. Would the herald perceive the innuendo in the next sentence? Louis hoped so. "The season for fighting is nearly past." A long pause followed this; Louis' sharp eyes studied the herald.

"The Duke of Burgundy is truly a defeated man," Louis went on now chattily. "And le Comte de St. Pol is an intriguer. We are well aware of it. He has two faces. I doubt, though, that he has two heads." Louis' voice became a bit grim as he thought of the Comte. He said plainly, "Le Comte de St. Pol will deceive all and any man as he is deceiving us and your King."

Herald was trying to memorize Louis' words; he was intent, mouth partly open, rehearsing Louis' words in his mind.

Now came the closing statement, the pregnant answer to Edward. "There are reasons why, therefore, your King should listen to overtures of peace, and they are wise reasons. You bring your master our overtures of peace."

Herald bowed. Louis had been sitting; the two men had been alone save for Lord Commines. Commines had had brief instructions. At Louis' rising he moved to the herald's side. Louis came over to Herald and took Herald's wrist and held up his palm and pressed a small bag of gold into it.

Herald bowed again and backed to the door. Herald was rather surprised when the great Lord Commines accompanied him close at his side, and Herald noted that other men melted away from them, though there had been instructions that no one else was to speak with him. He must remember to tell Edward all this, every bit of it.

Commines led Herald back to his own quarters. "A fine fresh horse for you, young man," Commines said with his engaging smile. "There are thirty ells of crimson velvet stowed neatly aboard for you."

Herald wondered why this great French lord was using sailors' talk. The French are crazy, he thought, but he bowed and mounted and Lord Commines himself escorted him to the gates of the camp so that Herald would be able to report no gossip, nothing but the words that came from Louis' own lips.

Herald put the bag of gold and the thirty ells of crimson velvet before his King. He and Edward were alone. Outside Edward's household men paced about the large tent; within, a single candle burned on Edward's table.

Herald repeated slowly the words of the French King. Edward asked to hear them again and again. He smiled slightly.

"Now we ask you to erase them from your memory."

Young Herald knelt. "They are gone, Your Grace. Completely forgot." He rose and grinned at Edward, and Edward patted him on the shoulder and put the bag of gold back into his hand and gestured toward the velvet. Edward admired it; it made him think of trade with France. "'Tis all yours," he said. "We ourselves are not able to accept gifts from our ancient enemy." There was not a trace of a smile on his lips, and Herald backed to the tent flap and disappeared into the night.

Using France as a master chessboard, Edward moved his troops into Boulogne and to the field of Agincourt. His men were his pawns; his two knights were Charles of Burgundy and le Comte de St. Pol. Edward was perfectly prepared to sacrifice them both, if necessary, but not Francis of Brittany which he likened to his castle.

The next day there were some skirmishes about the town of St. Quentin and Edward went on to Lihons de Santerre. But a French noble named De Grassay had been captured, and Edward ordered Lord Stanley to take him under his wing and guard and treat him well. Edward was busy entertaining Charles of Burgundy, who had arrived in camp with much fanfare but without his army.

Edward found it impossible to talk to Charles. "I might remind you," he said, "that you have broke our treaty and all our well-laid plans to set both our armies marching across France are now in the ashcan." Charles had been well fed and now he tossed off his cup of wine.

"I've sent my troops into Lorraine to pillage!" he said.

But Edward's spies said that Charles was afraid to let Edward see the remains of his army, now a raggle-taggle bunch of ill-fed, ill-clothed and ill-armed men, who might even be out of control, hence the pillaging.

"You should overrun Normandy," Charles said grandly. "Francis of Brittany will help and le Comte de St. Pol. My own quarrel with the Swiss continues."

Aye, and it will be the death of you, Edward thought. He rose to bid Charles good-bye; he shook his hand and smiled, his pleasant self. Charles had no notion that he was thinking how many of Charles' chestnuts he, Edward, should pull from the fire with no help from Burgundy's Duke. How much was Burgundy's Duke worth to England and could friendship between the two countries be ruthlessly sacrificed? That would bear much thinking, but when Charles left him Edward shoved that problem out of his mind and sent for Lord Stanley.

It was a beautiful warm starry night, but Edward himself closed the tent flap after Lord Stanley.

"In a few minutes, my lord," he said, "I am going to summon your prisoner, the Frenchman De Grassay, to my own tent. I shall not be here. You will—you and Lord Howard." Edward was very brief. "You will inform De Grassay that I am giving him his liberty and that he is to go straight to King Louis; you will give De Grassay a gold noble—here it is—" Edward held it out in his big hand, "and you will tell De Grassay to recommend you to his master, King Louis."

"Aye, Your Grace."

"That is all, my lord. You wait here. Lord Howard is escorting De Grassay." Edward went to the tent flap and out into the night; the campfires were burning; the men were gathered about them. Edward went over to the edge of one of the fires, almost unseen, and sat down and his busy mind roved from one subject to the other, one plan to another plan; the men were singing a ballad of which he was very fond. Suddenly he joined in.

While Edward was singing, the Frenchman De Grassay urged his fresh mount toward King Louis and his army at Compiègne with some misgivings. Louis le Terrible! De Grassay was only too well aware that his own brother served Charles of Burgundy. Would Louis have got wind of it? Indeed he had.

De Grassay shivered. But it was warm in Louis' quarters. "But I serve you, sire! And you only!"

"One of your brothers is in the service of the Duke of Burgundy," Louis repeated. His mistrust was very apparent and De Grassay shivered again. Louis' mistrust might easily cost De Grassay his head.

"Sire!" he cried. "I bring you commends from both Lord Stanley and Lord Howard. Both stand so close to the English King."

"You did not see the English King?"

"No. But Lord Stanley was very kind and—"

Louis scowled and waved his hand for silence. Dare he trust Edward? And yet—"*Mon Dieu!* I've no herald with me."

Commines said, "We can find a suitable young officer, sire, and borrow some suitable attire for him."

"Do it then," Louis snapped.

He sat crouched in his chair and wrapped in his cloak, his head bent, his eyes shrouded, while an hour passed. Commines reappeared with a young officer and Commines said cheerfully, "Well, my lord, does he not look handsome in his borrowed finery?"

The young French officer stood stiff but he managed to say he was overwhelmed at this honor, and his words and bearing made Louis smile and nod his head in approval.

"Memorize these words," he commanded. He did not dare commit anything yet to paper. Perhaps Edward would after he had received the message which the French herald would bring to him.

The French herald arrived at Edward's camp while Edward was at dinner. Edward, his appetite always splendid, was relishing the *petits pois* of France and had no notion of abandoning his pleasures of the table, so the young French herald waited what seemed an interminable time in the King's own tent with Lord Stanley eying him and Lord Howard saying no word at all. Suddenly there was Edward himself.

Herald knelt, glad for something to do. On one knee, looking straight at Edward's powerful legs, he commended himself to the King of England, direct from his master, King Louis. Then he was on his feet, the Lord Stanley and Lord Howard were both gone and he was alone with Edward. He swallowed and brought out Louis' first sentence.

"It has long been the desire of the King of France to have peace with England."

Edward smiled.

Herald, reassured, now remembered his master's words with perfect clarity. "Your Grace, never since my master's ascension to the throne has the King of France done anything willingly hostile to England. The King of France sheltered my lord of Warwick to discomfit the Duke of Burgundy and to punish the Duke and not the King of England."

Edward regarded his boots and then raised his eyes to Herald's face. So he had succeeded. The confrontation of Louis had taken place and Louis was going to apologize; indeed he was apologizing.

Herald had another sentence from Louis. "The Duke of Burgundy had invited the King of England to France—" Herald hesitated to get it right, "and the said Duke's only object was to get better terms for himself from the King of France. The King of France is prepared to be generous." Herald stopped. Had he said enough? Had he remembered it all? Evidently he had.

"Thank you," Edward said. "You will go seek refreshment, sir. You shall be summoned back into my presence in a few hours."

And now to business, Edward thought. Immediately he summoned his council and most of his nobles: his two brothers, Lord Howard and Stanley, Anthony, the Duke of Suffolk, the Duke of Norfolk, and Earl of Northumberland, Hastings and a dozen or more men. When they had assembled Edward told them in his usual direct manner that the King of France was suing for peace. And he put it to them whether or not they would accept the overtures.

Anthony's eyes were fixed on Edward in admiration and devotion. The border lord, Percy, grinned his hawk's grin like a baring of teeth. Hastings was openly jubilant. The Dukes of Norfolk and Suffolk were proud of their canny master: This was diplomacy at a high level, they thought. Clarence was boastful. "King Louis is afraid!"

"Aye, aye," they agreed with their King.

But not young Richard, Duke of Gloucester. Edward watched Richard, his brother, as he spoke passionately for using the army they had brought instead of weakly accepting peace. He is young,

Edward thought, even as Richard's dark eyes flashed with anger and intense and bitter frustration. Did not Richard see if he, Edward, could get what he wanted without fighting, it would be better? Well, he brushed it aside. The majority of his nobles were more sensible.

Edward said, "Richard, the majority rules."

Edward, putting a fist into a palm to explain each point, began to lay down the terms about which he had thought ever since he had first heard of Charles' defection, what could be saved and what could be gained.

Edward had three main points: first, the payment of seventy-five thousand crowns within fifteen days and twenty-five thousand crowns every Easter and every Michaelmas as long as both Kings lived: second, the marriage of Louis' son the Dauphin, to either one of Edward's older daughters and her endowment with rents up to sixty thousand pounds yearly; third, a private treaty between him and Louis to aid each other and a truce of seven years with a trade treaty of seven years and intercourse of merchandise to the mutual benefit of both countries.

These were Edward's terms.

The memory of the field at Agincourt where he had spent two nights had ceased to disturb him. These were different times. Gone was the old battle cry of the early part of the century; gone indeed were the provinces so hardily won by blood and lost so remorselessly piece by piece during the intervening years. Years ago he had said, and he could hear himself saying it, "We have enough land for one man to keep in our time." Surely it was more politic to marry the throne of Scotland and to marry the throne of France. But that truth was not so exciting as the old rallying cry, St. George for England! A King could not afford to be emotional, and an army was but one piece of his armor, a gauntlet which was well discarded sometimes not only to shake another man's hand but to receive his tribute.

So now Edward devoted himself to the actual arrangements of meeting Louis face-to-face, for which he was anxious; for years now he had dealt with a man he had never met, never spoken to, never beheld, a faceless spider, far away, whose vaunted charm and cleverness Edward could only guess at. Louis was

intensely curious too. Yet as always Louis was afraid and he kept
waking in the night with a nightmare that Edward had tricked
him. He kept remembering that a Duke of Burgundy had been
caught and murdered on a bridge, and perhaps all these plans
would go awry and the crafty English King would not keep his
word.

The place of meeting chosen was at Piquigny, where the
Somme was very narrow and yet too deep to ford. A wooden
bridge was hastily constructed, and on its rough boards were the
two Kings to meet. Edward set his men in battle array and set
them marching toward Amiens.

At Amiens the gates stood open. Louis had sent three hundred
cartloads of fine French wine and food, food, food. Into Amiens
flowed the English soldiers and Louis took fright again. They
were swarming all over the town! Why had he provided such
entertainment? Vainly, his officers told him they were all drunk.

"The streets and taverns are overflowing with Englishmen!"
Louis cried. "Commines, tell the English captains to take their
men away."

Commines said, "But they are too drunk to be dangerous."

"I will go myself to satisfy myself that that is so," Louis replied.

But meanwhile the same reports reached Edward. Furiously
he sent word to Louis to forbid his troops the town and to shut
the gates.

Louis said politely, "Oh, I couldn't think of doing such a thing."

"I'll set my own archers on the gates then," Edward replied,
and sent an order to all his captains to get their men out of
Amiens, and thereafter the gates of the city were closed to the
English under the orders of their own King. They had had the
satisfaction of having first made way with all Louis' wine, and
with that they had to be content.

The flags flew from neat rows of tents and the trundling guns
lay silent but formidable; and after the day's debauch the troops
looked sleepy and pale but neat. The sentries paced and the horse
park was ringed with carts; the cooks cooked and washing was
hung out and messengers came and went with the blowing of
horns and trumpets. Yet everyone heaved a sigh of relief when
the appointed day came and the two Kings made ready for the
historic meeting and treaty.

Edward wore a black-velvet cap adorned with a fleur-de-lis, an ironic gesture of which he was fully capable. His cape was cloth of gold, lined with red. The bridge onto which he stepped was guarded at his side by four Frenchmen; on the other side it was similarly guarded by four Englishmen. With him was Hastings, the Lord Percy, Earl of Northumberland, clad in brown velvet which showed off his hawkish, tanned face, the Bishop Rotherham, the Chancellor of England, and Anthony. Clarence was there too but the intense young Richard had refused to come. In bitterness he had told Edward he was making a terrible mistake; he had come to conquer France, not to make peace.

Louis stepped gingerly upon the newly hewn planks. Still fearful, he had dressed Commines in the same clothes as he wore so that if there were treachery someone might make an error and murder Commines instead. It was a dubious honor which Louis bestowed on his faithful adviser. But Louis' fear showed itself very plainly in the building across the center of the bridge of a barricade of strong bars. There was a small opening in it through which the two men could talk but could not admit a sword or dagger. Over this barricade was a wooden awning in case of rain.

It was the twenty-ninth of August. The whole English army was drawn up on one side of the Somme; Louis had but eight hundred men with him although the rest of his men lay within easy marching distance. On Louis' side the bridge was easily approached while on Edward's there was a morass with a causeway to approach the bridge. A dozen men apiece were allotted by the truce to each King, and so now under fair French skies each monarch set a foot on each end and approached the other and met at the barricade.

Louis had met Edward's terms. Louis was only too glad to pay seventy-five thousand crowns to get Edward out of France and to pay fifty thousand each succeeding year. Edward was glad to betroth his little Bess to the Dauphin of France, even though the Dauphin was as everyone knew neither strong nor well. The betrothal of their two children should cement the two crowns. The peace and trade treaty was for seven years. Through the barricade Edward eyed Louis, thin, yet smiling, his brown eyes eager, his manner almost unctuous, like a moneylender. Yet there was steel and strength in the voice and spirit; Edward saw it.

Edward's French stood him in good stead, for the conversation was conducted in it. Edward had seen the faint surprise in Louis' eyes when he had first greeted him as they both stepped to the aperture. Both bowed deeply and then both stood, Edward with cap in hand, the sun lighting the gold in his hair. He towered much higher than the aperture and had to bend down as they exchanged a brief kiss through the grating. Then Louis said, "My cousin, you are most welcome. There is no man in the world I so much desired to see as yourself, and I thank God we have met for this happy purpose."

Edward had answered in French, saying much the same thing as Louis, and then Rotherham, England's Chancellor, brought forth the documents to be signed, saying at the same time they were historic documents.

Anthony held the missal for Edward's hands to rest on as he signed, and one of Louis' lords performed the same office for him. This new treaty, as Rotherham said, provided for free trade and there would be no more need for safe conducts for Englishmen going to France or Frenchmen going to England, and the merchants of both countries were relieved of all taxes and payments they had had to bear previous.

Louis kept eying Edward through the grating. When the signing had been accomplished a rumble of thunder came and Louis jumped. A hasty glance up at the summer sky revealed tall thunderheads marching menacingly into the blazing sun. Louis whispered, "We would like to speak alone with thee."

Edward made a signal and the men clustered around him dropped away to the very back of the bridge and Louis' attendants did likewise. And so while the storm clouds gathered the two monarchs talked alone.

If Richard of Gloucester, alone and brooding in his tent, thought the storm was God's answer to this disgraceful peace, it was not a portent for Edward but indeed might have been for le Comte de St. Pol, for Louis wanted very much to compare notes with Edward on the Count's perfidy to both of them. In fact, although no one knows what the two Kings talked about, it must be supposed the Count was one subject, for soon after, he did—as Jacqueta had always predicted—lose his head to Louis' executioner on the charges of treason.

It seems certain they discussed the fate of Margaret of Anjou. Edward was anxious to give her up. Her charge cost money; his sister was getting tired of being Margaret's jailer; it was a trial to be the unwilling host of a Queen.

The storm was worsening and the lightning now flashed; the skies were dark and the air was heavy with the coming rain. The thunderclaps shook the bridge.

Louis motioned to Commines to come to his side. "Do you recognize him?" Louis asked.

"Indeed I do," Edward said, noting the two men were dressed exactly alike. Edward recalled the occasions he had met Commines when he had served the old Duke of Burgundy.

"Ah," said Louis, leading the conversation then to the present Duke of Burgundy. "What will you do if the Duke refuses to be included in this treaty?"

"I shall offer to include him again for his own sake," Edward said, indicating he was not going to abandon Charles, even though he was a fool.

"And then if he will not?" Louis persisted, leaning close to the grating as the rain now began to fall in slanting gusts of wind.

Crack! went the skies as they opened to let the lightning through.

Edward paid no attention. "I will have to wash my hands of the matter if the Duke refuses for the third time."

And now Louis leaned even closer. "What of Francis of Brittany? How if he refuses to sign?"

Edward's reply to this was as suddenly grim as the thunder. "In my hour of need," Edward said plainly with unvarnished truth, "I found no better friend than the Duke of Brittany." Suddenly his French made Edward quite Gallic. "I beg you, my lord, not to molest him!"

Louis instantly recognized that he should not pursue this subject now and yet he did. He hunched his shoulders a little and pursed his lips. Edward repeated, "If anyone should invade Brittany I will come back and defend him!" Edward let the temper of his tones speak for themselves. He wanted Louis not to mistake his intentions of defending Francis of Brittany.

The rain beat down. The lords gathered at the end of the

bridge were huddled in their fine capes, which were now beginning to look bedraggled and sorry. Louis motioned them toward
him and so did Edward.

"I wish you could come to Paris," Louis said. "I hereby invite
you. We have so many beautiful women in Paris."

He eyed Edward, who was thinking his reputation was worse
than he actually deserved, but Edward smiled. "I mislike to de-
cline," he said.

"Cardinal Bourbon here at my side will be glad to grant you
absolution for any frolic."

Edward grinned. "I wish it could be. *Quel dommage! Je suis
desolé!*" He laughed but he was thinking of Bessie. The rain
was pouring down, and it was time to take his leave. Politely,
not to turn their backs, both monarchs backed away from the
bridge.

Louis had offered to send him anything he needed, even to
candles, but Edward was already occupied with the problems
of getting his army out of France and remembering all Louis'
gestures, and trying to evaluate. The biggest worry right at this
very moment was how his troops would take to actually packing
up and going home without a fight. They had seemed content
enough up to now, but when it came to the actual leaving would
he have to deal with some hotheads, like his brother Richard who
wanted to stay, raise the banners, and fight and pillage France?

Immersed in his thoughts, he noticed the rain was stopping.
He looked up at the skies; the sun was coming out and bits of
cloudy blue blotted the whole afternoon sky. Edward walked on.
He saw his brother Richard at the flap of his silken tent, his
slight figure a reproach to the abandonment of the clash of arms
to the scratch of pen and ink upon paper. Edward was surprised
to see Richard come out of the tent, for Richard, he thought,
would have sulked all afternoon and closeted himself away from
his brother the King. And indeed Richard would have done so
except that he had been drawn from his lonely vigil by voices.

"Look! Look!" It was one of his own captains speaking, and
even while Edward came toward them from a distance men
gathered around and came from other tents and were quietly
advancing upon the King's own tent.

"What the devil is going on?" Edward muttered to Hastings
and both men quickened their pace.

The men around the tent were silent, but more and more of them were gathering. Finally someone perceived that Edward himself was almost upon them, so one slipped away and came and knelt before his astonished King.

"Your Grace! Behold! After the storm a dove came, a white dove, and sat upon your tent and it is still there!"

Edward raised his eyes from the kneeling man. One of the soldiers who had had to be dragged out of Amiens dead-drunk two days ago lifted his hands to heaven and cried, "It is the Holy Ghost, my lord. This peace is the work of the Holy Ghost. The white dove sits quiet on your tent."

The white dove ruffled its feathers and looked down its bony nose at all the soldiers and the lords and the King. It did not move.

All of Edward's soldiers saw the dove, its white plumage nestled in the fold of the tent. Edward called to him his confessor. He did not know whether the dove bore the spirit of the Holy Ghost, but he knew he should thank God that he had evidenced this miracle and that his soldiers thought so too.

Chapter 20

BESSIE THOUGHT, I am thirty-six years old and the hours, days, weeks and even years are gathering themselves, hastening onward in a furious rush. There was no time to go into a four-week retirement really, so she partly concealed from Edward that she was due early in November, and she did not enter her prepared chambers at Windsor until the twentieth of October, and even then the Duchess admitted her indispensable secretary and chamberlain of the household to her presence.

Edward had said that if the baby was a girl he wished to name her Anne in honor of the saint to whom he so often prayed, and he and Bessie remembered when he said it first, that day that seemed so long ago in Whittlebury Forest near Grafton.

The little Anne was born on the second of November.

"A new baby for Christmas!" Edward said. They were looking forward to Christmas already, the festival of Christmas, a time of lightened spirits always. November was behaving badly. It was very cold and very damp; the skies streamed with icy rain. But at Christmas, with the great halls of Windsor decorated and all the family gathered, it would be just like it always was, as though one weren't older and as though times didn't change, as though there really was peace on earth and goodwill toward men. As the year of our Lord fourteen hundred and seventy-five drew to its close, Edward worried about Charles of Burgundy who seemed to be behaving like a madman, and Clarence who was drinking heavily and who was worried about his frail wife; and Bessie worried about her mother, for the Duchess was not well; she was thin and pale and losing weight, and her bright eyes seemed remote and lusterless to Bessie; but there were good things too.

Anthony was bringing the little Prince to Windsor for Christmas; he was five years old. Gravely he regarded the new baby.

"We have the same birthday, Mother," he said.

It was almost his bedtime. The fire burned cheerfully on the hearth. Edward sat with his two-year-old son Richard, newly created Duke of York, on his lap while young Bess read the story of the Christ Child.

The other children sat in a circle around the fire on bright cushions, the candlelight gleaming on their blond heads.

"She brought forth her firstborn son and laid him in a manger because there was no room in the inn."

The Prince looked across to Edward as if to ask why or how could this happen?

Edward, remembering his own dictum that the child, his own firstborn son, should not go to bed in any but a happy frame of mind, asked Bess to read on about the coming of the Wise men and the angels in the fields and the great wonderful star and the music—the heavenly choir of angels, with music pouring from the night skies. Edward heard again the voices of his own choir as they had sung that day at evensong. Heaven on earth, he thought, closing his eyes briefly as the music poured again through his mind, each note rehearsing itself.

Exactly at eight the Prince was tucked into bed, this night by his mother and father, and Edward's own hand drew the curtains, his last glimpse of his son that of his head on the white pillow and the smile he was given as little Edward said, "Good night, Father."

Even the Duchess was feeling better; she was so proud of not only her grandchildren but of Lionel, who was now, as he had always prophesied, the chancellor of Oxford, and Edward was building anew at Magdalene and had sent his own nephews to be at school there. Anthony was excited not only at being at court but at his preparations to go to Italy, his long-deferred trip, the one on which he had set his heart so many years ago. He could be spared from the Prince's household for a few months.

So the Duchess had her own children with her; the court swarmed with Woodvilles, even to Kate's glittering head. She said to Anthony, "When you are with my husband (who was rich with royal blood) I wish you would at least let him finish a sentence, especially you and Richard."

Anthony looked at her in surprise. "Kate," he expostulated, "I am never rude."

"I know he never says anything but—"

Lionel was cogitating over Kate's request. "I believe that truly, Kate, your illustrious husband, the Duke, actually never finishes any sentence, so it is difficult to wait on him or his words."

Kate giggled. "You're so pedantic, Lionel."

"You're more witty than you know, Lionel," Richard Woodville said.

"You treat him in such an offhand manner," Kate said. "It hurts his feelings."

"When we're all together we're apt to do that," Anthony said. "But we don't mean to be rude. After all, we don't mind if someone interrupts us—"

"No, you're all just so positive!"

"So are you, my dear," the Duchess said. "After all it is up to you to draw your husband into the group."

"I try to, Mother," Kate said, a bit wistfully. Her marriage had been made for her by Edward and Bessie. The Duke of Buckingham was indeed the bearer of royal blood and Edward had thought he would cement him this way into the circle of Plantagenet and Woodville. Certainly no one could ask for a more bright and charming creature than Kate. She leaned forward and whispered, "He resents us, sometimes even me." Her red mouth was caught by her teeth and she looked so puzzled and wondering that her brothers and mother smiled at her indulgently. How could anyone not love Kate? It was impossible.

Lionel said, "There is always rivalry and friction in any royal court, in any government. I could give you many instances from Caesar to Alexander to the citizens of Athens."

"Spare us, I beg of you!" That was Richard.

"I expect that your husband, Kate," Lionel went on, "is simply a bit jealous of Edward's affections and thinks we push him aside. But I want to make it plain to all of you," Lionel raised his finger and waggled it, "that Edward does indeed rule the roost and that he simply follows the age-old theory of monarchs, *Divida et regna*, Divide and rule."

"Don't be so pontifical," the Duchess said. "My other sons understand Latin."

"Did Richard ever have Latin?" Lionel asked in surprise.

"I have less Latin than you, Lionel, and less Greek but much more charm," Richard said, bowing deeply. "And the ladies adore me."

The Duchess was immediately diverted. "Richard," she said, "you should marry."

Kate sighed. She saw that the discussion about her problems was ended and she would have to abandon the center stage for Richard. Still she would have to get her mother alone, for she was indeed worried about her husband. He was like a fretful child somehow. He was truly very different from her brothers; she had to treat him like a little boy instead of like the man she had hoped he would be.

But of course what Lionel had said was true: It was now Edward and only he who directed the courses of the realm, his the figure of the sun while around him revolved the court, always vying, each with the other, Woodville against Hastings; and while both Hastings and Anthony loved Edward entirely, envy slithered around and through the lords and nobles as green as a garden snake amid the roses of the King's garden. Yet Edward meant to be a stifler among them all and what truly and deeply troubled him was the problem of Clarence.

For a long time Edward had wanted to give his father and brother a decent tomb and a decent burial. He chose that moment and he chose it to see if Clarence, in the bosom of family grief, would amend his ways. Lately even at the council table Clarence would sit, arms folded, eyes either cast down or glowering, seldom speaking, and then in a grunt, far different from the way in which he used to be. Edward remembered one time at the council board when the mayor of London was present; the mayor's head had nodded and Clarence had leaned across to Edward and said, "Do lower your voice, my lord. The mayor is asleep."

Gone unhappily were those days. It seemed almost impossible to Edward that his brother should so openly covet his crown. Edward as King had no kin, only an heir. His only duty was to himself, his God and his subjects, and anything that interfered would have to be swept aside ruthlessly. With Clarence kinship, nay, brotherhood meant only a constant threat to the succession. And sooner or later Edward would have to act and when he did. . . .

Meantime he made elaborate plans to disinter the bodies of his father and his younger brother Edmund from their temporary resting place at Pontefract and arrangements for a solemn state funeral went forward. All of the royal family, its near and far kin and the entire court and ambassadors from foreign lands would pay homage to the dead father of their King.

On the twenty-fourth of July then the two bodies were taken from their humble coffins at Pontefract; that day, all day long, an image of the Duke dressed in an ermine-trimmed mantle and cap of estate lay in state in the choir of the church at Pontefract. Around the hearse was such a blaze of candles that the angel who guarded it, wearing a crown, seemed to be right of heaven itself instead of a man-made image, and so thought in wonder the common people who came to do homage to their King's father. They were each man given a penny to do honor to the dead, and each woman with child received twopence.

Early in his reign Edward had endowed, in fact, refounded a college at Fotheringhay and it was in the church there that he wished the bodies of his father and brother to eternally rest. The journey from Pontefract would take four days and the procession, led by Richard of Gloucester, garbed entirely in black and accompanied by many clerics, went through the land each day and by night rested in church, and in each church was solemn mass performed and all people came to do honor again.

On the twenty-ninth of July Edward in a blue habit and a mourning cap waited at the entrance of the churchyard with Anthony and Hastings, and Clarence and Bessie's firstborn son Thomas, Marquis of Dorset, who stood close to his stepfather. Thomas bit his lip hard as the cortege came close, for he could see plain the tears standing in Edward's eyes. The King went forward and leaned down and kissed the image of the dead Duke. Then Edward stood aside, his brown eyes bright with tears, and slowly he followed the coffins of his father and brother into the church.

The masses said the next day were three: the Mass of our Lady, the Mass of the Trinity and the Requiem were sung. The Bishop of Lincoln delivered the funeral sermon and as Edward disappeared into his closet men could see he had taken out his handkerchief.

The next day the Bishop of Lincoln preached the funeral oration. The church held most of the nobility of England. Then Lord Ferrers, dressed in full armor, rode the dead Duke's courser, holding in his hand the battle-ax, reversed, and after him came the King and Bessie with their two oldest daughters; they presented the mass penny for their grandfather.

About the church and castle, pavilions and tents grew like flowers. Edward had provided food and drink for all, fine food too; capons, cygnets, and butter and cream were on the menu. Five thousand people filed into the church to pass the bier and many more than that partook of the King's hospitality.

But the royal family dined in private. Clarence's wife, Isabel Neville, had just presented him with a daughter, but she was very ill and her sister Anne was with her. Edward felt his six healthy children and his radiant wife must be a constant reproach to Clarence, and he tried to put his arm around him and tell him that he was sorry, very sorry about Isabel. Clarence muttered something and said he should leave and go to Isabel. Edward agreed but when he walked away Edward felt a kind of impotent sadness come over him. How happy they had used to be when their father was alive, those days that seemed so many many years ago, before the shadow of the crown had fallen between them.

Nonetheless Edward had reason to be proud of himself. Although he had conquered no territory in France he had brought home safe to their wives the tillers of the soil and the lords of the manors. England was at peace. The treaties signed with the Hansards, the French, for trade assured the flow of commerce to and from her shores. Because he didn't need it Edward had remitted the last tax that had been levied before the war; back it went into the grateful pockets of his subjects. From Louis came the steady flow of tribute and Edward's trading ventures poured gold into his own pockets. He could devote now much money to rebuilding, to the collecting of *objets d'art*, to his precious books, to the founding of chantries, to all the good things of life which the Renaissance man cherished so highly. Cordial relations with Scotland meant at least a fairly quiet border. Little Cecily was betrothed to the heir of James III. In fact James was so enamored of the peace that existed between the two coun-

tries that he would later propose a wholesale marriage alliance
between the two houses of Stuart and Plantagenet.

Edward's relations with Francis of Brittany remained cordial
also, largely due to Edward's own restraint, for Francis was a
shifty fox and yet Edward could never forget how he had helped
him in his time of deepest trouble, as he had told and reminded
Louis. Francis now held as a pawn the only remaining heir of
Lancaster, young Henry Tudor, and his uncle Jasper Tudor.

But Edward's biggest worry was Charles of Burgundy, who
was indulging in such antics that the surname of "Bold" Edward
thought should be changed to "Rash."

He had affianced his only daughter to Maximilian, son of the
Emperor of Austria. Now Charles had it in his head that he himself should be the Emperor.

In front of Charles stood the firm and recalcitrant Swiss.
Charles' armies had overrun part of Lorraine and were besieging
Neuss, and heartily sick of him and ready to rend him they armed
their formidable mercenaries. Although Charles didn't know it
he was to meet death at their hands in the winter snow at Nancy
in just a few months.

But anxious to know what was going on, Edward commissioned Anthony to go to Charles. First Anthony was to travel to
Italy, to Milano, to the Duke and apprise him that the reason
Charles was fighting the Swiss was to get closer to Milano. After that Anthony was free to visit other cities but on his way
home he was to go to Charles who was in camp at Neuss.

Anthony did indeed see the Duke of Milano and then he traveled south to Rome. Anthony fell in love with Italy, as men have
done throughout the ages. But outside of Rome on the highway
the English Earl, rich and mighty, was suddenly surrounded by
very polite and bowing highwaymen, who relieved Anthony of
his plate and jewels, some of which he had purchased in Milano.
And of course all his money.

"Anthony is so damned naïve," Edward said.

Bessie hastened to send him a letter of exchange for four thousand ducats by way of the Medici bankers, which reached Anthony in Venice. In Venice also some of the shopkeepers turned
up Anthony's possessions, and the Venetian Senate met and de-

cided that any possession of the English Earl should be returned to him. So like even the present-day traveler to Italy Anthony left Venice in love with the Italians, for no matter what they did they did it so pleasantly and smiling. He proceeded to Morat where Charles of Burgundy waited in his martial array, his martial mind.

Charles asked him immediately whether he had come to stay and fight by his side.

Anthony smiled. "Is that your wish, my lord?"

The next day in light mail he toured the camp and rode out to see the forces of the enemy, the "froward carls," as the English called the Swiss. Anthony tried to talk with Charles at dinner but found him so supercilious that it was impossible to carry on a normal conversation; Charles was the same way with his own lords.

Anthony said to his secretary that night that he thought Charles had delusions. "If we stay here we will probably get killed for our pains," Anthony said. "The Swiss hate him and they're going to beat him soundly." Anthony politely took his leave of Charles before what he called the festivities began, and it was good he did, for Charles was soundly beaten at Morat and retired momentarily, licking his wounds but learning nothing from them.

Charles had one satisfaction though. He dubbed Anthony a coward.

But Anthony was glad to be home, and when he was home a new sign greeted his eyes, the sign of the Red Pale just a few yards west of Westminster Abbey among some almshouses. A man named William Caxton, an English merchant who had formerly lived in Bruges and done some negotiating previous for the crown, had opened up a shop with a printing press.

Edward's sister Margaret had patronized Caxton, and she sent him to England with his printed book on the play of chess. Caxton had dedicated the book to Margaret's favorite brother Clarence.

But while the idea of a printing press did not especially appeal to Clarence, who was too occupied in his own tangled affairs anyway, it did appeal to Anthony, who was fascinated and enthralled. Nothing must do but that he should see all of the shop and invite Caxton to count on his, Lord Rivers', patronage. And what of the first book to be published in England? What about Lord Rivers' personal translation into English from the French of *The Dictes and Sayings of the Philosophers?* Excited, Anthony got out his mass of papers and with the renewed diligence of any author whose work is to be published sat up late at night making sure of sentence structure and interest. He had to be in London anyway, for Edward had summoned a great council meeting for all the peers of the realm.

A grand council meeting was not summoned lightly; there were a great many problems on Edward's mind. So even Richard of Gloucester arrived in London, leaving his wife off at Warwick Castle to be with Isabel. Anne cared nothing about the court anyway; she was much more content in Middleham. She left it this Christmas with intense regret, and although she was worried about Isabel she was worried about her own delicate son, as she would be for the rest of his life.

It was always a shock for Anne to enter Warwick Castle and find her father not here, nor all the retainers and hangers-on she had known as a child. Her mother had stayed in Middleham at Anne's specific request, for she did not want to leave her little son without a close member of the family, and although she supposed she could have brought the little fellow by litter, all wrapped up, still she was afraid to trust the delicate boy to winter travel. And it was a bitter winter, as Charles of Burgundy was to find out.

But Anne found Isabel's quarters relatively unchanged; even the big old sideboard that they used to hide in occupied one wall of Isabel's withdrawing room. Isabel was in bed and if the furniture in the room was familiar, Isabel was not; Anne knew the moment she set eyes on her that she was going to die.

Anne, as she always did, felt her body freeze with terror and long shivers of the familiar hurt she had felt so many times before, but she managed a smile and came over to the bed; she took Isabel in her arms and kissed her, and then allowed her tears to spill over. "Oh, I'm so glad to see you," she cried, wiping her eyes openly.

Isabel smiled and blinked her eyes. "Give me that, Anne," she said and blotted her own tears.

"This is nothing to do," Anne said. "I'll pour us each some wine and we will celebrate."

For the next five days as Christmas approached Anne tended her sister, for her doctors would not let Isabel out of bed. The fires were kept blazing in her chamber, and Anne decorated it herself with boughs of holly and ivy and fir. Isabel loved the smell of fresh fir, and Anne ordered its fragrant boughs picked every day to freshen the air in Isabel's chamber. All manner of delicacies were brought to her, thin sliced breast of dove, a little portion of poached fresh-caught trout, a bit of roast capon, a little hot broth or a jellied soup, cold, for sometimes Isabel was so hot, so very hot.

The finest of wine was all that Anne would serve her. The chicken soup was laced with cream, strained through cloth so she could drink it with ease. Anne found much to do during the days; anything her fertile brain could dream up to divert and comfort Isabel. But it was during the nights, the winter nights, that her terror seized her anew, and she did not need to dream of the birth of Isabel's first child, whom she herself had wrapped in a white linen shroud. Then she had had her mother with her; now she had no one but herself, for she couldn't confide in Isabel's women; she was afraid they might tell Isabel.

As for Clarence, he was in attendance and now Anne saw for herself very plain that he was a confirmed drunkard. Gone entire was his vaunted charm; his eyes were shot through with bloodied veins and venomous thoughts. And all around her was the magnificence of Warwick Castle where she had spent many months of her youth, all around her the reminder of her father's greatness, the greatness of her family, all come to nought but grief and blood by a man's ambitions. Only women are sane, Anne thought. All men are mad.

Isabel's baby was born December nineteenth while thin snow scurried at the towering mass of Warwick Castle. And the baby was a boy, a tiny red-faced morsel who, if he could have been saved by love, would have survived more than the scant week of life allotted to him, for his Aunt Anne Neville poured out of her thin body a veritable cataract of love and joy. Isabel herself slipped quietly into death three days later, three days before Christmas.

And Christmas Day found Anne on her knees in church begging the Blessed Virgin to spare her sister's son.

The saints and Virgin turned a deaf ear to Anne's pleas. The tiny boy followed his mother quickly, as though indeed the world were far too unaccommodating for either one of them, too gentle to endure. Clarence gave orders for Isabel's body to lie in state for thirty-five days in Tewkesbury Cathedral; close by the bier, under the stones, resting perhaps uneasily, lay the young Prince Edward, Margaret of Anjou's son. Isabel lay with all the accouterments of a great Duchess, and young Edward had his plumed ostrich feathers under the stones with him. The cathedral had been cleansed by prayer since that bloody day when Edward had entered it, sword in hand. The man whom Clarence had betrayed and the wife he had never loved slept side by side; over their unhearing ears poured the music, the prayers and the chants of the priests. The New Year arrived with ice and snow; it was even worse weather in Europe. In London Edward was preparing to meet his grand council when startling word arrived from the Continent. Charles of Burgundy was dead, a bloody frozen corpse in the snow at Nancy. It was January 5, 1477.

Edward was assessing; it was a good time: the New Year. He had spent much time and more money wedding his sister to Burgundy's Duke, but there were no children of that liaison, unhappily, no male heir for Burgundy, only one previous daughter, the twenty-year-old Mary of Burgundy, now the greatest heiress in Europe. Now young Mary, with her stepmother Margaret, Charles' widow, faced the hungry wolves of Europe alone.

Charles' death was the finest gift the New Year could have brought to Louis. Instantly he went to church to pray for his sickly only son and to thank God for all his blessings. Burgundy would soon be his.

But Louis was facing two women more determined than he knew. Edward's sister, Margaret, Dowager Duchess of Burgundy, had instant plans. Her brother, her favorite brother Clarence, was now a convenient widower; what better than to wed the two, cementing once more the alliance between England and

Burgundy? Immediately she dispatched messengers to her brother Edward.

"Margaret is acting as though the coronet of Burgundy were a nice toy for a younger brother," Edward said to Bessie. "In effect she is saying, Poor Clarence, he wants a crown so badly. Why not give him a coronet instead to play with? For the mercy of God!" Edward's patience was wearing thin; his decisive no to the proposal was so quick and so definite that Clarence's mouth flew open and he stared at his brother stupidly across the council board. His whole body trembled with impotent frustration and self-pity.

"She needs a strong Prince," Edward said aloud, "to keep Louis at bay but if she wants an Englishman, then let her consider Anthony Woodville."

Clarence went red and puffed with impotent rage. But Edward's thoughts had already turned to King Louis. He was all too aware that Louis was indeed Mary's lord; the political animal that he was never let him forget it. Yet again Louis must be faced; without even a farewell to the glowering Clarence, after dinner Edward summoned the French ambassador.

"We are shocked by Louis' perfidy," Edward began sternly. If Louis didn't get his armies out of the vicinity of Burgundy and Calais, he himself would have to send troops; indeed Lord Hastings had already left for Calais with well equipped men-at-arms and a company of archers. After all, Edward said, his sister Margaret was the Dowager Duchess of Burgundy and he wouldn't tolerate her safety being threatened. So Louis resigned himself, signed a treaty of peace with Burgundy and the young Duchess married her Maximilian of Austria and Edward was left to deal only with the problem of Clarence.

For if Clarence had been a thorn in Edward's side for years, now he was an almost impossible threat, the dagger poised for the thrust.

"My brother means to put me out of the way," Clarence cried. "He practices the black arts on his subjects, will practice them on me and mine. He means to consume me like a candle. But I will requite him! I order my followers to be ready to lay on their harness in an hour for war against the King."

In Westminster Edward, who could be amazingly patient, could also be ruthlessly angry. "He'll regret this with every vein in his body," Edward growled, his big fists clenched. It would have given him intense pleasure to smash that big fist into Clarence's face, and for a moment it crossed his mind that maybe a good beating would sober Clarence. He ordered Clarence to come to Westminster.

Clarence came because there was no help for it. When he arrived Edward received him in the palace of Westminster and had taken pains to have the mayor of London present. Abruptly Edward, seated on his carved, high chair, accused the kneeling Duke, his brother, of taking the laws of the realm into his own hands and being a subverter of the King's justice.

Clarence was suddenly afraid. All his life he had plotted and planned against Edward, and he had never thought that someday he would have to account to his royal brother. Now suddenly at last there was no patience left in the heart of the King, no patience, only bitter resolve. Clarence on one knee looked straight ahead at Edward's casually crossed booted legs, which in the custom of the time were tight to his thighs and hips; the powerful legs now uncrossed themselves and both booted feet were planted on the steps up to his carved chair. Clarence raised his eyes up, past his brother's broad shoulders, to his face. Edward's eyes met his, a long look; there was contempt in that look, a searing contempt and dislike. There was the threat of a violent temper held rigidly under control; Edward's big hands gripped the arms of his chair, and the ruby ring on his finger blazed fire like to that which smoldered in his eyes.

"You may rise, my lord," the King said in icy tones. "We have summoned our guard. We are consigning you to our Tower of London."

There was no one very near. Edward said low but explosively, "By the Mercy of God, you fool George! You have forced me to this!" In louder tones he said plain for all to hear, "You will await our pleasure in prison."

Yet Clarence did not fear for his life. He stood and faced Edward, who by now didn't trust himself to speak. The mayor and the aldermen who were witnessing this, plus Edward's attending lords, hardly breathed; it seemed as though violence might explode in the King's chamber. Edward raised a big hand and the guards at the door stood at attention, the doors opened and with a blare of trumpets the King's guard marched solemnly into the room. Clarence made them a mocking bow. Edward sat rigid. He said no word until Clarence had passed from his sight. And even then Edward permitted himself no other mention of his erring brother; he had nothing further to say now anyway except he thought of the painful interview ahead, for the one person to whom it would be most difficult to explain away his actions was his mother.

If Edward was worried about what he would say to his mother, Anthony and Bessie and the whole Woodville clan were much more worried about the Duchess.

"She is very sick, Bessie," Anthony said.

They were walking along together to the Duchess' rooms. When they entered the Duchess was propped up on pillows, her eyes closed. As they approached the bed Anthony could see the very light labored breathing, as though her great heart had finally failed her. But when she opened her eyes to see her two oldest children, her old smile flashed out with effort.

"That book I gave you, Anthony, that beautiful one of Christine de Pisan, the proverbs—" she stopped for breath.

Anthony glanced at Elizabeth. "Mother," he said softly, taking her hand, "I gave it to Lord Gruthuyse."

"Oh. I forgot." The Duchess sighed.

"I made a translation though," Anthony said. "I could read it to you. In fact, I could probably recite from it by memory." He smiled and the Duchess squeezed his hand.

"Don't talk, Mother," Bessie whispered. She turned her head and the tears dripped down her face; one of the Duchess' women pressed a clean napkin into her hand.

"We will just sit here while you rest," Bessie said.

The Duchess had closed her eyes again. Presently she opened them and said, "I was thinking about your father. I wonder what women with two husbands do when they get to heaven?" The faintest twinkle was in her eyes. "You look so worried, Anthony. Don't be. I shall choose your father."

"Oh, Mother," Anthony said.

"Yes," said the Duchess, lapsing into French, "you are too serious, you and Lionel."

"Lionel is coming to see you," Anthony said. Bessie was sitting quiet, holding her mother's hand.

"Am I that ill?" The Duchess sighed. "If I feel better tomorrow, Bessie, I would like to go back to Grafton. I've been thinking of Grafton."

"Of course," Bessie said.

"I would like to see it, perhaps tomorrow," the Duchess said. She closed her eyes again and she seemed to be asleep. After awhile Bessie rose and she and Anthony tiptoed out of the room.

"I'll make all the arrangements about Grafton," Bessie said. "Do you think, Anthony, that she will be able? A fine comfortable litter?"

He knew that Bessie was talking into the wind and that it made her feel better to do something, and so he agreed with her, but the following day the Duchess did not rouse and her room was silent save for her labored breath.

"She feels no pain, Your Grace," Dr. Sirigo whispered to Bessie.

The gathered Woodville clan mourned. The Duchess would never see Grafton again.

Bessie sat on a tasseled stool at the side of the bed and the Woodville clan gathered, the Duchess' twelve children and the grandchildren and even the cousins from Lord Rivers' side of the family. But Bessie kept her vigil and only permitted her sisters and brothers into the room. She wanted the children to remember their grandmother as she had been throughout her gallant and joyous tilt with life.

So while the Woodvilles mourned and the chantries sang for the soul of the departed Duchess of Bedford, Edward's mother took the Duchess of Bedford's death as an excuse to come to Windsor. Cecily Neville had come to plead for her son.

It was as painful an interview as Edward had ever had in his whole life.

"There isn't anything I wouldn't grant you, mother," he said sadly. "Except I cannot give Clarence his freedom."

Every day fresh evidence of Clarence's treachery was being brought in to be laid before Edward's eyes.

"But what are you going to do?" the Duchess cried.

"I don't know," Edward said. "It is painful for me too."

"To rend our house in public!"

But Edward had made up his mind that there would be no

midnight murder in the Tower. "Whatever I decide to do, Mother, will be done lawfully and openly."

"It is the Woodvilles who hate Clarence, who have pushed you into this!"

"Mother, it is Clarence himself who has pushed me into putting him in prison. I had no choice." Edward flung out his hands. "Do you think that I have not exercised the patience of a saint? I have forgiven him time after time after time. I have lavished him with lands and gifts and titles." He was silent. "Worst, I have loved him entire."

Edward's voice was low; he was thinking of those long-past days when he used to go to see little George and Richard every day in London because their father was absent. "I was born with a strong sense of family," Edward said, "and by the mercy of God it has turned its fangs on me. I know it is difficult to be the brother of a King. And while you mourn about that I submit that it is also difficult to be a King and to be surrounded by self-seekers and treachery in the midst of one's family. And even on the bloody field of Barnet I sent two yeomen of the guard to try to save my cousin of Warwick and my trusty John. Who betrayed me!"

Edward stood. It was a warm day; he was dressed in a handsome doublet and matching close-fitted hose of blue. A heavy chain of gold was his only adornment besides his huge heavy ring, and the Duchess' heart was torn apart; her wonderful, handsome, magnificent son and poor, poor Clarence.

"God give me strength," she cried.

"Ah," said Edward. "And to me too, for God's sake!"

"I went to Sandwich to try and stop that marriage to Warwick's daughter."

"His first betrayal and Warwick's," Edward muttered. "And you see you did no good. I had warned him, you know. I'd warned both of them. The minute I heard of Warwick's plotting to marry my two brothers to his two daughters, I had them both confined to their rooms with my own gentlemen of the body on guard. I tried to teach them a lesson in obedience. There can be one King and only one."

"If I go to him and ask him to submit and sue for grace and pardon—"

"It would do no good," Edward interrupted. "That is a dream.

I've done that time after time. The truth is that he is no longer the son you used to know and love and no longer my brother. He is only a jealous man who would like to see me dead. On my oath were it I in the Tower now and he in my boots, I would have been long dead."

"No," said the Duchess. "He will always be my son and he will always be your brother."

Edward paused in his stride. "That is true, madam," he said. "The task before me is pure, plain hell."

He tried to forget Clarence and his political maneuverings.

Secretly he was arranging a marriage alliance between the Infanta Isabella of Spain and the Prince of Wales. This matter to be kept so secret that the letter from Ferdinand enjoined Edward to tell no one of it save his wife and his Chancellor, but since that letter to this day reposes with the seal of Ferdinand still attached, in the Bibliothèque Nationale of France, it must be supposed that Louis' spies were operating most successfully.

In August, while the Spanish ambassadors were in London and Clarence languished in the Bowyer Tower, Maximilian of Austria arrived in Burgundy and married its heiress. Booted and spurred messengers hastily carried the news to all the courts of Europe.

Edward swore and Louis grinned. Immediately he set his own armies to lay siege to St. Omer. Hastings flooded the land around Calais and made ready to resist. Louis sent his own messengers to Edward to invite him to join him in reducing Burgundy and promising to let him divide the spoils.

Edward, tongue in cheek, merely replied by asking what excuse Louis had to offer for attacking Mary of Burgundy.

Louis had lots of reasons. She had wed without his consent. Moreover she had wed an Austrian, so from that day onward Louis referred to Mary as Madame d'Autriche, always bringing out the four syllables in a fine flow of upward ascending accent. He assured Edward he had a *"très juste et raisonable cause"*; Madame d'Autriche had even the temerity to oppose the wishes of her sovereign lord.

Edward hedged because he had not yet received his reports from his own agents and they arrived the following day. They were quite illuminating, for Louis was in trouble. All over France the nobility were fretting; Louis had in the first week in

August executed the Duke de Nemours with complete aplomb, and his lords were uneasy in their châteaux and even uneasier at court. Louis le Terrible!

Secondly and most important to Edward, the Prince of Orange who was leading Louis' armies had defected; no doubt the shorn head of the Duke de Nemours had something to do with it. He and his troops revolted and went over to Mary. The town of Flanders wanted no part of Louis.

Louis threw up his hands, signed a truce and retired to the sun, in Touraine, to his favorite winter residence, Plessis-du-Parc-les-Tours. There he waited for the embassy Edward was sending, now with new instructions, as the two Kings continued to wage their diplomatic wars.

For Edward knew that Louis would do little or nothing during the approaching winter, so his ambassadors were instructed to say that it would be unpolitic for him to make war, for suppose Louis died. England would find herself fighting alone. Edward grinned when he told his embassy to remind Louis that he was mortal.

The Christmas season found Bessie ever more reminded that her mother would never again come to court, in the second week in December, her cheeks bright from the cold, her eyes snapping with love and humor, and all the children running to greet their *grandmère*. When one is young holidays are things of wonder, Bessie thought; when one is older they can be sad, a mourning and remembrance of things past. She sighed and yet there was more than the usual amount of tasks piling up for her daily. Each year she had increased her secretarial staff. But besides the holidays, besides the fact that Parliament was convening right after the New Year and that there were enormous amounts of entertaining and presents to be selected for important lords and servants, gifts to be sent overseas as gestures of amity, besides all this, she was pregnant again, and she was arranging the marriage ceremony of her little son Richard, Duke of York, who was four years old, and Anne Mowbray, who was all of six and who was the sole heiress of the Duke of Norfolk.

It was to be a great occasion. And it had taken some arrangement from Bessie and Edward, for the little Anne's mother had fully appreciated the value of her daughter's hand and had been bargaining shrewdly with the King and Queen for two years, and Edward had had to sign papers which returned the great inheritance to the family in case the little Anne did not live to maturity.

The tiny bride arrived at the palace on the fourteenth of January. Reassured by the presence of all the royal children, a smile of awed delight came onto her face when Edward came to bid her good night and to inform her solemnly that he himself would give the little bride away.

Young Richard was nervous. All those people watching!

"I'll take you myself, Dickon," Bessie said. "I will be right there with you and all your sisters too."

They had both rehearsed in their childish voices; they had both tried on their fine clothes. Edward had kept his promise to Bessie and had never parted her from her second son. At four the little Richard was quite tall, like his father, and healthy and smiling and very bright. He had his own council chamber "above the council chamber of our dearest son, the Prince, to have and to hold as his council chamber during his life," he had his own chancellor and an attorney and a chamberlain. But it was his mother who every night drew the curtains around his bed or read to him before the fire after evensong. "Goodnight, my dearest boy," Bessie said. He was sitting up straight in bed.

She leaned over a bit clumsily and he laughed. "Mother, you are getting fat."

Bessie sat down on the side of the bed and gathered him close.

"I'll tell you why," she said. "We're going to have another baby in the family. Maybe even a little brother for you to play with. In May. We can take the new baby for walks outside this summer, you and I together. Now close your eyes and pretend you are sleepy."

She pulled the curtains and as she pulled the last one he had indeed closed the dark eyes; to Bessie he looked like a little angel straight from heaven, the long lashes dark against the innocent young cheek. Bessie went down on her knees at the side of the bed and prayed to the saints and Our Lady to watch over him during this night. Richard poked his head out of the curtains and looked down at his mother's gilt hair. He hesitated. He should be lying quiet; he was supposed to be. But he put his hand on her bent head and Bessie looked up, startled.

"I was saying a prayer for you," she said.

"I know. Thank you, Mother."

Bessie lifted him and tucked him back in bed. In the shadowy room Richard's attendants watched this scene. They bowed when Bessie left her son's room; they would keep watch over him all the rest of the night.

The next morning Kate and Bessie helped dress the little bride and then led her into Bessie's chamber where Anthony was waiting to conduct her to the chapel. Then Bessie hurried away.

When she entered Richard's room he was dressed and waiting, and dressed in the latest style too, the short cloak edged with ermine. In fact, the French tailor that Bessie and the Duchess had discovered for the Prince and the young Duke now had Edward's patronage too; he could never understand how in the whole bustling city of London Bessie and her mother had unerringly discovered an obscure genius. Now Bessie took her son's hand in hers and together they left the room. They were to await the procession within the chapel with Edward and the Prince, their grandmother, the Duchess of York, and the three Princesses, Elizabeth, Mary and Cecily.

Bessie and Richard took their place under the canopy of gold and Bessie looked about herself. She was in the chapel of St. Stephen and the decorations for the wedding had been hers. She thought it looked wonderful and so did Edward, for he nodded his head at her, pleased. The walls were hung with carpet; the color was a pale azure, sprinkled all over with golden fleurs-de-lis. The gold canopy shimmered above their heads. And all the greatest lords and ladies in the land were present.

Anthony looked so handsome as he appeared in the distance with the tiny bride. When he was right beside them Edward himself stepped forward and leaning down placed her hand in his; she was much too small to hook her hand in his arm.

The ceremony began. It seemed almost unreal to Bessie, and yet her mind went back in time when those selfsame words had been repeated by Edward and herself. She glanced at him now. It had been dark that May morning; there had been few candles. Bessie had wept and so had the Duchess. Bessie could see her plain, wiping her eyes and then flashing her brilliant smile. And then the wedding morning when they had so utterly committed themselves to each other forever and ever.

The Prince was six. He stood alongside Bessie. He was betrothed to the Princess of Aragon and Castile. Young Bess, whose blue eyes were full of tears, her mother saw, young Bess who adored her little brother Richard, was going to be the Queen of France. Edward was so proud of her; he called her Mam'selle la Dauphiness. And just yesterday Edward had said to Bessie, "Mary of Burgundy is *enceinte*. If she has a son our little Anne would make him a fine bride." And Bessie knew he would pursue this, that it was not just idle talk.

I am ambitious for my children too, she thought, perhaps even more than he. And yet I pray God when these children grow up they are happy together.

Music rolled over her head. High mass would be celebrated before the altar. Bessie and Edward knelt side by side. She glanced at his profile. It seemed so long ago and yet just yesterday that they had knelt like this together in the village church at Grafton. At that moment Edward turned his head, feeling her glance, and he reached out and took her hand.

It fell to Kate's husband, the Duke of Buckingham, to lead the bride back to the King's great chamber where the wedding banquet was spread to feast all the guests. And the press of lords and ladies and the great of the realm was so great that the gossipers and writers of the period found them too innumerable to write them all down.

Anthony had had another function to perform too, for he was in charge of the great tournaments which would follow, and to please Bessie he had chosen her oldest son, Thomas Grey, now Marquis of Dorset, to assist him, and so weeks before, the notices had gone up all over London and Bessie had helped him pick the prizes: an A of gold set with a diamond, the E of gold set with a ruby and the M of gold set with an emerald. Little Anne Mowbray, the new Duchess of York, solemnly gave out the prizes. Anthony was dressed all in white in the habit of a hermit and his hermitage was of black velvet. His badge was the scallop shell, for humility. And Edward smiled down at all from the stands and watched with great interest, for he loved these contests, especially the sword play. Thomas de Vere, who was Oxford's brother, had challenged Anthony. Edward had pardoned him and was glad to see him here. To make things easier for the clan of De Veres he had restored Oxford's Countess, even though her hotheaded, unappeasable husband lay in prison at Hammes Castle. The Lady of Richmond was present too. Her only son, Henry Tudor, the last shadowy claimant to the throne from the Lancaster side, was in sanctuary in Brittany. But Edward's thoughts could not help going to the one who was not present, and it was neither Oxford nor Richmond; it was Clarence.

Parliament convened the next day. As he usually did, Edward suggested the theme of the Chancellor's address. The Chancellor quoted in sonorous Latin, *"Non sine causa rex gladium portat."*

Anthony sat motionless, looking across at Edward. "Not without cause, without a reason," he amended, translating for himself, "does the King carry a sword."

Anthony sighed. No one had more cause to hate Clarence than he, for it was Clarence's first treachery that had cost the lives of his father and his flamboyant brother John. And yet Anthony sensed better than most how painful and difficult this whole business was for Edward.

The Chancellor finished his admonitory words and all knew what would be next. The King himself rose and told Parliament that he had come to ask them for a bill of attainder. He mentioned no name. Then he said, "On divers occasions in the past we have been forced to punish many rebels and traitors. Yet after the great victories which God has given to us we have spared not only the multitudes in the fields but have pardoned—the world knows!—the movers and executors of such treasons."

Edward paused. He leaned forward. "Yet how have our leniencies been repaid? Only by further treason, unnatural, much more malicious than ever before in our reign."

He stood very straight, his face set. "What makes this treason much more to be loathed is that it has been contrived by one who, of all creatures on this earth, was most dutybound to love, honor and obey and thank him, by one who," Edward's voice lowered, yet all could hear him plain, "by one whom," he repeated, "it greatly hurts my heart to name. Our brother," Edward said, "our brother George, Duke of Clarence."

A sigh ran over the packed chamber.

"A duke should be accused by his peers and we shall now do so, point after point."

Anthony followed through the list of crimes of which, without doubt, Clarence was guilty. The foreign representatives who had squeezed themselves in jotted down notes. Anthony sat as in a trance, watching, and then Edward said the last words for which Anthony had been waiting, for he knew all of Clarence's offenses far too well.

"Even after all this," Edward said, now firm, "I could still have found the heart to forgive him if he would make due submission." Oh, Anthony thought, then Edward's mother did try to make Clarence submit and ask for grace and pardon. And he must have refused. "For nighness, nearness of blood," Edward said, "for the love, the tender love we bore him in his youth—this inclined me to mercy. But the Duke has shown himself incorrigible. The safety of the realm demands his punishment. Therefore, I am asking this Parliament for a bill of attainder of high treason that he be forever deprived of his dukedom, his estates and all other property which we have granted him under our letters patent. Your speaker will now call witnesses."

Edward did not deprive Clarence of his right to answer his accusers and Clarence took the stand. He denied everything of which he was accused.

The lords and commons stared at him in astonishment.

"I ask to prove my innocence in the wages of battle. An ancient right."

Too ancient, thought Speaker Alyngton contemptuously.

"This is a solemn and meaningful Parliament," he admonished the Duke sternly. "No man has spoke in your defense."

He looked about the hall.

"The accused will be removed and the Commons will consider the bill for which our sovereign lord has asked."

Since Clarence was brother to a King the Commons, after having passed the bill of attainder, appointed the young Duke of Buckingham to pass the sentence on the accused. On the seventh of February the Duke rose. There was not a sound in the chamber. Buckingham read solemnly and slowly that the sentence upon George, lately Duke of Clarence, was the death sentence. It was a cold, cold winter day, the seventh day of February.

But not colder than Edward's heart. This is what he had to do in order to secure the succession. And he had done it open and legal. And yet now he couldn't bring himself to sign away Clarence's life.

"I can't do it," he said to Hastings.

"Even if he is your brother, my lord, he is guilty of high treason!"

Edward glanced at him. None of his councilors had as yet said one single word in Clarence's defense.

I could imprison him for life, Edward thought.

Three days passed. And news arrived from Hammes Castle. Oxford had thrown himself in the water-filled ditch around the stronghold. He'd been dragged out by the castle guard and his life had been saved.

Edward could picture it clearly, the dirty water, the Earl frantic to escape his cell even into death. Edward shuddered. Could he condemn Clarence to that or was life precious even within the walls of a prison? Oxford had probably thought that with Clarence unable to help him all their plans were awry and in despair he had thrown in his hand too, for whenever Oxford had been active in his little plots Clarence and somehow the Bishop of Stillington were always caught with their fingers in the pie too. With some satisfaction Edward threw Bishop Stillington into jail too; why should he escape punishment? Meantime Oxford was cleaned up and dried off and put back into his more or less comfortable cell. A week had passed now since Clarence had been sentenced. Speaker Alyngton asked for an interview with the King; he pointed out that a man lay under attainder of high treason and Commons had to act.

Edward said, pounding his fist on his heavy chair arm, "I forbid a public execution!"

That much he would not have, no matter what.

Someone had pointed out that Louis had sent his brother to his death without a tear, perhaps even with a smirk.

"I am not Louis!" Edward roared.

But with Speaker Alyngton he was calmer. "Do what you must then," he finally conceded. "Only I will not have him slyly murdered. I will not countenance it!" He leaned forward. "He is to be informed of his approaching death. He is to be given the rites of the church and he is to be asked which manner of death he desires."

Now it was almost done. On the night of the seventeenth of February two men went to the Bowyer Tower. There Clarence was reclining on his bed. The room was quite comfortably warm, he had been provided with wine and he was, as usual, half drunk. He smiled contemptuously on his callers.

Stiffly they informed him of the Speaker's words in Commons and that the Commons had acted and tonight Clarence should prepare himself for his eternal rest. Clarence had taken a sip of wine and now he rinsed his mouth out with it and spat.

"The priest is here," one said.

Clarence sniggered. He dug in his purse and brought out a penny, and he tossed it to one of them. "My mass penny." He rose and poured himself another cup of wine.

"You will be permitted to choose the manner of your death."

Clarence threw back his head and laughed. His language was obscene. Hands on hips he regarded the two uncomfortable and embarrassed men. He avowed that it was most kind of Commons and his bastard brother, and the two King's men thought anew that he deserved to die. No one could call England's King a bastard and expect to live.

"Everybody looks at me the way you do," Clarence said. I'm going to weep, he thought, and he summoned all his strength of will to forbid to himself this final indignity. "I command you then," he said, sweeping his arm about, "to bring me here, right here on that spot, a whole butt of malmsey."

They stared at him and he laughed again. Thank God I'm half drunk, he said to himself.

"Do you hear me?" he asked insultingly. "You send me the priest and he can shrive my soul, what's left of it. And then you may open the butt of malmsey and when I've drunk my fill you can drown me in it. That is my way of dying, gentlemen, my dearest desire, it's always been my secret wish, you can tell my brother, oh, yes, do tell my brother that, that my blood is on his head, my blood all mixed up with wine, lots and lots of wine."

They still stared at him.

"Come, gentlemen," he said. "Send in the priest, send for the wine and let's get on with the night's festivities. We will drown our King's sorrows, my dear brother's sorrows, my mother's bastard's sorrows, in wine, in a whole butt of malmsey!"

"My poor brother," Edward said, "for whose deliverance no man asked." But at least he could give him a dignified funeral with attending lords and a fine hearse which took Clarence's earthly remains to Tewkesbury Abbey, where they laid him to rest beside the body of his wife Isabel, in a vault behind the high altar, with a plain slab covering it to this day. Edward could make amends to Clarence's soul and to his children, and this he did. He created Clarence's son the Earl of Warwick, Clarence's daughter had been named Margaret in honor of course of Clarence's favorite sister, and her name crops up in the household accounts: our dear and well-beloved niece Margaret, daughter unto our late brother, the late Duke of Clarence.

And when Bessie bore another boy in the early spring Edward christened him George, Duke of Bedford. In all of England only one man wondered with cynicism about the choice of name. Lord Hastings knew that Edward's astrologer had found a letter *G* as the next possessor of the crown. Was Edward really naming his new son after his erring brother or was he just taking no chances that one of his sons would not have a name which began with the letter *G?*

Chapter 21

SINCE HER mother's death Bessie had become increasingly dependent on Kate. Although all of Bessie's sisters—and there were seven of them—had married well, Anne to the heir of the Bourchiers, Mary to Will Herbert's son, and the court thronged with them, it was Kate to whom Bessie turned more and more, Kate who was so like her mother and who was the only one of them who had wed a Duke; Kate, the Duchess of Buckingham, of whom Edward was so fond. Kate who was so pretty and gay and so astonishingly dependable; Kate, who was the least happily married of them all.

For the Duke of Buckingham scorned the Woodvilles. The blood in his veins was partly royal and they seemed unaware of this important fact. Completely unaware. He might have been anyone for the way they treated him. Even his sweet Kate, even she was apt to glance at him in surprise and pat him on the shoulder with an impudent look in her eyes.

He blamed Edward. It was Edward and Bessie who had had his wardship and who had married him off to the Woodville tribe. And when he let Kate know that that was how he felt she would cast down her eyes and whisper that she was sorry, my lord, and then in the privacy of their room he would relent.

But Kate vouchsafed none of this to Bessie, even though she knew that Bessie guessed and guessed well. Kate was too full of life and far too French to let a nagging husband interfere in her headlong enjoyment of life. As for a lover, she would have had one in a moment had she found the man she wanted. But it would have to be a special man, a very special one, and until he came along Kate was content. Content as she was this summer day, sitting side by side with Bessie with the baby George tucked between them in his nurse's arms.

The children lined up in a row in the front of the royal barge. Down the river's bend they could see the flags flying on the silken tents and on the summer breeze wafted the smell of roasting swans; the trestle tables would groan with all kinds of delicate food and the finest wines from Burgundy would be poured into the chased goblets; for all that Edward's household was now governed strictly by the household book, even to the distribution of candles and ale and the strict setting forth of how much wood per chamber. When it came to the royal palate and to entertainment it was done as lavishly as the clothes the King wore and as lavish as his tastes demanded.

Kate was wearing a new dress. Around the deeply cut neck was a roll of the silk embroidered with suns and roses. When Kate was handed out of the barge, she saw Edward and she curtsied deeply. "*Regardez*," she said as he took her hand. "I too wear your badge."

Edward grinned and kissed her. "If I hadn't married Bessie I would have married you."

The Duke of Buckingham was standing alongside of Edward. He looked very pleased at Edward's words and Kate flashed her smile on both of them. Good, she thought, it's going to be a perfect picnic.

That same summer day in Brittany the hereditary Earl of Pembroke was reading in the garden of the castle in which he was warded, gently warded, it is true, but under guard, for Francis of Brittany knew that Jasper Tudor was an important pawn in the power game that Dukes and Princes like to play.

Jasper Tudor was an interesting man. His father was a Welshman and his mother had been Katherine, Princess of France. After the death of her husband, Henry V of England, she had married the gentleman by name of Owen Tudor, a plain gentleman, and from this unlikely union there was left only Jasper and his young nephew, the Earl of Richmond. Richmond's name was Henry Tudor and this thin, pensive, tense young man was the chiefest concern of his uncle, because young Henry's mother, who was at the moment on a picnic in England, was the direct descendant of John of Gaunt, and her only child was the last living claimant to the throne of England on the Lancastrian side.

In the summer garden, where the perfume-laden scents of a French summer made the slightest breath pleasant, Jasper Tudor laid his book on his knee and gave himself up to reverie. Despite all, he would have given anything to hear the pound of surf on the coast of his native Wales. And yet it would never be so.

His half brother, King Henry, was dead. Henry's son was lying dead in Tewkesbury Abbey, almost alongside of the faithless Clarence. He himself was an outlaw, virtually a prisoner, his life held at the whim of Brittany's Duke, who was not what Jasper Tudor considered a stable man. He had nothing, Jasper Tudor thought, but himself and what he happened to be wearing.

The door in the castle garden wall suddenly burst open and a figure stood there. Jasper Tudor leaped to his feet, dropping the book on the grass. He stepped over it and went over to his nephew holding out his hand in the pleasure of seeing him, and then it occurred to him he might be about to receive bad news.

"No," said Henry Tudor, anticipating his uncle. "No, it's not necessary for me to remain in sanctuary any longer. I may stay here with you."

Jasper Tudor smiled widely. He hugged his nephew and Henry Tudor looked up at his face, the eyes so direct and capable of humor. Henry Tudor thought, This is indeed a man. How fortunate am I. But he said nothing of the kind. "What were you reading?" he inquired, bending down to pick up the book.

In Scotland that same afternoon James III was receiving the emissaries of Louis of France, who were pointing out to him the dangers of alliance with England, for somehow James' brother had escaped from France and was now in England ready to make trouble. The brothers of Kings were a great nuisance and a terrible danger when they were backed up by the powerful armies of England. It might be best for Scotland to return to her ancient alliance with France, much better and much safer, for Louis of France had no designs on Scotland but Edward of England did. No one could gainsay that. James hesitated. He had put his brother in prison but he had escaped to France. Now he was in England. Had Louis deliberately let him go? James licked his lips. The throne on which he sat so unsteadily was bucking about; he gripped his chair arm with both hands. He was an uncertain King and sometimes the only thing he was certain about was his fear of losing his crown. And although in the end he lost it to his own black-browed son and lost his life to boot, he couldn't read the future any more than any other man, and it was his brother he feared. James licked his lips and told the Frenchmen to come back the following morning.

Meantime, picnics or no, the King of England was not unaware of the French intrigues in Scotland. The negotiations for the marriage between young James and Cecily Plantagenet had already cost Edward a good deal of money, and just as Louis considered Burgundy part of France, Edward considered Scotland part of England. But he also had his eyes on Burgundy, for new trade treaties had been ratified and he had a young daughter ready to be betrothed to the new little heir to its dukedom. Thus during that summer the Kings of England and France maneuvered and jockeyed, nudging their neighbors, betraying their trusts, lying, telling the truth, sending embassies hither and yon, signing treaties and tearing them up.

The autumn seemed to Bessie to hurl itself into winter. At Christmastime in Middleham Anne tended the deathbed of her young cousin, the young son of her favorite uncle John Neville. In Europe the plague showed its rancorous head and by January it had spread to London.

The court hastily moved. But it was going to claim one life from the royal family and that life was the youngest member, the little George, almost as though the curse of Clarence's given name had marked the infant from birth.

Bessie wept. He had been such a happy, sturdy little boy with fair hair and deep-blue eyes.

"My little son," she whispered. "God and the angels keep you, my littlest one."

She was kneeling by the small tomb. Edward had found her there alone and he put his hand over hers in the protective gesture he always used. She looked up at him and there were tears in his eyes too. He raised her to her feet and put his arm around her and took her to her own chamber.

"I'm worried about you, Bessie," he said.

Bessie wiped her eyes and cleared her throat.

"I've written to the Pope for a dispensation to permit my family to have meat and eggs during Lent but if it does not arrive in time I've given orders that both be served anyway. Your health and the health of your baby are the most important things in the world to me."

Only Edward knew that Bessie was carrying another child.

"My dearest wife," he said, and picked her up and carried her over to her big bed and laid her down. Her eyes were deeply shadowed.

Edward went around the other side of the bed and stretched out his long length, pulled the quilt over both of them and gathered her close, smoothing her hair back from her forehead. He could hear a tremulous sigh.

"We're going to take a nap," Edward said.

Another sigh came from Bessie. But she felt safe and comforted. She said sleepily, "Please, my love, let Kate and her family join the royal family and have meat and eggs during Lent too."

"Yes, of course," Edward said. "Of course. Now go to sleep, Bessie. Go to sleep."

He lay there long after she slept, his hands under his head, thinking. The room was so quiet, so still. He felt weary himself. But he too was grieving over the death of his son; he wrenched his mind from the remembered picture of little George, not yet a year old when he had died. As soon as Bessie felt better—she'd not eaten properly for a month, he thought—he would send her on a long tour with all her children and Kate. If the new baby were a girl they'd name her Kate. It would please Bessie, he knew. And he thought he should extend an invitation to his sister Margaret to come and visit; to cement again the ties with Burgundy and to worry Louis. Edward grinned slightly when he thought how annoyed Louis would be when he discovered that the Dowager Duchess of Burgundy was visiting her brother, the King of England. He must ask Bessie to write to Margaret also and entrust to her the task of preparing a fine house for Margaret and her entourage and for her entertainment. He sighed then himself. Bessie's eyes opened.

She raised herself on one elbow and leaned over and kissed him, putting her long fingers with their huge rings over his eyes. "You sleep too, my love, please," she whispered.

Edward drew a long breath. He turned over on his side, flung one arm over her and closed his eyes.

Chapter 22

MARGARET WAS arriving. It was her first visit to her native land in thirteen years and everything was ready for the grand occasion.

Bessie had fitted up Clarence's former dwelling in London, Cold Harbour, for the visiting Duchess and sent in a crew of workmen and later artists to repaint the ceilings and drape the beds in cloth of gold and fill the house with linen and plate from the royal wardrobe.

Edward sent a whole train of ladies and gentlemen to welcome her and bring her from Calais. Anthony prepared to receive the Duchess for a weekend gala at his estates in Kent. But all the parties didn't conceal the fact from Louis that the King of England and his sister, the Duchess of Burgundy, were conniving against him. To annoy Louis and give comfort to Burgundy, Edward lent Margaret ten thousand crowns and assigned fifteen hundred archers to duty in Burgundy. Next Margaret proposed a betrothal between Edward's daughter Anne and the new baby heir of Burgundy, Philip. This too was agreed upon by Edward, and one day Margaret and Bessie picked out two rings, one for Anne to send to her young fiancé and the other Margaret picked out in Philip's name and presented it gravely to Anne with a gold chain so she could wear it around her neck. Now came Margaret's final request: Would Edward himself take the field against France?

Edward pointed to his treaty with Louis, and at that moment word arrived from the Continent that while Margaret was negotiating with her brother for aid against Louis, Maximilian had signed a treaty and truce with the King of France.

Edward held his tongue and was affable. His tangled relations with Scotland, his desire to recover the city of Berwick, his deep involvement with the other countries of Europe, all made him certain that outright war with France was no advantage to him at all. He was more interested that very day in the ambassadors who were leaving for Spain, for instance, carrying a thousand pounds of bribe money and clothes of scarlet and green to smooth the marriage negotiations between the baby Princess Kate and John of Aragon and Castile.

However, Edward was perfectly ready to mediate between Louis and the Duke of Burgundy. He persisted in calling Maximilian the Duke of Burgundy, whereas Louis called him the Duke of Austria—was he a Frenchman? *Non! Il est Autriche!* Louis was further enraged when he suffered a defeat at Maximilian's hands and learned that a body of English archers had fought supremely well on the field from which the French retired.

Louis uttered a long, hissing sigh. He had been ill too. "When we recover our strength," he remarked, a sweet smile playing over his face, "we will set about killing boars. There's nothing we would rather do except kill Englishmen!"

He ordered a present sent to Edward. "For his natural history museum," Louis directed.

It duly arrived. It was presented formally before the whole court by the shivering French ambassador, the Bishop of Elne. It consisted of the largest boar's tusk Edward and the court had ever seen, plus the dried head of an animal so strange that no one could identify it.

Anthony recalled the present of tennis balls sent long, long ago by the Dauphin of France, the insulting present which had set English armies on their way to Agincourt. But this King of England permitted a merry smile as he looked down at the dried head.

"A most welcome and mysterious addition to our museum."

The Bishop gulped, his liquid eyes fastened on the repulsive head. Edward laughed. "Perhaps I should send your head back to your master," he remarked gently. "Dried."

The Bishop backed away hastily and bowed deeply. And so for at least a month the rumor ran around the courts of Europe that the King of England had cut off the French ambassador's head and sent it back to Louis.

Instead Edward went cannily about his treatment of the Bishop, bullying him and plying him with gifts which the Bishop fearfully returned; he could never face Louis with gifts from

Edward in his luggage and he suffered nightmares about arriving back in France with unknown bags of gold coins tucked into his chests by Edward's agents.

But Edward was adamant that he must sign the treaty he himself had drawn up, with the naming of a date for a Diet at which the Dukes of Brittany and Burgundy were included, for the King of England was their friend and the ties with Brittany and Burgundy were close, with marriage alliances arranged with both dukedoms. Then to give the French a bit of a cold shoulder, Edward went down to Windsor and when they sought audience told them brusquely he was too busy.

A few days later the representatives of the Duke of Ferrara arrived and came laden with gifts for Bessie and Kate and Bessie's daughters; among them were mirrors, wall mirrors and hand mirrors of such charm that the young Princesses thought they had never seen any gift so welcome. There were lots of parties and at this point Edward permitted the French to arrive too.

The Bishop of Elne traveled down to Windsor with his train and found himself in the middle of what he had always feared, a sudden erupting fracas between his servants and Edward's guard. One of Edward's archers so far forgot himself that he seized a club and knocked the Bishop's personal secretary senseless; he lay there bleeding on the court in front of the main palace at Windsor, and there was so much shouting and blowing of horns to summon the inner guard that the noise penetrated to Edward's own privy chamber where he was receiving the Italians. Into this elegant group, with Bessie and Edward seated on their thrones, burst Edward's personal guard dragging the offending guard, still club in hand, with the French following after, gesticulating wildly.

Ever since Edward's accession to the throne the rule had stood that any man fighting in the royal dwelling, be he a personal servant of the King or any other, should lose the offending hand which had struck someone else, for Edward was determined to have no brawling within his own castle.

The captain of the guard briefly indicated the guilty archer.

Edward said, "You know the punishment."

The French ambassador knew it too. A sudden flood of French came from his lips in such quantities that even Bessie and Kate had difficulty following him. The Bishop flung himself on his knees.

Bessie whispered to Edward, "He says spare him, spare him or my master will be displeased."

Edward was trying to make some sense of all this.

"Is your secretary dead?"

"He is unconscious," Bessie translated, using three words for the Bishop's forty. "Now he says tell the archer the King of France would not have any English blood on his hands."

While Bessie was saying this the Bishop now reverted to English. "My master, the King of France, would not wish to punish any Englishman so blood would flow!"

"This man caused a good deal to flow," Edward said, trying to keep from laughing for the expression on the archer's face was comical; he looked as though he would take pleasure in knocking the brains out of the aforementioned King of France. The club was still in one powerful hand and yet now suddenly he looked up at Edward with horror at what he had done, now that the excitement was almost over.

Edward couldn't resist gibing at him. "It is the King of France who spares you, not your own sovereign lord."

The captain of the guard waited. What was he to do with the prisoner?

"Take him away and confine him," Edward ordered.

"But do not, pray do not harm him, *je vous en prie!*"

"He won't be harmed," Edward conceded. "He can spend his time in jail meditating on the sweet mercy and goodness of King Louis."

While the Bishop was still in this unsettled state he signed the treaty Edward wanted. Edward had a last parting word.

"I hope your master won't have your head for this."

The Bishop trembled. The next day he left for France, and when Louis saw what he had signed he went into a paroxysm of rage and ordered the Bishop put on trial. During the next month the Bishop defended himself in court, saying pitifully he was forced to sign. He knew all the time that his royal master could say that he had been coerced and he had truly received no gifts; that little cup of gold had only two pearls on it, and the silver— he had lost money on the silver he had brought home with him and tried to sell.

Louis threw up his hands and the Bishop was acquitted. But Louis' crafty mind was exploring all the possibilities and probabilities, and when Edward's ambassador asked for possession of the Duke of Albany, who was the brother of James of Scotland, Louis agreed. He thought that was a fine idea. If Edward wanted to mix into the affairs of Scotland he would be busy there and too busy to interfere with Louis in Burgundy.

Edward immediately tied Albany to him by a series of bonds. He had already raised men and money by all kinds of methods, for he didn't want to summon Parliament to ask for more money; and as soon as the weather was more favorable, as soon as spring came, English armies would start north. Meantime Lord Howard was in command of the fleet; Edward had just recently purchased four fine new ships, and the young Prince was old enough to accompany his father, so off they set for Dover to review the fleet.

This time it was Bessie who stood in the wide, wide windows over the court, with bright, proud tears in her eyes as she saw her husband and son, mounted side by side; the Prince's entourage, which included Anthony and young Richard Grey, Bessie's second-born son, all of them so handsome, ranged behind and in front of him. The Prince was ten.

Once reviewed the fleet sailed, and sailed right up the Leith and captured a good many ships and sunk a very great many, raiding towns and terrorizing the coast of Scotland. On land and on sea Berwick was besieged; Edward was determined to get the English stronghold back into his own hands.

The sands were rapidly running out on the first year of the new decade. Taken in all, Edward was pretty well pleased by what had been accomplished and in Eltham, the lovely royal dwelling, the ladies of the court were concerned not only with the coming December and its festive sweetness but with the birth of another royal child.

In all the courts of Europe there was no court quite like Bessie and Edward's. While both were celebrated for their personal handsomeness, Edward for his towering strength and his handsome face and Bessie for her astonishing beauty, it was the beautiful children that excited the admiration of the foreigner and the admiration and pride of their countrymen. This child would be Bessie's twelfth child, her tenth by Edward.

She had never ceased to mourn Margaret and George; she kept the month mind of the death of each of the little ones and on those days she went early to church to kneel and pray for the soul of the little lost baby. Little Margaret had died on December eleventh, and the eleventh of every month found Bessie in chapel very early in the morning. This morning Kate came with her. It was the eleventh of October.

She would have been eight years old, Bessie thought. How fast have the eight years gone! Where are they? A handful of memories.

She knelt before the altar and Edward's magnificent sixty-voice choir raised their pure tones to heaven to intercede for the little girl whose soul was with the angels. How could it be otherwise for an innocent baby? The music enveloped Bessie almost as though it were surrounding her body and lifting it; it was a glorious assailment by sound, for music was Edward's greatest joy, even more than his illuminated books, and all parts of the country and foreign lands were searched for musical talent in voice and with instrument.

Kate and Bessie knelt then side by side, their women behind them; they were not in mourning. The rising sun sent its shafts of golden October light through the high windows and the colors of the rich velvets of their gowns were like to the colors of medieval tapestries, unfaded and brilliant.

The choir sang; the women knelt. When the mass was over Kate helped Bessie to her feet and arranged her voluminous cloak with its soft edging of sable. Bessie was going to retire soon, for she had but four weeks before the expected birth. Therefore, Kate had arrived at Eltham the day before, bringing her own women and her son. So the first thing they must do on this golden warm October day was for the Queen to see her nephew; it had been spring when she had seen him last.

Kate's son, Edward, named for his King and cousin, was two. He bowed gravely and Bessie leaned down and hugged him.

"He looks like Father!" Bessie said.

"I know," Kate said happily. "Bessie, I didn't tell you before but I'm going to have another baby too."

Bessie set the child down, smiling at her sister, and yet she felt a twinge of sorrow. This baby will be my last baby, she thought. Kate is young but I, I am forty-two.

"It will be our last child, Edward," she said.

"Oh, Bessie," he said. "Your mother had thirteen! Maybe you and I will do her one better." He grinned and sipped his wine.

Bessie said solemnly, "Edward, I am forty-two. Do you realize that? All these years we have been married I have just gone headlong into them and now it seems it is almost over and it makes me feel sad."

"Bessie, we have seven beautiful children and another one very, very soon. Now how can you feel sad?"

"Promise me," she said, "that we will give him or her a simple, sweet name, just as though, as you used to say, we were just simple folk."

The King stood and lifted her to her feet and drew her over to the wide window seat with its cushions. He put his arm around her and with his big hand laid her head against his shoulder. They sat there for a long time quietly. Edward was rapidly reviewing all the winter season would bring to Bessie in the amount of entertaining. The French were sending an imposing embassy; if Bessie delivered on time they would be on hand for the christening. No matter how many children Edward and Bessie had the christening was always most magnificent; it was so important to them, their children. Anthony would bring the Prince to court in early December and Edward had arranged to have his portrait painted with his mother and father and with Anthony presenting his new book to his ward, his nephew, Prince Edward. Also his mind was reviewing Bessie's request and it came to rest on two names.

"I think, Bessie," he said, "you should go into retirement soon. You weren't fooling me, were you? You look almost ready to deliver, Bess."

She shot him a glance from the cold eyes.

"Come, Bessie," he said. "When?"

"In about two weeks," she confessed, her mouth curving in a smile.

"All right then," said Edward, "because of that I won't tell you the names I've chosen and tomorrow, tomorrow you retire to your rooms and that's a command."

Edward wrote the two names on two slips of paper. Two names which had political overtures too, for was he not King of Ireland? Every day for the next two weeks he sent a gift, ranging through fruit and flowers to two new rings, for Bessie was very vain about her beautiful hands and was apt to wear at least three or four rings at the same time. One day he sent two folded pieces of paper, sealed with a note which he told her not to dare open then.

On the tenth of November Bessie's baby was born, a bald little girl with some golden fuzz on the very top of her head.

Bessie waited for Edward and when he arrived he smiled and kissed her, looked at his new little daughter and gave Bessie one of the pieces of paper. She broke the seal, looked at him and smiled and sighed.

"Now we will say the name together," the King began and then he hesitated.

"You like it Bessie? You really like it? Because I want you to say so plain and we could pick another."

He was very earnest and looked at her with concerned eyes.

Bessie bit her lips. "It's a perfect name, sweetheart," she whispered. "Just what I—" she broke off and Edward, relieved, said, "All right then."

Kate brought the baby; Bessie held out her arms for her. Edward said, with Bessie's voice mingling with his, "Our new daughter, we christen thee the Lady Bridget."

The weather was terrible; never had there been such a winter. Huge storms pounded Europe, the seas rose in anger, the mountain sides disgorged avalanches and floods. In France and Germany vineyard after vineyard shriveled and died in the bitter cold. In England all crops suffered. And the spring and summer produced a lean harvest; there was very little grain and the Kings of France and England had to look far and pay high for the oats, barley and victuals for their armies.

Edward was fascinated with the new engines of war and spent much time in the Tower watching over his new toys. Calais was heavily fortified against Louis, and the trustworthy Hastings was there to guard that bit of England on the Continent as Edward prepared for war with the Scots.

The war meant to Bessie that her oldest son would soon march with his own flying standards and his own retainers. She was doubly glad that Richard Grey was part of the Prince's household and committed to Ludlow and Anthony.

"In this day and age," Edward said, "a King should not have to take the field himself. There is too much to do for him to spend his time in military conquest."

He established a system of couriers. Their stations were thirty miles apart and news could be brought from the north right to

Edward's whereabouts. Ten men were assigned this task, the first postal system in England. They would keep Edward in close touch with the progress of the war; his brother, Richard of Gloucester, would have the command and under him, the stalwart Earl of Northumberland, Lord Percy.

The fleet was ready. Berwick would be besieged by land and sea; Scotland itself would be invaded as far north as was necessary to defeat her.

March was a nice month. For a change. Edward was in the north reviewing troops. In Burgundy it was even more pleasant, and young Mary of Burgundy set out on the afternoon of the twenty-seventh on horseback; she was an exceptionally fine rider and had been used to the saddle all her life. Mary, cantering easily along a wooded path, at ease, hands light on the reins, enjoying the brilliant afternoon, her gay escort forgetting for a moment the care of state and the hovering spider webs of Louis of France, suddenly before the horrified eyes of all her mare reared high, front hoof pawing, and Mary sailed over her head and her body lay crumpled against the bole of a huge tree.

The jolting news of Mary's death reached England as fast as a ship could sail. It reached Louis and his swarm of physicians and astrologers in Plessis as fast as Louis' system of couriers could manage it. A lathered horse reached Flanders with the news. First Charles and now Mary; there was no real ruler of Burgundy anymore save Mary's tiny son and her infant daughter. Their father, the beleaguered Maximilian, eyed his borders with fear and sent his messengers racing out with the news that he needed help.

In Westminster Edward weighed the dual problems. He hurried to win the Scottish war so his hands would not be tied against intervention of the continent.

And personal tragedy struck Bessie and Edward again; their pretty fifteen-year-old Mary died suddenly at the palace of Greenwich, and on May twenty-third she was laid beside her little brother George, under the stones at St. George's chapel.

In the Scottish War Edward was aided by the Scots themselves and James III. But James was also a Stuart, and so he set forthwith his favorites, his rude and ambitious nobles, his proud Highlanders with their skirling bagpipes and their inborn hatred of James' city friends.

He was not a very fine figure ahorse. Unlike his predecessors he rode poorly, cutting a comical figure. They had reached a small crossing called Lauder's Bridge. The structure of the bridge was too handy. The high wooden bars were an invitation to murder, and with swift violence James' favorites were seized and thick ropes slung around their thin necks. Cries for mercy had no effect on the Scottish lords; in five minutes five bodies swung over the muddied water of the burn, and James' hated favorites had breathed their last.

This news was brought posthaste to Richard of Gloucester and Northumberland and they blew up the trumpets and started north. A few days later Edinburgh was occupied by the English.

Edward had sent his system of couriers pounding through the nights and days, over muddied roads, through summer storms, with orders not to burn or ravage the capital city.

In Edinburgh the French agents quickly sent word to Louis, who raised his hands again to heaven and asked the saints how they could thus repay him.

Here was Edward with an army that hadn't been used.

So hunting for a new ploy Louis published the secret treaty which he and Edward had signed six months before, a treaty of perpetual peace during the lifetimes of the two Kings. It looks as though, Louis gibed in effect, that none of my vassals, including Burgundy, can count on help from the English King!

Edward sent Maximilian some good advice. Stall, he counseled. Louis is dying; make a truce or make an appointment for a truce. When one deals with Louis one has to try to be as clever and mean and treacherous. He is very ill, don't forget that; he won't live long; his days are numbered. But as Edward wrote those words and impressed them on his two envoys to Maximilian, neither could he know that his own days numbered less than Louis'. Indeed, how could he? Louis was old enough to be his father. He, Edward, was forty and yet already the span of allotted life was growing smaller and smaller until now it could be counted easily in days.

Edward didn't know it would be his last Christmas. He had issued the writs to summon Parliament in November; no doubt he expected trouble from Burgundy and France and perhaps he wanted more money for Scotland and its running fight.

Edward had put on weight in the last five years; but his height carried it off for him and this Christmas he was wearing the latest style from France, the doublet with padded shoulders and loose sleeves lined with fur—he was a magnificent figure. When the news arrived from Burgundy for which Edward was waiting, he and the court learned that Maximilian had signed a treaty of peach and that it provided that Maximilian's young daughter should marry the Dauphin.

Edward bore up nobly under Louis' double-dealing. He explained to young Bess, whom he and Bessie had called la Dauphiness, that the little Dauphin was always ill and that the intended marriage had been political, as she had always known, and other than the prestige of being *la Reine* she was losing nothing and gaining much. This was true of course but what anger Edward may have felt at Louis' treachery and his breaking of the treaty, we do not know. People said there would be war with France. Parliament had already been summoned; it was to meet in January.

As for Edward, in his canny mind, in his foreign policy that was evolved not from the age which glorified war but from the new age which looked first for a strong united country, solvent, trading, building, sailing, exploring, with a court which received embassies from every foreign land, his dealings with Louis were the first step and English Kings following after could do no better than to continue it.

Parliament opened on the twentieth of January and Edward was at Westminster to officiate.

The Speaker, the Chancellor of the realm, rolled out the sonorous Latin quotation. Looking back across the centuries it was very fitting.

The Chancellor had a splendid voice. *"Dominus illuminatio mea et salus mea."*

Under Edward's strictures the Chancellor, Rotherham, denounced Louis' wicked treachery and sounded the opening guns for—not war with France—but a grant of money for the King to defend and strengthen his realm.

But first Berwick. Their King had recovered it. It had been held so long by the Scots that it was "poor and desolate"; to encourage men to go there to settle and work it was granted the exclusive right to a monopoly of the salmon caught in the Tweed, and the act further required all trade with Scotland to go through the town to the benefit of its inhabitants.

Commons granted Edward the money he wanted; they enacted a tax on aliens and then exempted the Hanse towns, the merchants of Spain and Brittany, and Edward himself added an exemption of the Italians, so this turned out to be a blow against the French and the Burgundians. Commons also set aside eleven thousand pounds less for the household, according to Edward's careful household book, than he needed; undoubtedly he meant to make up the rest with his own rapidly ascending import-export business.

On the twentieth of February Edward turned to Brittany. He wanted Francis, its Duke, to be sure that he would come to his aid with four thousand archers, paid out of English money, in case Louis should turn his dimming eyes toward Brittany; and then a few days later messages went out to Louis, although the matter was so secret that it is not known what Edward advised his representative to say.

It is possible that Edward had picked up malaria in France. Sometimes he suffered from recurrent fever, but his magnificent physique had managed to throw off the worst of its effects. Bessie was at Windsor and in March Edward was there too; but on the twenty-fifth he returned to Westminster with all the royal family. And so he was at Westminster when the sudden fatal illness struck without warning.

Edward was so mortally sick that rumor about the country told the horrifying news that he had already died. The royal household was turned upside down in fear.

The first day Edward surrendered to pain and raging fever but the second day his mind told him he might die, and summoning strength he called for his lawyers; his will; he must add some codicils to the will that he had first made when he had left for France seven years ago.

But he did not die easily. Ever before his mind and his heart was the picture of his oldest son. The Prince was only twelve. Too young. Too vulnerable. And yet he had his stalwart uncle, the faithful Richard of Gloucester, who himself was barely thirty. Edward turned in his big bed, trying to summon strength.

"Prop me up," he said. The factions that had roiled about him in their fight for the royal favor, what if he weren't there to keep them from quarreling?

"Underset me with pillows," he commanded, and tender, shaking hands pulled his huge shoulders and body upright and tucked the pillows all about him.

The fever wracked him. He closed his brown eyes. "Bessie," he thought; she would be in the chapel praying, he knew, or else without the big closed doors. Under the closed lids her image ran around in his brain and his son, the young Prince, the King's dearest treasure, with his sweet smile and his flowing curls. And young Bess. His firstborn, his true love. And young Richard who was so merry and quick-witted, like a Woodville he was, his mother's joy from whom she had never been separated as he, the King, had promised. A long sigh rent Edward's chest. For years he had laughed when Anthony and Hastings, in sudden anger with each other, had laid a hand on the heavy dagger at his side. And Bessie's son Thomas, whom he, Edward, had always petted and spoiled; Hastings was jealous of him and yet why should he be so, for only a few days ago he, Edward, had told Hastings he loved him so entire that he'd given him permission to be buried in St. George's Chapel where Edward had commanded that his own body be laid to rest, the beautiful chapel he himself had built, each stone rising in clean beauty to the honor of King and God.

He roused himself. "Bring them, my lords, to me," he said.

His son. His fevered mind wrestled suddenly with a memory—was there something he had forgot to do? His son, the King's most precious and dearest treasure. Was there something he had forgot to do? No. His muscles relaxed. He had done it. Three days ago, still working at night he had signed a royal directive to Anthony, changing the Prince's bedtime from eight to nine, in recognition of his advancing years.

No, no, that was not important; his mind was too wracked with fever, just as his body. Try to think straight, he told himself, Edward, try. It does not matter what directive you sign for your son; he will be the King. I am going to die, he thought; tears filled his eyes helplessly. Anthony—if he could only speak with Anthony; Anthony was too far away; Anthony, Edward clenched his big hands as if willing Anthony to listen and obey. Anthony, you must make friends with Hastings! You must shake his hand!

The doors opened. Solemnly, fearfully, came into his sight young Thomas, Marquis of Dorset. Hastings, his familiar dear face, how long, how many years had Hastings stood faithfully by his side? From the very beginning Hastings had been there, a good and faithful servant.

They were gathered kneeling about his bed, Thomas' face that he had seen first in the forest at Whittlebury, the sun shining on his gilt head; now it was bared and still the selfsame color, the pure gold of his mother; Edward reached out his big hand and Thomas took it and kissed it. Edward felt his tears dropping slowly onto the back of his hand.

"Promise me, Tom, promise me you will live in peace and love for all my lords for the sake of your half-brother, your Prince. My son."

Thomas choked out that he would and so would his friends. This young gay faction that followed wherever Thomas went knelt behind him, heads bent; they had frolicked about the court, eager for service in Scotland or France, making merry always and at odds with the older Hastings, whom they thought considered himself far too important for words. What airs he put on, they mocked.

Now Hastings, his face older, the tears pouring down his cheeks, took Edward's hand. "My dearest liege lord," he muttered.

"Take the hand of the Marquis, my stepson Thomas Grey," Edward was summoning all his strength to talk, and Hastings now rose and bent over the bed.

"I can't sit up any longer," Edward whispered to him.

With trembling hands Hastings took away the pillows, one by one, until Edward could lie back. Then with a mighty effort he turned his wracked and dying body to the side so he could see the kneeling group before him.

"Take each other's hands and swear you will reconcile yourselves one to the other for the sake of—" Edward drew a little breath, "for my children." He saw them take hands and bow their heads as though they were oath-taking; he saw their stricken faces and their tears. He closed his eyes.

It was just a scant three minutes later when Thomas stumbled from Edward's room. Bessie was waiting outside the big doors. Her white face with its great eyes looked up at her firstborn son. He gathered her into his arms.

"Mother," he sobbed, "it is too late."

PART FIVE
Bessie, Young Bess and Kate

Chapter 23

THE COUNCIL was meeting. The wheels of government ground on even though the funeral drums and the muffled hoofbeats of the horses, and the masses and dirges and the mourning went on.

Bessie's figure was hooded and veiled, her forehead covered with a white frontlet, and a piece of lawn called a barb covered her rounded chin. Her great eyes looked steadily across the council board at Hastings, for according to Edward's will she had a place at the King's council board. Right outside the chamber door the faithful Kate and some waiting women sat with bent heads and clasped hands.

Bessie said, "Lord Hastings, Lord Stanley, it is our thought that at least four thousand men be sent to escort our son, the Prince, to London. Commands to that effect should go to our brother, Lord Rivers." Hastings moved in his chair, glanced at Stanley. The palace was already swarming with Woodvilles. Lionel up from Oxford, those two inseparables Edward and Richard, the Queen's son, Dorset; Haute, her cousin on her father's side—how many Hautes were there? Too many.

Hastings said suddenly, "Against whom is our young sovereign to be defended, madam?"

Bessie looked back at him. I must not weep, she thought desperately. I must not. They do not understand that I lean on my family because I know they love me and I can trust them. But I must try hard not to antagonize these others, for my son needs them. And I must remember that whatever I think of Lord Hastings and his escapades with Edward he would never harm my son.

"Who are his foes, madam?" Hastings continued. "Not his valiant uncle—the Duke of Gloucester! Or is it Stanley or me?" He flung out his hand toward Stanley.

Bessie swallowed and tried to keep the tears from her eyes. "Of course not, my lord," she said low.

"Is Your Grace's proposal intended to confirm the power of your kindred and violate the oath of amity—" Hastings bit his lip, because he too was truly torn with grief, "our oath of amity so lately sworn—by the deathbed of our royal master?"

Bessie clasped her hands so tight on her lap that her wedding ring bit into her palm and drew blood. "I am too near grief for those words, my lord," she said.

"I'll retire from court if our young King is brought to London surrounded by soldiers!"

Bessie saw that Hastings was emotionally unstrung. This steadied her. She glanced about the council board. Did they propose for a moment that young Edward have almost no escort? That couldn't be. But she would ask.

"My lord Stanley," she said, her voice composed, "it is, or should be, right clear to all at this board that our only and main concern is for our son. What is the proposal of others?"

Stanley cleared his throat. "An escort of fifteen hundred men, my lords?" He glanced about the chamber at the solemn faces. He thought the Queen had acquitted herself rather well.

"My lord Hastings," Bessie said, "our young King needs you."

Hastings said, "Then let it be resolved, we send word immediately in the name of this council that the Earl Rivers bring the King to London, having with him an escort of fifteen hundred men."

There was a knock on the door and Hastings waved a hand; Stanley himself went to the door.

"A letter for you, Your Grace."

Bessie saw it bore Gloucester's crest. She broke the seal and unfolded the letter. As she read, she was moved and grateful; the letter contained kindness, deference and submission. "A letter from our sovereign lord's brother, the Duke of Gloucester," she said and handed it across the table to Hastings. She rose then. They all stood. They bowed. Hastings handed back the letter. "We shall answer this this morning," Bessie said.

At Middleham Anne had read Richard's letter before he had sent it; he had called her into his privy chamber to read what he had just written.

"It's most kind and loving, Richard," she said. She could see he had been busy with his pen; the table was strewn with papers and wisps of smoke came from the sealing wax.

"I'm laying necessary plans," he said.

Anne thought it rather odd he didn't plan to leave for London immediately but she said nothing, for she was, as always, worried about her boy; he was ill again this morning. She herself, thin and pale, hurried off, thinking that at least it was the middle of April and soon May and the spring would greet the land, and if her young Edward could be out in the sun, oh, it would do him so much good. The first sunny day he could be carried out and later he would gain enough strength to walk.

The news of Edward's death had been brought to Ludlow Castle by a lathered horse and a weary rider. Four days later the council's commands were delivered to Anthony and slowly he made ready to obey them. Slowly, because young Edward was stricken with grief. Anthony gave himself up to counseling his new young King, his beloved nephew. Anthony was appalled not only by Edward's death but by the horrifying fact that this young charge of his was just a few years too young to face the tremendous weight, the uneasy burden, the awful dilemma, of the regal crown. Through his long years of service to Edward, Anthony knew only too well how hard the hands must be that handled the tiller. Now he put his own big hand over Edward's slender young fingers.

"My liege lord," he said. "There are many besides myself who will serve you with love, with fidelity, with all our best counseling, with anything you demand from us."

Edward tried to smile; he tried to remember how Edward was, but how could he imitate his towering robustness, the commanding figure that had been his father? He said, "I thank you, my lord uncle."

"You shall soon be within the circle of your own family," Anthony said.

This made Edward more sure and content. His beautiful mother. And Richard. "And I'm anxious to see Bess," he said. Bess was seventeen. He wished desperately he were seventeen. It seemed very old and as if one would be a true man and King if only one were seventeen. But he could depend on Bess. He visualized her swiftly; the gleaming blond hair and her intelligent merry eyes and her immense kindness and goodwill. Bess would be able to help him, he knew; he could count on Bess.

Not Edward nor Anthony had the slightest suspicion that neither of them would ever see Bessie or Bess again. The next day trustfully they set forth for London.

Chapter 24

IT WAS such a beautiful morning that day, the thirtieth of April, that young Edward felt his heart lift as he came out of his lodgings in Stony Stratford. Last night Richard Grey had arrived with messages from his mother and Sir Thomas Vaughn, his chamberlain, bent and old and kind, was at his side; they were so near London where his whole family waited.

Edward swung up into the saddle of his horse. His household men were mounted. He had sent letters off the day before, signed with the royal signet; he felt confident and proud. He gestured to Richard Grey as he saw that up ahead men were making way for a group of hard-driven horses.

"That must be our Uncle Anthony coming!"

Last night Anthony had heard that Edward's other uncle, Richard of Gloucester, had arrived in Northampton. He had ridden over to pay the young King's respects and had stayed to dine when Richard had insisted on his company for dinner. Edward looked ahead inquiringly as the ranks of his household men parted and made way.

"It's Richard of Gloucester," Richard Grey whispered. "And our uncle of Buckingham!"

Edward motioned a man to him and dismounted. Behind his Uncle Richard came a number of men and now they knelt in homage, and his uncle and Buckingham, who was married to his Aunt Kate, both knelt too. Edward extended his hand. Richard of Gloucester rose to face him. Edward was immediately conscious of unease, distress. His candid young face searched his uncle's face. The heart and mind of a tyrant are not pretty; did Edward, young as he was, get a glimpse of the twisted hatreds behind the grave mask of kindness? Edward asked, "Where is Lord Rivers, my uncle?"

Richard of Gloucester said, "I bring serious tidings."

Around Edward now had crowded Gloucester's attendants. "We had best go back into your lodgings," Richard of Gloucester said.

Richard Grey pushed past Buckingham and stood close to Edward; so instinctively did old Sir Thomas Vaughn. They walked by Edward's side as he followed his uncle back across the cobbled street and into the room Edward had left minutes before.

Edward stood in the center of the room. He was already taller than his uncle. And he could almost feel that his uncle hated him for being able to look down on him. What was he saying?

"My dearest nephew, you have my deepest condolences on the untimely death of your father."

Edward had been extremely well taught. He was very courteous as he answered, as he thanked his uncle, as he said that he himself mourned so deeply that it was painful for him to speak of it even to his kin.

"Aye," said Richard. "And yet it is evident that unwise councilors about your father drove him to excesses and ruined his health!"

Richard Grey said, "His Grace had eaten only vegetables that day he was stricken. In accordance with Lenten rule—"

"Be quiet!" Buckingham slapped his hands together sharply.

Edward turned to look at the Duke of Buckingham. His father had never admitted Buckingham to any council; Edward knew that his own father had considered Buckingham gay and pleasant and completely incompetent. Why was he here, a shadow to Richard of Gloucester?

"Where is my uncle Lord Rivers?" He stood straight, his dark eyes showing his distress, even though he was trying carefully to hide it.

"Your Uncle Rivers is in ward. He was arrested this morning." Richard of Gloucester added, "The men who ruined your father must be removed from office. Lord Rivers plots against you and me. My own safety demanded his arrest."

Edward stared at him, uncomprehending the enormity of this betrayal; then he looked to Buckingham, who nodded his head. "For our own safety," he repeated, glancing at the doors which were now securely blocked by his own men.

"Your father named me as your protector, my young nephew," Richard of Gloucester said.

Edward interrupted. "The Lord Rivers is my trusted friend, as is my half brother here beside me. As for the governing of the realm, we have good and trusted nobles and we have our mother, the Queen, who has a place at our council."

"You've been deceived," Gloucester said. "Women have no place at council tables. The ruling of the land is for men."

And I am not a man yet, thought Edward rapidly. Is that what he means? What does he mean? All that he had been taught rushed pell-mell into his mind; all the stories of great heroism and bravery that Anthony had read him; all the true tales of his father's own life, especially the struggle with Warwick—that was the one that pointed the way. But first Edward said, "My own father, my dearest father, set these councilors about me: Lord Rivers, my uncle, my half brother who is with me, and I will believe no charge against them until it should be proved! And I am asking you to release them."

Richard of Gloucester hesitated. "We will go back to Northampton now with Your Grace, till we find out whether London is safe for us."

Edward thought, Anthony is there in Northampton. I will do as Father did when Warwick held him prisoner. He nodded his head. "I am content to place myself in your hand, my dear uncle. But I must insist that when we come to Northampton you heed my request. I believe no charge against my kin and I must ask you to release him."

Thus far Edward had conducted himself very well and had his opponent been another Warwick he might very well have succeeded. And now as he walked out to his already saddled horse, he walked tall and unafraid, smiling upon all the mounted men. Richard his uncle rode at his side with Buckingham right behind, showing every kind of honor to him as befitted a King. But when they arrived at Northampton, Richard Grey and Thomas Vaughn were not with them.

Edward felt cold fear in his room at Northampton. He washed and prepared for dinner; he tried to shove it away as he went across the hall to the dining room, and with some ceremony he joined his uncle for dinner.

"My Uncle Rivers," he began. He hoped his voice didn't quaver.

Richard of Gloucester said genially, "We sent a dish from this same table over to Lord Rivers, Your Grace. Be of good cheer. All will be well!"

But he didn't tell young Edward that Anthony had sent the dish back with a courtly note that if they pleased, would they send the dish to young Richard Grey, his other nephew, who was unused to adversity and needed comfort the more. Buckingham and Richard of Gloucester had sneered at that note, but they didn't dare do it in front of Edward.

They were very cheerful. Edward ate little; they didn't seem to notice. But when Edward rose to say good night they both bowed deeply. Richard himself escorted the young King to his chamber. And there Edward realized that his own personal household men were missing and in their place were some creatures of Richard's. Upon this young twelve-year-old boy had fallen the terrible tragedy that his father had feared; on his dead brother's memory had Richard of Gloucester committed the greatest betrayal of all. But young Edward did not yet fear for his life; he feared for others who were most dear to him. When the curtains of his bed were drawn he could hear the other strangers in the chamber who guarded him (for he would have tried to escape had not soldiers ringed his bed). He could hear their shuffles and noisy breath in his room. In the darkness behind the drawn curtains young Edward V of England prayed for his friends and committed his cause to the Lord. Then, like his father, he said a special prayer to St. Anne.

Chapter 25

THE SANCTUARY looked just the same. There was the circular hearth—Bess remembered it. Only now around it were branches and green things and flowers and on the stone floor, fresh green rush; there was the intricate, carved oak paneling, with its tiny door and curving stone staircase leading to rooms connected by quaint Gothic arches. The woodwork was laced with corbels and foliage. It came back to young Bess in a rush of memory.

She held in one hand the small hand of little Kate, who would be four in August. In the other hand she carried, according to her mother's instructions, all her jewelry in a small case, all of it, Kate had commanded, "even to the trinkets, Bess, the smallest trinkets." Bessie, her head and shoulders cloudy with her veils, carried Bridget, who would not be three till Christmas and who was upset and tearful with all the haste of moving and packing and the household men struggling with boxes and chests and packages.

Richard, who was not yet ten, supervised his own servants and his younger sister Anne. Cecily came last, herding her two juniors in front of her. Thomas was still in the royal apartments, making sure that nothing had been left behind.

The night wore on. Thomas and the household men came and went, with Bessie still in the room with the circular hearth, the candles guttering, a Bessie overwhelmed with fatigue and fear and sorrow. The coming dawn would usher in the merry, merry month of May.

The news had spread quickly all over the city. Richard of Gloucester had taken possession of the young King and arrested Anthony Woodville by a trick of inviting him to dine first, and then he had arrested old saintly Sir Thomas Vaughn, the young

King's chamberlain and counsellor, and his half brother Richard Grey. For the safety of the royal children their beautiful widowed Queen had fled into sanctuary at Westminster.

The news had been brought to the Chancellor of the realm, Archbishop Rotherham, in the early hours of the morning and straight away he had word from Hastings, and in panic and loyalty he called for his servants and set out to the Westminster sanctuary.

There he found Bessie in the main chamber. She sat on a low cushion on the rushes; her long bright hair had escaped from its veiled coif and fell straight down her cheeks and back, and she kept pushing it aside with one white hand, trying to make it lie smooth over one shoulder. All about her lay boxes and cartons and the household men struggled in with more, the Archbishop following after until he came to the Queen. There he knelt on the rushes before her and in trembling tones he blessed her and the royal family, and he said he had brought to her keeping the Great Seal of the realm.

Bessie clasped her hands together. "To me?" she whispered.

"Aye, and I bring you cheering news from Lord Hastings. He says to tell you that if there is any crowned than your eldest son, we will on the morrow crown his brother. Here is the Great Seal which your noble husband gave to me, so I deliver it to you for the use of your son." The Archbishop had been kneeling in front of the sitting Bessie, so their faces were on a level and now he rose creakingly to his feet. "Be of good comfort, madam!"

He hastened off. By the time he reached his home and looked out the window, in the dawn the Archbishop saw riverboats full of the Duke of Gloucester's men, clustered about the landing stage to the abbey so that none might enter the Queen's asylum. There they waited, the water lapping at the gunwales of the overloaded boats.

Hastings said, appalled, "But my lord, you may not, you've not the power nor the right, to give the Great Seal to any! It was entrusted to your keeping!"

Bishop Morton nodded emphatically.

Hastings said, "Go to the Queen and assure her of my support. Tell her to trust us and bring back the Great Seal."

"The sanctuary is surrounded now." The Archbishop quavered,

then drew himself up. "I shall enter through the abbot's chambers."

Hastings was thinking, Have I been wrong? Have I been misled? Is there treason and treachery here? And the doubts stirred in his mind, but no, he himself had written to Richard of Gloucester, pointing out the danger of allowing the Woodvilles to possess the young King. All that Richard had done so far was to take rightfully under his wing his own nephew and so ensure that he and he alone would be the King's protector, and that, Hastings thought, was right and well. And besides that his faithful spy Ratcliff was watching Richard, Duke of Gloucester. It never occurred to Hastings to wonder whether he could trust Ratcliff.

For Ratcliff was reporting to Richard, Duke of Gloucester. He was telling the dark-browed Richard that Hastings was leaning already to the Queen's party; that Hastings' loyalties were bound up inextricably with the young King and that to seize the crown he would have to first rid himself of Hastings. And it would have to be done quick.

Hastings attended the council meeting that very morning called for the Tower, and he was a bit uneasy because he had learned that the council had been divided in half. That was odd, he thought. But within the council chamber was the Archbishop, the Chancellor of the realm, Rotherham, and the Bishop Morton, two faithful friends and Lord Stanley and the young Duke of Buckingham.

An hour passed. It was nine and still Richard of Gloucester had not appeared. Suddenly there he was, saying politely that he was most sorry, he had overslept.

He was very pleasant. He talked about strawberries. "I hear you have the most wonderful berries," he said to Bishop Morton. "I'm so fond of them. Why not send out a servant for some?"

The Bishop was delighted to comply, he said. He did send a servant; Richard excused himself for a moment and then he didn't come back. While in Bishop Morton's garden a young boy named Thomas More helped gather a mess of strawberries, in the council chamber desultory talk went on among the men; they were wondering when Richard would return.

Then the door burst open. Richard stood there, his face drawn, biting at his lip as he did when he was tense, drawing and fiddling with his dagger.

"I am surrounded by traitors."

Hastings stared at him.

What he was saying hardly made sense. Something about lords conspiring, his shrunken arm.

"To keep and rule the realm as my brother commanded me I must rid myself of traitors. And I know their names." His eyes swept the board from Hastings to Rotherham to Bishop Morton. Richard licked his lips. "I divided my council myself this morning. Divided the loyal from the disloyal. For in here is the man who protects the harlot who drove my brother to excesses and who breathes curses on me."

Hastings went white. Only early this morning had Hastings' "faithful" gentleman Ratcliff assured him again of Richard's love for him. Hastings looked helplessly at Bishop Morton, helplessly, for Hastings had long been the foremost man in the kingdom, so sure of Edward's love that he couldn't encompass this attack on him. Just last week when he had ridden into London, he had been preceded by four hundred men to honor him.

Hastings said, "But that is not true, Your Grace. What you imply. About traitors. Not true—" his voice trailed off. For he was gripped now by terrible emotion. Richard had flung open the door behind him; armed men were crowding into the room, half running behind the seated council, filling the room they were, with drawn daggers.

Ratcliff has betrayed me, Hastings knew surely. He had lied to him. It must be that this man Richard, the faithful Richard, whom he thought he could trust, was going to kill him.

"My lord," Hastings said, "I writ you myself and—"

Richard screamed, "There is the traitor. He who sleeps with the wicked harlot Jane Shore."

For one fleeting moment Hastings would have given anything in the world for Anthony Woodville at his side. As always Edward had been right; he had warned them to stand together; he had glimpsed the danger though he had no notion from whom it would come.

"Seize him!" Richard cried, pointing at Hastings. "And him."

This time his finger went to Bishop Morton and the Chancellor Rotherham. "Seize them."

Lord Stanley protested. He drew his dagger. Instantly he was knocked to the floor; blood poured from a wound over his ear.

Bishop Morton in his robes was shoved roughly through the door; after him was hustled the ponderous Chancellor, his robes marked by Stanley's blood. Hastings felt his arms seized and bound behind his back.

Richard of Gloucester was breathing heavily. "We shall give you time with a priest to shrive you!"

Hastings said, "I shall pray for your soul, that you do nothing further to stain it for the sake of your dead brother, my own dear liege lord." He could hardly speak the words. He saw quick there was no hope for him, no possible hope, no avenue of action left now except to join Edward in death. It had been done so quick there was no proper block, and they laid Hastings' head against a piece of timber, a heavy green log on the green, green grass in front of the Tower Chapel.

Chapter 26

UNEASE AND fear roamed wide in London's narrow streets. Men barred doors at night. Everywhere there were Gloucester's soldiers; men with the badge of the boar. And already in the taverns the men were calling it the badge of the pig. The pig. It was the eleventh of June, the summer sun was warm, the coronation of the young King was set for June twenty-sixth. Richard called a council meeting in the star chamber and there he laid before the assembled lords and clergy the problem, the big problem. How could the young King be crowned while his brother was in sanctuary? It was a disgrace to the realm. The Duke of York, ten years old, was being held a hostage by his mother!

He was calm now. The Archbishop of Canterbury inclined his ear to the argument; it touched him on all points.

"My lords," Richard said, "here, very near us, almost within hearing distance, lies the Duke of York, held hostage by his mother and the Woodvilles. We have this to consider: A child who has done no wrong, does he have right of sanctuary? I think not, my lord. I think I have the right to take him from it and set him in his lawful place beside his brother."

Richard paused. He was the faithful Richard this morning. His eyes, deep-brown, steady and sad, found those of the Archbishop of Canterbury. "My good lord," he said, "I've no wish to violate the sanctuary. But I'll do it if I must."

"You cannot!" The words burst from the Archbishop. It would be far too dangerous a precedent. The lay world encroaching on the ancient rights of the church. It was so dangerous a doctrinary idea that the Archbishop would defend it with his life.

"I may be forced to," Richard said quietly. "Think you, my lord, the disgrace to the realm and to me. The young King crowned while his brother lay in sanctuary."

The Archbishop bit his lip just like Richard, and the other lords, Buckingham included, began to argue. The argument waxed heated and it is true that they were within earshot of the Queen's sanctuary, for Bessie and Bess could hear their voices, shouting at one another in the heat of passion.

The Archbishop hardly heard what the others were saying because Richard leaned forward across the polished board and said, "Children can commit no crime that needs asylum. Therefore the privilege of sanctuary cannot apply. I can possess myself of him by force." The steady, sad eyes in his sensitive face burned into those of the Archbishop, who found himself trembling from the force of his emotions. Let armed men once enter a sanctuary and the whole church would be defiled, and his God would be basely betrayed. He rose to his feet. "I go to the Jerusalem chamber to see the Queen," he announced. His eyes swept the board; he signaled to two Bishops and two lords to attend him.

Within the Jerusalem chamber Bessie was waiting, for the distraught abbot had announced he was coming. The Archbishop stood in the doorway, came forward and bowed deeply; around him were his lords, temporal and spiritual, and beyond in the corridor Bessie could see the armed guards of Richard of Gloucester. Then the door shut on them.

"I have come to beg you, Your Grace," the Archbishop said bluntly, "that you relinquish your precious son to us, who love him. So that he may be with his brother who needs him and wants him."

Bessie breathed fast. "Does his brother lack a playfellow then, my lords?" A slight smile swept over her face. "It's been my experience as a mother that Princes, young as they are, could play without their peers or their kin with whom they often agree worse than with strangers."

"I know that brothers bicker," the Archbishop blurted. "But, madam, what of his place at the coronation? He should take part."

Bessie seized on an untruth. "He is not well."

The Archbishop faltered. Then he said, "Madam, I pray thee. If thou dost not agree to surrender your son, my lord Protector will possess him by force. And once this sanctuary is invaded by armed men there will be no sanctuary for anyone and the Lord's will shall be violated. Madam, are you prepared to have that upon your soul?"

Bessie said, "The Protector says that? I pray God he may prove to be truly a Protector."

Her great eyes swept the faces of the men with the Archbishop, but they were grim and uncomprehending and she saw clear that they thought she held her own son hostage. She clenched her hands. There was a stool at one side and because she was trembling she sat down on it and arranged her skirts. She raised her head and looked up at the Archbishop, who was speaking.

"Madam, he must take his place at his brother's side. He must stand at our King's side when he is crowned next week. It is not lawful to keep him here. You have no right. He has done no harm to anyone. And no one will do him harm, we vow it. I vow it, madam, I give you my oath, my solemn promise, my word under God!"

Bessie bent her head.

"I vow it, madam, before my God."

Bessie slowly rose to her feet. "My lord, and all lords now present, I don't want to be so suspicious as to mistrust your truths, your vows."

"Oh, madam," cried the Archbishop, "trust me. I have given you my oath."

"No!" cried Bessie suddenly. "My sons are safe if they are apart!"

Her adamant words struck the Archbishop with force. "You will not be permitted to keep him, madam."

Bessie looked again at the circle of lords behind the Archbishop, at their grim faces. I have no choice, she thought desperately.

"Madam, we come in goodwill!"

It was the Archbishop's last plea and Bessie heard it plain. She turned and went to the doorway, went through it, and when she came back in just a minute she had Richard by the hand. She stood there with her second-born son and the lords bowed deeply.

Her voice was clear and steady. "Lo, my lords, here is the gentleman whom I would keep if I were permitted." She did not dare remember what Edward had said—"I'll never separate you from him, Bessie." Don't think, don't remember, one small part of her mind commanded.

"My lords," she said, "the desire for a kingdom knows no kindred. As I reminded you, each of the children is safe if they are apart. Notwithstanding I deliver him now into your hands and I shall require of you—before God and man—that ye be faithful. Ah, if you think I fear too much, beware you fear too little."

There were murmurs of "Dear madam, we shall by our oaths," and murmurs of greeting to their young Duke. Richard was very appealing but Bessie heard none of it really, for she had turned to the child. "Farewell, my own sweet son," she whispered.

Richard looked up at her although he was quite tall for nine.

"God send you good keeping, Richard."

"Mother," he whispered. "I'll be with Edward. And the Archbishop."

Bessie said, "Let me kiss you before you go."

Whenever any of Bessie's children said good-bye it was her custom to bless them, and now Richard automatically knelt for his mother's blessing.

Bessie laid her hand on his forehead. "God bless you and keep you, my dear son, and remember as always my love and my prayers follow you wherever you may go." She lifted him up and kissed his cheek. Then she turned and, taking his hand, led him to the Archbishop, who bowed deeply.

"Welcome, my lord," he said, his voice shaking with emotion. "Welcome with all my heart!"

Chapter 27

ANNE NEVILLE had parted from her only son with hugs and kisses. He was not nearly strong enough to journey to London and she didn't want to leave him at all. She never left him but her husband had ordered her to come to London, and willy-nilly she obeyed.

When she reached London one of the first things she told her husband was that the citizens of York were growing impatient about their plea to have their taxes reduced as he had promised. Richard was annoyed. He had been up half the night before; it was hard and straitly demanding work to seize a crown and to dispose of each problem in order. For now that Hastings was removed and since he had persuaded the Archbishop of Canterbury to give over into his custody Edward's other son, the way was clear for the ordering of the execution of Anthony Woodville and old Sir Thomas Vaughn and young Richard Grey. It was quite necessary that they should die, for he, Richard, knew well enough that alive they would plot and plot and plot to restore young Edward to his throne.

His quick mind told him though that the citizens of York were the ones who would respond to his call for arms, so he said gruffly he would write and explain he was too busy to consider their complaints now but would surely tend to it when he was able, and then he told Anne that Bishop Stillington, who had been such a good friend of Clarence's, had come to him and vowed that Edward and Bessie had never been legally married, because Edward had affianced himself to someone else before he married Bessie. So it was necessary for him, Richard, to assume the throne, and instead of young Edward being crowned on the twenty-sixth of June, Richard and his wife would be crowned early in July.

Anne stared at him. Her mouth fell open. "Is that true?" she asked.

"The Bishop is going to speak tomorrow," Richard said. "My brother's children are not legitimate. Therefore, they are not heirs to the throne. I am."

Anne backed away from him. There was something in his face that terrified her.

Richard, angry, rose and banged down his fist on the table. A wine cup rolled off it and the red, red wine lay like spilled blood on the polished floor; it spread slowly and Richard stood there, looking down at it, sliding his dagger back and forth in its sheath.

Anne was at the door. "Wait!" he commanded.

Obediently Anne turned.

"You'll need a new dress."

A faint frown creased her forehead. Anne Neville was not interested in clothes; they meant nothing to her.

"For the coronation," he said angrily.

"Oh." She half dismissed that with a wave of her thin arm. "I can have a dress made in two days."

He stared at her. She seemed impervious to him, his ambitions, his desires, his needs. All her life she has been a great heiress, he thought angrily; she just waves her hand and lo, a dress is produced; she doesn't care—it is just another thing.

"You act as though you are sleepwalking, as though this is a dream!" But he could already hear the cries: King Richard! King Richard!

Anne steeled herself against the old familiar fear. She looked straight back at him. Then she turned slowly, turned her back on him and went down the long hall. It was shadowy in the distance, as though she were walking toward eternity.

The weary rider wearing Anthony's badge of the scallop shell reached the London town house of the Duke of Buckingham on the twenty-seventh of June. He was admitted immediately to the presence of the Duchess, who knew him of old, who raised him up, looked long at the grim and grimed face and took into her hands the last letter from Anthony.

Kate's voice trembled. "You wish food or drink?"

He couldn't answer. Seeing her was too much of a reminder; he could remember so vividly the two of them together for so many

many years, their glamour a kind of cloud about them. So he went over to the sideboard and poured himself a cup of ale to clear his throat of unshed tears.

"He died very brave. I waited for the burial. He was wearing this, madam. Even I hadn't known it."

He swallowed and Kate whispered, "What is it, Will?"

"It's a hair shirt, madam. He always used to say he had to remind himself constant to be humble, to show humility to his God."

Kate couldn't speak.

"Madam, I would like to ask you to let me wear it till our rightful King is on his throne." Instinctively he had lowered his voice. He glanced at the heavy, closed door; he was standing in the house of the arch traitor, the Duke of Buckingham.

"Aye," said Kate. She held out her hand, a single enormous ring, a ring with Edward's favorite stone, the ruby ringed with pearls, blazed on her third finger. "His Grace's gift to me last New Year's," Kate said steadily. "I wear it only till young Edward is crowned." She pointed that fine finger at him. "But you are too well-known to stay. My brothers Lionel and Richard are with my dearest sister, the Queen, in sanctuary. But my brother Edward has escaped with three ships and followers to France. You join him. I'll provide you with my livery and money."

He knelt and took her hand and kissed the ring. "I vow to live only for this cause!"

"I, too," Kate said. "And never forget, all over the realm there are men and women vowing just the same as you and I."

But after he had gone, brave in his new livery of the Duke of Buckingham, Kate Woodville went over to the window seat and opened the letters he had brought. He would reach her brother Edward safe and carrying messages from Kate and Lionel and Richard, for Richard already had plans for escape and Lionel had got messages out to his diocese, where he'd be welcomed.

Kate had locked her door. She opened Anthony's letter and his will. "I wish to be buried alongside of my dear nephew, Richard Grey," Anthony had written. He had loved young Richard entire; he had acted like his father. Kate could remember Richard Grey never left Anthony's side when he would come home to Grafton. It didn't seem very long ago when one spring morning Anthony had said, "Today, Richard, this morning, my little man, is the day when you are big enough to learn to—" Anthony stopped.

"What?" cried Richard. "What?"

Anthony held out a shiny new saddle. "Happy May Day," Anthony had said, laughing.

Kate laid down the will, her hands shaking. A sheet of paper fell out. Kate read:

> Somewhat musing, somewhat mourning,
> In remembering th'unsteadfastness;
> This world being of such wheeling,
> Me contrarying, What may I guess?
> Me thinks truly, Bounden am I,
> And that greatly, to be content;
> Seeing plainly fortune doth wry,
> All contrary from mine intent.

It was Anthony's last poem, written in the early hours of the morning of June twenty-fifth in Pontefract Castle. Kate couldn't read anymore. She lay face down on the cushioned window seat and wept helplessly.

Chapter 28

"BASTARD SLIPS shall have no roots!" thundered Bishop Stillington, Clarence's good priest whom Richard had picked as Chancellor. The crown had been placed on Richard's head and on Anne's, Anne who had shivered uncontrollably when she stood before the altar. They had stripped her naked to the waist and anointed her with the holy oil and placed a coronet on her head, and then wrapped her in purple robes. She was the Queen.

It was July and even the summer sun did not shine this year; instead the rain and fog swept in from the sea and it was cold, cold, and the stone floors sweated under the rushes and the south wind didn't come, or when it did it came laden with sea fogs, drifting over England. In the country Kate spent most of the days with her children; thus the rumors that swept London all of August didn't reach her until the third week in August.

She had been kept well informed, had Kate. She knew that her brother Lionel had slipped out of sanctuary and was in his diocese, gathering adherents and loyal men for young Edward. Richard was in Berkshire with the family of Stoners, raising men for the same cause. Thomas had escaped from sanctuary also and was with Lionel, and all over the country men gathered, secret and openly both, to raise an army and rescue their young King from the Tower and to crush the tyrant who had seized his rightful throne. But the news that Kate received that August morning sent her hastening toward London and the sanctuary with the single compelling motive of her sister Bessie.

When Kate arrived at the outer gates of Westminster she found the sanctuary guarded by a creature of Richard's, a man called Nesfield, and a rough-looking crew of soldiers. But Kate had attracted quite a few onlookers and behind her impressive retinue hovered a great many Londoners, who had divined the situation and were anxious to see what would happen.

"Make way! Make way!" shouted Kate's foreriders.

The soldiers sullenly obeyed. Nesfield came stamping up to see what the trouble was and came face-to-face with the Duchess.

"Let me pass, fellow," Kate said contemptuously, "or my husband, the Duke of Buckingham, will have your head!"

Nesfield swallowed. The Duke indeed was an ally of his master Richard. But this woman was a Woodville. The trouble was, thought Nesfield, watching the crowd press closer, that the Woodvilles were popular in London. With as good grace as he could muster, he bowed. Kate sailed through the opened gates and into the abbot's chambers. There she spoke with him, and he himself took her into the sanctuary quarters where the Queen was. The abbot pointed silently to the closed heavy oaken door.

"Her Grace is within."

"How long has she been there?" Kate cried.

Young Bess said, "All last night and this morning, Aunt Kate!"

Kate turned about to look for a weapon. There were green logs piled on the circular hearth. "Summon two monks, Father," she said, "and force the door."

But first she went to the closed door. She bent down. She put her lips to the crack. "Bessie," she called. "It's Kate. Let me in, Bessie."

There was no answer.

"Bessie. Bessie!" called Kate desperately.

There was silence.

"We'll have to force the door," said Kate. The abbot nodded. The two monks chose a log long enough for two of them to hold. They charged the door with a shattering crash, once, and again.

Kate said to Bess, "Who told her?"

"Tommie did," said Bess. "He had to—"

There was another series of crashes; the wood of the door began to splinter.

"Tommie got out. He was helped by the dog Lovell, that minion of Richard's! We got word back from Tom that it was true. No one has seen my brothers for weeks and no one knows where they are."

"Oh, my God," Kate whispered.

"Mother fainted." Bess looked at Kate with eyes that spilled with tears. "Both of them," she whispered. "My brothers. Mother said, 'My sons? They—'."

The battered door collapsed. Kate rushed forward with Bess after her. Within the small room there had come no sound. There was none now. On the floor, her head pillowed on her arm, her long bright hair spilled across the back and shoulders, Bessie lay half naked and mercifully unconscious.

She was burning with fever. Kate and Bess turned her over; her eyes were closed and she breathed quickly. The monks lifted her gently and laid her on the bed. The abbot knelt beside the bed for a brief prayer, and then the three men left Bessie to the care of her women.

They undressed her, taking from her the torn garments which she herself had seized and wrenched. For when Bessie had entered that room and shot the bolt, she had done so in such agony of mind that she had been sure she was losing her reason and that she was going mad with grief and hate. For she could not rid her mind of the struggle of her sons under the murderous hands that killed them, and she could hear that they must have cried out for help, to her, to Edward, and she kept hearing those cries and she could not bear it, she could not look on the faces of other people, she could not talk, nor eat, nor stay with other humans. She had fled here and locked the door, and then she had lain on the cold floor and beat her fists against the stone until they were covered with blood. She had torn at her clothes and rolled on the floor, using the mortification of the flesh to clean the mind, the heart.

"Edward," she cried. "Edward! Help me! Please help me!"

The cold seeped into her body, numbing, bitter. She stretched out and welcomed it, laying her bare arms ahead of her body, ripping away the last of the tatters of her sleeves so that the icy cold could reach all through them and she had laid her cheek down against the stones too, first to one side then to the other. The cold, the numbing cold.

She cried now. Helpless sobs. Her tears fell down her cheeks and over her arms all during the night. She turned over on her back, and she began to shiver uncontrollably, and it was a relief to shiver; she could feel the long convulsions of it going through her body. At dawn she drifted slowly into unconsciousness.

When Kate and Bess took from her fevered body the torn

clothes and bathed her face and hands and arms with warmed
perfumed water and wrapped her into one of her furred bed-
gowns, she knew it was happening. She heard Kate's voice and
she opened her eyes. And she heard Bess' voice. Her hands hurt;
they were putting ointment on them and wrapping them around
and around with soft linen. Bessie submitted. She began to dream.

She dreamed of the Duchess. She could hear her mother's
voice. She could hear Edward too. He was saying, "Bessie. My
Bessie. Go to sleep now, go to sleep."

Bessie closed her eyes. She began to drift endlessly on a sea
of heat, heat, heat.

The fever rose and rose. They propped her up on pillows so
she could breathe more easily. The pain was through her chest,
stabbing her with relentless kniving strokes.

"She is delirious," Kate said. "She thinks I am Mother."

Three days went by. Three days in which the bodily sickness
helped the bruised and crazed mind. Three days in which Bessie
suffered only physical pain while the muddled brain slept.

On the fourth day, early in the morning, as Kate kept her vigil
by candlelight, Bessie opened her eyes.

"Kate," she said plainly. "Kate, I am covered with sweat. Please
fetch some water and bathe me."

Kate laid her hand on Bessie's head. "You are cool!"

"Yes," said Bessie. A cough rose in her throat.

"Don't talk," cautioned Kate. "You have been very ill."

Gentle hands lifted her and bathed her and changed the linen.
She drank a little wine. Kate brushed her hair and tied it back
in a ribbon, and then plaited it. Bessie said, "Kate, my boys are
dead. The Archbishop broke his promise to God and someone of
Richard's has killed them."

Kate couldn't speak.

"I know it, Kate. They are gone from the Tower. No one has
seen them for weeks. I know they are dead. When I speak to
them in my mind I get no answer. You know how you can do
that, Kate, when you are away from your children? You think of
them and you suddenly see them smile," she coughed. She
reached out her hand and Kate took it gently; it was still purple
with bruises.

"Bessie," Kate tried to say.

"I went mad, Kate. That's why I locked myself in this room. This morning when I wakened, I wondered why I hadn't died because I would just as soon die, Kate, because I am afraid—" Bessie hesitated, "I am afraid it will happen again."

Kate sent for the abbot. The first day he stayed near Bessie, praying. The second day she was stronger. She was able to repeat the prayers with him. The third day, when the frightening revulsion began to rise within her, she was able to get out of bed and kneel on her cushion and repeat over and over into her clasped hands, *"Dominus illuminatio mea et salus mea."*

Bessie was stronger. Bessie was able to sit outside in the garden when the sun shone at noon. The monks could see her sitting there when they came out from their noonday meal, her needle flashing in the sun; she was remaking a dress of little Kate's for Bridget, who toddled nearby with a painted hoop. Kate always was near too. And Bess. But this time Kate taught the French class, for Cecily, beautiful Cecily, was but thirteen and little Anne eight. Kate had a birthday party that week; she was four. The monks came and wished her happiness and at the door of the sanctuary were left toys, carved wooden animals and painted dolls, and a beautiful illustrated book that Jane Shore entrusted to one of the monks. At night Kate would think about the children and then about Edward and then young Edward and Richard. How carefully they had been brought up. The last time she had seen her nephew she had been so charmed and taken with him; he reflected all of Anthony's courtliness, and there was not a book he had not read, she thought, or that Anthony had not read to him; he could discourse on any subject and he was splendid at his mathematics; his father was proud of that. And he had the swift brilliant wit of the Woodvilles and of his father and his love for music. When Kate realized that this was what Bessie was thinking too she wondered how she indeed could bear it, and she wondered how long it would be before the wound was at least healed enough for Bessie to take stock of the future, for there was a future and it had to be faced, and Kate kept remembering Edward's voice in those early years: "Look at her, Kate! My dearest daughter, my beautiful daughter. Aye, if she is to be my heir I'll be more than satisfied."

The last week in August Jane Shore arrived at the sanctuary with a message. It was from the Lady Margaret, Countess of Richmond. She had heard that the Queen's Grace was ill and she was sending her physician. A Dr. Hall. He would arrive the following morning.

Dr. Hall was escorted to Bessie's presence by the abbot; Bessie received him in her bedroom, propped up on her pillows in her bed. Bessie knew the reason for Dr. Hall's visit. She had given instructions that Bess and Cecily be dressed in their finest afternoon dresses and that they should come and meet the doctor. When that was done Cecily was sent from the room and the door was closed. Dr. Hall had made a pretense of asking Bessie about her cough. She lifted a white hand. "I am getting well, sir. You have brought me a message, haven't you?"

Her face was white and set. Kate knew what Bessie was going to say; to say it she had to admit to herself once and for all that hers and Edward's dearest treasures, their sons, were dead. The plans to rescue them had to be abandoned. And other plans had to be made. Bessie said, "Sir, you see before you the heir of York. My dearest daughter, the Princess Elizabeth."

Dr. Hall took her hand and kissed it. "Madam," he said, "the countess sends you her heartfelt sympathy and her devotion. I too, madam," he blurted, his lips trembled a bit under his beard. His glance went to young Bess. He thought, I see Edward in her; her eyes look direct and honest just as his did and she speaks that same way, for Dr. Hall knelt now before the standing Princess, and he said, "Your Grace, I will do all in my power to serve you."

Bess said, holding out her hand, and with a small smile, "We thank you, sir. We need your friendship and we shall accept it gratefully."

Just like her father, Dr. Hall thought.

"Madam," he said, turning to Bessie, "There has been much bloodshed, roiling and misery in the realm. It is time to end it."

Bessie nodded. So Kate thought, Here are three women and one woman who sent the message to bind up the wounds that men have caused. Will we be able to do it?

"The Countess proposes what my husband had voiced a few

years ago," Bessie said. "That we wed my daughter and the Countess' son, the heir of Lancaster. Is that not so?"

"Yes, madam," Dr. Hall said. "It is so."

Kate left for Wales and her children the following day, for it was necessary that Kate be on the outside of the sanctuary walls and able to do as much as she could for the new cause to which they were all committed, for now they had a shining cause, a cause for which the houses of both Lancaster and York could sound the horns, blow up the trumpets, unfurl the brilliant banners, a cause which would rescue their beautiful Princess, shut up behind stone walls, guarded by knaves. Was there a man who wouldn't hasten to buckle on his harness to set her free to marry her Prince, to put on her blond head the coronet she was born to have?

Kate hastened home. She had hardly given her husband a thought; it was as though he were dead. Before she saw her children, she went up to her chambers to wash the travel dust from her hands and face and to change her gown. She was standing in her petticoats when her door burst open.

Kate, startled, knew it must be her husband, for no one else would dare enter her room thus but him. And Henry, Duke of Buckingham, went forward and knelt before his wife and put his arms around her waist.

"Oh, Kate," he cried, "Kate, you said you never would but forgive me! Forgive me! I didn't know what he was going to do!"

Chapter 29

RICHARD III, King of England, was asleep. He stirred and smiled, for he was halfway between waking and sleeping and he was dreaming of a night long ago. It had been a Friday, the twenty-sixth of June, and that day, riding at Edward's side, he had entered London with his brother, the King. Four hundred citizens in green and the aldermen in scarlet had met them. And that evening Edward had made him a Knight of the Bath.

Richard turned over. What a sumptuous Bath it had been! Three knights of the order and squires and musicians singing, and they had told him what it meant to be such a knight as this; they told him all the ideals of chivalry and honor.

A priest took him to the chapel where all night he had prayed and made his confession and in the morning he heard mass. Then they had put him to bed and he had slept like this, half awake, too tense to sleep, but they had roused him early and dressed him and brought him before his brother, the King.

Edward had commanded the two knights to fasten the spurs on Richard's heels. All Edward's lords watched, smiling, kind. They liked him, Richard. And then the King himself, his towering brother, had stepped down and embraced him and kissed him, and with his own hands had put about his slender waist the sword belt and girded him with it. Edward had said, "Be thou a good knight." He kissed him again and set him back. "Be thou a good knight," Edward repeated, smiling, fond.

Richard sat straight up in bed, his face twisted, breathing fast. Why had that scene been recalled to him now? "Be thou a good knight." He could hear Edward's voice plain, speaking to him. Richard's eyes searched the shadowy room; the dawn was coming; he could see into the corner and there was no one there. Edward slept, slept forever in the chapel he had built, the Chapel of St. George at Windsor, beneath the stones. And he, Richard, was now King of England.

"I was but nine then," he said aloud. And his mind told him he had been the same age as little Richard, Duke of York, whose merry laughter was not heard anymore.

Richard got out of bed. Silent and twitching he allowed himself to be clothed, and when he strode from his chamber he was met by the news that the Duke of Buckingham had writ a letter, which was published throughout the realm, calling the country to arms.

He went rigid with rage. To think that Buckingham had actually written to Henry Tudor, offering him Richard's throne and Richard's niece, the Princess Elizabeth, as his Queen! The Countess of Richmond, Henry's mother, was undoubtedly behind this and the former Queen. He would have liked to seize the Countess of Richmond but he didn't dare; she was wed to Lord Stanley now and he, Richard, needed the Stanleys; he couldn't afford to offend them, for now all over the country the counties were stirring and the names like St. Leger, on whom he should be able to count, were slipping away, slipping away.

Anne said, "They say that the sons of Edward are dead, murdered." She looked at him wonderingly with her brown, steady eyes. "No one has seen them for two weeks. They are gone. Disappeared. And they say they are dead."

"Buckingham is a foul traitor and Dorset is full of lust and seeks out women! I've said that publicly."

Anne said, "Richard, to stop the dread rumors, why don't you show the people of London your two nephews? Then they would know they are not dead. Why don't you show them to the people?" He bit his lip hard and continued to worry, fussing with the dagger at his side. For a long minute Anne regarded him, puzzled. "Why don't you show them to the people?"

In Brittany Jasper Tudor read Buckingham's letter. Then he passed it back to his nephew. He rose and laid his hand on Henry's shoulder, looking down at the thinning blond hair. It was raining hard, and he took a turn about the room and then flung himself down into a chair and looked across at Henry Tudor with affection and concern. A gust of rain blew a shutter hard against the narrow window.

"Someone will have to go to England and it cannot be you," he said. "It is dangerous enough for you here." Jasper Tudor didn't quite trust their host Francis of Brittany, especially since he was not well. What if he became too ill to issue orders? There were plenty of men who would betray them for the money offered by the homicide who called himself King of England.

"I know it should be quick, our descent on England, but not too quick or we'll be like to fail, Henry. This damned weather."

The rains which had plagued Europe and England all summer were continuing, rivers were at their peak and the sea tossed restlessly and angrily between Brittany and England. "It will not be an easy crossing," Jasper Tudor said, in great understatement.

Henry regarded his slender hands. He was twenty-six years old. A serious young man, he had always been very conscious of his destiny, holding himself aloof from any entanglement or marriage, ready to be proudly the heir of Lancaster. He was well taught, very intelligent, quiet, sparing in dress and purse and all things secondary to the dedication of his life to be indeed the last heir of Lancaster and thus ready to be a King. A steadfast belief in his own destinies had marked him as unusual for a good many years and Jasper Tudor recognized this very plain, and he was beginning to believe in it himself.

"I will send this messenger back to Buckingham," he said, "and set a time when I will slip across to England."

It was still raining the night of October first. Jasper Tudor leaned on the rail of the small, tossing vessel and heard the voice of Sir Edward Woodville issuing the commands as the sails were furled, all but the sprit, which bellied taut against the wind, hardly above the waves; spray flew high. There was a wry smile on his face; never had he thought that the day would come when he and a Woodville would join hands.

Edward Woodville came bounding down from the higher deck and Jasper turned to face him. "I've been trying to see the coastline, sir," he said.

"It's been a long time, hasn't it?" Edward said genially, wiping off his face, for they were suddenly drenched with seawater.

"There's a cove in there," he gestured. "We'll try to slip in. Should be no trouble, no other vessel." He ran his eyes over

Jasper Tudor, who was dressed as a common sailor. "You'll do, my lord, but be careful. The men with you are clever and will be calm in face of betrayal. They'll get you back. I'm going to sneak in very close to shore. *Regardez! Votre amour*—Wales!"

Jasper Tudor could see nothing but white water. He did indeed *regardez!* with dismay. The sailing ship leaned perilously, righted, bounded across the foaming breakers and there, there was the coast!

The anchors, fore and aft, sheet anchors, slipped overboard. The boat was hoisted over. Hands helped Jasper Tudor, hands received him in the rocking dory, then the oars dipped and it was a short row; on the hard shingle the dory scraped its bottom and Jasper Tudor set his feet on his native Wales for the first time in twelve years.

It was very dark. That was as it should be. But there was a rocky path and Jasper Tudor followed the stalwart, plodding figure of one of the men that Edward Woodville had assured him were clever, steady and calm. He hoped he needed none of those qualities.

They followed the rocky path up and up a little farther. There was a hut ahead; in it was burning a dim light. The sailor ahead of Jasper Tudor reached the rude door and opened it gingerly. Within was a single figure who held out, in the light of one rush, a large glittering ring and an envelope sealed with the crest of the Duke of Buckingham.

The sailor nodded and stepped aside. "The messenger from His Grace, the Duke of Buckingham, my lord."

And so Jasper Tudor stepped inside the crude hut and closed the door.

In that dim rushlight Jasper Tudor's eyes went to the messenger, a slight figure. Under the cap he could see the gleam of blond hair. There was something wrong! For this was not a man, not even a boy. "Who are you?" he asked grimly.

The eyes into which he looked were suddenly merry and the figure made a small curtsy. "I am Kate Woodville," said the clear voice. Jasper Tudor was incapable of even an oath.

He stared and stuttered, "Sir Edward brought me over."

"Please give him my deepest love and love from all of his family," Kate said.

She seemed perfectly assured while he felt like some kind of dolt. "I am Jasper Tudor," he said.

Kate made him a small bow, flaring her cloak open, and her figure under her man's costume—he told himself sternly to pay attention to business.

He held out his hand for the packet; Kate relinquished it and slipped the heavy ring of her husband's back onto her thumb. She said, "The whole south is ready to fight. All the southern counties."

He said, "There's not enough time."

"The time set is the eighteenth. This month."

He didn't want to say that he didn't trust her husband. So he said, "The weather is so damned bad, it should be better in two weeks. But the plan to land His Grace in the south at Poole or Plymouth—I'm not too sanguine. I'd rather it were Wales."

"My husband will rouse Wales. And march to meet you."

"I gather," said Jasper Tudor, "it is all in here—the complete plans?" He held out the thick packet.

She nodded. "Even to crowning at Bodmin."

"Why did you come?" he asked. He looked down at her from his height, suddenly urgent, demanding.

"Because it is a matter of great moment to me, my family, my dearest sister. So I came."

Jasper Tudor thought it was foolish. "You took a great risk."

Kate looked surprised. "No risk. Good-bye. Give my love to Neddie." She held out her hand forthright, like a man.

He took it. Her grip was firm and their eyes met. Kate looked up at him and her fingers tightened on his as though she were going to lose her balance. Then she stepped back.

"I felt unsteady for a minute."

He smiled, suddenly. "It is the magic here in Wales."

She thought, Oh, what a man is this one. It rushed over her that she was meeting him thus because Bessie's boys were dead and Kate's eyes were suddenly haunted. She said, "I wish that my two nephews had such an uncle as you have been and are, my lord."

He wanted to gather her slight figure into his arms and hug her tight. Instead he stepped to the door.

"Your Grace," he said formally, reminding himself she was another man's wife, "Your Grace, please relay my thanks, affection and loyalty to your husband. And now you will permit me to give you a command. You are never to indulge in this kind of rendezvous again. It is too dangerous." He paused at the door, then opened it cautiously. The sailor outside nodded his head; he looked at Kate and she was smiling at him.

"Thank you for thinking of me," she said. "Good-bye and God speed."

The door closed behind him; in the tiny cabin Kate carefully extinguished the rushlight, pinching it between her gloved hands. Then she gathered her cloak tight around her and went slowly to the door and out into the night. Something had happened to her that had never happened before.

On the eighteenth of October it was still raining. Later they would call it Buckingham's Flood. For as Jasper Tudor had told Kate, it was too quick, the plans too unreadied, and yet the whole of the south was aflame with hatred and rebellion against their so-called King, the murderer of his nephews, Richard III.

The rain had begun again on the sixteenth. The south lay like a drowned rat as the rivers overflowed their banks and the roads became impassable, and in Wales Buckingham was bottled up with his troops like rabbits flushed from their burrows by floodwaters, so the chroniclers put it.

Nonetheless the Woodvilles and Bishop Morton, the St. Legers and the Courtenays marched to the meeting place. But Buckingham never appeared, and when Jasper and Henry Tudor appeared off Poole there were indeed soldiers on the shore who beckoned. Jasper Tudor shook his head. King Richard had got there first; they were King's men there, and so Henry and Jasper turned their vessels about and made for the safety of their exile once more.

Luck had been with the wicked King, the people said. In Westminster sanctuary Bessie trembled for the life of her son Thomas; the price on his head was enormous. But Thomas and Bishop Morton in disguise fled to Ely, the Bishop's faithful diocese, and from there to the safety of Flanders. Lionel crossed the Channel in a small boat and so did Richard Woodville, and this news was smuggled to Bessie along with assurances that they would return; it was only temporary.

In his palace the King raved against his rebels; they were not only false traitors, but they were men of dreadful morals who slept with women and committed adultery. In his moral rage he singled out Jane Shore and made her walk in penance through London in her shift.

The people gathered around her in sympathy. The beautiful Jane, head high, her hair streaming down her back, drew crowds who murmured encouragement. Richard raged.

But what of Buckingham, his chief rebel? In Brecon Kate watched the muddied road for news; his troops had melted away, sodden, unfed; poor soul, thought Kate, he was never a military man; if he had only just not tried to be bigger than his boots! She wept for him, knowing he was alone and afraid in hiding and whom could he trust? For he was not well-liked; no one knew that better than his wife.

The King had marched quickly to Salisbury when Buckingham's army collapsed. Buckingham himself was brought to Richard there, a prisoner.

"Take me to the King," Buckingham ordered. He had a dagger in his sleeve; he would kill Richard himself!

Richard refused to see him. His execution was ordered. Buckingham pleaded now. Let me see the King. He sent Richard his ring; he begged. Please!

Adamantly Richard refused. He would grant no interviews to traitors. The royal presence would not be demeaned by wicked men. In despair Buckingham resigned himself to death and the realm was shocked, for it was the thirty-first of October; it was All Souls' Day and Sunday, the day that the Duke of Buckingham paid with his head for making the dreadful mistake of helping Richard III to seize the crown.

But from now on there was no sleep for the tyrant, for he had unloosed the whirlwind. His mind coiled uncertainly, fearfully, about the men around him; whom could he trust? He didn't dare imprison the Countess of Richmond. And he was helpless to punish her, to ward her in a remote castle; he had to leave her free to plot with the former Queen, with the Duchess of Buckingham—all these women who hated him!

And what of Northumberland? What of the proud Percy in his northern stronghold? Richard needed him too, he who had in the early days been a good friend. What was Percy thinking now? Did he brood in the north? Did he believe the tales told about his moral, driven monarch who couldn't sleep anymore at night? That week Richard ordered a hundred masses to be sung for his soul. It was an inordinate amount; no one had ever heard of such an amount. He needs them, said the people; he needs more than a hundred.

Christmas was coming. In France Jasper Tudor welcomed into their ranks the Woodvilles, Bishop Morton and hordes of lesser fugitives from the King's justice. The ranks were swelling rapidly, and Jasper Tudor was worried about how to support all these people until they could make another and final descent upon England.

"But we will wait until the plans are perfect," he said. "If it takes two years we will wait."

His nephew's eyes looked past him and into the future. He had no doubt now that he was the rightful King of England and he had no doubt that he would successfully uncrown the tyrant. The purpose which had burned within this strange, serious young man for years, a fire untended save by his own inner resolves and surenesses, now flamed open for all to see, with a steady fire. Henry was also a fine politician.

"On Christmas Day," he said, "I shall kneel in the cathedral at Rennes and ask God's blessing on my union to the Lady Elizabeth Plantagenet, Princess of England, and vow before God and man to wed her and to make her my Queen."

This was the Christmas present that young Bess received. And on that same day in the sanctuary chapel young Bess and Bessie knelt too and prayed that their marriage be blessed and that their faith could indeed work a miracle.

Bessie tried very hard to make a little Christmas for her young children. There were gifts for the littlest; once again the sympathy of London washed about the walls of the sanctuary, and Bessie knew the people of London prayed for the safety of the Princess and her little sisters.

Bessie had gift rings from her jewel case for Bess and Cecily and one for the kind abbot.

"But we have to be careful, Bess," she said, "for my jewels are what we are living on. They are paying for our food, our wood, our candles."

How long had they been in sanctuary? The winter wind howled about its thick, thick walls; those walls were so thick that when that building was taken down two centuries later, the workmen grumbled mightily that it was indestructible. How long had they been hiding here? Almost eight months.

On New Year's Day little Bridget and Kate and Anne, escorted by Bess and Cecily, came to their mother's bedside in the morning with their handmade gifts. Their love spilled over onto Bessie. She knew she must do something for them, must get them out of this confinement, but how? How? There was nowhere to flee and how could one flee with five daughters? It wasn't like slipping alone into the night, uncaring whether or not the life which one held not preciously were lost.

But if Bessie wanted freedom for her children, Richard the King wanted them out of sanctuary too, for how did it look to foreign lands when the foremost lady in the kingdom and the Princesses hid in a sanctuary, as though he, Richard, were a monster? And would murder them all if they dared to step out from under the church's protective walls? As a matter of fact that month the French Estates General did brand Richard as a homicide and pledged France's aid in helping the exiled Henry. Richard would have liked to throw an army against France but he was helpless to raise it in his cause. So he bent his efforts to try to force Bessie to leave Westminster.

Bessie had given the problem a great deal of thought and so when Richard's request came she was ready. Her secretary wrote exactly what she dictated.

"The Queen's Grace and her daughters will leave the sanctuary on the very day that Richard, King of England, will swear on oath before the mayor and the aldermen of London and his own council and his lords temporal and spiritual that he will not harm but that he will take care of and shelter the daughters of his late majesty, Edward IV of England."

Richard raved.

Anne said, "She asks for nothing for herself."

"No, and she'll get nothing. I'll keep her bottled up!"

Yet he couldn't bring himself to do what she asked. It was on the horns of a dilemma that Richard sat and Bessie knew it.

Bess said, "Mother, you shouldn't even give him that choice."

"I must," Bessie said. "For your sakes. The money will run out soon."

"How can I be a member of his court?" Bess stood trembling, hands clenched.

Bessie rose. She said, "Once your father was a prisoner of my lord of Warwick. If he could do it you can."

Cecily's blue eyes were wide as she looked from both Bess to her mother. Bessie caught the look. "And you too, Cecily," she said.

But she insisted that Richard swear his oath before all and then, as if Edward himself were nudging her elbow, she added another provision. Richard must swear never to place the Princesses in the Tower and swear to guide and demean them as befitted the daughters of the late Edward IV.

"Thus you shall be received at court as you should," Bessie said. "And given the honor due you and the place due you. And by this oath he shall have admitted publicly that we hold him suspect till he swore before God and all his lords."

Not for nothing had Bessie lived with Edward for twenty years. And she won her battle with Richard. His hand on the Bible, in the presence of his council and lords, Richard swore the oath word for word and one can guess what it cost him.

Bessie dressed the littlest ones, Kate, Anne and Bridget, in their best gowns and brushed their hair till it shone. "Never, never forget," she told them, "that you are the daughters of King Edward. It is your father who steps forth from here with thee at your side, proud, kind, brave. His hand will be holding yours and mine, my dearest daughters. We are ready to go."

Thus they set out once more into the workaday world from the sanctuary. First young Bess and Cecily, then Kate and Anne, then Bessie holding Bridget's hand and close behind Bessie the faithful Grace Plantagenet, whose devotion would serve Bessie all her life.

Bessie was forty-seven years old. Grace thought that day she had never seen her more beautiful. Her great eyes blazed from her thinned face; she looked forward to the halls of Westminster as though Edward himself would be coming to greet her, so sure she walked. She had been a Queen for more than twenty years and she had never looked more queenly.

Richard had chosen obscure apartments in Westminster Palace

for Bessie and her daughters. But as they passed through the myriad halls and corridors to the place he had picked the hurrying servants perceived her and the Princesses. Instantly they knelt in homage.

Four ladies-in-waiting instinctively sank into low curtsies with bowed heads as Bessie passed. Her guards stared uncomfortably straight ahead. Behind them struggled servants with cartons and boxes, all that remained of twenty years of living.

The doors of the apartments closed finally with the last of the boxes that Thomas had packed for her that night long ago when she had left the royal apartments for the sanctuary.

Bessie spread the fine counterpanes on the beds. She hung the pictures and displayed the plate. The few rugs were laid and the books unpacked. There was a scrap of garden outside; it would be fine for the little ones.

"It looks wonderful, Mother," young Bess said.

"It looks wonderful and pretty, Mother," said little Kate, smiling.

"You may go outside," Bessie said. "Imagine. Outside to play." She turned to young Bess. "But you and Cecily must wait upon the Queen. It is your place in the realm and you must take it. And the Queen is kind. You shall get to know her."

There was nothing left of Anne but her goodness. In the early spring her only son had died. The chroniclers said she went almost mad with grief and now she moved like a shadow, painfully thin, already renouncing the world in which she had lived so tragically and in which she had so little time left. As the fall passed and Christmas approached, young Bess tended Anne who was often too sick to leave her couch. Bess read to her and summoned Anne's confessor and helped her dress and led her, leaning on Bess' arm, to her gilded chair, where she leaned her head back against the wood and closed her eyes and listened to the music her ladies made for her.

Anne was dying and she was ready to die, except sometimes a bit of her old spirit would flare up. One day before Christmas she suddenly summoned Bess.

"Come with me to my husband," she commanded, and Bess obeyed and waited outside a closed door.

She could hear Anne's voice. "It is noised all about the palace!" Anne cried. "They say you complain of my sterility! And that you will not share my bed because of my sickness which offends you!"

Bess could hear the low murmur of Richard's voice.

"How can you say such things?" Anne cried. "I have been a good and loyal wife, God knows, I have! And you—"

They came out the door together, Richard escorting her, smiling, his brown eyes kind. Bess could see that Anne had been comforted somewhat and that night she and Bess looked over some material from the royal wardrobe. There was some happiness in her face, Bess thought, as a great ell of red velvet was unrolled for her view.

"I shall have that," Anne said.

"It is beautiful," young Bess said. "It will look handsome on you, Your Grace."

Anne smiled at her. "You shall have it too," she cried. "Make exact the same dress for the Lady Elizabeth. Exact the same." She smiled like a child bestowing favors, and Bess took her thin, thin hand and kissed it. "Thank you, Your Grace. It is very kind."

"We shall be gowned just the same," said Anne. "You and I."

It was the last Christmas that Bessie and young Bess should spend in these rooms and the last Christmas for both Richard and Anne. For the forces which Richard had unleashed were gathering slowly, slowly. Each day brought a new defection from Richard's dwindling ranks and each day Jasper Tudor welcomed a new and famous name to the growing group of exiles about his nephew Henry.

My lord of Oxford had arrived, for instance. Oxford had been warded in Hammes Castle but his warder was one of the Blounts, faithful to Edward, and now both of them swelled the restless group, waiting, waiting.

In January Anne took to her bed. "She is dying, Mother," young Bess told Bessie. "She coughs blood."

Richard was revolted by it; he could hardly bear to be in the room with her. "What the gossips said was true," Anne whispered to Bess. "He waits for me to die. He wants me to die. The father of my son."

She had forgotten everything, Bess thought, except her dead boy and the years she had cared for him and lavished upon him her love; he was the only human who had ever truly loved her. She spoke of him constantly, telling Bess tale after tale of his goodness and his quick mind and his doubtful smile, for he was always so frail, so sick. "I tell him I am coming, his mother, to be with him." Then the tears would well up in her brown eyes and young Bess would tremble with pity and sorrow for her, but she would try to smile and say, "Oh, Your Grace, when spring comes you will be well. You must rest and get well and when April comes you can go out in the sun. We will wrap you all up in rugs and take you out in the sun."

"I used to do that with my own dearest Edward," Anne replied.

But Anne was not to live to see the April sun. She died on the sixteenth of March, a day the wind howled about Westminster and the moon came across the face of the sun in a fearsome eclipse. She was not quite thirty-one years old.

The ladies sent Bess to tell the King.

Richard bent his head in what Bess thought might be sorrow, even though all the palace had known that Anne was dying and had known it for months. Then suddenly he raised his eyes and looked at her. Bess backed from the room.

"You will excuse me," she said. "I am distraught with grief."

She went immediately to her mother. Sitting at Bessie's feet on a cushion she told of Anne and her last hours and then she spoke of her uncle.

Bessie put young Bess to bed and gave out she was ill. The country seethed. Somehow the people began to know that the tyrant coveted his own niece as a wife. Bessie's small, obscure apartments were like a beleaguered camp.

"The Princess is ill!" Bessie stood foursquare in the doorway.

"No one may enter!"

In London on the walls of Westminster men wrote a rhyme:

"The Cat, the Rat and Lovell our dog rule all England under a hog!"

Catesby was the cat and Ratcliff was the rat—good friends of Richard they were. And yet they were now afraid, very afraid. Catesby took it upon himself to tell the tyrant; he took it upon himself boldly, as one miscreant to another.

"You will have to openly disavow the rumors," he said. "You cannot marry your niece!"

All during that weekend and Palm Sunday Bessie wrestled with the problem and its danger to young Bess. So on Holy Thursday she sent by secret ways Grace Plantagenet with a note to Richard the King, and late, late that night he came to Bessie's chamber, alone.

Two candles burned, for Bessie was allowed only seven hundred crowns a year and couldn't afford candles. The wind sighed. The small room was shadowy and silent as though the past sat there, unspeaking, brooding. Bessie had steeled herself for this interview. Her hands trembled; her knees trembled as she made a small curtsy. Then she forced herself to look at Richard.

His face was drawn. It was sad, haunted. He was dressed in black, in mourning for Anne, black unrelieved by any color or any jewel. His slight figure was thin.

"Please sit, my lord."

At the sound of Bessie's voice he seemed to quiver. Then he did sit.

"I have called you here—and I thank you for coming—because I know that my dearest daughter and the plans for her marriage to Henry Tudor are a threat to you. A very dangerous threat."

He looked at her, almost unseeing, reading instead the future.

"I was the Queen for twenty years," she said, trying to remind him she was well versed in politics.

"And to stop the rumors," Bessie went on as evenly as she could, "to stop the terrible rumors and to quiet my daughter's fears there is only one thing to do. And that is, as you well know, to again go before your knights and swear publicly on oath that you do not desire to marry your brother's daughter."

Your brother's daughter. Richard flinched from the words as though he'd been dealt a physical blow. As though he were asking what had he ever done that people could say and think such dreadful things about him.

His eyes haunted Bessie. Deep within her pity stirred. He hadn't answered her.

It was so shadowy in this little room. We are both ghosts, Bessie thought, held in thralldom to the past, to all those years.

She swallowed. "My lord, if you thus swear in public I shall write to my son Thomas and tell him to come home and tell him that the plans he is making for my daughter are too dangerous for her and there must be no more blood."

His eyes met hers coldly. For they were both thinking that no matter what Bessie wrote to Thomas the plans would not be abandoned, so Bessie's offer was a mere gesture. But it was better than nothing, Richard thought; it would stir up trouble for Bessie; it would sow some seeds of discord; it would reflect on Thomas' loyalty to Henry Tudor. Richard spoke for the first time. "If you allow me to place the Lady Elizabeth in my own castle of Sheriff Hutton for her safekeeping I will swear I do not seek to marry her."

Bessie's eyes studied his face; she tried to judge. She leaned forward. "You swear you wouldn't harm her? You will swear before God to keep her safe?"

"Yes," Richard whispered. "I swear it before God. She will be safe."

Bessie could hardly speak. "You swear to God you'll keep her safe?"

She rose, standing over him. Richard stood too, rigid, scarcely breathing.

"You swear you'll never harm her?"

He inclined his head. One arm was held close to his body as if to protect himself; he stepped toward the door. He was leaving her.

Bessie thought, Have I been wrong? Are my sons—are my sons . . . ?

"Richard," she cried to stop him. "Oh, my God, Richard, where are they?"

She flung out her hands to him in desperate appeal. "For Edward's sake," she whispered.

He couldn't answer. He didn't take his eyes from her; he backed the two steps to the door.

And now Bessie knew; she knew surely.

Great tears brimmed over and down her cheeks. Grief buried her heart. "Oh, Dickon, how could you?"

"Bessie." The one muttered word.

Bessie took her hands from her face. She stood stiff. "A bargain then. Between you and me. You swear to keep it?"

"Yes."

They would never meet again.

Richard said, "No one knows I came."

Bessie nodded. She could not bear his presence. She raised her head; she gave an order in her old imperious way. She was arrogant and cold. "Never attempt to see my Bess again. Your brother's daughter."

Chapter 30

YOUNG BESS leaned against the parapet of the frowning castle of Sheriff Hutton and on clear days she could see across the Yorkshire moors to the great castle of Middleham, where Anne Neville had been brought up and where her own father had been held prisoner by my lord of Warwick.

The wind blew. The sun shone. It was spring. Young Bess looked out over her greening England with love. And it looked back at her with a smiling face. Young Bess had learned much from her imprisonment; she had remembered, as her father had taught her, to be kind, to be direct and open, and she knew that her demeanor had served her exceedingly well, for the complement of the castle, to a man, was half in love with her, their royal prisoner. I have become a woman, she thought; I think Father would be proud of me.

She gazed across the moors; beyond them lay the sea and beyond that lay her Prince. When would he come?

On the first day of August a flotilla of small ships set sail from France. They were coming, the Woodvilles—Edward, Richard and Lionel; sturdy Blount and the rakish hot head, the Earl of Oxford, with the ensign of the streaming stars flying brave in the wind; Bishop Morton leaned on the rail, looking down at the summer blueness of the seas; even the ocean seemed kind that day.

Jasper Tudor was aboard the leading vessel; with him was the slender, quiet man they already acknowledged as their rightful King.

They steered for Wales. The disembarkment was solemn, as solemn as had Henry Tudor's life been and would be. He stepped out of his small boat onto the shores of his Wales. About him his followers poured out of their own boats, and if there were shout-

ing or commotion or excitement it suddenly ceased. All men
bared their heads. For Henry knelt. He leaned toward the
warmed August earth and kissed the soil of Wales with his thin
lips; for him it was a moment not of triumph but of devotion.

Jasper Tudor looked down at his head with its thinning, blond-
ish hair.

Henry began, in low tones, the Psalm:

"Judica me, Deus, et decerne causam meam."

That day was August seventh, and it would be the eleventh of
the month before Richard knew that Henry Tudor had landed
in Wales and was marching toward Shrewsbury, because Jasper
Tudor had been right—Wales had welcomed them and helped
them and had kept its silence.

Richard was at Nottingham. He had already assembled some
troops and now letters poured forth in all directions, summoning men to his aid. In the field he was capable and he was quick;
Edward had taught him well. He summoned the Stanleys and
Lord Percy, Earl of Northumberland, and they came.

Richard hadn't seen Lord Stanley for quite a few months, as
he had asked leave to absent himself from court so he could
spend time with his family. But he had sent his son, Lord Strange,
to take his place. The young man regarded Richard steadily and
the King scowled.

"I summoned your father."

"He is ill."

"Advices have reached me that he is on the march."

Young Lord Strange looked back at the tyrant King. Anger
beat in his heart. "I know nothing about what my father is doing
but my uncle, Sir William Stanley, has joined with Henry Tudor."

Richard's eyes burned with hot anger too. "I'll send word to
your father," he said, "that you will die unless he joins me."

Lord Stanley was indeed marching on the road toward Leicester, where Richard was also moving. On Sunday, August twenty-
first, Richard moved out of Leicester toward Market Bosworth;
he left Leicester riding proudly, a coronet encircling his helmet,
the master of England and the master of some ten thousand
men. He went about a dozen miles that day and encamped for
the night in rolling, hilly country that gave a good view over the
flatter countryside through which Henry Tudor was approaching. The tents were put up. Richard's couch looked comforta-

ble; it was not due to its quilts and coverings that he was not to get sleep. He slept poorly and dreamed much.

Lord Stanley's forces had arrived. Lord Percy, hawk-faced and saturnine, was camped with his Borderers, his Northerners in their odd garb: They wore jackets of wool that had been clipped from the legs of the sheep and their gear was old, so worn one knew they were well equipped to handle it.

Richard paced his tent. He knew there was no sleep for him. But he had ten thousand men and Henry only five; why then was sleep denied him? His restless spirit roved the night trying to see into men's hearts; would they fight for him tomorrow?

The dawn broke in grayness. Richard sent word to Lord Stanley to come to his side or he would execute his son, Lord Strange, immediately. A soldier bore back Lord Stanley's defiant reply.

"My lord says to tell you that he has other sons."

Richard ordered him to stand and watch while his soldiers beheaded Lord Stanley's young son. There was shouting and confusion while some men ran to drag out Lord Strange; men gathered around and then there was quite an odd silence, and the soldiers shifted their feet and watched sullenly.

Catesby, the "cat," whispered to Richard. "You had best not shed more blood."

Richard trembled with anger. But his eyes saw another figure. The tall figure of Lord Percy.

"I think that order had best not be carried out," he said.

Percy's tanned, hawk face and deep-set eyes looked inscrutably into those of his present King. And what he said sent a chill of fear through Richard.

"I shall take the rear. I shall remain posted on the ridge in the rear."

Richard could not penetrate those eyes. His mind darted back and forth. Was there treason in his camp? Lord Percy bowed and strode away.

Lord Percy went back to his Northerners. It was getting quite light. He was camped on a ridge and could see plain over the two opposing forces. Percy reckoned quickly that Henry Tudor had expected Lord Stanley to join him during the night; instead Stanley was encamped quite near him, Percy, a little to the west. Henry's forces looked quite strung out to Lord Percy, who narrowed his eyes against the rising sun. The sun was at Henry's back; to his right was a marsh and he was looking up at Richard's forces strung along the hill.

The trumpets and horns sounded, the sun glinted and Percy called for his horse. When it was brought he mounted; his men waited patiently; they knew he just wanted to see better; they knew he wouldn't lead them into battle ahorse but would fight on foot with them. They waited and watched; they would fight if he did, even if they had no quarrel with Henry Tudor; they would obey their hereditary lord. Meanwhile Lord Stanley and his forces waited and watched too.

And Henry came forward bravely.

Oxford commanded the archers in the very front. And he had learned the lesson Edward had taught him at Barnet very well. Regardless of the forces opposing him, he forbade his men to go more than ten feet from their standards, to keep a solid wedge driving forward into the center of Richard's line. From his eminence Lord Percy watched, and he realized before Richard did that already Richard's troops were scattering and falling back for the simple reason they didn't want to fight. Richard was branded.

Richard was being defeated because he was the murderer of his nephews, for Percy had no doubt that he was guilty; even if he hadn't given the order he had sent them to the Tower and seized the throne. Percy was a man of the fifteenth century. The murder of women or children broke the code by which he lived. How long would it be, he wondered, astride his small border horse, before Richard would raise the futile cry of treason?

Richard's troops were hesitating and Oxford's were not. They drove forward with the Earl's shouted commands. He was right among them; on his two sides Percy could see the flying standards of the Talbots and the Savages; so they had come over to Henry's side, had they? Percy rubbed his brow, lifted off his helmet and held it in his brown hand; that gesture suddenly told his troops they were not going to fight at all and that the cold appraising eye of their lord was telling him he didn't need to shed the blood of his Borderers, nay, nor the blood of even a horse.

Norfolk's standard was gone; he had followed Richard to his death, Percy thought. Now he could see the King plain as he rallied his household men, his inner circle of hated cohorts; he was setting forth fast toward the standard of Henry Tudor himself.

Percy squinted his eyes. The King stopped at a well and drank. He closed the visor of his helmet and then mounted. He was making, in a furious onslaught, for the standard of Henry Tudor.

The fight was sharp and short. Richard rode forward wearing his crown; he had killed for it; he would die for it.

Percy watched, on the ridge of Ambien Hill, the seething struggle around Henry's standard and at that moment Stanley's troops began to move. Lord Stanley suddenly made up his mind. He threw in his lot with Henry Tudor; his horns sounded and his troops rushed pell-mell ahead toward the remains of Richard's army.

Percy glanced at the sun. He reckoned the battle had lasted but a brief two hours and no one needed his help. But he ambled down the hill with a few of his captains to pay his respects to his new King and to shake hands with his old crony, my lord of Oxford, while Lord Stanley's troops now pursued the fleeing troops of Richard. King Richard was dead. They had stripped his body and tied it, perfectly naked, over the saddle with the arms and head hanging down on one side. They were leading the horse across a small stone bridge; it was narrow and Percy saw the King's head bang against the stone walls of the little bridge.

He averted his eyes. In the distance he could see the spire of the church at Stoke Golding. Percy sighed. He thought, Vengeance is mine, saith the Lord.

Chapter 31

BESSIE WAS standing on one side and Kate on the other of the stairway at Shene; young Bess was coming down the steps, smiling at them.

"I was saying good-bye," she said.

Bessie turned and looked up at Cecily and her three other daughters. She waved a hand. "Go to the front windows," she called; they could wave good-bye from there. This was young Bess' day, the day she would travel to London; this week she would be wed. Her sisters could come tomorrow; today Bess should have all the attention, Bessie thought. The people were waiting to see their Princess enter London, to marry the Prince who had set her free from her prison at Sheriff Hutton and given her over to Bessie's care until she could be married.

The escort was waiting in the courtyard. Flags and standards and caparisoned horses, an open carriage draped with blue. Out there in the court Jasper Tudor dismounted and came toward the doors, which were thrown wide for him as a voice announced him.

"His Grace, the Duke of Bedford."

Bessie and Kate and young Bess stood, the three of them, at the foot of the stairway and Jasper Tudor came forward quickly. He knelt and kissed Bessie's hand and the Princess' and while he did that Kate had time to think, Why, Henry Tudor has given him the title of Bedford! Her blue eyes were wise and direct on his as he took her hand, and when he saw her smile he leaned forward and gave her a quick kiss. He meant to marry her as quickly as he could. There would be another Duchess of Bedford at court, and he guessed that if the Duchess were looking down from heaven she would mightily approve.

Young Bess waited until her mother and her aunt were settled in the seat, and then she took her place, alone, facing them. They both smiled at her. She is going toward the life for which she was born, Kate thought, and she will do it well. She will love and cherish her children, her husband and her realm; she is gentle and kind; she is steadfast and honest, and yet she is not dull. She is as lovely as the white rose and yet she is not vain.

Bessie thought, Indeed she will be a better Queen than I. It will be different for her; she goes forward now to a prescribed mate; I pray she will love him and that he will love her. It was different with Edward and me; so different. Edward, she thought, oh, Edward, I was not strong enough when you left me and my boys. I failed you but Bess will not. She will not.

The carriage was nearing the village. Bess was looking ahead, her hand raised in greeting, her smile pure and young as she turned from side to side to acknowledge and accept the love and homage which was hers. The tossed pine and fir branches, sweet-smelling, lay in the road and were crushed under the painted wheels; the carriage rolled on, carrying the three women, two Woodvilles and one Plantagenet, toward London.